MW01125212

EL DORADO DRIVE

EL DORADO DRIVE

- A NOVEL -

MEGAN ABBOTT

G. P. PUTNAM'S SONS
NEW YORK

PUTNAM
— EST. 1838 —

G. P. PUTNAM'S SONS
Publishers Since 1838
An imprint of Penguin Random House LLC
1745 Broadway, New York, NY 10019
penguinrandomhouse.com

Book design by Laura K. Corless

Library of Congress Cataloging-in-Publication Data

Names: Abbott, Megan, 1971- author.
Title: El dorado drive : a novel / Megan Abbott.
Description: New York : G.P. Putnam Son's, 2025.
Identifiers: LCCN 2024043485 (print) | LCCN 2024043486 (ebook) |
ISBN 9780593084960 (hardcover) | ISBN 9780593084977 (epub)
Subjects: LCGFT: Thrillers (Fiction) | Novels.
Classification: LCC PS3601.B37 E43 2025 (print) |
LCC PS3601.B37 (ebook) | DDC 813/.6—dc23/eng/20241004
LC record available at https://lccn.loc.gov/2024043485
LC ebook record available at https://lccn.loc.gov/2024043486

Printed in the United States of America
1st Printing

The authorized representative in the EU for product safety and compliance is
Penguin Random House Ireland, Morrison Chambers, 32 Nassau Street,
Dublin D02 YH68, Ireland, https://eu-contact.penguin.ie.

For Mom

Over the Mountains
Of the Moon
Down the Valley of the Shadow
Ride, boldly ride, . . .
If you seek for Eldorado!

—EDGAR ALLAN POE

EL DORADO DRIVE

All I want is to be innocent again.

She would always remember her sister Pam saying that, murmuring it as she dropped to her knees on the icy grass, that blond, blond hair of hers—the Bishop hair—glowing in the dark yard.

Harper had followed as her sister bolted from the house, back door swinging wildly, the Merry Mushroom cookie jar under her arm, coffee-stained. Holding it like she held her stuffed Pooh doll, age six, screaming that her sisters were pinching her, pulling her hair, scaring her, making her pee her pants.

Charging across the backyard, both sisters shuddering in the night air, Harper's bum right knee throbbing, teeth aching from the cold of it, until Pam stopped short, in the far corner, under the soaring elm, its branches bare and veiny.

Harper watched, the March wind screaming in her ears, as Pam dropped to her knees like the drunk girl at the high school party, the private school boys circling.

All I want is to be innocent again.

But they both knew it wasn't possible.

Life only goes in one direction. And experience only gathers itself, accumulates, thickens.

P am was digging with both hands.

The elm branches, blowing, whispering all around, Harper watched her sister's ragged French manicure plunging into the black earth like when they were little, making mud pies, digging out earthworms for Mr. Loccrichio next door.

What's wrong, Pammy? What is it?

And Pam, her knees sliding in the dirt, had looked up at her, those gray-blue eyes of hers bright and startled. Like she'd forgotten Harper was there.

Help me. Please. Harper, help.

H arper ran to the toolshed for a shovel, for anything, her breath squeaking, fumbling for a rusty shovel, a metal spade.

Later, she remembered seeing her face in it, pulled and strange.

T hey dug and dug, the frozen soil cracking, giving.

Soon enough, Pam's collie, Fitzie, joined them, churning his paws into the dirt, too, wanting to be a part of the game, the mad adventure.

Harper's arms were so much stronger than Pam's, strong from her three decades' work at the Hunt Club stables, and soon enough the hole was big, bigger.

Big enough for the Merry Mushroom cookie jar, stuffed to the brim with curling green swirls of bills packed like tight little cigars.

The Merry Mushroom jar that, an hour before, Pam had plucked from its hiding place in the basement, stuffed deep in a bulk Tampax Pearl box next to the wobbling dryer.

Their forearms aching, their hands split and bleeding, but at last the hole was deep enough for the cookie jar, for five cookie jars stacked on top of the other.

Kneeling, her knees cracking, Pam wedged the Merry Mushroom deep inside, nesting it against a wall of dirt.

Harper staggered back, trying to catch her breath, Fitzie licking her fingers.

She heard a clicking sound, Pam's teeth clattering from the cold, from an unnamed fear.

He can't ever find it, Pam said.

Or, *She can't ever find it.*

Or, *They can't ever find it.*

Which was it? The roar of the winter wind. It had all gone away.

All she remembered now were Pam's eyes, so wild, so frenzied, her headband sliding down her forehead and her turtleneck sprayed black with dirt.

Oh, Pammy, Harper promised, *it'll be okay. It'll be okay.*

But Pam only laughed, laughed in a strange, strangled way, her Tretorn slipping suddenly in the dirt mound, her ankle turning.

Harper reached for her just in time, their hands interlocking, stopping Pam from tumbling into the shallow grave.

Harper saved her from falling, but not from what came next.

In a few hours, Pam would be sprawled on the floor of her kitchen, her face pulped red.

In a few days, Pam would be deep in the dirt herself, her hair shellacked, her face put back together again, stiff and strained, her lips Clinique-painted, her nails shorn and clean, her body stuffed in the shiny emerald-green dress she'd bought at Jacobson's and worn for every birthday, Christmas, New Year's Eve, since her divorce three years before.

But Harper would never think of her like that, not ever. Instead, she always remembered her in her old house—the grand one, sold after the divorce.

She could picture her there now, standing at her glossy kitchen island, her hand curled around her clinking glass, her eyes dancing. Her eyes promising you that she loved everyone and everyone loved her and she would never die. It was impossible that she should ever die.

After, they began filling the hole again, a much more joyous activity, Pam's shovel clanging against Harper's spade and Fitzie running ragged circles around them, yelping and howling into the night.

The top of the cookie jar, a white curl and then gone into the earth.

Is it gone, is it really gone? Pam asked, and Harper promised her it was.

Pam, her face dirt-speckled and her mouth open in the dark yard, reached for her sister's forearms, Harper lifting her to her feet.

Crying and laughing at everything. Laughing at the both of them, covered in mud, *dirty as a dishrag,* their mother would have said, *my slobby sues.*

And the ground packed tight beneath them and somewhere on El Dorado Drive a neighbor's hound howling at the moon. Fitzie howling back, scratching at the storm window. A bird crying in the night. The smell of the earth, wet and pure.

1

Nine months ago

E verything's changing," Pam said softly.

"It always is," Harper said, squeezing her sister's hand as they sat, uncomfortably, on folding chairs sinking heavily into the football field lawn.

Onstage, Pam's son, Patrick, gauntly handsome in his goblin-green Norseman robe, rose from the folding chair to accept his high school diploma.

Harper felt her eyes fill. How was he still not age six, elbows on the table, meticulously removing the plastic and eating two rolls of powdered mini-donuts in one sitting, his fingers, his face, even his long eyelashes, dusted white?

An average student, Patrick had devoted most of his energies to running track, to all his jobs—painting fences and mowing lawns until he was burnished brown, his arms like carved banisters. And, most of all, to the care and maintenance of his little sister, Vivian, who sat beside Harper now, chin trembling, shaking off mascara tears.

But if you looked at Patrick on that stage—so solemn, his polyester robe glinting like spun satin—you might think he was valedictorian, class president, most likely to succeed. It was the way he carried himself, so regal, very grand, and Harper wanted to cry, too, Pam sobbing beside her now.

"I'm just so proud," Pam kept saying, but Harper wondered if there was some strange kind of relief too. Relief that he'd made it, he'd graduated, and, thanks to a modest track scholarship, he was going to some college in Chicago—*away*, further away than any of them ever had.

When he turned to wave to them from the dais, the look on Patrick's face reminded Harper of a skittish colt, eyes darting. He'd made it through a calamitous childhood, scissored in two by his parents' ugly and endless divorce. He had gotten out. Somehow, Pam had gotten him out. Or he had gotten himself out.

So Harper decided not to see it as an omen when his diploma slipped carelessly from his long fingers as he glided across the stage, the kid behind him accidentally stepping on it, flattening it under his penny loafer.

It was only when the caps flew in the air that Harper realized her niece, Vivian, had abandoned them, a flash of chlorine-blue hair slinking behind the football stands with another girl. The two of them nearly disappearing inside their spray-painted hoodies, their bare legs poking through.

"This is going to be hard for her," Harper said.

Pam nodded gravely.

No one knew what they'd do about Vivian, once a sweet, earnest little girl who followed her big brother everywhere and loved nothing more than riding. Harper herself had put her on her first, an old gray quarter pony named Lumpy, at age five.

Now a surly sixteen with a midnight-black manicure and pierced tongue, Vivian spent most of her time riding around in strangers' cars, a vodka bottle necked between her knees, pouring for a parade of sweet-faced girls, many of whom would kick off their sparkly sneakers in Vivian's bedroom and slide under her satin comforter, licking Vivian's laughing face, insisting, if Harper opened the door, *It's a slumber party, we swear.*

Pam didn't seem to register any of it, but Harper marveled over their ease and comfort, Vivian and her girlfriends. Times were so different now, she wanted to say.

How do you keep track? Harper would tease her niece.

And Vivian would remind Harper in that scratchy voice of hers, thick with tar, *I'm young.*

But that was before her mother laid down the law on New Year's Eve—Vivian cuffed inside a patrol car, kicked out of some warehouse party in Corktown, jaw clenched and hands purple, something about a potato chip bag full of MDMA. That was before her father threatened to send her to boarding school—*and not the kind you'd like,* he warned in the all-caps text Vivian promptly showed Harper.

But Patrick had stepped up, taking Vivian everywhere he went, to the mall movie theater with the sticky carpeting and the neon arcade games, to National Coney Island for chili dogs or to Sanders Chocolate Shoppe for hot fudge ice cream puffs at the counter, like the hundred times Pam had taken them as little kids, as their mother had taken them.

Every day after school, Vivian sat high in the stands, watching her brother run track, pretending to do her homework while carving graffiti on a bleacher bench, but—at least—behaving, staying still, *keeping,* as Pam would say with a sigh, *her panties on.*

But now Patrick was leaving.

It'll be just me and Vivian, Pam had said that very morning, her

7

brow damp from making a hundred mortarboard candy pops for the graduation party. Adding with a laugh, *One of us is coming out in a body bag.*

It wasn't until after the ceremony that their big sister, Debra, finally appeared, her husband, Perry, trailing behind in the same linen Hickey Freeman sports jacket all the fathers in Grosse Pointe wore, trying to catch his breath.

"We weren't late," Debra insisted. "Perry couldn't make it up the stands. I can only guess you forgot to reserve us seats on the lawn. . . ."

"It doesn't matter," Pam said, winking at Harper, who tried not to laugh. That morning, they'd made a twenty-dollar bet on how quickly Debra would complain about the seating.

"Well, it matters to *me*," Debra started to say, then stopped herself, kissing Pam on both cheeks.

"Hell, Pammy, you did it," Perry said, squeezing Pam's arm. "By hook or by crook, you got your boy through."

"Hook *and* crook," Pam laughed. "And a lot of sweaty glad-handing at the PTA."

"The question is," Debra asked, looking around, fanning herself with her program, "where's the proud papa?"

It had been the big unknown, whether Patrick's father, Doug, would show, *maybe in a puff of sulfur*, Pam had joked, knowing her ex-husband all too well.

"It's okay, Mom," Patrick said after the ceremony, slipping one arm around her and his other around Vivian. "He's been working a lot. I figured he might not make it."

"He could still come to the party," Vivian said softly, her eyes raccooned from crying all day, a bandage hanging loose, her brother's name newly tattooed on her calf.

"I'm sure he'll try," Harper said, curling her arm around her niece.

But you never could be sure with Doug, and part of her was relieved he hadn't yet appeared. All day she kept thinking she saw him from the corner of her eye—a flash of madras, the smell of his clove-thick aftershave. It made her nervous. It had been so long.

The sky heavy with looming rain, there was an anarchic, spooky feeling in the air as the parking lot filled with crushed graduation caps and trampled robes, with sweat-slicked parents trying to corral their whooping seniors, some of them jumping on random car hoods, a champagne bottle crashing, spattering green glass, foam.

Zigzagging through the crowd, Harper ran into her nephew Stevie, Debra's sweet burnout of a son.

"Where'd everybody go?" he asked, scratching his head.

It turned out his parents had left without him, *forgotten him,* as Stevie put it, laughing in his slouchy jeans, his eyes red and sad. Stevie, who had no driver's license after last year's second DUI.

Harper offered him a ride in her beat-up minivan, a cast-off of Pam's, twelve years old and two hundred thousand miles.

Nudging their way to the school exit, Harper and Stevie witnessed two separate fender benders and a dad-on-dad shoving match, a bristle of panic rolling through the lot.

"I can't believe it," Stevie said, punching the cigarette lighter. "Patrick's doing it. He's really doing it."

"Going to college?" Harper said, pulling at last onto Vernier Road.

"Getting out," Stevie said, his sunglasses falling over his nose as Harper hit the gas. "The great escape . . ."

Harper guessed the unremarkable school Patrick had squeaked into was as exotic as the Sorbonne to Stevie, still technically a freshman at Mercy College three years after his own high school graduation. Even if he'd had the grades to get into a state school, Debra and Perry couldn't have helped pay for it, not after Perry got sick.

No one knew how Pam planned to swing Patrick's tuition. *Hope and lottery tickets,* Pam said whenever Harper asked. Or, *Hope and witchcraft.* Or, *Hope and dollar slots.* Lately: *Hope and turning tricks.*

Hope and big loans, more likely. High-interest loans, car title loans, payday loans, towering credit card debt, who knew what else.

You have to give them everything, Pam had said to Harper that very morning, stuffing an envelope with a thick ripple of cash to give Patrick later that night. Everything left in her checking account minus two months' rent.

Pammy— Harper started, but what could she say?

I've never done anything, Pam said, turning her head away, sealing the envelope, *but I can say I did this.*

Everyone assembled at Pam's rental house on El Dorado Drive for the party she had been planning for weeks, maybe months. Planning it like it was a wedding, a royal wedding even, and Harper half expected Patrick to arrive in a horse-drawn carriage.

Mom, you don't have to, Patrick kept assuring her, worried until the last minute that he might not make that gentleman's C in trigonometry. *We can just hang out. It's cool.*

But Pam was the sister who planned parties, who hosted, who threw herself into everything with the sweaty fervor of a general readying her troops for the final battle, the one to win the war. It made sense when she was married to Doug, when she was president of the Junior League and chair of the Parents' Club, when she lived in a five-bedroom, six-columned mansion on a canopied boulevard near the lake and hosted three or more parties a month—dinner parties, fundraisers, meet-and-greets, luncheons, receptions.

But those days were gone, long gone, which was maybe why this party meant far more, why it had the weight of a coronation, the eerie desperation of D-Day.

I t's beautiful," Harper told her, barely catching her sister as she flitted in and out of the house with trays, bags of ice, bug spray.

"I tried," Pam said with a sigh, the back of her hand on her forehead like a soap opera actress. "I just want him to remember it forever."

They both stood for a minute to take it all in: the backyard glimmering with candles and string lights, Norseman-green-and-gold balloons, a half-dozen rented tables draped with gold linen, branches strung with miniature graduation cap streamers, garlands shimmying with graduation tassels, the ancient elm tree thick with bright paper lanterns: *Class of 2008!*

More than twenty years ago, Harper and her sisters had celebrated their own graduations on the grand lawn of the Hunt Club, formal affairs that ended with all the parents drunk, their chairs tipping onto the grass, and all the kids escaping to the after-parties in paneled basements and rec rooms all through Grosse Pointe.

Now, as the auto industry's fortunes sank, most graduation parties resembled this one, stuffed into the backyard of Pam's split-level rental house on the optimistically named El Dorado Drive, a street that would forever remain aspirational, close as it was to the shaggier St. Clair Shores, a different county near the water, strange smells forever rising from the storm sewer drain. *That ten-mile drain's giving everyone cancer,* everyone always said. *But would the people who live there even know the difference?*

But somehow Pam made it all work, as she always did.

You never even noticed the pitted aluminum siding, the yellowing lawn, the painted-over window latches and sagging gutters.

All you saw was Pam's magic.

Within an hour, more than a hundred people had arrived, many of them with go-cups, roadies, what her parents used to call "driving drinks" for the ten-minute car ride to a party.

They needn't have bothered. Pam had set up a potting-bench-turned-makeshift-bar for the adults, who rarely left it, but soon enough one of the Styrofoam coolers disappeared, only to find its way to someone's van and another to the basement, and by six o'clock, half the teenagers bore telltale rum-punch-red tongues.

One by three, three by six, they came and in every other hand an envelope for Patrick. Some of the adults—like Marty, Pam's divorce attorney—just pulled out their wallet as soon as they saw Patrick, slapping bills into his hand like he was the maître d' at the Stork Club.

Harper hoped her nephew would do the right thing with all those checks, those fluttering bills tufting loose from the card holder sleeves. But she feared somehow he wouldn't, didn't understand money or what it meant, only that his parents never stopped arguing about it and piling up debt.

But who was Harper to talk, anyway.

How many Bishop sisters," Perry shouted out, "does it take to carry a cake?"

And everyone laughed as Harper, Pam, and Debra lugged their mother's sterling silver cake tray across the yard to Patrick, his graduation robe ballooning behind him in the June breeze.

On the tray sat the teetering party centerpiece: the "Money Cake," a towering creation that had taken Pam hours to make, rolling dozens of crisp dollar bills around toilet paper dowels and glue-gunning them to a Styrofoam pillar at least three feet high.

Everyone gasped as they saw it, pulling out their digital cameras, their disposable cameras to capture the spectacle. *Money Cake! Money Cake!*

"They're all the rage this year," Debra said, clearly relieved that all her son, Stevie, had wanted when he graduated was all-you-can-eat Buddy's Pizza, a rented slushie machine, and a keg of beer pumping for all who surrendered their keys at the door.

"Jesus," Patrick said, running a finger along the dollar bills wrapped tight as their grandfather's Dunhills. "Mom, Jesus."

"May the road ahead be paved with gold," Pam said, throwing her arms around her son, "and the wind forever at your back."

"I don't think that's how it goes," Perry whispered to Harper.

"May the road ahead be paved with gold," Harper replied, lighting a cigarette, "but we're stuck on a cul-de-sac."

Everything felt both glorious and painful, Harper thought, like all family events.

"The beauteous Bishop sisters," Perry said, taking a picture of them under the string lights wrapped tight around the elm tree. "The blond Bishop sisters, the bodacious Bishop sisters, the bountiful, the bona fide, the bold, the brilliant . . ."

"That's enough, honey," Debra said at last, taking the camera with one hand, his Scotch and soda with the other.

"Patrick's the best thing I ever did," Pam whispered to Harper, thankfully out of her daughter's hearing.

A half hour later, when the toasts came, Patrick hoisted his mother in the air to wild applause, like a football hero with his homecoming queen.

"Best mom in the world!" he shouted to loud cheers. "Best mom ever!"

Pam, legs dangling, in her yellow Laura Ashley sundress and matching apron, threw her head back and laughed, kissing her son's stubbly cheek as everyone cheered and began singing, loudly and with full vibrato, that song from *Titanic*.

"Damn," Debra conceded, standing alongside Harper as they watched their sister high in the air, "Pam always could throw a party."

A s the crowd swelled and spread, the air grew heavy like it might storm, a pressure building under those white Michigan skies. It reminded Harper of her childhood summers, running around the Hunt Club pool, their towels like capes, screaming *it's gonna rain, it's gonna storm!* as their mother murmured from under her straw hat that she once knew a girl struck by lightning on the high dive.

That feeling—the exhilaration of time running out, bare feet slapping on the concrete, rain spots scattering hotly, a constant low rumble in the distance—gave the graduation party a particular intensity, a sensual dread.

Or so it felt watching the teenagers—Patrick and his friends and Vivian and hers, young and heedless and tattooed, buzz cuts and pink-tinted ponytails, jocks and freaks all blurring together, screaming and singing along to Patrick's graduation mix, crying and shuddering with the bigness of the day, the night. The end of childhood, or so they hoped and feared.

"It's the same but different," Debra said as they watched them dancing on the cracked patio, shirtless and shoeless, the bass thrumming from Stevie's speakers hoisted on the windowsill. "We were all going to Michigan or Michigan State, we all knew where we were heading and when. Jobs at twenty-two, married by twenty-eight, house, kids, country club . . . It was all mapped out."

Except we were wrong, Harper thought.

Only Debra was still married and Harper never had. None of them owned their house or had the careers they had planned. Harper couldn't even remember what she'd planned, or hoped for.

The storm somehow held off, or at least lurked only in the wings, and no one seemed to want to leave, and that was when the rented photo booth arrived, wheeled in by two deliverymen who patiently waited for their cash tips from Pam's apron pocket-turned-money belt.

Instantly, the graduates swarmed the booth as Pam set down a basket stuffed with sunglasses (*A future so bright!* the sign hung around it screamed) and another with glow sticks, rhinestone tiaras, Grosse Pointe Norseman mascot horns, corny little signs on Popsicle sticks that said things like, *The tassel was worth the hassle!*

For the next hour, the booth never stopped jostling with tangles of teen limbs hanging out from under its swinging velvet curtain.

"Jesus," Debra whispered to Harper, watching the spectacle, "when did Pam hit the lottery?"

"Stop counting other people's money," Harper replied, imitating their mother's hectoring tone, and they both laughed.

But there was something beneath it. With family, there always was.

Suddenly, there was a loud whoop and a whoosh, and turning, Harper saw the bottom branch of the elm tree instantly ablaze.

"The string lights!" Pam screamed. She'd wrapped them too tight around the tree, or maybe an errant spark from the grill had landed near them.

Patrick charged over with a waterlogged cooler and Perry grabbed another and soon there was a whole bucket brigade, like something out of *Little House on the Prairie*, Pam kept saying, her face terrified and excited at once.

The flames were smothered in under a minute, but for the next hour, guests would continue to slip and fall from the scattered ice, or roll their ankles over beer cans punctured and sizzling with foam. And every time, Pam would cry out, running to them, joking that a fire would have caused less damage and been so much more beautiful.

Pam," Harper finally asked under her breath as her sister passed for the hundredth time, "how can you afford this?"

Pam stopped, brushing the hair from her sweat-sheened forehead.

"What makes you think," she said, laughing, "I can afford it?"

"Is Demon Doug helping out?" Debra asked, that old nickname they'd all given Pam's ex-husband, first as a joke and then less so.

"What do you think?" Pam said, bending down to drag a metal tub of ice from the kitchen to the back door.

"Maybe it's for the best," Harper said. Then softly, "But he's not coming, is he?"

"No," Pam confided. "I called a few hours ago. Last-minute business trip. For Volkswagen. That's what his new assistant said. The one with the sultry voice."

Typical Doug, Harper thought. With his electric-green Mustang, his bachelor condo downtown, deep in the shimmery bowels of the Renaissance Center. His high-living ways, everything leased, rented, loaned, or hustled.

My kids'll pay the price forever, she once confided to Harper, *for my god-awful taste in men.*

"Would it have killed him," Debra said, bending down to help her, "to at least stop by, hug his son, drop off a check—"

"—that would bounce by Monday," Pam said as the tub rattled over the door ridge.

Pam looked across the yard at Patrick, a glow stick in his hand, a dazed look on his face, like his legs weren't sure to hold him. *Stoned,* Harper thought.

"Patrick won't talk about it," Pam said, a hitch in her voice, "but I know he's heartbroken."

S tanding at the bathroom sink, Harper took a breath.
There was a shiver of dread she couldn't name. Something to do with Patrick's leaving, Doug's no-show, all the talk of money. The money, the money. Always the money.

The tiny bathroom smelled forever of sump, the narrow vanity, glued to the floor, keening to the right with the summer heat, the sink glowing from Vivian's latest dye job, a searing ring of aquamarine.

You're crazy, she told herself, looking at her sun-pouched face, her dull eyes. *Everything will be fine.*

Her phone buzzed, shimmying on the vanity counter.

Doug. Impossibly, it was Doug. Speak of the devil . . .

Harper didn't answer and the phone kept buzzing until it shimmied into the sink, landing in the blue, blue ring.

B y nine o'clock, the party was throbbing with energy, the churning pleasure and terror of graduation, of what came next.

The music boomed, teen anthems of regret, power ballads of youthful melancholy as graduates snuck around the side of the house or slunk into the basement, pilfered forty ouncers or an errant bottle of champagne swinging between the folds of their robes.

All while the adults reigned in the backyard, waxing nostalgic over their own graduation parties on the water or even downtown at the Belle Isle Boat House, the Detroit Athletic Club, the grand affairs that no longer existed. That feeling they could barely remember: of everything beginning. "Like a fat peach," Perry said, lighting a cigar, his match sparking on the concrete patio, "just about to turn ripe."

Looking around, Harper realized she knew more of the teenagers—many of whom she'd given riding lessons to—than the adults. Pam had so many friends—from the PTA, the library benefit committee, the Junior League. Beverly Linebaugh. Caroline Collins. Women with smooth yellow hair, Lilly Pulitzer sheaths, men in Florida tans, plaid madras. They flitted in and out, bright birds alighting, then moving on to the next party, the gold-lined envelopes passing from hand to hand.

Even now, her big house gone, the money gone, Pam's life was so different from her own.

Let me help," Harper said, spotting Pam, now shoeless and in jeans, trying to clean up the mess as it was making itself, squished hot dog buns in the grass, cigarette butts singeing the tablecloths where Debra and Perry sat.

"Jesus, Pammy," Debra said, looking at Pam's bare feet. "Are we hillbillies now?"

As if on cue, Pam's ankle bent over a broken beer bottle, sending her sliding across the grass, nearly into Debra's arms.

"It's my fault," Perry insisted, his feet bare too. "I made her show me her old dance moves."

"Can't do the Running Man in strappy sandals," Pam said breathlessly, leaning on one of the table benches while Harper plucked a green glass shard from her pink foot. "Remember, Deb?"

Debra didn't answer, balling soiled napkins into her fist.

Moments later, they were in the kitchen, Pam tugging the sink hose nearly from its root to wash off her foot, bleeding even more now, and Debra talking about getting stitches.

"The kids are the ones supposed to end up in the emergency room," Debra said.

The blood blotted the linoleum and Harper saw Pam's face go white and reached for her, sitting her down in one of the rust-pitted chrome chairs.

"I just got dizzy all the sudden," she kept saying, her head down.

Harper and Debra exchanged looks, then sat down with her, chair legs scraping on the peel-and-stick linoleum.

Like Pam as a little girl, the whirling dervish at every birthday party, every family gathering, spinning and sparking until she fainted or threw up.

"It's okay, Pam," Debra said, taking her hand. "It's all okay."

We're out of the top-shelf," sighed Debra, draining the last vodka into her glass.

Debra rarely drank, but the evening had that quality where everyone wanted to keep it going somehow.

For the past hour, the three sisters had been sitting around the kitchen's rickety Formica table, one Pam had found at a garage sale and rolled home when she'd first moved into the rental two years ago. Their lives all so busy and messy on their own, it was maybe the first time they'd sat alone together in years and Harper realized, with a piercing pang, how much she'd missed it.

"Found one!" Pam announced, climbing up the basement stairs with a shiny new jug of dubious gin. "Vivian's hiding place."

"Shit," Debra said, dumping more tonic in her cup and Pam's, "you could floss your teeth with that grain."

"Harper's being good," Pam said, noting the Coke can Harper had just opened.

She'd been good for nearly three years, since she first tentatively ducked her head into an AA meeting in the basement of the public library.

It had been harder tonight, all the frenzied exultation, the way the past and the future kept rushing back or rushing toward you at the same time. It was so much easier when she was alone, in her routine, in the barn, the barracks.

"Don't tell on me," Pam said, reaching for one of Harper's cigarettes.

"Or me," Debra said, taking one, too, as Pam pulled an ashtray from the kitchen drawer.

"That looks familiar," Harper said.

Flipping the ashtray over, Pam showed them the familiar logo on the back.

"Mario's!" Harper said, curling her hand around its heavy cream porcelain. "God, it's so heavy. How did you pinch it?"

"I stuck it in Mom's handbag," Pammy said, scrunching her face mischievously, like when she was four years old and had shoved a tiddlywink up her nose without telling anyone for three weeks. "Luckily, *she* was half in the bag at the time, so—"

"Other kids' moms made pot roast," Debra groaned, reaching for a cigarette. "Ours took us downtown in our stiff Sunday dresses."

"Mary Janes pinching our feet."

Every Sunday night through their whole childhood, their parents stuffed them into the backseat for the twenty-minute drive from serene Grosse Pointe to the battered city, midway through a long decline from which it had yet to recover.

"Remember how Frankie would bring out the relish tray?" Pam said, smiling. Frankie, their favorite waiter, so elegant in his waistcoat and bow tie.

"And we'd fight over the four Genoa salami and sweet pickles?"

"—and Mom would always say," Debra said, lowering her voice dramatically, "*The house Cab, please, Frankie, honey.*"

"Dad loved that sauce they'd pour on the steak."

"Zip sauce."

"Zip sauce!" They all laughed, Pam limping around, her feet bare on the kitchen floor.

"It was really just steak sauce—"

"—steak sauce with four sticks of butter."

"But Dad acted like it was the elixir of the gods."

Harper and Pam cackled as Debra went silent, her cigarette burning down between her fingers.

"Slices of Alinosi spumoni for dessert," Harper said. "How it'd shiver on the plate."

"Usually, they were drunk by then," Pam said, her voice softening. "Remember when he pulled her arm too hard. He told everyone he was trying to help her on with her coat."

"Broken collarbone," Debra said coolly. "Wifebeater's Special."

But sometimes it was beautiful, Harper thought, remembering driving home in Dad's sapphire-blue Caddy with the bench seat. Bouncing over the potholes on Jefferson, the glittery lights on the Detroit River.

Like a charm bracelet, their mother used to say. And it *was* like that. A charm bracelet strung from bridge to bridge.

The three sisters bundled in the backseat, warm and full and watching their parents' hands strung together on the console, never doubting it would last forever.

B y midnight, everyone was gone, mostly. The guests had moved on to other parties, or drunken rides home. Patrick and Vivian had decamped with cousin Stevie and their friends to the dingy marina a block away. There was no swimming because of the lethal current and usually some kind of troubling bacterial alert, but somehow they always found some seawall to jump from and you couldn't stop them, even as Pam and Debra always tried.

Only Perry remained, lulled to sleep on Pam's La-Z-Boy by the easy drone of the Tigers game, staggering into its eleventh inning. The sisters could hear his snore two rooms away, occasionally rising to a snort-whistle like Popeye, making them all laugh.

Harper had always liked Perry, who'd had a hard run. Like so many of their friends' husbands, he'd spent the last ten years drifting from a high-powered, white-shoe law firm to a more modest one and then to a strip mall office of his own, before getting sick.

It was hard seeing him now, his perennial tan a leathery jaundice, courtesy of the cancer he seemed determine to ward off by sheer will, by his lock-jawed WASP reticence, the perpetual easy grin and bored shrug.

"He's never been good with this stuff," Debra said with a sigh.

"With cancer?" Harper said. "Who's good with that?"

"With money," she said. "Practicality. A budget."

They were in arrears, she confided, on his medical bills. "Rear even of arrears," Debra added. "High five digits of arrears."

Harper thought of poor Perry and his shrinking body, his pale, thinning hair, the strange smell emanating from him. So different from the Perry she knew at twenty, Debra's handsome law-student boy-friend with the Brooks Brothers suit and repp tie, the smile careless and light.

Later, Harper would try to remember when the conversation had turned, when they'd gone from the comforts of nostalgia to more pressing concerns.

"If you can't afford the party . . ." Debra was saying, a slight slur to her words by now.

". . . how am I gonna afford the tuition?" Pam finished. "Great question."

The gin made Debra ask, and the gin made Pam finally talk, even opening the kitchen junk drawer and showing them the appalling bills for the day's celebration.

"What about Patrick's trust fund?" Harper said. "I know that's supposed to be for after twenty-one, but . . ."

"Trust fund?" Pam said. "You mean bust fund."

Harper felt herself jolt forward. "Pammy," she said. "What do you mean?"

That was when Pam told them a ghastly story. About her visit to the bank the week before. How the manager, a nervous man with a curlicue of blond hair he kept stroking across his pate, sat her down and showed her the ledger, the steady but increasing withdrawals from first Patrick's trust fund, then Vivian's, transferred directly into their father's own account.

They'd set up the trusts a decade ago, when business was still flush for Doug, before the separation, the lawsuits, the IRS audit, the bankruptcy.

It raised a red flag for us, the bank man said. After all, an irrevocable trust means the money cannot be taken out by the grantor, or creator of the trust. *But your husband assured us—in fact, insisted—he would be using it for his son's tuition.*

Pam nodded, everything about this so familiar, so tragically expected.

I assume this is correct? the bank manager asked nervously.

No, Pam had told him, *absolutely not.*

There had been no tuition payments, no dorm deposits. Pam wasn't even sure Doug knew what school Patrick had decided on. He kept telling people Patrick was going to Northwestern.

Sitting there at the bank, behind the stanchions, Pam felt nearly sick from it all, the deceptions so deep. Sweat rising, tingling. As delinquent a husband as he had been, she never anticipated such epic con-artist malevolence from the man she'd shared a bed with, shared countless whispered intimacies with, for nearly two decades.

What kind of man, the bank manager added, almost to himself, *would raid his children's future to save his own?*

Pam, unfortunately, knew just what kind of man.

Nearly twenty years ago, Pam had married dashing Doug, a rising star in finance, a big shot on the cover of *Crain's* by age thirty-two. They had fifteen starry years together, Pam on his arm for gala dinners attended by Lee Iacocca, even the Fords. And then there was the glory that was their two children, Patrick and Vivian, impossibly world-weary by adolescence, when their father's flameout began.

And what a flameout.

First, Daddy lost it all, Pam always said to her sisters, *then Doug.*

But to Harper, it wasn't the same thing, not one bit. Their own father had worked devotedly for two dozen years as a company man before finding himself unceremoniously canned in 1987 after GM announced it would close eleven of its plants and started cutting costs upstairs.

Doug, on the other hand, had never worked more than six months for anyone, hired first by Ford and then—briefly—Chrysler, where he became famous for issuing the directive that his team move their watches from their left wrists to their right so they would never forget that *it is always time to change!* Eventually, he went solo, starting a series of "groups" and consulting firms, none ever panning out, sinking them deeper into debt. Now, he'd just begun some consulting gig for Volkswagen, whatever that meant.

So, despite selling their house, their three cars, and their cabin up north, Pam had less than six thousand dollars in the bank and a mound of marital debt, while Doug, as Pam told it, had yet to pay one slim dime in alimony or child support.

I went straight from the bank to Marty," Pam said. "It's catnip for a divorce attorney. He was practically licking his chops."

A father stealing from his own children! Marty had clucked, paging through the bank statements.

Even as Pam knew she would never be able to pay him, any attorney.

We'll garnish his salary, Marty said, looking up at Pam, *we'll take his house.*

But Doug had no salary right now, and no house anymore, none of them did.

L istening to it all, Harper didn't know what to say, or think. But she did know now why Doug hadn't shown up for Patrick's graduation or the party. And she did know why he'd called her.

———

Fuck that guy," Debra muttered finally, breaking the tension holding them tight to the kitchen table, the air even heavier around them.

For a moment, Harper didn't know what Pam would do. Debra had always hated Doug and never stopped reminding Pam of it when things went wrong.

But Pam, bless her, laughed. She laughed even as she looked like she might cry.

"Fuck that guy," Harper echoed, pounding her fist on the table.

Soon enough, they were all pounding the table until the plastic gin jug flew off the top, Harper catching it with one hand inches before it hit the floor.

"Fuck that guy!" Pam finally said, too, holding her cup out for more gin.

As if on cue, a peal of thunder rumbled outside and the screen door blew open and shut and Pam ran out into the yard to bring in the Money Cake before the rain came at last.

She set it in the middle of the table, the bills rippled from the humidity, sticky from the mosquito spray. They all joked how Pam better start unrolling them from the dowels if she wanted to make first semester tuition.

But there was an anxiety buzzing beneath all of them now. *What would Pam do? What would any of them do?*

"Harper," Debra said, a mischievous look in her eye, her speech slurring so sweetly and all her usual edge gone, "did you know Pam's been looking into cash spells?"

Pam covered her face in embarrassment.

"What the hell is a cash spell?" Harper asked, feeling drunk through osmosis, drunk with rage. "Double, double toil and trouble?"

She thought Pam might laugh, but she didn't, her face softening, her hand running along her neck tiredly.

"Pam"—Harper reached for her hand—"you're not in this alone. We'll all help."

Pam smiled and held Harper's hand, a moment so sweet that—

"How about me?" Debra said suddenly. "I should show you my bills from Cottage Hospital. They'd put hair on your chest."

"What is this?" Harper asked, laughing. "Bankruptcy poker?"

"I'll take your dwindling trust fund," Debra said, teetering on the narrow line between joking belligerence and true belligerence, "and raise you twenty-seven thousand dollars and counting!"

"Until the IRS starts filing liens and confiscating your property," Pam countered, "you don't even have buy-in at this table."

It was playful and it wasn't, Harper thought, like everything between sisters.

"I told Perry I was considering selling my body," Debra said. "And he paused and said, 'Well, maybe your *blood*?'"

They all laughed even louder, Harper pointing out that Debra always did have nice tits, and they all toasted the tits their mother gave them, "If nothing else!"

"Let's toast to a windfall," Pam said, reaching for the gin again. "For each of us."

She refilled Debra's cup and her own, then let the jug hover over Harper's water glass.

Harper looked at her. Thirty-five months since she'd had a drink, even if she almost never talked about it to her sisters. No one ever talked about those things in their family, or any of the families they knew.

"Pammy," Debra warned. "Leave Harper be."

"I'm sorry," Pam said, pulling the jug back. "I'm just superstitious. A toast with water—"

And Harper looked at them both for a long minute and then decided.

"Ah, what the hell," she said, shoving her cup toward the glugging jug. "Just one. For Patrick. For Pammy."

"For the beauteous Bishop sisters," Debra said, lifting her glass.

Later, Harper would wonder why she'd done it, but it was simple, really. She loved her sisters so much and she wanted the moment to last forever.

And they all drank, and the gin tasted so good Harper pronounced it even better than zip sauce. And the talk about money went on and on, about credit card interest rates, about selling things on eBay, about working as a mystery shopper. About how a few of their friends had discreetly started selling Mary Kay cosmetics, magazine subscriptions, vitamins.

"And what about you, Harper?" Debra asked, reaching for the gin, one finger left. "Don't you have debts?"

Were there debts? There were. To Mastercard and two different kinds of Visa, to the IRS (failure to declare, failure to file, late payment penalties). Debts from student loans, their father having died long before he finished payment. Debts from root canals, debts from car repairs. Her Hunt Club paycheck was never enough.

But there was another debt, the biggest one, one her sisters couldn't have known about. She hoped they never would.

"I mean all that time with Leigh," Debra said, shaking her head. "She had champagne tastes."

"You're going to mention my ex," Harper said, watching Debra empty the last of the gin into her glass, "while you top me off?"

And they all laughed and laughed. They laughed until their faces hurt, a crazy kind of laughing, pounding the table, the three sisters, the miniature table Pam had rolled four blocks, the sooty ashtray between them and so much love Harper thought her heart might burst.

Y ou'll puncture the cooling coils," Debra was shouting.

Pam was standing before the frost-thick freezer with their father's engraved mason's hammer. *wBE* for *William Edward Bishop*. The one they gave him after twenty years at GM. *It used to be a gold watch,* he'd said, tossing the hammer down on the dining room table with a percussive thud. Two weeks later, they laid him off.

The drinking went faster and faster after that, the night churning around them. At some point, Harper plucked one of the long dowels loose from the Money Cake and was waving it like a magic wand.

"Pam," she trilled like Glinda the Good Witch, "you've always had the power to go back to being rich."

And Debra reached for a few dowels of her own, punching them over her fingers, doing "jazz hands" with the rolls of cash.

"Don't you bitches," Pam shouted, "think you're gonna walk out of here with even one of those bills."

T he sky cracked open just before two—just when, sitting on the concrete patio with her sisters, Harper thought the clouds couldn't get any heavier, hang any lower than they hung, nearly touching their foreheads, tilted up.

Patrick and Vivian had finally returned from the lake, soaking wet, their hair algae green, their friends gone. Patrick draped himself across a chaise, Vivian at his feet, her pointy black nails flicking the phone in her palm, speaking inaudibly to her brother in her low and husky voice.

Some kind of melancholy had fallen over them, an awareness of the bigness of the night, that heavy nostalgia that only teenagers have, a

nostalgia for the moment as it's happening and you're already imagining remembering it later and longing to get back to that time again.

"Where's Stevie?" Debra asked, but no one answered. Poor Debra,
forever wondering where her son had gone, since age five when he'd
wander off at the mall, Tigers stadium, Woods pool.

"Mom," Patrick said, looking up, "I love you so much."

"I know, baby," Pam said, crying now and so happy and too drunk
to get out of her folding chair.

They hadn't drank like this, the three sisters together, since high
school (even if Harper drank like this for a long time without them).
But the night had a kind of power and maybe it was less the gin than
the feeling, the glimmering foreboding.

And the rain came at last, like a promise long kept, even forgotten.

But it was a warm, faint rain and no one wanted to go inside and
the speakers twitched to life and some song came on, a grungy roar that
seemed to jolt everyone to life again.

It brought even sullen Vivian to her feet, wrapping herself around
Patrick, letting him swing her around *like a potato sack,* a game their
father played with them when they were little.

"Patrick, dude!" a voice cried out and it was their phantom deejay:
the forgotten Stevie, standing dazedly by the speakers, a tiara stuffed
in his tufted hair, his eyes glazed and beatific, his fingers dancing along
his iPod, spinning the click wheel like a turntable.

The best you ever had, the singer belted jubilantly, *is just a memory.*

Soon everyone was on their feet, Harper huddling under the awning,
the empty gin jug under her arm, while Pam and Debra had found a pair
of abandoned glow sticks and were twirling them like parade batons.

Even Perry was awake now, watching from the patio door, wiping
his sleepy eyes as the rain glittered over all of them.

"Shit," Perry said, "they almost make me want to be young again."

It felt so good, watching them dance, Vivian's hair whipping around as Patrick spun his sister dizzy, Stevie joining them, jumping up and down like a pogo stick, his highlighter-bright hoodie streaking across the yard. The numb, neon beauty of the kids, free of hope but also expectation, their breathtaking fearlessness, the sense that nothing mattered at all, *what did it matter because what could possibly be next?*

Harper felt a hand on her shoulder and heard Pam's sweet purr.

"Oh, Harper, aren't they lovely? Everything's going to be perfect for them."

And it was only then that Harper realized, at some point, she'd put on one of those novelty sunglasses (*for a bright future!*), now spattered with rain, with chaos, giving everything a plastic iridescence.

She wondered if she was drunk and had somehow missed it.

"You wear it well," Perry said, sweeping her into his arms and twirling her round.

And then a heavier feeling fell upon Harper so fast she felt nearly knocked back.

The next day, hungover and lost, she would try to remember it. It was something about how their childhood was so different from Vivian and Patrick's, who grew up amid far splashier wealth and lost it so much more abruptly. Harper's own father was a well-paid company man, meant to work in the same place for decades, the kind of career that didn't exist anymore. But Vivian and Patrick's father—a speculator, an entrepreneur for the "new economy"—made and lost fortunes overnight. The world had changed.

The best was long past now, a decade ago, or a generation. We'd left these kids with nothing, less.

Just after three, Harper crawled into her minivan, deciding she was sober enough to drive home. A few glugs of gin could hardly count, not after what her body used to take.

That was when she saw the message pulsing from her cell phone. A six-hour-old voicemail.

Doug. Doug. Pam's Doug, Demon Doug.

It had been waiting for her all this time.

E ven inside the minivan, she could hear the thumping bass and the scatter of voices from the backyard. The way the sound carried, she could even hear Pam shaking a rattling limbo stick and Vivian singing in that throaty voice of hers, the squeak of the picnic table beneath her.

She could hear all that as she, one finger pressed to her other ear, listened to the message, Doug's smooth voice, her phone slick against her ear.

Harper, honey. Bet you were worried I might come by. Guess you know by now what your sister's up to. Trying to empty my pockets, bleed me dry. I have this fond, perhaps naïve hope you'll talk some sense into her. It would be to our mutual advantage. Call me.

Harper stuffed the phone back into her pocket and went back inside for more gin.

2

Five months later

ater, the police would ask her why she'd left—skipped town, fled the coop, bolted. It looked suspicious, or something.

You leave and everything starts after that? Kind of convenient, isn't it?

But it wasn't convenient or even logical. She just knew she had to go.

It was the graduation party, the hectic intensity of it, Pam's ardent determination to make it all special, like the last party on a sinking ship, in a burning house.

And that fatal jug of gin passed round and round, the sisters bemoaning their toils and troubles, like three witches, like midnight hags, hand in hand, conjuring a spell . . . it all felt too much. Her sisters, their burdens and hunger and rage.

Most of all, it was hearing Pam talk about the money, about Doug.

And then Doug's message. It had hovered in her head all night, like a warning, a tolling bell.

She had to leave.

The following morning, through the haze of her first hangover in three years, she had remembered that horse camp gig, far away, the other side of the state.

"Is it too late to sign on?" she'd asked, her fingers trembling on the old rotary dial.

"Not if you can get here by Saturday," they'd told her.

The next day, she threw two duffel bags in her car and drove nearly five hours, from one loamy stable to another, north of Grand Rapids, the 4-H money even less than she was getting at her job at the Hunt Club.

Then what's the difference? she could imagine her sisters saying. But the difference was it was *away*.

It turned out to be just what she needed. Every morning a mounted lesson, followed by barn chores and grooming, handling, saddling and bridling lessons, lunch, then trail riding three days a week, drills four days a week, followed by untacking, brushing, cleanup. All the western Michigan girls with their long, Sleeping Beauty hair tied up with ribbons, their seriousness and obedience, gold crosses around their necks, hoisting hay and saddles and wheelbarrows. Every aspect of every day accounted for, regimentalized, soothing.

It was what she needed.

The same smell of ammonia and oil, manure and wood chips, the same soulful girls—their swinging ponytails and furrowed brows—that she remembered from her own horse camp days. Every night, sitting in the stone meeting lodge or around the campfire singing with that sleepaway camp solemnity: *Mmm-mmm, I want to linger here,*

Mmm-mmm, a little longer. The songs never changed, the same ones she'd sung thirty years ago.

It could make you cry, Harper thought. But she didn't.

Y ou're *where*?" Pam had asked the first time Harper called home. "But, Harper . . ."

The disappointment in her voice.

"I just needed a break. I just needed . . ."

And then Vivian came on the line. "I can't believe you left me here alone," she whispered fiercely. "Patrick leaves next month and it'll be just me . . ."

"And your mom—"

"And *her*," Vivian snarled. "You left me with *her.*"

The tension and tumult back home crackled across the line and Harper would have to take long nighttime walks after every call, chain-smoking smuggled cigarettes and hoping for the best.

T he last week of October, she finally returned home, long past the end of summer, helping set up the camp for fall hayrides and church retreats, Girl Scout trips and autumn trail rides.

She arrived at her apartment door to find the locks changed.

Her shoulder heaving, she'd nearly pushed in the door when the building manager, a sour woman with blazing red hair, appeared at the end of the hallway, dragging a canister vacuum cleaner behind her.

"Gone," the manager kept saying. "It's all gone."

"What do you mean, *gone*?" Harper said. "This is my apartment."

"It's *my* apartment," the manager said, letting the vacuum hose fall to the carpet as if readying for a fistfight. "You were renting it and when the rent stopped, it stopped being yours."

Harper sighed. "I was paid through the summer."

"Funny how little that matters," she said, one hand on her hip, "on this, the day of our Lord October thirtieth."

Harper stared a moment at the door, cardboard thick, all the scuff marks at the base, the smell in the hallway of Pledge. The sonic click of the plug-in pest repeller. She guessed it had never crossed her mind the landlord could get anyone else to take her place.

"My stuff . . ." she started, only then realizing how tired she was, her foot aching from the gas pedal, those long hours on I-96.

"I could have given it all to Goodwill," the manager said, tugging the vacuum cord loose from the wall and winding it and winding it as Harper watched.

"I guess so," Harper said. She wasn't sure if she wanted to cry or put her hand through the door. Or maybe around this woman's neck.

"But I called your sister instead," the manager said, the cord like a snake coiling around her arm.

"Samaritan of the year," Harper said, stepping on the last wagging tail of the cord. "What about my security deposit?"

"Cleaning fee," the manager said, her lips curling coolly into a smile. "See how it all evens out?"

Harper was still cleaning out her minivan in the parking lot, tossing all the Big Gulp cups and sticky maps, when a car pulled up beside her. A Lexus. Platinum, glowing orb-like in the sun.

Improbably, it was Pam, blond bob flicking behind the windshield.

Maybe, she chuckled to herself, her sister had won the lottery, or scored a gangster boyfriend.

She had been bracing herself to see her sisters, ready to be scolded, or something, but as she watched Pam bopping in the front seat to some pulsing dance beat from Vivian's playlist, all the trepidation fell away.

"Hey, hotshot," Harper called out. "Where'd you get the swanky new wheels?"

Stepping out, sunglasses glinting, Pam leaned on the car door, tanned and trim in her suburban mama capris, her sensible flats.

"Just a lease," she said. "Vivian calls it Grandma Gold, but I love it."

Harper grinned.

"Get in, Harper baby," Pam said, grinning too now. "I have so much to tell you."

3

———

The whole summer's been like this," Pam confided. "With her."

They'd arrived back at Pam's house on El Dorado Drive to find Vivian dyeing her hair again, in the kitchen sink this time, boombox shattering every windowpane. There was purple everywhere, spatters on the linoleum, on the cheap particleboard cabinets, on their mother's linen tablecloth.

It had started with a newly pierced nose (swollen, oozing), then the ugly pigeon tattoo (*Jesus, Mom, it's a dove!*). Then there was the time Pam had to pick up Vivian and three of her friends at the police station, taken in for "drag racing" in the parking lot of the abandoned mall in Harper Woods, tearing up a curb, bending a handicap sign, dumping unrecovered substances down a sewer drain.

"Drag racing?" Harper asked. "Like *Rebel Without a Cause?*"

Pam laughed, but there was something in the laugh, tense and tight.

"You got out, Aunt Harper," Vivian murmured, purple rivulets down her chest, staining her Mountain Dew–green bra, her cutoff shorts, watching her mother mopping up the floor with dish towels, anything. "Why would you ever come back?"

It's been rotten," Vivian said through the shower curtain as Harper sat on the chenille toilet lid cover.

And she explained how it had been the worst summer ever, grounded for half of it, all for stupid shit like skipping school to drive to Cedar Point because Cassie wanted to go on the biggest, tallest spinning pendulum ride in the world.

"Who's Cassie?" Harper asked, even as she could tell by the way Vivian whispered her name throatily, a catch in her voice.

"Cassie's *everything*," Vivian said, her palm on the shower curtain, ducking her head out so Harper could see her beatific smile.

It all made Harper think of her own first love, Stephanie Modelli, her eyes dark and flashing, the ruff of her thick hair gathered tight in French braids, the three beauty marks below her collarbone on which Harper first dared to rest her fingertips.

"And Mom can't stand it," Vivian said, whipping the curtain shut again. "You know how she is."

And Harper did know.

But instead she said she was sure Vivian's mom was just looking out for her.

Because she had heard Pam crying in the kitchen earlier, and could, too, hear the sorrow in Vivian's voice through the curtain, her hand reaching for a towel, a purple pool at her feet.

Did she tell you what she's doing? To Dad?" Vivian asked, her hair now dried to a soft violet under Harper's calloused hand.

They'd lain together on Vivian's clothes-mounded bed for an hour,

Vivian spilling everything and showing Harper her pierced nose, maybe kinda infected, and her belly piercing (*Mom doesn't even know about this one!*).

"What do you mean?" Harper said.

"She's suing him. Mom's suing Dad."

Harper paused. She didn't know what Pam had told Vivian, about Patrick's trust fund and her own.

"She's not suing him," she said finally. "She's just trying to protect you. Your future."

"Is that what she told you?" Vivian said.

"Viv, I know it's hard—"

"She spends all the child support on her own shit," she said, digging into her pillow with her dagger-sharp nails.

"Is that what your dad told you?" Harper said carefully.

"You should have seen the big party she threw here last month," Vivian said, not answering. "Do you know what she served? A caviar mold. All the soccer moms and Botox biddies sinking their fingers into it. Just looking at it made me sick."

"Caviar—how dare she," Harper said, adding pointedly, "And who pays for your weekly manicure at Madame Suzy's?"

"She won't pay my stable fees," Vivian insisted, ignoring the question. "Pleading poverty. She said when you came back, it would straight itself out."

"I get a discount," Harper said. "It makes sense."

"Does it?" Vivian asked. "Dad says Mom's got everyone snowed."

Harper almost laughed. Sweet Pam and sly Doug. She still remembered their wedding. How their mother, three Tom Collinses in at the reception, leaned over to Harper, whispered to her with junipered breath, *Look at the two of them. The fox and our little hedgehog.*

I don't think, Harper had replied, *that means what you think it means.*

The bunny rabbit, her mother said, sitting back, her lips pursed, *and the billy club.*

"Honey," Harper said, "the bank called your mom. Months ago. Your dad's been taking money out of your brother's trust fund."

Vivian looked at her. "That's not true," she said, her voice cracking hoarsely.

"Viv, it is," Harper said, putting her hands over her niece's. "I'm sure he thought he'd pay it back. Long before Patrick turned twenty-one."

Of course, Harper wasn't sure, but she wanted to give Vivian something, anything.

"The fucking money," Vivian whispered, pulling her hands back. "The two of them and the fucking money."

Harper nodded vaguely, wearily. The fight over money, over assets, had taken over everything. And for Vivian it must've seemed like forever, so much of her young life.

She wished she could tell her niece how in love her parents once were, caught up in their shared dream of a bountiful life together. Thinking of their wedding again, Pam, barefoot, in her poufy dress, screaming with laughter. Doug spinning Pam around on the dance floor, under the lights, spinning her until she was dizzy, until she was bent over in her poufy dress, laughing so hard—she told her sisters later—she nearly threw up.

All through dinner—pizza from Bommarito's and iceberg lettuce with ranch was all anyone could manage—Harper kept thinking of what Pam had said earlier: *Harper baby, I have so much to tell you.*

She wondered, maybe feared, Pam's "so much" was a new man and she tried to think what she would say if it was true.

Other than a few interchangeable college boyfriends, she'd never seen Pam with anyone but Doug. *I finally met my dream guy,* she'd whispered to Harper from her dorm phone all those years ago. *And he's just like I always imagined. The only boy at the frat party in a seersucker suit!* All these years later, she didn't know if she was ready for it, or if Pam was.

And she couldn't imagine how Vivian—sullen at the kitchen table, flattening a paper towel over her pizza slice, watching the grease soak through—might respond to her mother dating. Her violet mane soft and fragile, like cotton candy. Her nose piercing angry, weeping.

"Now that Aunt Harper will be back at the Hunt Club," Pam was saying, one of many attempts to rouse her daughter from her post-tantrum stupor, "maybe you can start up your lessons again, V."

"Maybe," Vivian said, reaching for the two-liter of Diet Coke. "Maybe not."

An uncomfortable silence, one of many, returned.

"Well, I sure hope so," Harper said, stealing Pam's crusts. "You were one of my greatest success stories." Vivian had been a promising show rider when she still tried, placing eighth in the state championship in her division.

"You made it look so easy," Vivian said.

"Your aunt was a great rider," Pam said. "She was a star."

Harper said nothing, a funny weight in her chest.

Another silence fell. Vivian lifted the pizza to her nose, smelled it.

"Remember that paint mare you used to love," Harper said, looking at Vivian. "Hopscotch."

"Butterscotch," Vivian said, her voice husky and high. "I can still feel her under my hand."

Harper knew what she meant. She'd had a horse like that, at that age. A quarter horse named Fidget.

"You were never happier than in the old barn," Harper said. "Grooming her on the cross-ties. She was beautiful."

"You gave me your favorite currycomb," Vivian said, closing her eyes as if she could see it.

"Hobbies give you discipline," Pam said, listening but not listening, sweeping Vivian's crumbs off the tablecloth into her palm.

"You taught me to start at the neck," Vivian continued, ignoring her mother. "Small circles the size of your palm. To the dock of her tail."

Harper wanted to curl her niece's chin under her hand. Still so soft-hearted, a girl who'd been through so much, her parents' long, loud marital collapse.

"You did love that horse," Pam said, sighing loudly. "I told your father that any expense, it was worth it. We had to keep her. He makes Vivian so happy."

Harper watched Vivian's face fall. She looked down at her plate.

"But you know your father," Pam said, slapping the pizza box shut.

For the next two hours, Pam and Vivian tangled over school and how in the world there could not be any homework the week after midterms (*That's exactly WHY there's no homework, GOD!*), all while Harper showered and did laundry and took Pam's collie, Fitzie, for a walk.

When she came back, her sister was standing before the open freezer door with a hair dryer in one hand and their father's mono-grammed hammer in the other.

Every two weeks, she had to defrost that freezer of hers, the ice so thick inside that the refrigerator was leaking all over the floor.

"Don't tell Debra," Pam said, rapping away with the hammer, chipping off big slicks of dirty ice.

"*Pammy,*" Harper said, imitating Debra's dour tone, "*you'll pierce the cooling coils!*"

"*I'll impale,*" Pam said, laughing, "*its tender aluminum skin!*"

———

Finally, after eleven, the freezer was freezing again and Vivian was at last in bed, or at least in the glowing cocoon of her bedroom, huddling her squirmy body under quilts and throws and dirty clothes, the light from her phone incandescent.

I hope I got it all," Pam said. "It was hard to concentrate with that building manager shouting in my ear the whole time."

They were standing in Patrick's bedroom, full of boxes. All of Harper's things, hastily packed and striped with blue tape, along with her TV, wrapped in her mother's daisy afghan, a set of hangers bunched.

"I'm sure it's more than enough," Harper said, staring at the repurposed faded yellow Gordon's London Dry gin boxes, like the ones that lined their childhood basement.

She fingered the flap of the biggest one, a porcelain figurine popping through the top: two white horses running, their legs nearly interlocked. A gift from Leigh, a few months after everything started between them, feverish and magical.

"Thank god, you saved this," Harper joked, both of them laughing as she held it up to Patrick's halogen floor lamp. It was an extravagant gift, a Staffordshire, but if you didn't know any better, it was just an old-lady tchotchke, the horses white, their eyes black and haunting, their mouths open as if barely catching their next breath.

"What if I dropped it, accidentally?" Pam said, reaching for it.

"No," Harper said, pulling it back. The creak in her own voice surprising her. "No."

"Sorry," Pam said. "Sisterly loyalty. She did you wrong."

Harper nodded but said nothing. It *was* loyalty. She believed Pam, but she thought of what Vivian had said: *You know how she is.* How

Pam is. About girls loving girls. It was *fine, whatever works for you,* but it wasn't . . . serious.

"I hope Patrick doesn't mind all this crap in his room," Harper said, returning the figurine safely to the box.

"Nah," Pam said easily, sitting down on his bed. "He's abandoned us, after all."

They both laughed emptily and Harper looked around again.

There was something about it. How all her belongings fit into a teenage boy's bedroom, not more than a hundred-twenty square feet.

"You know," Pam said, "you could stay here."

"That'd be great," Harper said. "It'll only be a few nights. I've got my last paycheck coming and—"

"I mean you could stay here awhile," Pam corrected. "Live here awhile."

Harper looked at her. "That's so nice of you, but—"

"You'd be helping me," Pam insisted. "Vivian is so happy you're back. This summer, things got so . . . out of control. She . . . she needs the discipline of riding."

"It's good for that," Harper said noncommittally. She was thinking of how many lessons Vivian used to miss or disappear from, tantalized by that sly stable girl awaiting her behind the paddocks or the barn cat meowing for her in the tack room. But somehow, on tournament days, she'd still show up, bladelike and precise in her canary breeches, a champion's gleam in her eye, ready to dominate.

"I know she's a handful. I'd insist you be paid for your time."

"I get paid," Harper said, wincing a little. "The Hunt Club pays me."

"That's not what I mean," Pam said. "I'm sorry. I just . . . You could save on rent. Help me manage my delinquent child. Save me from a homicide charge."

"Chasing after Vivian all night, cruising 7-Elevens and skate parks?" Harper said. "Very appealing."

"She's crazy about you," Pam said. "She loves you more than anyone."

Harper smiled. "It's easier to love your auntie than your mom," she said gently.

"There's other stuff too," she said. "The trust fund and Doug—I think we're going to have to go to court. There's so much paperwork to dig out, so many documents to gather . . . Doug hid stuff everywhere. I had to hire someone just to find all the money."

Harper didn't say anything, wondering what she might uncover.

"It's just been so hard," Pam said, her fingers touching Patrick's things. "I'd love to have my sister around. I'd love to have you here."

Harper looked at her, could feel the need radiating off her.

"And there's something else too," Pam said, bouncing on the balls of her feet. "That thing I wanted to tell you about."

Watching her, Harper had to laugh. "Have you taken a *lover*?"

"In a way," Pam said, hands on her hips. "You can keep a secret, can't you?"

"Sure," Harper replied.

Secrets came naturally to her. She'd kept them all her life.

So my doorbell rang," Pam said, "and it's this guy standing on the front step, and he's kinda cute and maybe giving me the eye."

They were sitting on their parents' aging Adirondack chairs on the crumbling patio, that impossible stillness of Michigan evenings, the faint squawk of boat horns from the marina beyond, the fuzz of their radios.

Pam was drinking Cape Codders with gin, the green glory of Tanqueray and a crimson jug of Ocean Spray at her feet. Harper was sticking to the cranberry juice, just tart enough to not make her miss the gin.

"And I'm thinking," Pam continued, "is this going to be like one of the dirty paperbacks we used to pass back and forth in middle school? Is he going to pull out a vacuum cleaner extension and offer to tidy my cushions?"

"Vroom, vroom," Harper said.

"No such luck," Pam laughed. "Did you know collection agencies can show up at your house?"

Harper did know. And she wanted to laugh at her sweet sister, who'd never worked a day in her life, married at twenty-two, going straight from the Chi O house to Doug's first brick colonial. Even if now Pam had to cash out her IRA to make rent.

"Accounts receivable, LTD. Or LLC," she said, her brow crinkled, her face pink and full of woe. "I swear, he *was* looking at my tits, and honest to god, I thought . . . *Would I? Would it help?*"

"Pammy," Harper said, wagging her finger, "the guy they send is never the one who can clear the debt."

"So my new financial manager tells me," Pam said. "My lawyer introduced us. We talked about my quote-unquote prospects."

"Is that your big secret? You're sleeping with your financial manager?" Harper said.

Pam assured her she wasn't sleeping with anyone except Fitzie, currently rubbing his snout against both their legs.

"But things are looking up in other ways," she said, reaching for her tumbler, rolling it between her palms. "In fact, everything's changed."

"Robbed a bank? Embezzled from the Parents' Club?" Harper teased.

There was something in how her sister was acting. All the witty patter, she didn't like it but couldn't say why.

"Better than that," Pam said, finishing a long sip, her mouth stretching into an infectious smile. "Everything's changed. I've changed. And you can too."

T hose words, they hovered uncomfortably in the air. Didn't all worrying conversations begin this way? A new diet, a new religion, a
new man (*He swept me off my feet!*). All the things women were always
telling their friends with the zeal of a convert. It always led to trouble.

"I know how it sounds," Pam said, reading her mind. "But listen."

I t all began a few months ago, not long after Harper skipped town.
Pam had run into Sue Fox at the returns desk at Jacobson's department
store.

Pam had been trying to return an expensive Reed & Barton silver
serving bowl a distant relative had given her and Doug for their fif-
teenth wedding anniversary. Separated soon after, she'd never used it,
never even taken it out of the box.

The pinch-mouthed customer service representative, however, kept
insisting on a receipt, and then began aggressively pointing out the tray
appeared to have been used, spider scratches and oxidation, and, to that
end, they hadn't carried this particular model in four or five years.

Are you suggesting I'm lying? It had been a hard week for Pam.

*Well, it's obviously been used. And damaged. Damaged goods are
not our problem.*

That was when Pam raised her voice, nearly in tears.

But it came this way! You sold it this way!

A firm hand landed on her pilled sweater, along with a cloud of
Houbigant, and Pam turned to see Sue Fox, former Parents' Club president and recruitment chairwoman of the Junior League, her dark bob
shimmering.

Within seconds, Sue had swiftly stepped in, genially noting to the
customer service lady that she herself had seen that very bowl up in

Home Furnishings last month, and, well, to be honest, she didn't buy it because of how beat-up it looked, a half-dozen scrapes from sitting on the aisle, knocked about by ladies' handbags, all those Burberrys with the studded bottoms. And, by the way, is it really worth losing a lifelong customer like Pamela Bishop, whose father had served as general counsel to the president of General Motors, over such a minor matter?

An hour later, Pam sat across from Sue at the Wooden Nickel, two hundred dollars cash newly nestled in her worn Coach purse, sipping three o'clock martinis and wailing over the recession and the latest wave of auto industry layoffs, even after the emergency government loans to GM and Chrysler, and the endless hours all the husbands now spent, depressed and drunk in their recliners, moaning about politics, the shunting of manufacturing overseas.

Did they ever think, back when they'd made their enviable marriages to their hotshot husbands, that they'd end up as the fiscally responsible heads of struggling households? Scrambling for substitute teaching jobs and taking on countless "housewife hobbies"—selling essential oils or special vitamins, mystery shopping, hosting Pampered Chef dinners—all just to hold on to their mortgages?

But then Sue looked at Pam, a twinkle in her eye.

It doesn't have to be like this, you know, she'd whispered, the tang of the vermouth tingling Pam's nose. *There is a solution.*

Valium? Pam asked, chuckling to herself, her fingers poking around the plastic tray of snack mix.

She didn't know how seriously to take it. Sue Fox always seemed to have ideas, notions—*schemes,* she'd jokingly call them, rubbing her hands together with glee.

But Pam had to admit Sue was good at getting things. She'd once talked the Parents' Club into charging members an annual hospitality fee for all the meetings she hosted for the bond drive, which *she herself had pitched.* And didn't Sue also end up securing a series of high-end items for the holiday raffle she'd started to raise money for the Hunt Club's paddocks renovation, even winning a David Yurman cable buckle bracelet herself? And she always had a Midas touch when it came to securing product and service donations, sweetly assuring everyone they could take a substantial tax write-off with which her accountant (once CFO) husband could surely help.

Our mothers—well, many of them—held Tupperware parties when we were young, Sue reminded her. It was true.

In the late '80s, after the collapse—the first collapse—of Ford, of Chrysler, their own mother, who wouldn't have deigned to touch a vomit-pink Mary Kay eye palette, or Avon perfume in a bottle shaped like a cat, seriously pondered getting her real estate license before their father died and the insurance money kicked in.

Their mother, like all her friends' mothers, wasn't built for economizing, much less for employment. But they did know charity luncheons, fundraisers, with—and among—each other. So selling to women just like themselves made sense. *For pin money,* they used to say, a discreet term for house payments, the grocery bill, back taxes.

Women helping women, Sue said, *and I don't mean by sharing Valium.*

And that's when Sue told Pam about the Wheel.

They all needed money. Some needed more, some less, but they all needed it.

So why not help one another?

It's called the Wheel because it never stops moving, Sue said. *Twice a month, we meet.*

A different member hosts each time, and the meetings were just parties, really. And at these parties, they took turns giving and receiving gifts to one another. To lift one another up. *As women should, as they must.*

What kind of gifts? Pam asked, feeling a little tipsy, a little light-headed.

That's the best part, Sue said. *Cash. The gifts are cash.*

But if I had the cash— Pam started.

You only need it once, Sue explained. *A joiner's fee. All new members bring cash. That cash is pooled and becomes the gift. See how simple it is?*

It sounded simple, sure. But why had no one thought of it before?

Before Pam could ask, Sue plowed ahead, explaining how the gifts were, in many ways, the least of it. The Wheel gave them "sisterhood" they'd long missed, that they hadn't known, really, since Girl Scout camp, since high school lacrosse, or never. An opportunity for support and empowerment, for social and professional networking, to help those in need, for charitable works, even (sometimes, occasionally). But also the power not in receiving but in giving. Gifting. What a gift.

Listening to Sue Fox, Pam couldn't help but notice her expensive highlights under the bar's recessed lighting, or the Burberry envelope clutch with the tartan lining every time she opened it for another cigarette. Whatever this club was, with its parties and its gifts—well, it seemed to be working out for Sue.

Women changing their lives. Just by doing what they do best, what they do anyway. Gather, celebrate one another, believe in one another.

That sounds great, Pam admitted, a burning in her chest from the vodka, from the dream. *Really great.*

Within a week, Pam had attended her first party. She figured she had nothing left to lose. And there, she was inducted into all the secrets of the Wheel.

And, growing up a Bishop, Pam found keeping a secret was the easiest thing in the world. All three sisters did.

They'd all been in a sorority, after all. It was just like that, wasn't it? Secrets and rules and oaths of omerta.

Too good to be true," Harper said to Pam now, curling her legs beneath her on the splintered patio chair. She was thinking of what Vivian said, that her mom had thrown an extravagant party, the caviar mold, everything.

"That's what I thought at first," Pam said. "You have to see it to believe it."

"Is that what Sue Fox told you?"

Harper knew Sue from high school lacrosse, where she played attack. On a field of braids and ponytails, Sue was the only one who played with her hair loose, her trademark barrel curls swinging toward the goal line.

These days, Harper saw Sue, the barrel curls long gone, nearly every day at the Hunt Club. She was one of those very active member committee chairs who was always telling everyone—*just so you know*—about which employee she'd seen smoking behind the barracks, how the drapes in the dining room might need a cleaning, and had Harper ever considered covering the gray because she had the most wonderful colorist, very reasonable rates.

"But I don't get it," Harper said. "Giving each other money—how does that help any of us?"

"After your first party, I can tell you everything."

"Why can't you tell me now?" Harper said. "What is this, like Dad's lodge with the crazy handshake?"

"You think Dad was in the lodge for fun? He was in it for business. Old boys' network. Why shouldn't there be something for us?"

Harper raised an eyebrow. "An old broads' network?"

"Speak for yourself," Pam laughed, her cup empty now. She eyed the gin. "Do I dare?"

"Go on," Harper said. "Life's hard, we must take our pleasures as we may."

Which is something their mother used to say, near the end of her second round of chemo, making her meal of V.O. on the rocks and two Cadbury chocolates.

Pam looked at Harper. At Harper's cup. Maybe she saw something in Harper's eyes.

"Just a drop," Harper said, extending her cup.

"Are you sure?" Pam asked.

"What harm could one splash do?" Harper said.

We must take our pleasures as we may. Besides, the fall chill was coming so swiftly as Harper sat there, no home to speak of other than this, her sister, her dear sister.

"Okay," Pam said, tilting the bottle over Harper's cup. "Just enough to toast."

"What are we toasting?"

"The future!"

"The future," Harper repeated softly, drinking, her nose tingling, the sweet warmth of the gin, of Pam's ruddy hand on hers as the rental patio turned blue, cold.

Just after midnight, Harper curled up in Patrick's twin bed, her feet twitching against the scratchy sheets, her thoughts heavy and complicated.

Somewhere in one of those Gordon's London Dry boxes sat her stack of unopened mail, all those telltale *PAST DUE!* envelopes. She had no plans to even plug in her answering machine, much less listen to the usual long messages from creditors, threatening legal action, catastrophe.

There had been something intoxicating about Pam's excitement— well, it reminded Harper of the Pam she'd known all her life but who had been tamped down these last few years, nearly snuffed out through her punishing divorce. Pam giddy, Pam active, Pam with her hands gesticulating, her voice strong, her laughter resounding.

And clubs had always been a part of their lives. All in the same sorority, Pam as Harper's legacy, Harper as Debra's. As children, spending summer afternoons, holiday galas at the three different country clubs their parents belonged to—the Hunt Club (for riding), the Lochmoor Club (for golf), and Grosse Pointe Club, quaintly called the Little Club (for drinking, and not a little).

In fact, it was a mere three days after their father was laid off that he drunkenly snuck back into the Little Club at night, slipped on a dock, hit his head, and died.

Harper was a junior at U-M at the time, a rising equestrian. Pam was a sophomore, Chi O's starry social chair. Debra, the oldest, had started an MBA.

After their father's declining estate was divvyed up, Debra left school and married Perry, a scant seven months before Stevie was born.

Pam took a semester off, helping their mother sell everything in the house, even the family's storied Scrabble set, which the mayor's wife accidentally poked her heel through. *Seeing your friends and neighbors plod through the house,* Pam told them, *offering two bucks for the Baccarat crystal flutes from Mom and Dad's wedding night*—she never forgot it. That night, Pam confided, their mother cried until she was sick.

The insurance money from their father's fall came late and got Harper through her final year at U of M. Her equestrian days, however, were over. She couldn't even afford the tack. But quitting meant she had plenty of time for Smirnoff shots with her roommates. *Dad's parting gift,* they used to joke, gallows humor even then.

After that, the debt started.

L ate, very late, Harper saw her phone light up.

Come outside, the text message insisted.

She'd known it was coming, she just didn't know when.

She lit a cigarette on the edge of the bed, hands shaking.

I can see you, the text taunted. COME OUTSIDE.

S neaking out the patio door, she saw a flash of something in the deep black of the backyard, the neighbor's garage laced with ice.

Something pale, the color of orange sherbet. A man's face, red and puffy.

"Shit," Harper whispered. She'd been hoping it was a bad dream.

From the shadowy reaches, Demon Doug emerged, cell phone glowing in his hand. Grinning like a monkey in a way that made Harper shiver.

"Jesus, Harper," he said. "Don't you ever return a call?"

"Did you call?" Harper said, dropping her cigarette onto the grass with a hiss.

He chuckled, walking toward her, the frost-tipped grass crunching under his boat shoes.

Harper felt her breath catch. It was something in his face, in that grin. She could nearly catch a whiff of Cutty Sark, his favorite.

"So you hightailed it all the way across the state to dodge me, eh?" he said. "Your sister only made it to the other side of town."

"I had a job opportunity," Harper said, averting her eyes.

"Got one of those for me?" Doug said, gesturing to the cigarette pack in her hoodie pocket. "Come on. Like old times."

"Doug, your charms faded long ago," she said, feigning coolness even as she fumbled for a cigarette. "First, when you left your family high and dry. Then, when you started stealing from your goddamned kids."

"I never stole a goddamn thing," he said.

"Except you did," Harper said, her teeth chattering in the chilly air. "The bank manager told Pam everything."

"That fucking bank manager," he said. "I was going to pay it back. Long before anyone even knew it was gone."

"Like you were going to pay child support? So my sister and her kids didn't end up in this shitbox by the sewer hole?"

He looked up at the house, the aluminum siding rattling in the wind.

"Posh Pam on El Dorado Drive," he said, smirking, cigarette still hanging, unlit in his mouth. "That street name! Some city planner's wishful thinking."

"Your kids live here," Harper said coolly. "On El Dorado Drive. Thanks to you."

"Come on, Harper. You always had a sense of humor," he said. "Listen, I could bore you with business. I could tell you how, to make money for my kids, to plan for their future, I need to be liquid. I'm liquid and that money's coming back, for everyone. But right now I need the capital to—"

"I don't want to hear it," Harper said abruptly, backing up. "I'll leave."

"Okay, okay," he said, patting his pockets for a match. He never had matches.

Harper dug her lighter out and held it toward him.

"You know why I'm here," he said, their faces close, the flame licking between them.

Harper pulled back, the lighter hot in her hand.

"I'll raise the money. It'll just take time," she said, her voice with a funny tremble in it. It was humiliating, but she couldn't stop it.

He looked at her and laughed, so loud that Harper glanced nervously back at the house. She didn't want Pam to wake up or, worse still, Vivian.

"Honestly, Harper, I don't see how," he said, inhaling deeply, his face red. "What, you're back at the Hunt Club? Making, what, twenty an hour at most?"

Fifteen, she wanted to say. A figure too humiliating to say aloud.

"Here's the thing," he said, his docksiders digging into the dirt. "I'm gonna need you to put in a word for me. With your sister. A kind of trade-off—"

"Doug, no," Harper said, her head instantly throbbing. "No."

"We're a lot alike, you and me," he continued, cigarette bobbing in his mouth. "Both of us deep in the hole. Too deep to get out without help. I'm just saying—"

"I'm nothing like you," she blurted.

Doug's face tightened, the cigarette hanging from his thin lip. "I don't think you're really in the position here to take the high moral ground."

"I'm going to get the money," Harper said. "I have to."

She had to, didn't she? It was a secret she'd kept so long, from Pam, from everyone. But especially from Pam.

He looked at her, glowing in the light from the neighboring houses, the spidery streetlights. This is how he once seemed, she thought. This glowing thing. Pam's glamour boy. Seersucker and an MBA, the kind of intoxicating, unearned confidence that made other men, older men, say, *He's a comer,* and that made women, younger women, say, *Get that ring, Pam! Leave it to Pam,* even Debra used to say, *to grab the brass ring.*

Rescuing her from the family debt, restoring her to the high tower where princesses belonged.

Suddenly, with a high, buoyant bark, Fitzie came bounding toward them. Harper bent down and grabbed his collar just before he leapt toward Doug eagerly.

"There's my boy," Doug said, rustling Fitzie's fur tenderly. "Who loves you best?"

It was, Harper thought, watching him, the same thing he did with Vivian and Patrick. The thing that made Vivian say things like, *He loves us and Mom can't stand it!*

"Doug," Harper said. "Don't come here again."

Doug smiled, a funny kind of smile, a little sad, maybe.

"Whatever she tells you, Harp," he said softly, "remember, everything's more complicated than it looks." He paused, looking at her, hands in his pockets like a little boy. "You know how that is. Don't you?"

Harper didn't say anything. She was thinking of something, a long time ago. That icy morning at Dawn Donuts, the windows fogged and the smell of burnt coffee, the bell ringing over the door and there was Doug, digging his hand in his raincoat pocket, slapping the fifty grand on the laminated table. *If you need it, it's yours, Harper.*

She felt a heat under her eyes, but it was so dark and she stepped backward, nearly knocking into Fitzie, circling her legs.

"We'll talk soon, yes?" he said.

"Soon," Harper said. "Yes."

He nodded then, as he turned away, added faintly, "It better be soon."

And it sounded like desperation or a warning. She guessed it might be both.

It had been nearly four years ago. She needed the money. At the time, it felt like the most important thing in the world, and she would have done anything to get it, even take money from Doug.

Pam and Doug were still together then, but barely. The marriage was forever skittering half off the road, into the dark woods. *Sometimes I wish he was cheating,* Pam was always saying back then. *But he only cheats with our bank account.*

Every time Pam said it, Harper felt a twinge of guilt.

But Doug never told Pam about the loan, not even through the worst of the divorce, the endless battles over the settlement, the trust funds arrangements. Except now it was starting to feel like he'd merely been saving it for the right moment. The chit he'd call in when he needed it. An anvil he held over Harper's head.

The minute Harper took the money from Doug—*fifty grand!*—she knew she'd crossed some kind of dark threshold.

No one could ever know, least of all Pam.

4

―――

"Have you thought about what we talked about last night?" Pam asked, standing in the bathroom doorway as Harper brushed her teeth.

"Jesus, I just woke up," Harper said, spitting into the sink. "I've got a lot to do today. I gotta talk Mr. Bingham into giving me my job back. He's probably replaced me with two fifteen-year-olds he can pay minimum wage or school credit."

"All the more reason to think about it," Pam said, bumping Harper's hip with hers, making room for herself at the sink. "The Wheel."

"Okay," Harper said, spinning her finger. "Right. The Wheel."

"I'm just so excited," Pam said, reaching for her toothbrush. "You know I wouldn't bring you into anything that hadn't worked for me."

"I do know that."

"And think of all the money you'll be saving staying here!" Pam said, her mouth thick with foam.

"I didn't say I'd—"

"Just for a few months." Pam smiled winningly. "Till you get on your feet."

"I'll think about it," Harper said, surrendering the sink to her. "But let's just let the other thing go for a while, okay? Till I get my sea legs back."

In the furze of last night's gin, both their fingers red and numb around their tumblers, Pam had been so convincing, her voice lilting, enticing, and wistful all at once. About how she was part of something now and it was going to fix everything, and she wouldn't need to fight so hard anymore. She was so tired of fighting.

But in the light of morning, Harper found herself pondering if her sister had joined a cult or, worse, Amway, like Pam's friend Jill Fleischer, whose husband would corner you in the grocery store parking lot and say, *We have exciting news to share with our friends!*

"Sure," Pam said, spitting into the sink. "Think about it. And you can talk to Deb, if you want."

"What?"

"I invited her over tonight. I know she's missed you and she may be better at explaining how things work. You know how anal she is. Remember her teaching us how to balance our checkbooks?"

"Wait," Harper said, feeling a funny kind of wince. "Deb's doing this too?"

"Since August," Pam said, her face disappearing into a washcloth.

"Oh," Harper said. An unspoken sister energy shuddered between them.

Pam dropped the washcloth and looked at her. "You weren't here, Harper."

"I know."

"And she called me crying over medical bills," Pam continued. "Harper, she'll tell you. It's changing everything for her too."

That language again. In Harper's experience, nothing changed anything, much less everything.

"Does Deb know?" Harper said suddenly. "That you invited me?"

But Pam only laughed, that lovely, inviting trill of hers.

"Of course she knows," Pam said, still laughing. "It was her idea!"

It seemed like Pam was lying, probably to make her feel better.
Debra didn't like to share. *Threes squeeze!* their mother used to be-
moan, observing their shifting alliances. Someone was always out. Except, Harper had to admit, it was never Pam. Pam had always been the
one to offer up her new cashmere sweater if you complimented her on
it, to insist every invitation included her sisters, too, to throw you the
surprise party you never knew you needed. You wanted to be around
Pam, all that blithe, booming energy. If Debra was the one who pro-
vided the sense of order their parents couldn't be bothered to (*Financial
aid applications are due Tuesday, Harper! This is the only sorority
worth your time!*), then Pam was the one who showed the love.

And now her two sisters shared this new thing, and was it wrong
to want to see what it was all about? To maybe be a part of that? The
electric secret crackling between, among them, drawing them close,
closer than they'd been in years, than since they were little girls in
matching Christmas velvet coats, doing figure-eights together at Windmill Pointe Park.

At the Hunt Club, Mr. Bingham scolded Harper over rancid coffee
for her sudden "leave of absence" in their busiest season and *who
do you think you are, anyway, disappearing for months?* Still, within an
hour Harper was back in the barn, stroking all the horses' manes, apol-
ogizing for abandoning them, singing softly in their ears.

But by the end of the day, after dealing with the demanding parents, the latest girl drama on the junior team, and a trainer she caught getting high in a hay loft, she wanted to crawl under the hay and hide.

She couldn't help but think of everything Pam had said the night before.

A small price to change your life.

The truth was, Harper had long ago given up on changing her life. She couldn't even imagine what that might look like. Maybe because her older sisters, in the early years of their marriages to go-getter men, had more of a taste of it.

In her youth, Harper had had plans, dreams. Riding, competing, maybe even going into breeding. But the horse world was expensive, it was for rich people. And then, rather abruptly, they weren't rich anymore. They weren't even comfortable, barely *just getting by*. And going from rich to *just getting by* was maybe the hardest thing because you'd never learned how to do anything. How to accommodate, how to budget. So your debts only grew. It took Harper years to learn.

And, besides, so much of what Pam had said sounded like one of those late-night infomercials for the "Greatest Vitamin in the World."

And yet, and yet . . . a coldness spread through her chest.

I'll raise the money, she'd told Doug on the dark lawn. *It'll just take time.*

She didn't dare do the math.

That evening, Harper returned to Pam's house to discover her sister had unpacked all her things, all her grubby things. She'd washed her clothes, it seemed, and put them in Patrick's bureau drawers. She'd plugged in Harper's cheap Walmart clock radio alongside Patrick's glooping lava lamp. She'd put Harper's battered trophies on the shelf alongside Patrick's shining ones.

A pretty little peach pillar candle glowed on the bedside table *to get rid of eau de teen boy*. It draped everything in a dreamy Creamsicle haze.

"Does it feel like home now?" Pam asked, peeking into the room.

Harper sat on the bed, dragging her boots off, weary from her first day back at work.

"It's only going to be a few weeks."

"Sure, honey," Pam said, winking. "Whatever you say."

What does she know about love, the way she talks to my father?" Vivian said, arranging herself in front of Patrick's full-length mirror, posing in a stretchy buttercup minidress.

There'd been a fight over curfew and how Pam was clearly trying to sabotage Vivian's love life, to stand between Vivian and happiness.

"You and Dad always got along," Vivian said to Harper. "Remember how you used to go to Red Wings games and the Auto Show together? You know he's not like she says."

Harper didn't say anything. It was true, of course. In some ways, neither she nor Doug ever quite fit in, neither caring about the *Social Register*, or spending Saturday nights nursing warm gin and tonics at the club. And it always seemed that, at every family event—weddings, birthdays, holidays—they ended up together. Gossiping over whiskeys in the far corner of the big ballroom, sneaking out for smokes. Outsiders even from the inside.

But Harper didn't want to talk about Doug.

"Tell me more about her," she said, closing the bedroom door, trying to settle her niece, to calm her. "Your girl."

Vivian smiled at Harper in the mirror. "Cassie. My girl Cassie."

And she told her how, many months ago, she'd met her in the bowels of the community hockey rink, a cluster of ski-jacketed teens passing forty ouncers and Cassie, in pink, fuzzy mittens, had smiled at her with a crooked front tooth, smelling of butterscotch schnapps, and the two of them huddling under the bleachers, heads knocking against each other, hands grasping. That night, Vivian felt her whole life shudder to a halt just from the girl kissing the inside of her thigh.

For hours after, Vivian kept finding the fuzzies from Cassie's pink mittens on her jacket, the slope of her belly, *everywhere.*

Cassie Dove was her name. Wasn't that crazy beautiful?

"She has a work-study at the attendance office, so I'd seen her. But it wasn't until Fourth of July that it really happened," she said, smoothing her hair. "I spotted her at the fireworks. She invited me over to her blanket, sprayed Bactine on me, and kissed me behind the ear."

They'd been together ever since and it was perfect and would definitely last forever.

"Of course it will," Harper said.

And then Vivian pushed one of the cutouts in her dress to one side, displaying the secret stick-and-poke bird tattoo on the small of her back.

A dove for Cassie Dove, Harper realized.

She wanted to cry out to her sister, *That's no ugly pigeon. That's Vivian's heart.*

"Have you . . ." Vivian started, her fingers going to her mouth, chewing on her thumbnail, "have you ever been in love like that?"

Harper looked at her niece a long time.

"You *have,*" Vivian said excitedly, moving closer, resting one knee on the bed where Harper sat. "What was her name?"

"Leigh," Harper said, the first time she'd said the name aloud in so long. It felt dangerous. "Her name was Leigh."

"What was she like?" Vivian whispered, both of them like teenagers now, leaning close, not wanting anyone to hear.

"Difficult," Harper said, smiling a little. "And lovely. And lonely."

"Lonely?"

"I guess we both were," Harper said. "And we found each other for a little while."

"Just like Cassie and me," Vivian said. "We talk about it all the time, how lonely we were, even with everyone around."

Harper nodded, a funny feeling in her chest. Her hand gripping one of Patrick's pillows.

"I'm sorry," Vivian said, watching her closely, her eyes heavy like she might cry for both of them, for all four of them.

"Nothing to be sorry about," Harper said, shaking her head, letting go of the pillow. "Now let's get another look at that dress."

Vivian nodded and rose from the bed, spinning around one last time before Harper, her eyes on them both in the mirror on the closet door.

"That's the one," Harper said, her voice thick.

"I'm glad you're back," Vivian said to her in the mirror, tugging anxiously at her minidress, the Lurex snapping back into place.

"Me too," Harper said, not a lie, not the truth.

If she closed her eyes, Harper could still see Leigh riding, the nape of her neck and her elegant hands. She rode like she was floating.

It had started—like all wonderful things—like a movie. Five years ago, they began riding together at the Hunt Club, and fell in love while riding.

Those first few months, it was all heat and magic. And the next year, it was all drama—fights and confusion and furtive meetings at motels by the freeway; in the Hunt Club tack room, everything smelling of liniment; in Leigh's gold Eldorado. Even now she could see the bobby pins slivered in Leigh's hair, the narrow blue vein on her collarbone. It didn't matter then that Leigh was married, with a little boy. It didn't matter because no one would ever find out. Until they did. Until he did. Leigh's husband.

It all happened so fast. The divorce filing, the accusations. His threats.

He's hiding assets! Leigh would tell her, sobbing into the phone. *The accounts are all frozen.*

She needed a lawyer, fast. The lawyer needed a retainer, fast. And so did the forensic accountant who promised to find the money Leigh was sure her husband was hiding.

I need money, Leigh kept saying, crying into those elegant hands. *I need money or he'll take away my kid.*

Maybe it wasn't Harper's fault (though Leigh liked to say, *You enticed me*), but it felt that way. And maybe, too, she thought she needed to do something, make the grand romantic gesture, even if that gesture required her to lay her hands on fifty thousand dollars.

Fifty thousand dollars for the retainer. Fifty thousand dollars Harper didn't have until Doug set it on that orange-topped table at Dawn Donuts and it passed straight from her hands to Leigh's.

Are you sure you don't want to wash your hands? Doug had said wryly after she took the money from him. *Pam would want you to.*

Soon after, Pam and Doug separated, and Harper never told her sister or anyone.

We're a lot alike, you and me, Doug had said the night before, the red ember of the cigarette like an exclamation mark. *Both of us deep in the hole. Too deep to get out without help.*

And Doug had helped. And now there was no escaping it.

"Pam, I swear to god," Debra scolded, "you're going to kill yourself one of these days."

Because Pam was wielding their father's hammer again, chipping away at the feathery frost lining the freezer.

"When you bring better wine," Pam said, pounding the hammer, "we won't need the ice."

They were sitting around the kitchen table, just like they'd been all those months before, at Patrick's graduation. The confessions, the Money Cake, the cash spells.

There was the questionable wine Debra brought from the grocery store and the two-liter of Pam's favorite Diet Coke on the table, even as they all admitted it would have made their mother roll over in her grave if she saw they were now the kind of family to dine with a two-liter on their table. And Debra had brought her signature lasagna, with nutmeg tucked in the béchamel. (*It always tastes better than mine,* Pam admitted. *Patience,* Debra said. *As Perry always says, you gotta let the bitch rest.*)

At first, there was the pretense of catching up, Debra and Pam feigning interest in Harper's horse camp experience, Harper listening to them complain about their children.

But quickly talk turned to their new venture, which seemed to consume them. The Wheel, whatever that was. Harper still wasn't sure.

"It was so hard not telling you," Pam said to Harper. "We vowed to wait until you got back."

"And yet you couldn't wait one more night," Debra said with an arched brow.

But Harper could tell Debra was excited too. Debra excited was a rare and striking thing.

Debra, with her newly highlighted hair. Caramel highlights that took five years off her. And didn't her eyes look a little brighter, tighter too?

It seemed the Wheel was working magic on Deb too.

It's a circle of giving," Pam said. "Get it? The Wheel."

"Like an investment club," Debra said.

"But we don't use the word *investment,*" Pam clarified. "Only *gift.* We gift one another."

And these gifts were given at parties held at least twice a month, depending on the number of new members. At each one, they crowned a new recipient, the woman who'd worked her way up to the "receiving position."

"Jesus," Harper said. "Receiving position. This sounds about as fun as a course in tax law."

"But it *is* fun," Pam said. "You'll know most of the other women. Sue, of course, and Becky Schloss and Beverly Linebaugh from the Hunt Club, and so many other women. Women like us."

You mean like you, Harper thought.

"It's parties," Pam said, "and bonding and sisterhood and—"

"Money," Debra said.

"Money," Pam admitted.

"Don't you want the money?" Debra asked, that whiff of impatience Harper had known since childhood, waiting on her sisters to tie their shoes, *bunny ears, double-knot them, Jesus, c'mon, what a spaz,* back when people still said unforgivable things like that.

"What does Perry think?" Harper asked.

Debra tapped her cigarette on her dinner plate.

"Are you asking because he's my husband," she said, winking at Pam, "or because he's an attorney?"

"Or because he's a man?" Pam said, tsk-tsking with her fingers.

Jesus, the two of them tag-teaming her, just like when they convinced her she had to pledge Chi O or she'd spend four sexless, pleasure-free years on North Campus like a loser. *Don't you wanna ride something other than a horse, Harper?*

"I'm asking," Harper said, "because I'm wondering how secret this secret is."

Debra told Perry everything, after all. She had since she first let him slip his fumbling hand up her shirt in tenth grade.

"I asked," Debra said. "And Sue said I could tell him."

"Husbands are okay. So long as they're the kind who understand what a secret means," Pam replied. "Or the kind that can't be bothered to listen."

"So Perry knows," Debra said, a grim cackle, "but he doesn't *know* he knows."

"No one's telling Deb what to do," Pam said. Then, reaching for Harper's hand, asking, "But what kind of sisters would we be if we kept it to ourselves?"

As they spoke, Harper began picturing a massive sisterhood of one-to-one confidences, like the girl who first gave you *Flowers in the Attic* or Jackie Collins, who first demonstrated how to use a tampon, how to get birth control, or the girl—Tiffani Lambert—who first showed Harper the things she could do with her hands, with her mouth. Things that made her punch her mattress, see stars. Sweet Tiffani, with her soft gray cross-country hoodie and the click-click of her retainer, and how her knees were always skinned from the hurdles, how high she jumped, how fast she made Harper's heart beat.

Harper's head was swimming.

The longer they talked, the more inevitable it felt.

Their energy was, Harper had to admit, intoxicating. Both her sisters so caught up in it, their faces bright. They seemed happier than they had in years, since their buoyant twenties, showing off their preening new husbands, attorney Perry and businessman Doug, shooting out of U-M law and business schools like cannonballs, ready to conquer the world.

This is how you're supposed to live, they had seemed to tell her, even if they never said it out loud. *This is how you should be living, Harper.*

But it hadn't worked out for either of them.

And now they were trying again, in their creasy middle age, their hands on the captain's wheel this time. Get it, *wheel*?

"Just imagine it," Pam said, "the three of us, building something, sharing it. Like the pillow forts when we were five."

But didn't the pillow forts, Harper thought but didn't say, *always come tumbling down?*

J ust come next Wednesday," Pam said finally, "and see for yourself."

"Next Wednesday, though? I'm not ready," Harper said. "I need to get back into my routine at work and—"

"All you need to do is show up," Pam insisted. "You won't be the only new one."

"Just show up?"

"And bring your gift," Debra added.

"My gift?"

Debra turned to Pam. "Didn't you tell her?"

"Of course I told her," Pam said. "The new member contribution."

"You told me," Harper said, "but you never said how much."

"This," Pam said, "is the hard part."

A long pause followed, full of darting glances between her sisters. It made Harper nervous, on edge. How much *had* her sisters laid out?

"Five thousand," Pam said, making a face.

Harper laughed, nearly a bark. Pam might as well have said a cool million.

"I thought it was crazy too," Debra said. "I had to apply for two new credit cards to get there. But I'm about to make it back five times over."

"It all comes back to you," Pam said, her hand on Harper's. "That's the power of the Wheel."

The screen door screeched, then came the thud of Vivian, shoulder against the composite wood door, whipping it open.

They all watched her race past them, the soft blur of her lilac hair, her feet plunged into what Pam called hooker heels, her phone curled in her hand, still caught up in whatever drama of the night had consumed the last few hours.

It was like a switch went off and Pam began clearing the table, Debra rose to find her purse.

Harper guessed the Wheel really was a secret, everything suddenly sotto voce, as if Vivian might have her ear pressed to her bedroom door, straining to hear. As if Vivian cared at all.

"Remember: It's just one gift," Pam said softly to Harper. "One time and you're golden."

"No one's making you do this, Harper," Debra said, slinging her purse over her shoulder. "It's up to you."

"But we'd love to have you," Pam said, her hand on Harper's arm. "And for you to have *this*."

Harper nodded, stacking the dinner plates. Five thousand dollars, it seemed impossible. But her sisters had done it. And it had paid off, or so it seemed. Pam with her leased Lexus, Debra with her meticulous highlights. And that was just the beginning, or so they said.

As Debra hunted her coat out in the living room, Pam leaned down, whispering into Harper's ear, "I can help get you there. We'll talk later, okay?"

Harper nodded, unsure what she meant. She was thinking, her brain buzzing, her chest humming. *What if this is it?* she thought. *The thing to pull me out of the hole, to let me start a life that had never really gotten off the ground.*

Debra reappeared in her nubby old Talbots windowpane coat. "Either way, we're glad you're back, sis."

"Just think about it," Pam said again, for what seemed like the hundredth time.

"I'll think about it," Harper said, a funny, jumpy feeling in her chest. "But if I end up losing five K, I'm coming for you two bitches."

B ack in her room, Harper looked at the box of bills, all those cellophane window envelopes demanding *IMMEDIATE ACTION!*

You're like me, deep in the hole. Too deep to get out without help.

Demon Doug's voice skittering around her head like a rat.

I'm nothing like you, she thought now.

For the first time, she had a plan, or at least the promise of one. She had something.

5

Tonight! The home of Beverly Linebaugh, six o'clock sharp!

Harper was nervous, putting on her Clinique face, which she almost never did, the pressed powder so old it seemed to disintegrate in her hand.

She had the money, barely. It had taken her all nine days to raise it. One thousand came from an advance on discounted riding lessons offered to two sets of Hunt Club parents (Pam's suggestion). Another thousand from a cash advance on a new credit card (Pam's suggestion).

But most of it came from Pam herself.

Three thousand dollars cash Pam pulled out of the ceramic Merry Mushroom cookie jar on her kitchen counter.

It had been their mother's, improbably from Sears, which was not a place her mother shopped. But it turned out it was from her own youth, before she'd married well.

It was never worth opening, their mother not one to bake, stuffing the jar instead with Stella D'oros and stale dietetic cookies. But, as a little girl, Harper used to love fondling the funny, chipped handle—a mushroom cap lain flat on the jar's top—while watching her mother lift the plastic off deviled eggs before a summer party, hosting all the GM men in patchwork pants, their wives in seashell-dappled wrap skirts.

"Are you sure?" Harper said, staring at the cash.

"Don't give it a second thought," Pam said, showing her the inside of the jar, a thick whirl of bills like a flower.

It was the least she could offer, Pam insisted, given how much help Harper was with Vivian, driving her to swim practice, to the sad mall, to Doctor Rumson to swab her infected nose and scold her just as he'd scolded Harper thirty years ago for the oozing stud in her ear.

"No way. I'll pay you back," Harper said folding the bills, still warm from the chugging dishwasher under the counter. "It might take a while—"

"It won't," Pam said. "It's because of the Wheel that I have it to give, baby."

Then adding with a wink, as Harper folded it in her palm, "Just don't tell Deb."

Later, that remark would hover in Harper's head. Especially all the times she would hear Debra mutter, "Pam's gotta stop inviting women who really can't afford to be here. It causes problems."

"What kind of problems?" Harper would ask, thinking, *But I'm one of those women.*

"There have to be some kind of controls," Debra said. "If you invest your own money, you've invested in the idea of the Wheel. Its power. And discretion."

"Right."

"If it's not your money, it's Monopoly money," she said. "You start thinking the rules don't apply to you."

Harper didn't think of Pam's three grand that way. But, at the same time, she wasn't sure she'd invested in the idea of the Wheel, not yet.

It reminded Harper of something her boss Mr. Bingham once told her, over cigarettes behind the paddocks. When she held lessons at the Hunt Club for free, to draw new members, only half of those who signed up would show. Sometimes fewer.

You gotta have skin in the game, he said.

Those people only respect you if they've paid, he said.

All day, the cash stuffed in her cubby, padlocked, she could think of little else.

She could still change her mind. Give the money back. Give Pam her three K to stuff back in her cookie jar. Picturing Pam's look of disappointment, hearing the cluck-cluck of Debra's disapproval. Reminding Pam that Harper *never wanted to do anything with us.*

It was true that she had never been a joiner, not like her sisters with their book clubs, ski trips, garden club, historic preservation council, spa days, girls' weekends—Debra even went to church.

Maybe you don't like women, Debra had once said.

Maybe, Pam had added, with a wink, *she likes them too much.*

The night before, her sisters had prepared her, advising her what to wear (or really what not to: *Please, Harper, not that ratty fleece*) and how things might go.

They told her that there would be four other new members.

And, as always, one woman would be in the "receiving position." One woman who had "run the Wheel," as they put it.

This time, that woman would be Sue Fox herself.

Sue Fox, who had involved Pam, who had involved both Debra and Harper, would be collecting the new members' spoils.

"So I'm giving five thousand dollars to *her*?" Harper asked.

To Sue Fox, who drove a paprika-colored Mercedes and showed off her backhand every Sunday at the Hunt Club, shimmying around the courts in her Lacoste tennis skirt.

"Everyone gets their turn," Debra explained. "It'll be you soon enough!"

"You're not giving it to her," Pam added. "You're giving it to yourself. So it can grow eight times its size or more."

"Is that what Sue Fox told you?" Harper asked. "How many times has *she* walked away with the money bag?"

"Believe me," Debra said, "she's earned it."

"How?" Harper asked. "By getting more people to open their wallets?"

"No," Debra said, "by making this all happen."

"Harper," Pam said, "forget about Sue Fox. This is about you. Don't you want to bet on yourself?"

Harper nearly laughed, thinking what a bad bet she was.

"Don't you," Pam said, looking her straight in the eye, "want something for yourself this time?"

There was something in that, Harper had to admit. She'd spent more than half her life leading six-year-olds in two-hundred-dollar breeches around the riding ring, tending to their finely bred Arabians, hanging their bridles and leads, spare crops and helmets in the tack room and making nice with their parents, many of whom didn't think twice about dragging mud across the tennis courts and forgetting to tip the valet.

And when she thought of the things she had thrown away money on over and over in her life—horse feed and tack, Grey Goose, Camel Lights, packets of Valium in the restroom of the Rustic Cabins bar in the old days if you went after six P.M.—maybe throwing it down for this roulette spin just once wasn't a bad idea.

Harper took a breath, then reached inside the cubby, resting her hand on the cash envelope tucked in the back, under her hoodie. It still felt hot. Maybe money always felt hot.

The envelope in her hand, then in her purse.

Hot, hot, hot.

By five o'clock, Harper was no longer thinking of returning the money, abandoning ship. By five o'clock, she was thinking of Pam's cookie jar full of cash, the fat green swirl. It was a kind of freedom, wasn't it? Maybe she would never be free of some things, but to be free from Doug felt like a start.

Harper put her minivan in park at every red light, trading her boots for a borrowed pair of Pam's plaid flats, sliding off her barn jacket for the camel houndstooth she wore only at Christmas services, a coat so old her mother—dead fifteen years—had given it to her. Her high school graduation pearls in her ears.

The ride along Lake Shore Road was one she had made at least twice a day her entire life, passing the sparkling, bottomless waters of

Lake St. Clair. Maybe a handful of residents in their Patagonia and Ray-Bans, walking their Irish setters, their golden retrievers.

When she was a kid, they lived a mere two blocks from the lake, but she could never remember her parents walking along the water. No one ever did. It was like a painting you hung in the front hallway and forgot.

Parking three doors down from Beverly Linebaugh's sprawling ranch house, she turned off the ignition, catching a glance of herself in the rearview mirror, trying to ignore the Clinique powder cracking in her crow's feet, stamping between her eyes.

The house smelled like fairway dew, Polo cologne, carpet cleaner. Like their own childhood, long gone, all gone.

"Thank god!" Pam exclaimed, rushing toward her, eyes twinkling.

"Am I late?" Harper whispered.

"Debra was sure you'd back out," Pam whispered back conspiratorially, grabbing her hand as she stepped inside.

"I never said that," Debra said, clutching a clipboard in the crook of her arm. "Not exactly."

The living room was full, overflowing with cashmere and Elizabeth Arden, smooth coos and light chatter.

Through the patio doors you could see Beverly's ex-husband's putting green collecting frost.

"I'm thinking," she heard Beverly saying, "of dynamiting it."

Three of Pam's friends, all cool blondes, formed in a creamy fist at the center of the room: Caroline Collins, Jill Fleischer, and Becky Schloss. Three PTA moms with stiff blowouts and ears, wrists, and throats draped with family pearls, tennis bracelets.

"Harper," Jill Fleischer, the friendliest of them, waved toward her limply.

"We thought it was just a rumor," Becky Schloss said.

Up close, Becky looked so different since the last time Harper had seen her, a Hunt Club luncheon a year or so ago. The same narrow, knifelike face, but now so tight her right eye was forever winking. Discreetly, she patted at it with a cocktail napkin.

Her husband likes her tight as a drum, Pam had told her. *I don't think he understands physics.*

But Harper had heard other rumors, too, like, *Her husband likes to push her around. You know the type.*

As the room filled, Beverly held court from the rolling bar cart. A lithe, reed-thin woman with wristbones popping like marbles, she had rarely been seen in fall or winter until last year, the first in seven she hadn't spent in Sanibel Island, her first ever as a divorced woman, with a husband under indictment for embezzlement, bank accounts frozen.

"Welcome, how lovely," Beverly cooed, clutching the tips of Harper's fingers in hers, that odd crab pincer pinch of the ladies who lunched.

"Good to see you," Harper said.

"You have worked some kind of horse girl magic on my darling daughter," Beverly said. "Her diagonals are crisp as a dollar bill!"

Twice a week, Harper gave private lessons to Beverly's eleven-year-old, Elektra, who rode, aggressively and badly. The money came from somewhere, Harper thought. Maybe it came from here.

"Can I get you a cocktail?" Beverly asked. "Any clear liquor. I have all the clears."

Clear liquors to match all the pale creams and paper-whites of the upholstery, the wallpaper, the shampooed carpets, the drapes like icicles over windows so clean they squeaked.

"Club soda, thanks," Harper said.

Beverly wrinkled her nose in disappointment.

All the women were drinking vodka sodas except Caroline Collins, the coolest of the three cool blondes, who drank aquavit straight from the freezer.

Harper tried to disappear into the drapes, holding one of the swiftly passed hors d'oeuvres—a Ritz cracker with pepper jam and cream cheese, a WASP delight for four generations—over her open hand to catch the crumbs.

"Harper!" cawed a voice and Harper turned to see Sue Fox, tanned and serene, gold bracelets dancing along her brown wrists as she raised her arms to her. "I told Pam weeks ago that she absolutely had to invite you."

Her embrace, redolent with White Shoulders, felt light as air and Harper was reminded of her own mother's careless hugs, engineered so no garment wrinkled, no hair nudged out of place.

The sound level in the room rose as new faces began appearing—two eager women with matching black bobs who Pam didn't know, a few more she faintly recognized from the Hunt Club, or the carpool line from dropping off Vivian at school.

"We're so excited," one, then the other, kept saying, bouncing on the balls of her feet, her purse swinging aggressively at her side.

Alongside their antic energy, Harper started to feel less awkward, less the bull in the bone-china shop.

And, if she really thought about it, Debra stood out even more, with her planner's energy, hovering over everyone, monitoring attendance and watching the clock like the strictest homeroom monitor you ever had, her drugstore reading glasses pitched on the end of her nose.

"Deb, for god's sake," Sue Fox kept teasing her, "if we wanted to be bossed around all night, we would have invited our husbands."

But somebody needed to collect their "gifts," which Debra did with great fanfare, hoisting an ivory drawstring bag like the bride at an Italian wedding.

Of the five new members, Harper was the only one who'd merely stuffed her five thousand dollars into an old bank deposit envelope, which she dunked into Debra's bag with all the gusto her lone club soda could muster.

One of the black-bobbed women—a recruit from Debra's book club—brought hers in a long blue Tiffany box. The other presented a heavy embossed envelope tied with red ribbon.

The final new member to arrive, an older woman Harper recognized from the sales counter at the League Shop, swept in late, in one manicured hand a department store gift box of the size when you order a gravy ladle or nut bowls from a wedding registry, and in the other a Gucci leash, her cocker spaniel, Fredo, yipping and whirling at her feet.

What did it matter, Harper would later wonder, *what you put the cash in?*

But, somehow, it mattered, all of it. Like the right Ralph Lauren sweater in high school, the L.L.Bean duck boots, laces forever untied.

An hour or more later it began. By then, they'd all had a few drinks, save Harper, who watched it all like a woozy tableau, the smiling women, highballs tinkling in their hands, meandering past an untouched shrimp toast platter on the glass-and-brass coffee table.

(*Don't WASPs ever eat?* Doug, a lapsed Irish Catholic, had asked her once, that first Christmas Pam introduced him to the family. Confided as if Harper wasn't a WASP, was more of his kind, honey. And maybe she was. *We're a lot alike, you and me,* isn't that what he'd said the other night? *They do eat, but such tiny bites,* Harper had replied, grinning. *Is it,* he'd asked, leaning close, *because their teeth are too soft from the quinine?*)

Becky Schloss—once the wealthiest of them all with a mansion on the lake and a husband with some kind of connection to the notorious Tocco family—rang a large silver bell, drawing all attention to the white center of the white room.

"It's time, Sue!" Pam called out, heel snagging in the white carpet. "It's time!"

And Sue Fox—deep in conversation with Debra by the shivering French doors, cracked open for their pluming cigarettes—turned to face the room, a smile spreading across her face.

"It's time! It's time!"

Pam reached for Harper's hand, swinging her arm excitedly, whispering, "I've wanted this for you for so long."

There was a ritual to it: the women forming a circle around the coffee table, faces shiny, flyaway hair and lipstick smudged, heels off, tossed in the corner, pedicured toes dancing in the carpet plush.

"We are only as strong as the weakest among us," Sue began, reading from a mimeographed page from her big watermelon-pink binder. "Therefore we take an oath to one another and ourselves: We the women assembled pledge our loyalty to the Club, our adherence to its rules, our discretion in all matters, and our silence to the outside world. We pledge to protect one another at all times, to commit to the secrecy of the Wheel, and to trust in its promise. All together now: *Women trust, women give, women protect.*"

"Women trust, women give, women protect!" everyone repeated. Harper watched them, her mouth open but not moving.

"I know a woman whose eyes are opening," Beverly began chanting, the other women joining in.

"Who is strong, stronger than anyone knows . . .

"Who is wise, wiser than anyone realizes . . .

"Who is hungry for life."

Debra, her face slick with sweat from the crowded living room, put her hand on Harper's shoulder, then reached for Pam, playfully tugging her hair.

Debra's drunk, Harper noted to herself, hiding a smile. *Debra's never drunk.* There was something sweet about it, lovely.

"I know a woman who is passionate," the women continued, their voices rising.

"Who makes use of the lessons life has taught her, the challenges she faced."

Pam, her face piping with color, her voice strong, her winter-white turtleneck crowding her neck, her hand tight around Harper's.

"Who refuses to limit herself!

"Who recognizes her own value!"

Debra, nearly shouting now like a tent revival meeting, her eyes avid, leaning over to Harper between the verses and whispering, "This is it, this is what we've all been waiting for."

"I know a woman who believes in her power.

"Who has surrendered the desire for approval, for pleasing others.

"I know a woman who is ready for change.

"I know these women. They stand before me now. We are those women."

84

Something about it didn't quite seem real, Harper thought, watching them.

Nothing about it seemed real.

Like so many of those secret sorority rituals, things with laxatives and pubic hair or prescription pill roulette. They were real, but they weren't, because you never told anyone and you never even talked about it to each other. It was sacred, in its way. And you would be embarrassed to even say something so sacred aloud.

Beverly rolled in the chrome bar cart, its top cleared save one glistening bottle of Dom and a thick, heavy gift box that reminded Harper of her girlhood. Christmas mornings with a princess coat, a pair of ice skates wrapped in Jacobson's silver paper, crimson grosgrain ribbon curling at her feet.

"That's twenty-five thousand dollars," Pam whispered in Harper's ear. "Cash!"

"Spread the energy!" Beverly whispered throatily, lifting the top off and holding the box in the air, high above her head, then passing it to Debra at her left.

And one by one, the money box passed.

From Caroline to Becky to Jill to Sue, manicured hand to manicured hand, prim clear polish or Ballet Slippers.

By the time it landed in Harper's own rough, horsewoman's grasp, she—even with all eyes on her calloused palms, shorn nails—couldn't help but feel her heart skip a beat.

"Feel it! Feel it!" the women chanted, their breaths thick with gin and olive brine.

Inside the tissue paper tufting was a stack of cash thick as a boot heel. Their envelopes and boxes emptied, the bills counted, sorted, gathered neatly behind the kitchen door as they'd all drank.

The stack, banded with a thick velvet ribbon—green, of course. You just wanted to hold it and never let it go.

Harper held it, feeling the crisp edges, the creamy weight of the thing.

The women around her were giddy. "Flip through the bills," they urged her.

"You have to feel it. Did you feel it?" they all asked her.

"What am I supposed to feel," Harper finally whispered to her sister.

And Pam looked at her, lipstick smeared across her front teeth, and said, *"Power!"*

"Power!"

And—in spite of herself—Harper felt it, and more. Felt, in that minute, her whole life opening up like a bloom of vodka in her chest.

Sue Fox began chanting again, the velvet ribbon tugged loose now and the bills seeming to dance up her arms like a magic trick.

"I know a woman who believes in her power!

"I know a woman who is ready for change!"

And all the women joined in, surrounding Sue, as if to shimmy against some of her fortune, her power.

Sue lifted her arms high, bills scattering, her head tilted back like a minister on TV, like a preacher at the state fair, where Harper rode from ages ten to nineteen in the Equestrian Pavilion, competing alongside the sheepshearing and the pig racing.

But most of all, Sue reminded her of the queen bee at the Chi O house at U of M. The one who made everyone insane and miserable and ecstatic with such intensity that there were two suicide attempts during the freshman rush she commandeered with imperial exactitude and cruelty.

Y ou're in it, now, sweetie," Pam said, sidling next to her. "In a few months, that'll be you."

Harper nodded, looking longingly at the vodka soda curled in her sister's hand, feeling like the nun at the orgy.

She wanted to be a part of it. The vodka soda, yes, and the cash foremost. But maybe also that frenzy too.

These women, their faces glowing orgiastically, what could be wrong with that?

P op! came the bottle of Dom, Beverly wrestling it between her thighs like a champ. All the women rose, tilting slightly in their velvet flats, black and red and ecru, bows and buckles, crests or monograms.

"I know a woman who believes in her power!

"I know a woman who is ready for change!"

I n a few months, that'll be you.

I t was after midnight when Harper and Pam got home, but Vivian was still awake and possibly high on something—Adderall, untold party drugs, or maybe just the epic thrum of teen girlhood.

They sat, all three, on the rental sofa, microfibered and overstuffed, and Vivian told them the saga of her day, how that asshole substitute soccer coach claimed Cassie flashed her pierced nipple at him in the attendance office and it was really just a way of scaring her into not reporting the time he demanded to see their bloody tampons as evidence of menstruation.

Eventually, Pam slipped into sleep on the sofa listening, the hypnotic taffy pull of Vivian's words *it's all bullshit and misogynist and everyone knows that coach is a big perv*—

So Harper made Vivian her favorite hot cocoa with the mini-marshmallows and a dash of cayenne like after PonyPal classes when she was little and still riding quarter horses. It seemed to soothe her.

"Did you have fun at the party?" Vivian asked, breathless after her tale, which—Harper had to admit—was legitimately harrowing in ways that would have been impossible in her own youth, long before you carried all your secrets in the hot palm of your hand. And how all those secrets could be revealed in an instant, it terrified her.

"It was okay," Harper said. "You know. A lot of women."

"So it's like a woman empowerment thing?" Vivian said. "I thought Aunt Debra called it an investment club."

"Yeah," Harper said, after a pause, "something like that."

"Are you joining too?"

"I guess," Harper said, looking over at Pam, sound asleep, her right arm twitching. "Yeah, I guess I am."

Vivian made a little face, unreadable to Harper.

But then she leaned back on the sofa cushion, watching her sleeping mother.

"Mom's so happy now," Vivian whispered, licking her lip like a kitten with cream. "I never knew she could be happy before."

In bed, Harper couldn't fall asleep. She found herself paging through the guidebook they'd handed out to new members. Its piglet-pink pages and fading laser print reminded her of the purple-print dittos her kindergarten teacher used to pass out, and of her grandmother's old spiral-bound church recipe books, with mimeographed instructions for peach melba, Harvey Wallbanger cake, something called "company casserole."

"If we abide by this booklet," Sue Fox had told them, "and our own common sense, we have nothing to fear. The main thing to remember is that this is our thing. We don't talk about it to others."

"It's our thing," Becky Schloss chuckled. "Cosa nostra."

"Our thing," Sue said, smiling a beauty pageant smile, "minus the machine guns."

The first few pages were all about sisterhood, how we all held immense power we only had to tap into.

But most of the book was about rules. How to talk about the Wheel (*don't!*), how to recruit new members (with great care), how to make sure the Wheel is safe (*and legal!*). About what to do when you "run the Wheel" and get that cash.

Not cash—*gift*.

As her sisters had told her, *gift* was the key word. The magic word.

But that was just the beginning. There were more rules:

- *Use our secret magic language. Invite, not recruit! Gift, not invest!*

- *Never hold meetings or discuss Club matters in public places or over email or phone.*

- *Never wire or transfer gifts. If you can't make a party, entrust a fellow member with the cash. In a pinch, wrap in foil, insert into your thickest magazine, and send overnight via FedEx. Never U.S. mail!*

• *Don't deposit your gift all at once. Instead, do so in increments of less than ten K.*

Because banks report cash deposits of ten thousand dollars or more, Sue had explained. And why draw attention?

But the most important proviso was the last one:

• *Since the money you receive in the Wheel are gifts (not income, not investments), they do not need to be reported on your income tax form.*

Because gifts up to twelve thousand dollars were tax-free. *No need to report!* After all, why would the federal government discourage gifts? Wasn't it the dream of America, a community rallying around a friend in need, like George Bailey at the end of *It's a Wonderful Life.* But women! All women. What if Mary Bailey had had the Wheel?

Harper had never even thought of the IRS. *Or* federal laws, it was beyond her pay grade anyway. Harper had never made enough money to even worry about anything other than what could be contained on her 1040-EZ, so what did it matter.

*W*hy, Sue Fox had said, *should we hand our money to some stock trader, some man at Merrill Lynch, some man you never see, much less trust, when we could give it to our friends? To one another?*

The first time I was gifted, Becky Schloss had confided, *I brought the cash home and spread the bills all over the bed and my husband said, You mean this actually works?*

And it was true, wasn't it? The men they knew had been doing this kind of thing all their lives. Cutting corners, finding write-offs, riding on credit, living by technicalities.

Besides, Sue Fox assured them, her husband, a CPA, had reviewed everything. And Caroline Collins's husband, an attorney.

It had all been vetted, cleared by men, you see.

Female empowerment and male assurance—it seemed like a mixed message to Harper, but what of it? What did it matter, so long as it worked?

But the more gravely phrased provisions made Harper wonder if there had been trouble in the past.

Above all, we must be careful whom we invite into our special circle. The Wheel isn't right for most women, nor are most women right for it. Invite women who you respect and trust. The woman who invited you is someone who believes in your rich potential and that you will be an asset to the Wheel.

Harper lingered on that last sentence awhile.

I've wanted this for you for so long, Pam had said, slipping her hand in Harper's like when they were ready to ride the Gemini at Cedar Point.

Pam has brought us Harper, Beverly Linebaugh had said, introducing all the new members, *whom many of you know and love already. Harper, we're so happy you've joined us.*

You make us even stronger!

The words silly, maybe. The language canned. But the looks on their faces, mascara flecked, the catch in everyone's throat when they talked about changing their lives.

The women all so warm to her, embracing her, Sue Fox even kissing her flush on the mouth.

I always wanted to be a part of something, Debra had confided to her as the party broke up, nearly rolling her ankle on a fallen champagne flute. *I always wanted this.*

It reminded Harper of old feelings, feelings she tried not to have anymore. The smell of Leigh's hair, the soft baby strands at the base of her neck.

Is it okay to want things? Harper wondered but didn't say out loud.

Collapsed on Patrick's twin bed, her eyes shut tight, her nephew's old, cracked headphones over her ears, Harper willed herself to sleep just after three.

She dreamt of orange sherbet, vodka sodas, the click-click-click of women's heels on a marble floor. Of lipsticked mouths, open and chanting.

Of Sue Fox grinning, her hands sunk in a big bowl of caviar, the black muck gleaming on her fingers.

I know a woman who believes in her power!

I know a woman who is ready for change!

Of Pam's embrace, her cheek hot against hers.

You're in it now, sweetie. In a few months, that'll be you.

Are you ready," Pam said the next morning, twirling the drawstrings on her Hunt Club hoodie, "to accept Jesus into your life?"

They both laughed as Harper followed Pam down the blue-painted stairs to the musty basement, a chill to the floor despite the rag rugs Pam had thrown everyone.

It was time, she said, for Harper to learn all the secrets of the Wheel.

Holding a big coffee to stay warm, Harper sat on the old sofa, one rind of the serpentine sectional they'd grown up with and on, from its original home in their parents' stately Tudor, to their widowed mother's ranch house to the rec room of Pam and Doug's rambling colonial, and now, finally, to the ever-flooding basement of Pam's split-level rental.

A sofa once so chic that it had been the talk of the neighborhood, with its abstract pattern, sizzling pink and lilac splatter and a darker chevron overlay. A coked-up fever dream of Manet, pleated on the front, smooth on the back, and how many hours lying on it in childhood wonder or teen agony, her fingers digging under its accordion pleats.

It was on this same sofa Harper had first slid her hand down Stephanie Modelli's jeans, Stephanie whispering, *There, there, there!*

But those days were long over and the sofa now smelled of dog pee, well water, who knew. Harper wasn't even sure how Pam had ended up with half of it, and whether the other half was in Debra's basement. It would be like their mother to split it between the two of them. *Harper, darling,* she could imagine her saying, *is this the dowry you really want to fight over?*

Harper watched as Pam began sliding out an old classroom easel from behind the dented furnace with great ceremony.

The night before, Harper had heard the women talk about something called the Board. What would happen when the Board was reordered and *have you gotten a look at the Board yet? Has Pam shown you the Board?*

"Ta-da!" Pam said, flipping the easel around like Vanna turning the tiles.

As if on cue, the clothes dryer changed cycles loudly, rocking on the cement floor like some psychotic drumroll as Pam dragged the easel directly in front of Harper.

Harper wasn't sure what she expected, but it wasn't this: a garage-sale corkboard, studded with bright thumbtacks connected by yarn. A Jackson Pollock array of squiggly colored lines that formed a pyramid.

It reminded her of Pam's reigns as Parents' Club president, as Girl Scout leader, as sorority president, even as student council president back in their own high school days. Pam with her highlighters, thumbtacks, stickers, and foil stars, trying to organize everything, make sense of it, make everything seem fair and logical and true.

Harper squinted, leaning forward, noticing that under each thumbtack was an index card with a name written in bright colors: deep green, sparkling silver, metallic gold.

Harper's was the newest one, her name in red.

"What do you see?" Pam asked, very much in teacher mode.

"A pyramid," Harper said, noticing her card sat at the bottom.

"Wrong." Pam shook her head. "It's not a pyramid."

"Sure it is. The shape—"

"It's a triangle," Pam said, her hands tenting for effect.

"Okay," Harper conceded. "Triangle. What's the difference?"

"There's a big difference," Pam said, eyes glittering. "There's no hierarchy in triangles."

"But there is a hierarchy," Harper said. "I'm at the bottom and Sue Fox is at the top."

"No longer!" Pam said, plucking Harper's card from the bottom and moving it up one row. "No one ever stays at the top. No one ever stays at the bottom. It's always moving."

Harper wasn't so sure. But she waited, listening, watching her sister twirl around the board, chattering with such contagious energy.

Pam explained that there were four tiers, starting at the bottom with the five new members.

It was simple, really. You started at the bottom, with the five K in cash. The buy-in. The outlay. The bite.

After that first night, your only job was to invite new women, fresh blood.

Once you brought a new woman in, you moved forward. *Not upward!* Forward!

"After every party, the Board shifts," Pam said. "All the new members invite new women and move forward. Moving up and up at each party until you receive your gift."

"Okay," Harper said, her head aching a little. "But now, after last night . . ."

". . . we need to update the Board," Pam finished.

And with that, she yanked Sue Fox's card off the board, flicking it with gusto.

"Sue's done," she said. "She ran the Wheel."

"So she's out?"

Pam punched Sue Fox's card to the bottom, so far down it nearly drifted off to the floor.

"Once you reach the top," she said, "you can start again at the bottom. Or start a new group with new members. Or both. And rise again."

Harper's eyes flew back up to the top of the pyramid. There were two cards there: Becky Schloss and Pam herself.

"Who's next?" Harper asked. "You or Becky?"

"Me," Pam said, smiling. "She invited one last night. I invited two."

Harper smiled back. "I put you on top, huh?"

"Honey," Pam said, squeezing Harper's wrist in her soft hand, "you don't know the half of it."

———

Harper stared at the index cards, edges fluttering from the furnace draft, fluttering like pinned butterflies.

"But how long does it take?" she asked, looking at all the names. "I mean, it seems like it's working out pretty well for Sue Fox, but . . ."

"It can happen very fast," Pam said. "As fast as you want it to."

Sue Fox, it turned out, had risen to the top four times in eighteen months.

"Sue never explained this part," Pam said, "but I figured out pretty fast the only way to keep it going—to really work the Wheel, you have to multiply your efforts."

"What do you mean?"

Pam flipped the corkboard around to the other side. A second pyramid appeared, empty so far, except for the tacks and the yarn.

"You need to have more than one group of women going," she said. "The growth imperative."

"Quoting Doug now?" Harper said, raising an eyebrow.

But Pam only laughed.

It reminded Harper of something from the night before, how Debra, a little tipsy by the powder room, confessed, *Pam said you weren't sure I wanted you in. But I did. Even before her. I told her months ago. But you know how she is. Pam.*

And Harper did. So many of the women there last night were Pam's friends. Pam had always had so many friends. It was like elementary school. How even though she was the youngest, Pam would be invited to every birthday party, even by girls in Debra's and Harper's own grades who'd forgotten to invite Debra and Harper themselves.

Everyone loved Pam.

———

And the hard part is over for you now," Pam was saying, maybe seeing something on Harper's face. "You already paid in. You already took the leap."

"Okay, but—"

"You're already one step closer to all the things you want," Pam said, looking at her. "Harper. Baby. Aren't there things you want?"

And in her sister's face she saw a million things. Even pity.

Wouldn't you like to be free?

Harper walked up to the Board, flipping it around again, staring at it. She found her card, pressed her palm over the tack in its center.

Reaching past her, Pam plucked it loose and, with a grin, dragged it up the Board, past Beverly and Caroline, even past Debra's, to the very top. Pushed the tack over the spot Sue Fox's card had been.

"See what the top looks like," she said softly. "Feel what winning looks like."

Harper closed her eyes. She couldn't imagine it, but maybe she could touch the edges of it, electric.

"Now all you have to do is one thing."

Harper nodded. "Recruit?"

"*Invite*," Pam corrected her, flicking the card with her fingers, spinning it.

"Invite," Harper repeated.

"Bring us more women."

Later, much later, Harper would remember this conversation as the key to something.

If only new members paid in, well, everything depended on getting new members.

How does giving away your money solve your money problems?

By expanding the Wheel. Power in numbers. More women, more power.

It was all right there if one only looked at the Board, did the math, reviewed the mimeographed manual she'd given her:

The Wheel is always moving, active, circulating the energy of giving and receiving.

We don't invest, we gift.

We don't recruit, we invite.

The key is always new women!

Once a member receives her gift, the group buds off into two new groups with all existing participants shifting up a level.

And the bottom of the pyramid—the triangle—needs to be filled again, *with the lucky new members you bring in!*

Remember: *You are not taking their money; you are blessing them.*

It's all about inviting new members, so you can rise, rise, rise!

So it wasn't a pyramid, it was a triangle. And technically, you weren't selling anything—not raffle tickets, not Girl Scout cookies, as they were used to. Nor were they selling vitamins, kitchen knives, magazine subscriptions, cosmetics, penny stocks, as some women they knew had taken up with the first round of layoffs.

Except, in a way, you were. You were selling the Wheel. New recruits—members—were the raffle tickets, the vitamins.

You were selling the women you knew. Even the ones you loved.

But, Harper thought, you only needed to do it for a while. Or she only did.

You could make back your money times four and get out.

Or she could.

What could be the harm in that? The men they knew had been doing it all their lives. Maybe the women should, too, only better. And maybe, sometimes, for better reasons. For their children's tuition, their husband's medical bills. Or to erase a private debt that filled you with shame.

H-a-r-p-e-r, Doug cooed into her voicemail that night. *Have you thought more of what we talked about?*

Pam listens to you. She trusts you. We could help each other. We always have.

Harper deleted the message. She knew the words behind the words.

The threat humming in there: *What would your sister think if she found out you owe fifty large to the man she's telling everyone in town stole her money?*

It was a thought she couldn't hold on to. A poison.

6

Sit down and think of everyone you know (aunts, cousins, friends, coworkers). Check your address book, church directory, school directory. Start up a conversation. Share your story. If they respond in a negative way or ask intrusive questions, drop the subject and wish them well. Write down everything they say in your log—their financial worries, their pressures.

We love women who say, "I've been waiting for this!"

These are the women with the nerve and the need. These are the women who need us.

Harper didn't think she could do it, didn't know how.

She wasn't like Pam, the life of the party, the extrovert and social butterfly, the honeybee hopping from flower to flower. She wasn't even like Debra, the font and the planner, her organizer energies, the forever class secretary, the meticulous treasurer of every group, league, alliance, association.

Pam could just draw aside one of a dozen friends at a holiday party, her book club, the PTA meeting, the school's College Night. Pam could start up a conversation in the line at the post office, the bank.

And even Debra, forever joining things, could just open her phone book, her Filofax, could pull aside a fellow member at the Junior League or the Rotary Club or one of the wives from Perry's old softball team or his lodge and tell them, in that Debra way, what they must do, should do, if they had any sense at all.

"But you don't have to do any of that," Pam assured her. "Just do what *you* do. Do it your way. Like you always did."

"What do you mean? What do I do?"

"Like in high school, the Varsity Club. And at Michigan, at Chi O. Rush Week." She paused, looking at her. "Harper, you *know*."

But that was different, Harper thought. It was so easy, she never even had to try.

For Varsity Club, all she did was make a pitch in the girls' locker room after lacrosse practice, standing on a bench, promising twenty-minute meetings and a keg party, making them cry over the Special Olympics until they agreed to a charity car wash, arriving in their tiny shorts, every dad and uncle and granddad shaking their wallets into soap-streaked buckets passed around. Her teammates *wanted* to be in the Varsity Club after that.

But Chi O was trickier. Recruitment chair three years in a row because she never wanted to have to organize events or run meetings. She certainly didn't want to keep the books.

It came surprisingly easy, like stringing pretty pearls.

You knew the ones, the way they looked at you. Thumpers, Harper called them. Big eyes, hindfoot wagging. Quiet, sweet girls easily spooked by the more intense girls, the sorority princesses.

They came for the Rush Week mixers, the happy hours, the tailgate parties, the house tour meet-and-greets, blowouts and hot-pink minis, buffed and polished head to toe, go-cups of vodka and Hawaiian Punch, the frenzy of Jens and Heathers and Katies and Lisas.

The intensity of it all, hopping from house to house, oohing and aahing, screaming and laughing, hugging and toasting, and at least one girl crying.

Harper hung back, watching it all. She herself had never had to try because she was a legacy, and Debra worked damn hard to get her bid.

Just be yourself, she would tell the rushees, meeting up with them, coming straight from equestrian team practice, still in her breeches, and watching it all, their girlish frenzy.

Maybe that was why so many would come to her room after, or even throw a rock at her window at two A.M., drunk on the back lawn. *Can I come in? Can I come up? Harper!*

Harper would say sure and give them one of her fleeces to throw over their party dresses and they practically jumped into her bed. *Thumpers.*

They loved Harper's lazy energy, that's what Pam used to say. How her hair hung long and over her eyes, how she'd laugh at their twitchy, teary nerves over who liked them and ask them why any of that would even matter, *a girl as cool as you.*

Before long, they'd get under Harper's covers, so soft, like kittens, so sweet they'd hurt your teeth.

In the morning, Harper's pillow always smelled like coconut. One eye half-open, she'd see the girl wiggling back into her party dress, chugging water from Harper's thermos, fingers shaking from the hangover, from all the stresses of Rush Week, from the first month of college, from all the boys, from everything. *Harper, Harper, can I wear your fleece home?*

Once a girl stole a pair of her breeches. She said she loved to press the velvety inner patch against her cheek and remember.

The fleece, the breeches, sometimes a sweatshirt, a tank top.

It smells like you.

Like barn? Harper would laugh. But she knew what they were really talking about was themselves, their coconut sweetness, their once-hollow centers, made suddenly interesting to someone else for the first time. Harper could make them feel interesting.

That was twenty years ago," Harper said, looking in the hallway mirror. "No one tells you your face will turn into a three-day-old balloon after forty."

"I bet you find one within the week," Pam insisted with a smile.

And Pam was right.

There was a first, awkward attempt at the Hunt Club. Mrs. Ferris, who liked to watch her youngest daughter, Kirsty, ride in the morning, whose hands always shook when she tried to light that first cigarette. Mrs. Ferris, with her Burberry scarves, forehead tight as a hard-boiled egg.

Harper didn't know anything about her financial situation other than the fact that her burgundy Lincoln Town Car had a conspicuous fender dent that, according to Mr. Bingham, was a "goddamned eyesore" in the Hunt Club parking lot.

"A room full of women?" Mrs. Ferris said, interrupting Harper even before she could finish her pitch. "I could kill myself just thinking about it."

But then Harper came up with a new idea. She came up with Sandy.

Sandy Gutowski née Hall, a sophomore on the lacrosse team when Harper was a senior. No one paid attention to Sandy, a timid girl, her mouth thick with braces, until one day in practice Harper noticed that Sandy was both ambidextrous and double-jointed and, with the right attention, could be a star on long-stick middie. Which she was, for a brief time before she blew out her knee cutting late to the net, sitting out most of her junior year on the bench.

(She took it hard. There were rumors she swallowed a full bottle of Tylenol the night of the championship. That she'd had her stomach pumped at St. John, crying over missing the game.)

In the intervening years, they'd rarely crossed paths until Sandy started working part-time at the library. Harper saw her there at least twice a week when she dropped off Vivian for swimming classes next door, or whatever Vivian did from five to seven, which, more likely, was find her way to Cassie's bedroom, or to Bronco's, the liquor store just off the freeway where all the teenagers bought their Mad Dog and their beer. Her hair was never wet when Harper picked her up, and she never smelled of chlorine, but she was always smiling.

But there was Sandy at the library's front desk, fidgeting endlessly with her rubber stamp and her ink pad, with her glue stick and silver barcode wand and—as Harper learned—not making a dent in the eighty-seven-thousand-dollar debt she'd carried since her husband died, a heart attack at the exact wrong moment in the stock market, his secret day-trading habit gone into overdrive since he'd been laid off from Chrysler's auditing division. His buyout was gone, kaput, not even enough to pay for an economy casket.

So Sandy, left with twin boys and a double mortgage, checked out books for three hours a day four days a week—the most hours the library would give her since, as they told her, she *really needed to read more books*—seated shakily on a swiveling stool and waiting for her life to change.

Sandy's debt was what the mimeographed guidebook called her *pain point*. The problem or need that the prospective member faces.

Identifying and addressing pain points, the guidebook noted, *will convince them to change their lives through the Wheel.*

Sandy earned, by Harper's calculation, about eight dollars an hour, barely above minimum wage. But her manicure was immaculate, and you couldn't miss it because Sandy was forever lacing her fingers through her springy curls, a nervous tic. A poker tell.

Which made sense, it turned out, because Sandy loved to gamble. Harper had clocked the MGM Grand Rewards parking tag on her sad little powder-blue Ford Escort in the library parking lot a few days before.

"So pretty," Harper said, watching Sandy stamp the Elmore Leonard novel. "Your nails, I mean."

Damn if Sandy didn't blush.

"I do it myself," she said, a smile so faint you might miss it, slapping the plastic cover shut on the hardback, "these days."

"You could charge for it," Harper said. "If you wanted."

Sandy looked up, surprised. "Do you think?"

"Sure," Harper said. "If you're looking for extra money. I know I always am."

That was when Harper confided she was on her way to Greektown, to the casinos.

Sandy looked at her. "Sometimes I go," she whispered. "Just the slots."

Harper smiled. "I love the slots."

Sandy's hand went to her curls, tugging at them, drawing them straight in anxious repetition. Harper wondered if it had driven her husband crazy. It already drove her crazy.

"But," Harper said, another lie, "I get a little scared downtown by myself."

Sandy's face tightened, went pale. "I know. You hear about things. My husband never let me set foot in Detroit alone."

"Maybe we could go together," Harper asked. "After you get off."

"Maybe," Sandy said, barely a whisper, "we could."

Watching Sandy at the slots, Harper thought: *Well, gosh, I'd be helping her.*

It was just like Pam said, *You're giving them this opportunity. To empower themselves.*

Because there was nothing empowering about sitting among the somber crew of daytime gamblers that surrounded them, oxygen tanks and bad skin.

The MGM Grand was Sandy's favorite, she said, though she'd had some good luck at the Greektown Casino. Her husband always said blackjack was the only game you had a chance at, and if anyone knew numbers it was the former chief auditor of one of the Big Three. But she could never do the math in her head fast enough. She could never stop her hands from shaking on the felt.

The slots, it turned out, were where Sandy belonged.

Her first time, she won one hundred and sixty dollars.

It's the best and worst thing that can happen to you, Harper thought. Winning the first time. Feeling that feeling.

It reminded her of when she was a teenager. How all the girls had Pappagallo belts, the ones with the interlocking twin gold buckles shaped like teddy bears, spouting whales, lion heads, seashells, kissing mice, the satisfying click as one met the other.

The click-click of your belt against another girl's as you rolled on the sofa together, or in the backseat, Tiffani Lambert's teeth knocking hers, the smell of watermelon gum and orthodonture, the twin golden clamshells on her belt pressing hotly against Harper's pelvis. The click-click, finally, at last and her lacrosse-calloused fingers inside, on her patterned underwear—sprigs of cherry, watermelon slices.

Tiffani Lambert and the click-click of the belt. You could chase that forever.

The slots were like that for Sandy. She couldn't get enough. She'd started them to get out of a hole and dug herself one five feet deeper.

They stood, side by side, plastic cups of gin and tonic in hand, at Sandy's favorite machine: I Dream of Jeannie, a dazzling pink and aqua with spinning genie bottles animated on-screen. *Make a wish! Make a wish!*

Sandy pressed the fat neon-green button over and over, her sensible flats tapping on the swirling carpet. Each time, the TV show's bouncy, bounding theme song boomed, pink lights flashing.

She lost and lost and lost until she had to run to the ATM, making Harper leave the Wheel of Fortune machine to hold her spot.

Sandy, pink under the pink lights' tinkling, clicked and clicked again, her hand drifting to her hair, pulling the curls loose, letting them spring to tightness again. Biting her lip.

A baby chick ready to be plucked, Harper thought. A Thumper, eyes so big, hind foot twitching.

Two hours later, Sandy was crying in the powder room, the attendant handing her tissue after tissue from the tall lavender box.

Sandy was in what Pam and Debra and Sue and the guidebook would call *the bottom of the funnel,* wherein the prospective member has considered her pain points, explored her options (the library, the slots), and is on the brink of opening herself up to the opportunity and changing her life.

It was all so easy. Harper couldn't believe how easy it was.

Always remember, Pam told her, *you are giving them a gift.*

Vodka and cranberries at the round bar, spinning on the stools, Sandy's eyes red, tissue balled, her voice slurring now.

"I shouldn't have gone for that credit card advance, I shouldn't—"

And Harper assuring her, "I'd've done the same thing."

Most of all: listening. Which is what Harper had always done, with those sorority pledges, with girls and then women crying in bathrooms everywhere, with nervous mothers at the Hunt Club, biting their nails to ribbons as their gangly daughters attempted their first jump, as Mr. Bingham warned them their dues were, well, overdue. Six months overdue in fact.

And then, at the critical moment: placing her hands on either side of Sandy's spinning stool, leaning forward, and asking her to come to Jesus.

"You never had a chance," Harper said.

"What do you mean?" Sandy said, one hand clawing through her hair.

"You know those sounds you heard? The way the machine lit up each time? It's a trick."

Harper had read it in a magazine once. How they program it so all the sounds and lights go off even if you lose.

"They ran these tests on gamblers," Harper said.

And she took Sandy's hand in hers.

"To see how fast your heart would beat," she continued. "How hot your skin got."

Sandy looked down at Harper's hand around her wrist, her finger on her vein.

"So even though you lost," Harper said, "once you hear those bells, see those lights, all you want to do is play again."

"Shit," Sandy whispered.

Harper could feel Sandy's heart beating like Thumper's tail.

"You felt like a winner," she said, moving her finger from Sandy's wrist to her hot palm, "so why would you stop?"

Sandy's legs shaking, her plastic vodka-and-cranberry cup wedged between her knees.

In the article, they talked about slot players getting in a state called *dark flow*. The losses disguised as small wins—it lulls them. They sink into the pleasure and escape even as they're drowning.

"I'm in trouble," Sandy whispered, her tongue curling around her tiny straw. "So much trouble."

"We all are, Sandy," Harper said. "But maybe there's another way. A way you won't be alone."

Sandy looked at her, those doe eyes.

"Where you'll meet women like you, and me, and we're in it together, hand in hand, hip to hip."

"Where's that?" Sandy asked, and Harper could hear her mouth go dry. Could feel the yearning.

"Can you keep a secret?"

She didn't tell Sandy what the casino owners also learned, but it was the key: *There's no sound at all if you lose right away and stop playing.*

It turned out no one could bear it. The silent machine, just staring you in the face.

You'd do anything to end that silence, to stay in the game.

"I can keep a secret," Sandy said, leaning closer to Harper. Bending down slightly, her breasts close against Harper's arm. "I promise."

A week later, Harper held Sandy's moist hand as they stepped down into the sunken living room of Sue Fox's classic colonial, red brick and green shutters, all-American.

"I'm so nervous," Sandy whispered.

"Don't be," Harper said, squeezing her hand. "It's just a party among friends."

"But these women aren't my friends," Sandy said, looking around.

"They are now."

As elegant as Beverly Linebaugh's party had been, there'd been so little food, but Sue had laid out large trays of salmon pâté and dainty crabcakes from Tom's Oyster Bar, a fleet of mini-cheesecakes alongside a champagne punch. Sandy and the two other new women huddled over it all, their eyes wide at the splendor.

"It feels good being on this side, doesn't it?" Debra said to Harper, passing her near the kitchen.

And it did, in a way. She couldn't imagine ever handing over five thousand dollars to anyone again.

But she did wonder about Sandy, who'd called her late the night before, her voice high and strained. *I went to four jewelers before I found one who'd do it,* she said. *My husband paid fifteen thousand for it when he proposed, so my wedding ring should've been worth more than three, shouldn't it?*

Harper had suggested other things from the guidebook. A new credit card, a cash advance, borrowing against an insurance policy.

But Sandy had done all these things already, to make her mortgage payments, to pay for her sons' orthodonture.

It's okay, Sandy said, a faraway voice, on some ancient cordless phone. *I never liked that ring anyway.*

Thankfully, Pam approached her immediately, looping her arm around Sandy's waist, complimenting her manicure and her figure (*What I would give for your waistline!*).

Pam was always the first, but others followed suit, Jill Fleischer handing Sandy a vodka soda, Beverly telling her she must try Sue's Roquefort-rolled grapes.

"How is it different from my husband's office football pool?" Jill was saying. "The one he loses every year. Here's the answer. With the Wheel, everyone gets to win."

"My husband wouldn't even let me buy a lottery ticket," Sandy said softly.

"We know the drill," Pam replied, squeezing Sandy's narrow waist. "Just another case of men trying to put the thumb on women and keep us down."

Pam and Sue Fox. Neither would have ever called themselves a feminist, and yet both knew how to talk like one. Both knew how to organize and get things done, to agitate and persuade. To inspire. To get what they wanted.

I t's Pam's night, ladies," Sue reminded everyone, turning up the music, breathy, bouncy pop songs they all remembered from high school.

It was Pam's big night, as it had been Sue's last time.

But watching her, she saw a tension, too, in her sister's eyes.

"Are you okay?" Harper asked her.

———————

B ecause something had happened hours before. An upsetting thing.
Pulling up to the driveway after work, Harper saw Doug's acid-green Mustang sitting out front, its front door hanging open like he'd leapt out so fast he hadn't bothered to slam it shut.

The garage open like a mouth agog, Pam and Doug were screaming at each other inside, the door's pull cord swinging between them, Doug holding a sack of something heavy in his hands.

"Don't you dare!" Pam cried out. "You are not permitted in this house."

"You think you can take any more from me?" Doug asked, lifting the sack. "Because this is all I've got!"

"Get out! Go back to your bachelor pad! Your perky blond assistant! Your secret bank accounts in the Caymans!"

At first, Harper thought she was seeing things because, improbably, Doug swung the sack high in the air until pennies began spilling forth like confetti, scattering across the garage floor.

"Take them!" he demanded. "All my wheat pennies. Collected since I was six years old. But they're yours, you greedy bitch! All yours!"

Her feet skittering over the pennies, Pam hurled open the door of her Lexus, the heel of her hand on the horn, the sound blaring like a reveille.

"Someone call the police!" she cried out, her voice blending with the horn.

Harper couldn't move, paralyzed by the spectacle. Thinking of Vivian, hoping she wasn't inside, hearing it all, seeing it all, her mother in sweatpants, screaming bloody murder. Her father raging in his Nantucket Red golf pants. Her father, probably three Scotches deep and swinging that half-full sack at her mother, swinging so close Harper wanted to cover her eyes.

112

It felt like he might do anything.

"We're in the money," Doug was singing now, stomping on the pennies like grapes. "We're in the money! Is that what you want?"

An opera of marital discord, histrionic divorce drama, but there was a darkness in it too. In their relentlessness and in the way neither of them seemed to feel they had anything to lose.

"Harper!" Pam said, seeing her at the foot of the driveway. "Call the police. Tell them we caught a deadbeat dad in our garage."

Harper wanted to hide, but it was too late.

Doug had spotted her, an odd smile on his face.

Harper felt a sharp shock of fear. *He's going to tell,* she thought. *He's going to tell Pam about the loan and Pam will never talk to me again.*

"I'm calling," Harper lied, holding her phone in the air. "I'm calling nine-one-one!"

But Doug was already careering past Harper with a wink that said, simultaneously, *Do you believe this shit?* and *I'll deal with you later.*

"You saved me," Pam said, both of them watching Doug's car disappear down El Dorado Drive. "You saved the day, sis."

I think Fitzie ate half the pennies before I swept them up," Pam joked to Harper now, her hands curled around her highball glass, sweating a deep ring into Sue Fox's sideboard.

Adding, with a whisper, "He'll be sorry. For what he's doing. But never half as sorry as he's made me."

Harper put her arm around her just as Debra approached, a Xanax in her palm.

"They give them to Perry," she said, as Pam plucked it from her, "but he has a few to spare."

H arper's phone kept buzzing in her pocket, a throbbing thing. After Doug's tantrum in the driveway, she didn't dare look.

Instead, she stuffed it in her purse and dumped the purse in Sue's bedroom, on the California king with all the other handbags.

"You know, I wasn't sure about you," someone said.

Harper turned around to see Sue herself in the doorway, velvet headband matching her velvet belt, a newly filled ice bucket in hand.

"If I'm being honest," Sue continued, "I wasn't one hundred percent."

"Okay," Harper said.

"I thought you were too much of a . . ." Sue started, pausing as the door closed behind her.

Harper looked at her, waiting.

"Too much of an individual," Sue finished. "You always did your own thing."

"I guess," Harper said. "But remember, we were teammates. You were one of the best attack players we had."

Sue smiled, the first genuine one Harper had seen since joining. Almost kittenish.

"I fucking loved lacrosse," she said, swinging the ice bucket by its handle, almost coquettishly. "But you didn't let me finish. I wanted to say I was wrong about you. Sandy is a good get. I can tell she'll throw everything into this. She'll bring all the Al-Anon women here."

"Sandy's in Al-Anon?" Harper said, surprised. She was pretty sure you weren't supposed to recruit at an anonymous meeting.

"Don't you remember that time in high school, Sandy's mom throwing up in the parking lot after a game?"

"I forgot about that," Harper said. But they'd all seen it. And no one said a word to Sandy after. At least not to her face.

"I guess she's a regular at the meetings," Sue said, smoothing the bedspread—strewn with Coach saddle bags, the wood-handled Bermuda purses, the top-handled satchels—with her free hand. "That really opens us up to huge numbers if Sandy's open to it. Do you think she is?"

"I don't know," Harper said, a little guiltily. "Probably. She really needs money."

"Anyway," Sue said, hugging the ice bucket to her chest, "it means she's good at keeping secrets."

know a woman who believes in her power!

"I know a woman who is ready for change!"

In the hot center of the hot swirl of women, Pam shone in the wine-colored silk blouse she'd bought at the Somerset Collection for this very occasion.

At home, she'd fiddled for twenty minutes in front of the mirror, sucking in her stomach, trying different belts, working to master something she called the French tuck.

But now, hours later, the blouse hung half-loose, dappled with other women's lipstick, taupe foundation, as they cheered her on.

Harper assumed it would be like last time, when Beverly had rolled in a bar cart laden with cash.

But Sue had more dramatic plans for Pam, emerging from the kitchen with an enormous gold-foil dollar-sign balloon, a cascade of ribbons twirling around her arm.

"I know a woman who believes in her power!" everyone chanted as Sue handed Pam a giant pearl stickpin.

"That Sue," clucked Debra behind her, "she knows how to present."

And suddenly it was happening, Pam taking the stickpin with one hand and covering her eyes with the other, as if this were a piñata, and reaching out and all the women chanting and—

"I know a woman who is ready for change!"

BAM! Like a Looney Tunes cartoon, the balloon exploded gold confetti, fifty, hundred-dollar, five-hundred dollar bills floating everywhere and all the women screeching and cheering and Pam whirling around, her palms open like a little girl's first snow, until she grew dizzy.

"Happiest I've seen her," Debra said wryly, "since her wedding day."

"Your sister," Sandy whispered, startling Harper, who'd forgotten she was there. "She's a goddamned queen."

After, Harper was smoking on the frozen deck when Pam, smirking, slid the patio door open, a pair of champagne flutes hanging between her fingers.

"What?" Harper said. "We're toasting again?"

Without saying a word, Pam thrust one of the flutes into Harper's hand, bottom first.

"Baccarat," Harper read. "So what?"

"Look at the inscription," Pam said, plucking Harper's cigarette and taking a drag herself.

Harper looked closer, then saw it. Her parents' initials and their wedding date.

"But . . ."

"The estate sale," Pam said. "After Dad died. Remember how some bitch offered Mom two bucks for their wedding glasses?"

Harper didn't know what to say, recalling only how nightmarish that day had been for their mother, watching all their family heirlooms stuffed into the L.L.Bean totes of friends and neighbors.

"Turns out that bitch was Sue Fox," Pam said.

Harper looked at her, dazed.

But then she saw Pam's lip twitch and the laughter came, loud and strident, vodka-powered, even a little scary. "Come on," she said. "It's funny."

It was funny, maybe. And Pam's laughter was always so contagious. Harper started laughing too. They both couldn't stop. The more they laughed, the funnier it seemed.

The party went longer than Beverly's, far longer. And Beverly herself, after too many vodkas, was splayed on Sue's brocade sofa, her blond hair streaking the dark pillows.

All the women's shoes were off, a tumble of spiky heels and sensible flats cluttering the entryway, Becky Schloss's perpetual red-bottom pumps.

Among the new members, Harper thought she recognized a woman in a faded Laura Ashley dress, a Peter Pan collar.

"Isn't she from your church choir?" Harper asked Debra.

"Yes," Debra said. "Maggie Mueller."

"Did you bring her?" Harper said.

"No," Debra said. "She's Pam's."

"Oh. So she—"

"I was going to invite her. I'd been talking to her for a few months about it. She was waiting on some insurance money. I guess it came in, and then . . ."

"Shit," Harper said. "Does Pam know you'd been talking to her?"

Debra shrugged. "It's okay. It doesn't matter."

You weren't supposed to poach, but Harper supposed it was inevitable. They all knew the same people, especially Pam and Debra.

"I guess I wasn't aggressive enough," Debra said, finishing her drink. "You snooze, you lose."

———

117

In the kitchen, Caroline Collins and Becky Schloss were taking turns
stuffing Pam's take into her cleavage as Pam purred along to a song
Harper recalled from Vivian's repertoire: *Dom, cash, and ho-ho-hoes!
Pop that cork, baby—oh-oh-oh!*

Sandy, so excited to be a part of it, sat on the kitchen island, clap-
ping along with glee.

"Harper, honey," Pam said, waving her over, "come sit with us."

They were passing around a dusty bottle of mezcal someone had
found in Sue's husband's library, marveling over the worm floating in
the amber, "like a frozen crinkle cut," Caroline decided, holding the
bottle to the light.

All the laughter, the women in the warm kitchen and Pam hooking
an arm around Harper, making her sit on her lap like in high school,
playing quarters with a purloined bottle of Malibu.

"Who's gonna chance the worm?" Becky kept asking, swinging the
bottle, mezcal sluicing, Pam still singing about champagne and hoes.

"Worm! Worm! Worm!"

Later, she'd try to figure out why she'd done it, backsliding into
bad habits. First, a swig of gin, now a sluice of mezcal.

Was it Pam's gorgeous relief, tufts of U.S. currency poking from
her bra?

Was it Sandy, her first recruit, elated to be there, cradling the bottle
like her lacrosse stick on the bus after a game?

Or was it the thought that her big night was coming too? Some
week soon this would be hers, her turn to run the Wheel?

Whatever it was, when the bottle passed carelessly from Caroline
to Pam to Sandy, the blur of their faces, watching Sandy's mouth opening for the worm, Harper—elbows out—grabbed for it instead.

"Harper! Harper!" the women chanted.

And her fingertips pressed against the mottled glass, the bottle tilting into her mouth, the worm, musty, curled and plump, dancing along

her tongue, the mezcal sliding easily inside her like sweet smoke, vaporous, potent, dangerous, like everything yet to come.

Later, stepping out of the powder-pink powder room, Harper found Sandy waiting for her, one of her curls tight around her fingers, corkscrewing.

"I never told you how much it meant to me," she said, her words tumbling out like two over-rehearsed lines in a school play, "back then."

"What do you mean?" Harper leaned against the doorjamb, wishing for a Diet Coke, a cigarette, something.

Sandy paused, her face reddening. "Lacrosse."

"I didn't do anything," Harper said, putting her hand loosely on Sandy's shoulder. "You were good."

"Those were my favorite times," she said, her eyes inexplicably filling. "I think about them all the time."

"I know what you mean," Harper said, the mezcal misting up her throat. "That's how I feel about riding. I—"

"Remember how, on that trip back from Stony Creek, we sat in the back of the bus. We shared your headphones . . ."

"No," Harper said. "I mean, maybe."

There had been so many bus rides home, from lacrosse games, from horse shows, interscholastic meetings, the state fair. Two dozen, three dozen different girls, arms tucked inside letter jackets, Blow Pops and Diet Coke, the bus so dark and everyone's headphones sizzling with different songs, the flash of passing car lights, the soft down on a bare arm, thighs brushing against thighs.

"You remember," Sandy said. "I know you do."

"Sure I do," Harper lied, not a lie really. She remembered it all, just smudged together, like the punch-soft Neapolitan ice cream melting on Sue Fox's kitchen counter.

1

The text came close to midnight.

It was the last of a dozen from him she'd found on her phone as the party finally rolled to a close.

I think it's time we rendezvous-ed again, don't vous?

Doug. Demon Doug.

Or you want me to come there instead?

Harper set the phone on the mattress beside her, watching it. She didn't know what to do. How to make him go away.

The last thing she wanted was a repeat of the penny cascade in the garage. That look on Doug's face, the red bulge in his forehead. What would stop him from saying something in round two? *I may owe you, Pam, but you know who owes me?*

Finally, Harper punched the phone's tiny, sticky buttons.

Where?

Lit for Christmas year-round, Rustic Cabins was nearly empty. A few bleary old men watched *SportsCenter* over whiskey and beer backs, and a man who looked like Harper's old lacrosse coach shot pool alone, his fingers slipping drunkenly on the soft felt.

Smelling forever like pine and Pine-Sol, it knocked Harper back to her drinking days, to Leigh. They'd come a few times, nestling in one of the high wooden booths, no one ever bothered them. It wasn't the kind of place you were bothered.

Which was probably why Doug liked it, seated amiably at the Lincoln Log bar rail. Doug, lit like Paul Newman under the twinkling lights and giving her his thousand-watt smile.

"You're late," he said, looking cozy in his forever wrinkled chinos, his country-club-pink V-neck.

"Mr. Punctuality now," Harper said. "You were late to your own wedding and the births of both your children. You didn't even show up at all for your son's grad—"

"Those days are over. New assistant. Monique. Army reserves, no shit. She keeps me on schedule with freaking military precision. To be honest, it's kinda hot."

He signaled to the bartender.

"One for her, one for me," he said, pointing to his glass, amber. Back in the day, they used to drink Jameson's together when all the other Bishops stuck to vodka, gin.

"No thanks," Harper said uneasily. *His kisses are always sweetest,* Pam used to say, *before the punch to the gut.*

121

"You a friend of Bill's now?"

"No," Harper said. Then, feeling the weight of everything, she added, "I'll have a beer."

Barstool to barstool, it was the closest she'd been to him in three years or more.

All those decades of a perpetual tan, like he'd just returned from Pebble Beach, had taken a toll, his skin looking like a manila envelope, like it might crack. But those green eyes of his, they still danced, and that smile, how it seemed to slide onto his face at unexpected moments, Doug always so amused, or bemused by people, by life.

People are fucking inexplicable, he told her once. *Until they're totally predictable.*

Adding, *I like you, Harper. Because you've always been explicable.*

"What was that today?" Harper asked, a sticky mug of beer set before her, sad and soapy looking. "What the hell was that?"

He looked at her innocently, sipping his whiskey with his pinkie out in a way that used to make her laugh.

"Those pennies," she continued. "Trying to humiliate Pam. What if your daughter had seen that? Isn't it enough, stealing from your goddamned kids?"

He shook his head. "Jesus, you believe everything she tells you. I guess you gotta now that you live with her."

"She's my sister!" Harper said. "Of course I believe her."

"Well, your sainted sister is murdering me," he said, his index finger stamping on the bar. "She's boning me. She's eating me for dinner."

"Here's how I see it," Harper said, pushing the beer away. "My sister's dirtbag ex is robbing her blind, sneaking down the chimney and stealing her kids' gifts from their stockings."

He paused a second, then let out a laugh so loud that the bartender flinched.

"And yet, when you needed it," he said, "you deigned to ask for my help."

A nd there it was, the money. There was no avoiding it. Not anymore.

I 'm working on it, Doug," she said. "I'll have something for you soon."

He gave her a long look.

"C'mon," he said, laughing lightly. "Where the hell are you getting that kind of money?"

"I . . . I've been giving private lessons." She stammered in spite of herself.

He smiled at her.

"I'd like to know what kind of private lessons bring you that kind of coin."

Harper didn't say anything. That feeling suddenly that he was fishing for something. The way he kept swiveling on his stool coyly. The insinuating tone.

"C'mon, Harp. We always got along. We never fit in with the rest of 'em, did we?"

"I don't know what you—"

"And we operate the same way. Keeping things close to our vest."

"Compared to you, I'm a fucking open book."

"Really?" he said, bemused. "So you told your sister about our arrangement?"

Harper pulled the beer back, taking a sip, then another.

"I told you," Harper said, her voice tight, strained. "I have a plan—"

"What kind of plan is gonna get you fifty grand?"

"I'm part of this women's club now," she blurted. "We help each other with our finances. Getting out of debt."

As soon as she said it, she regretted it. He looked too interested too quickly, tilting his head, a faint smile lurking there.

"What kind of club?"

"I just told you."

"How did you get involved in this . . . club?"

"It doesn't matter," she said. "The point is, your money's coming."

He paused, as if treading with care. It made her more nervous somehow.

"So how much money are we talking here?" he asked. "The kind that can help you pay off your credit card?" He took a long sip of his whiskey. "Or the kind that can get you a gold Lexus?"

"That's a lease," Harper said. "Pam's car is leased."

"So she tells you. Do you really know everything? Because, if there's one thing I know, Harper: Money ain't free."

Harper leaned back on the stool, her hands gripping the bar's edge. The Christmas lights twinkling, her eyes blinking. It felt like he knew something. Like he was playing with her.

"I have to go," she said, pushing the mug away again, beer sloshing.

"Aha," Doug said, watching her. "Well, now I'm interested. Tell me more about this club. Something tells me it isn't Mary Kay."

"You don't know what you're talking about," she said, on her feet now, grabbing for her coat.

"Okay," Doug said, a smile curling up his face. "But thanks for this bit of information. It's useful."

Heart thudding, Harper was halfway to the door when he called out.

"Just watch yourself," he said, so loud she nearly flinched. "Things can get pretty complicated pretty fast when money's involved. People have a tendency to get attached."

The old men at the far end of the bar lifted their heads vaguely and Harper rushed back to Doug.

"Doug, please," she whispered. "This has nothing to do with Pam. You'll get your money. Isn't that what matters?"

Doug paused, then nodded.

"Sure, Harper," he said, hands in the air as if in surrender. "Okay, sure."

But as she turned away again, his hand found her arm and held it.

"But keep in mind," he added, his voice suddenly heavy and low, "a little money can be a dangerous thing."

In the minivan, Harper tried to catch her breath.

Glancing at the rearview, she looked at herself, feeling drunk, shaken.

It was only then that she thought about Vivian. Had she said something to her father about the women, the parties? *Dad, you should have seen the caviar mold Mom put out.* She couldn't guess what Vivian knew or thought she did, or how she'd frame it.

For five minutes, maybe ten, she sat there, waiting for her heart to slow down. Waiting for her breath to come back. Wishing she were seven again, not wanting to go to the Girl Scout meeting. Standing outside the gymnasium door, all the prim, pretty girls in a circle, their ponytails tied with thick ribbon.

And then, suddenly, Pam was there, running across the gym floor, her blond braids whipping. Pam, always making her feel wanted, making everything okay.

Come on, Harper, she said, grabbing her hand in her warm fist. *It's time! It's time!*

———————

Back at the house, she could hear Vivian in her bedroom. At first, she thought she was talking on the phone, but then she heard another voice, one as husky as Vivian's, and full of knowing laughter. *Cassie.*

Harper sat at the kitchen table for a long time, making calculations on the back of a takeout menu. Puzzling over how long it might take to get her twenty-five K once and then a second time. Two spins of the Wheel.

"Hey."

It was Vivian in the doorway, an oversize tee and her skinny legs, her *Patrick* tattoo snaking up her calf.

"Cassie's here," she said, shuffling toward Harper, a giddy smile on her face.

"Does your mom—"

"Mom doesn't care," Vivian said. "She came home so plastered. She wouldn't shut up about how you ate a worm and everything."

Harper made a face.

"The Scientology meeting must've gone amazing," she added.

"Fabulous. We're all ascending," Harper said. "Now go to sleep."

"Mom wondered where you'd gone to," Vivian said. "She thinks you're very secretive, you know. I told her you were probably meeting your lover."

If she only knew, Harper thought.

"Will you take Cassie and me to breakfast in the morning?" Vivian asked, lingering as Harper hunted out a water glass in the cabinets. "Like last weekend."

"Sure," Harper said. She'd come to like Cassie's growing presence, sleeping over, brushing Vivian's hair at night, her fingers covered in rings, untangling Vivian's tangles, soothing her to sleep. A sleepy, sweet girl with a crooked front tooth, her head forever tilted in wonder at Vivian's energy and rage.

"Aunt H," Vivian said, "was Dad here today?"

Harper looked at her. "Why do you ask?"

Vivian shrugged.

"Did he say something to you?" Harper asked cautiously.

But Vivian was silent, staring at a chip in her eggplant-purple manicure.

"Vivian," Harper said, "I know it's hard, but your dad—and your mom—they both . . . they're just so disappointed. In each other. In themselves. And that makes them so angry."

Harper wasn't even sure what she was saying, how to articulate it.

"How did it end?" Vivian asked.

"What?" Harper opened the dishwasher, still looking for a clean glass. "You know your parents were unhappy forever and—"

"Not them," Vivian said. "You and the woman you were in love with. Leigh."

Harper felt a jolt, forgetting for the moment that she'd told Vivian her name.

"Well, it's complicated."

Vivian rolled her eyes. "Adults always say that."

Harper smiled. "Because it is. You'll see."

"I see already," Vivian said, and Harper thought she was probably right.

Harper sighed. "Well, she needed my help, badly. She'd gotten herself in some trouble and she needed my help. So I helped her."

"And?"

Harper paused, turning away to the steaming dishwasher, her eyes clouded. "And then she didn't need my help, or me, any longer."

"I'm sorry," Vivian said throatily.

"I'm not," Harper said, still pretending to hunt for glassware, staring into the wet rack. "When you love someone, you'll do anything for them, Vivian. No matter what. You have to, or it was all for nothing."

She didn't know what she was saying, and suddenly she felt Vivian's hand on her back.

They stood there for a long time, it seemed. And then Harper saw them. A pair of glasses in the back of the rack. Their parents' Baccarat champagne flutes. She reached for them and started to laugh.

"What is it?" Vivian asked. "What's funny?"

And Harper laughed louder, too loud, thinking of Pam stealing those flutes back from Sue Fox. Picturing her stuffing them in her cardigan pockets at the party. And putting them in the dishwasher, no less. Their mother would have been horrified.

It was the funniest thing and she couldn't stop laughing.

H arper had imagined they'd be together after. She and Leigh. Not right away, but eventually. Once the divorce was finalized, the custody arrangements settled, after her husband stopped raging at Leigh and leaving threatening messages for Harper.

After all that, they'd ride away together in Leigh's Eldorado.

And they'd find a way to, slowly, pay off the debt together. Even if she couldn't imagine Leigh, with her English tweeds and J. Tod loafers, ever having a job or even filling out an I-9.

But many months passed and then many more and Leigh had long stopped answering her calls when Harper overheard the news at the Hunt Club. Leigh was back with her husband. They'd bought a big new house on the west side and whatever affair she'd embarked on was clearly over. A happy ending, everyone said.

So much for the retainer, the divorce attorney. In the end, Leigh had lost her nerve, and Harper's money. In the end, she wanted a husband to take care of her.

I'm just not the type of person who does this . . . Leigh used to say, a wicked grin on her face, running her hand down Harper's throat.

And it turned out, she was right. So she returned to the type of person she was supposed to be.

It would have been a shame to throw away a family over whatever that was, everyone at the Hunt Club said at the time.

But what was it? Harper found herself asking. *What was it.*

8

Three months later

The soft thump when it opened, it was almost erotic. It *was* erotic.

"Shit, Debra," Pam whispered, "it's beautiful."

Debra's eyes lit up, and they all gazed inside the steel box.

"Perry insisted," Debra said. "He told me I couldn't keep treating our refrigerator like an ATM."

"The tip to the newspaper boy," Perry said, "smelled like vermouth."

Everyone had developed a different strategy for handling their gifts when they received them.

For months, Debra had stuffed hers in an empty ice cream carton in the freezer. Most just made two to three bank deposits over a few weeks. Because, as the guidelines—and Sue Fox—reminded them, banks must report cash deposits of ten thousand dollars or more and why draw attention?

But many, like Sue, no longer trusted banks at all after New Century collapsed a few years ago. Or like Becky Schloss's husband, who moved all their money "overseas."

"Let's not get ridiculous," Pam had said at the last party.

"Spoken by the woman who keeps most of her money in a cookie jar on the kitchen counter," Debra replied. "What if you have a grease fire? What about the steam?"

Harper laughed, wondering what their mother might think about using her ceramic Merry Mushroom cookie jar as a stash spot.

"You're not still doing that, are you?" Sue asked, shaking her head. "Pam, what did I—"

"It's still in the jar," Pam said with a laugh, "but the jar's now in the basement."

A few weeks before, Pam had caught Vivian *literally with her hand in the cookie jar.*

She thought it was pizza money, Pam had assured Harper, carrying the jar downstairs and stuffing it inside a bleach-stained Tampax Pearl box, between the washer and the dryer.

Let's hope she doesn't need a tampon, Harper joked.

But later she'd asked Pam what she might have told Vivian about the money, the Club.

Nothing, Pam had replied, barely listening. *Believe me, she has no interest in what her lame mom is up to.*

Debra's new solution to the cash was, like Debra herself, far more traditional.

But when she told them she'd bought a home safe, Harper was expecting one of those tiny metal boxes with a three-digit combination lock, like the ones they slung around their ten-speed handles.

Instead, with great ceremony, Debra had ushered her sisters into her bedroom closet to show them the Sentinel Plus, a floor safe the size of the mini-fridge Pam had ordered Patrick for his dorm room. On one side was a keypad, like in a Bond movie, or on the ship on *Lost in Space* reruns.

Debra punched in the numbers, her chunky new ring, pearl as big as a cocktail onion (*a gift to myself for living through the last decade,* Debra had said), discreetly concealing the code. They all gasped as an electronic ping sounded and the safe door popped open, revealing carpeted shelves on which were nestled several ziplock freezer bags stuffed with cash.

"Two-inch-thick steel, five live-lock bolts, pry-resistant hinges," Perry said proudly, tinkling the ice in his Scotch. "And it's fire-resistant. It'll protect its contents from fires up to two hours."

"A two-hour fire," Harper murmured. "How do they *know?*"

"They test it. It can handle up to fifteen hundred degrees Fahrenheit for thirty minutes."

"But not blowtorches," Debra said, a whiff of disappointment. "That'd cost another grand."

"If I had one of these in my basement," Pam teased, "it'd be ankle deep in water twice a month."

"It's water-resistant too," Debra insisted.

"Basements are best because it could fall through the floor in a fire," Perry assured them, running his jaundiced hand along the door.

"Are you *planning* on a fire?" Pam teased. "I'd be more worried about a burglar walking off with it."

"This is TL-15," he explained, "which means it can survive fifteen minutes of sustained attack from drills, hammers, crowbars, your everyday hand tools."

Harper hadn't seen Perry this excited since before he got sick, and it was nice to see.

"What's stopping a burglar from wheeling it out the door?" Pam said, a little edge in her voice. "He can open it back at his—what do you call it? His chop shop? These Detroit pros can strip a Chevy Impala in four minutes. You think they can't tackle that?"

Harper looked at Pam. In this small way, forever like their mother, how her anxiety could turn spiky, a little mean. Like the way she talked to Vivian, if Vivian pushed or prodded her. *Why couldn't I have had a daughter who wanted to shop for prom dresses with me, get our nails done together?*

"Honestly," Debra said, ignoring Pam, "I'd love to have it embedded in the floor. But they told us we'd have to cut a cavity into the solid concrete, which is another couple grand."

So much had happened.

So much to lead to this: *How do I safely stash fifty, seventy-five thousand dollars or more in cash?*

"It's everything I promised, right?" Pam asked Harper late one night, their now daily ritual of gin and something on the frozen patio out back.

"It's good," Harper said, face warming, Fitzie curling under her hand.

She hadn't run the Wheel yet, but she was close, so close.

It had taken her longer than her sisters—mostly, as far as she could tell, because the Wheel had grown so large, swelling to thirty-six women.

But Harper had recruited five new members in the last few months and it was easier now. It turned out that perfect candidates came to the Hunt Club every day: women ages thirty to sixty or more, velvet hats and tight breeches, glistening blowouts and Elizabeth Arden skin, frustrated and lonely and, often, in these recession times, cutting corners, worrying over their bills, cutting their housekeeper's services to weekly, monthly.

There were dark rumors of Chrysler and GM declaring bankruptcy, even after the bailout. Everyone was saying 2009 would be a make-or-break year for the auto industry. It was something they'd heard every year of their lives (*Live by the car, die by the car, and we are dying, man . . .*). But it all seemed to have a special urgency now. Harper avoided the news, the headlines so apocalyptic. *Is this the end of Detroit?*

Sometimes she'd see the Chrysler and GM men sneaking smokes behind the clubhouse, the aura of desperation. Or she'd see their wives fingering the pricey Breyer horse figurines in the gift shop, assuring Harper that they were only looking for their daughter, granddaughter, niece. But none of them were buying. Not these days.

And Harper need only flip through Mr. Bingham's Filofax to know who was six months behind in dues, lesson fees.

Her mistake with trying to recruit—*invite*—Mrs. Ferris all those months ago had been her direct approach. Now, she focused on nurturing the relationship, the connection. And then, it would just happen.

Soft hands, she told Mrs. Langley in the dark barn. *Let me show you. Here, soft like you're holding a baby chick. Knuckles vertical like this. See, feel that. And forward, nudging her to work into the bridle from behind.*

The attention was intoxicating for them. Mrs. Langley's excited gasps as her beloved chestnut mare responded to her as she never had, how grateful she was. Like Leigh, back in the day. Oh, she so loved Harper to come up behind her in the round yard, gently correct her, then more firmly. Mrs. Langley had been married fourteen years to a banker with too many teeth, a glad-hander who once backhanded his son by the pool in front of everyone. He still had his job, his money, but none of it was hers, after all.

And didn't Mrs. Langley deserve something of her own, after all? Didn't she deserve something more?

I do, she whispered, her voice suddenly low, nearly a growl. *I do, Harper, I do.*

Doug had receded for the time being. The late-night texts and calls had stopped. It was almost as if Harper's turn at the Wheel was coming and he'd wait for it.

But, of course, he couldn't know and sometimes his silence made Harper nervous rather than relieved.

Once or twice, he'd come by El Dorado Drive to pick up Vivian for a daddy dinner and Harper would see his neon Mustang idling in front of the house and wonder.

She'd watch Vivian dart across the lawn and into the dark car, Doug's halo lights—the *pimp lights,* Pam called them—glimmering.

She'd watch and wonder.

But Harper couldn't recruit as fast as Pam, or even as fast as Sandy Gutowski, who'd seemingly brought in every fragile or brittle member of the Christ Church Al-Anon chapter.

Sandy had really thrown herself into the Wheel in every way and seemed to feel Harper was her mentor, guru, sponsor. And she was always calling Harper—for advice, tips on what to wear (*Do I look like the person to ask for fashion advice?* Harper would say).

Once, she called Harper, her voice small amid the unmistakable sound of electronic bells, whistles.

Sandy, you're not at the casinos, are you?

She was, of course, and had lost so much she didn't dare say it aloud. And now she was drowning her sorrows at some place improbably called the Amnesia Bar, sixteen floors high in the MotorCity Casino, or the Agua at MGM Grand, too tipsy to drive home after downing three of their specialty cocktails, the Dimmer (vanilla vodka and Sierra Mist).

I'm at work, Sandy. Get a cab.

In Detroit? Harper! Such ancient horror in her voice, the infinite, blinkered horror they had all grown up with, the worst thing that could ever happen to you would be to end up in Detroit with no way home.

But Debra had come through.

She's yours. You brought her in, Debra said at first. *She makes me crazy with the fidgeting and the talking, talking.*

Please, Deb. I'll owe you, Harper pleaded, then adding, *She talks when she's drunk and who knows what she'll say?*

That was all she needed to convince Debra.

But if she throws up in my car . . .

I'll clean it out with my toothbrush.

Deal, Debra said, almost a chortle in her voice.

After that, Debra took Sandy under her wing in true Debra fashion, assigning her various secretarial tasks to keep an eye on her and keep *those goddamned twitchy hands busy.*

B ut who could be worried about such small snags when everything was going so well?

The parties! How they grew and plumped and ballooned to bursting. Almost entirely because of Pam's precedent. Even in her cramped house on El Dorado Drive, the side of town none of the women ever ventured to by choice, she made it special. Crab mousse and champagne cocktails, boozy bourbon balls and shrimp on skewers, silver tablecloths and tall white candles. Once even a tower of cream puffs held together by caramel that she called a croquembouche.

After Pam's example, Jill Fleischer could no longer get away with the freezer-burned lasagna she served back in the fall, nor could Debra, with her pecan cream cheese spread set on card tables heavy with plastic tumblers of Inglenook blush zinfandel or Gallo dry Chablis for a sure-fire sugar hangover the next day.

And, thanks to Pam, the women were finding more and more creative ways to present the gift. Becky Schloss had called upon that origami class she once took to present an intricate money lei, and over the holidays, Sue Fox decorated a silver Christmas tree garlanded with cash.

Best of all, though, was Pam's Money Cake for Beverly Linebaugh, a variation on the one she'd made for Patrick all those months ago. An ingenious spectacle in which the recipient lifted the festive cake topper to find a hundred-dollar bill wrapped around a dowel that, once tugged, unfurled a long ribbon of bills that stretched across the entire living room like a Busby Berkeley musical come to life.

These were the good times, and everyone wanted them to last. Harper hadn't had such a busy social schedule since she was twelve years old, the most popular girl at horse camp. Metal bunkbeds, bodies still vibrating with the day's intensity, Tretorns or K-Swiss dangling off the upper bunks, whispering above or below, swinging in time to your Walkmans, both playing the same stuttering cassette of OMD at the same time. You shared this thing, secrets tucked in secrets, hands curled over mouths, the same smells—hay and feed and the sticky Prell and toxic Rid from camp showers—sharing everything and no one else in the world would ever understand.

She felt closer than she ever had to her sisters. Even reticent Debra let her mask fall sometimes, crying on the shabby back patio one night, sharing her fears over Perry's cancer, over her son, Stevie, whom she found in the garage nodding off in his parked car, the engine on and the air thick with poison.

And she and Pam closer even than when they were five and six, even if much of their time together was spent in the mildewed basement, going over the Board, the member prospects, or the "leads" as Sue kept calling them. Pam kept track of them on dozens of color-coded index cards. Green for women with wide social nets. Blue for women with high financial need. Pink for women who may not have the financial need but may be drawn to the sorority, the empowerment, or for charitable purposes.

And Yellow, the largest stack of cards, for those women requiring further inquiry. (*Do we really think she can bring in new members, after all those rumors—you know, the "nervous collapse"? I heard she slashed her wrists in her ex's bathtub. I heard she slashed the tires on his mistress's new car.*)

This wasn't how Harper thought about finding new members.

"That's because you've only had to find three," Pam said, riffling the cards like a blackjack dealer. "But we need to think bigger. More creatively."

"How big do we need to get?"

"Harper," Pam said, setting the cards down, "if we don't grow, the newest members will never get their money back."

For Pam, recruiting had become almost evangelical. The woman at the post office who kept putting off her biopsy. The nurse at Vivian's school with three kids under six and an auto worker husband laid off while on disability. If only she could sit down with them, with all of them, and explain how they, too, could change their lives.

At the last party, the nurse arrived without her five K. *Look, let's show her what it's like first,* Pam said. *Then, if she can't gift next time, I'll sponsor her. I promise.*

Sue Fox clucked her tongue. Debra made a face. Sandy Gutowski wondered softly if that was really fair. But Pam didn't seem to care.

Sometimes," Pam confessed to Harper one night, "I see the Board in my sleep. All these cards, bright and shiny, filling out the bottom row. All the women who need our help, the secret we get to share with them. How they come to us so hungry, hungry and open, like their big, hungry hearts."

Harper didn't know it then, but everything was already starting to turn.

None of the women knew it then, but everything was about to blow apart.

9

——

D o you like it?" Jill Fleischer asked, spinning around.

They were in Caroline Collins's cool blue living room for Debra's big night.

All the women were staring at Jill—or, more specifically, the brand-new full-length lynx fur from Lazare's in Windsor draped over her bony shoulders.

"You guys," Becky Schloss said, sashaying over to Jill to fondle the goods, "Elizabeth Taylor is in the house."

"It's stunning," Sandy said, anxiously smoothing her rayon blouse. "Like a queen's."

Soon, all the women were surrounding Jill—her smile wide as Caroline's modular sofa—taking turns stroking her fur.

Sue Fox, however, remained planted by the fireplace, a dangerous look in her eye.

"You have to take it back," she announced abruptly, booming over all the coos of pleasure. "You must return it immediately. Throw it into the back of the truck it fell off of. At least until tax season's over."

"Take it back?" Jill said, clasping it around herself.

"C'mon, Sue," Pam said, rolling her eyes. "If she wants to play *Scarface*, that's Jill's choice."

"You should talk," Jill barked back at Pam. "What about your gold-plated Lexus?"

"Leased," Pam said, her perpetual refrain. "It's leased."

"I don't get it," Maggie Mueller said. "Isn't this what we're here for?"

Maggie—no longer in the faded Laura Ashley dress she'd donned at her first party all those months ago—had arrived that night in a leopard-print Calvin Klein cocktail dress she insisted was a gift from her mother.

"We need to be safe," Sue said, walking over to Jill. "We need to be careful. Do you want people to start asking questions?"

"What does it matter? It's all quote-unquote legal, isn't it?" Beverly Linebaugh said, yawning over her gimlet. "Isn't that what you've been telling us all these months?"

But Sue was already tugging Jill's fur off her knobby shoulders.

"No peacocking," she said crisply. "No drawing attention. These are the rules we abide by. Now take the fucking coat back."

"Sue!" Jill cried out, nearly stumbling as her wrist caught in the sleeve.

"Get rid of it. And I don't want to hear that you're swanning around the fine dining room at Da Edoardo in it. Got it?"

For a brief second, Harper thought a fight might break out, like on *Dynasty*, Alexis and Krystle in the lily pond.

But Jill was embarrassed now, rolling up the lynx in a flurry, and some of the women started giggling, breaking the tension even as they all looked like they might have made more discreet big-ticket purchases of their own.

———

These women," Debra whispered to her by the kitchen later, "they don't have any discretion. And they still don't know what money means. They throw it all away for a fur coat, a logo on a handbag."

"I know," Harper said, even if Debra, in that moment, reminded her of their mother, the way she used to talk about the Catholics, how tacky St. Joan's was, its service like a magic show. *All the incense and bells,* she'd say, clucking her tongue. Then, a disgusted whisper, *And the crucifixes!*

"Sue Fox really shouldn't talk, though," Debra said. "She's run the Wheel so many times, her HVAC guy found fifteen grand trapped in the ceiling vents. She'd been hiding it in the crawl space."

Harper couldn't pretend she hadn't thought about the risks. Even though Sue's accountant husband had supposedly reviewed everything, had guided them on their language, on the latest IRS guidelines, it all felt like a loophole, following the letter of the law, *probably,* but maybe not the spirit.

"What does Perry say?" Harper asked.

"Business, my dear," Debra said, imitating her husband's WASP drawl, "is always a racket."

Harper laughed. "An ex-corporate lawyer should know."

You should see my ex's tax returns, Jill Fleischer had said only hours before, that sluggish Xanax slur of hers as she defended her lynx to everyone. *Writing off escorts as a business deduction? Taking a loss on his mistress's botched boob job? Those are loopholes.*

Even Pam once told everyone how, the first time she did her taxes after her divorce, Doug refused to give her copies of any of their joint returns. When she finally wrangled them away and gave them to the H&R Block accountant she could afford, he spent an hour sitting across from her, paging through them and laughing.

"But . . . do *you* trust all these women?" Harper whispered, almost like she was ashamed to ask. *Sisterhood,* after all, was the word they all used all the time, to the point of meaninglessness.

These women filled her life. But only because they all *shared this one thing.* Because the parties kept going longer and longer, and the cocktails never ending, she knew so much about all of them, but far more than she wanted to know, like Beverly Linebaugh's drunken revelations about her marriage (*by then,* she confided, clutching a cocktail napkin in the knot of her anorexic fingers, *he could only get it up if I wore riding breeches*) or Becky Schloss opening the chest freezer in her garage to show Harper her lawyer husband's stash of clients' semi-automatics.

"Well, once I clear my debts," Harper told Debra, told herself, "I'm out anyway."

"That's what I said too," Debra said, smiling at Harper, ashing her cigarette on the marble counter.

Originally, Harper had assumed most women cashed out once they reached their goal—the credit card debt gone, the mortgage payments up to date. But it was increasingly clear that no one ever stopped.

All the women were saying it now. The key to real success was to keep going. Start running two or three new groups at once. Diversify and grow. You could do that if you recruited heavily enough, "thickly enough," as Pam liked to say. With more than one group of women going, you didn't have to wait months to ascend. You might be a lowly five-grand initiate in one, and nearing the top in another. Instead of once every five or six months, you could reach the top, run the Wheel five or six times a year.

Remember! When this is done properly, you can make seventy-five to a hundred grand a year, the updated guidebook promised.

No one knew how many groups Sue Fox was running, or how much she had made by now. There were rumors she had a binder fat as a phone book of her own charts with names of dozens of women she'd recruited in Oakland County and beyond. Or a Board that took up an entire wall of her home, like one of Churchill's war rooms, Perry used to joke.

Harper couldn't even conceive of it. Just keeping track of one group of women was overwhelming. They were already big enough to make her occasionally mistake blond Caroline for blond Jill.

But she knew Pam had started another. She'd seen the corkboard down in the basement, tucked behind the other one. She didn't know who the women were and something told her not to look. Even when Debra asked.

"I'm just curious," Debra said. "Well, Sue is. You know how she is."

And Harper did, the way Sue was always inquiring about the new members Pam brought in. The week before, on a planning call, she'd asked Pam about the two prospects she was bringing in, a pair of sweet women from Harper Woods, both nurses at St. John's.

"There's no way they can afford to be here," she insisted. "*You* paid for them."

"Who told you that?" Pam asked. "Why does it matter?"

"It matters," Sue replied coolly. "This isn't a charity."

Harper noticed that Sue hadn't answered the first question. Who *had* told Sue, she wondered.

Everyone fell silent until Pam put on her sweetest smile.

"But, I mean, *isn't* it?" she said. "Just like you told us. Women helping women."

If they can't pay their way in, how can they succeed? That's what Sue said. Some of the others too. Everyone wanted Pam's numbers.

They don't bring in the right kind of people. That's what Sue meant.

Harper didn't say anything, but she wondered, not for the first time, if Sue had said the same thing about her.

Pam's gotta stop inviting women who can't afford it, Debra had said too. *It causes problems.*

But Harper knew she wouldn't be among them if Pam hadn't loaned her three thousand dollars. If Pam wasn't her sister, she thought now, would she be here at all?

That night, Harper fell asleep in Patrick's bed, drifting off after hours of sipping vodka and tonics with Pam, doing the postmortem on Debra's big night: how Caroline Collins had presented Debra with an elaborate queen's cape made entirely of bills.

It had taken her all day, collecting the gifts early and delicately stringing them together. *Long Live the Queen,* the women chanted as Caroline hung the cash cape over Debra's shoulders, shaking.

There was something lovely about it. It was finally Debra's turn. Debra, *the oldest sister with the middle-sister personality.* That was how Doug used to put it.

Debra had been through so much, with Perry, his illness. And Pam had always been the bubbly beauty, with personality to burn. Harper had been the horse girl, the athlete, the outsider. (*Did you know about Harper? She likes girls!*) But what was Debra?

And finally, all these months since Sue first recruited her, it was Deb's turn to take center stage.

Oh, to see her face, bills like fish scales shushing as she paraded through Caroline's living room, a cocktail shaker as her scepter. *Long Live Queen Deb!*

The next day, there were many calls, many texts about Jill's lynx and the guidelines and perhaps they needed to be updated, or at least better enforced.

And Harper kept thinking of Pam. Everyone teased her about the Lexus, but that wasn't the only luxury she'd procured.

Just a few weeks before, Vivian had told her of another.

They were in the barn, Vivian brushing Jackpot's mane and tail with hypnotic slowness, cooing to her softly. The goat's hair bristles shushing softly. Jackpot was a Hunt Club horse, one everyone loved.

"You guys party more than *I* do," Vivian had said. "But I don't understand what you *do* at these parties."

"What does anyone do at parties?" Harper asked. "What do you do?"

Vivian raised an eyebrow and they both laughed.

"It's really more about supporting women," Harper said. "That's all."

"But supporting them how?" Vivian asked, loosening a knot in Jackpot's mane with her bright silver nails. "Like, does someone cry and everyone group-hugs them?" She let out a mean little laugh.

"Exactly like that," Harper said. "And then we eat cheesecake in our muumuus. Don't you have SAT prep at four?"

"But you said it's an investment club," Vivian said, watching her, "right?"

"I didn't say that," Harper said, instantly uncomfortable. "It's really more about educating ourselves about business, savings, retirement planning. Financial literacy. Our generation of women—no one taught us anything, not even how to balance a checkbook."

Vivian didn't say anything at first, resting her head against Jackpot, palm stroking her neck.

Then: "But, I mean, where's the money coming from?"

"What money?" Harper said, face warming.

"The money you need to invest, or whatever you call it," Vivian said. "Mom doesn't have, like, a job."

Harper paused. Technically, it was true. Pam had dabbled a bit in real estate after the divorce, but never enough to get her license. No one was buying then, not after Ford and GM went into "reorganization" following losses of ten billion dollars. Besides, managing Patrick and Vivian through their boisterous high school years and dealing with endless legal issues with Doug—it took up so much of her time.

How does a middle-aged woman who's been out of the workforce since college get a job? Pam had moaned.

But, of course, Pam had never really been in the workforce in the first place and her degree in communications had always felt vague, even to Pam.

"It's been hard for your mom," Harper said. "Building her own life after the divorce. That's why the group is good for her. And, well, she loves it. She's so damn happy to be good at something."

Vivian looked at Harper very closely. "Well, she must be a fucking Wall Street titan, then."

"What?" Harper said, thinking suddenly of the Merry Mushroom cookie jar, now hidden in the basement.

"Did you see the perfume she just bought?" Vivian said. "Did you know it's the most expensive in the world?"

Harper paused, fiddling with the trough heater, moving it out of Jackpot's way.

She had noticed Pam had purchased a few new things, including a brand-new coin purse and fanny pack from some Louis Vuitton outlet. *It's not a fanny pack,* she kept insisting when Harper teased her. *It's a pochette.*

But that phrase: *The most expensive perfume in the world.* Had Vivian come up with that? It sounded more like her father. She could practically imagine Doug saying to Vivian, *Only the finest for your mother. She can detect a knockoff like a pro.*

"I don't know about any perfume," Harper said, "but your mom never gets to treat herself. She deserves some treats."

"Is that what the parties are for?" Vivian asked, swinging the brush. "Treats?"

"No," Harper said. Again, not a lie, not the truth.

Vivian's hand fell abruptly, Jackpot shuddering with surprise.

"Well, let's hope it lasts, whatever it is," she said, throwing the brush into the groom box.

Then adding, as she turned to exit the stall, "Because every time I show at SAT prep, the tutor asks when she's finally gonna get paid."

Moms aren't allowed to want things," Pam said, running the mini-vac along the nubby wall-to-wall, forever gritty under their bare feet.

"I don't think—" Harper started.

"Middle-aged women aren't allowed to want things," Pam continued, voice lifting. "Doug can buy sports cars, stereo systems, new girlfriends. But god forbid I want something. And get it for myself."

She opened the drawer of the oak dresser, the one with all the brass fittings that long sat in their parents' bedroom. Jabbing her hand inside—a swarm of nylon underpants, five for thirty dollars, up to her wrist—she plucked out a curvy black bottle the size of a small peach, a tiny gold cord around the top.

Harper paused, moving through a memory she couldn't quite name.

"Joy," Pam said, fingering the gold letters. "Jean Patou. Remember?"

"I think so," Harper said, her eyes on the red plastic stopper that, when they were little, looked like a cherry atop a sundae.

"It was supposed to look like a Chinese snuff bottle," Pam said. "We looked up *snuff* in the encyclopedia."

She plucked the cherry off the top and took Harper's wrist in her hand, dapping the stopper on the inside.

The scent, like a storm.

"Mom," Harper whispered, her eyes full. "That's Mom."

"After she died, it was all I wanted," Pam said. "To remind me of her. Doug kept forgetting. Finally, for our tenth wedding anniversary, Deb intervened and marched him to Hudson's to buy me a bottle."

Harper couldn't speak quite yet, her mind fizzy with recollection, a pressure over her heart.

"A week later," Pam added, replacing the stopper, turning away, "we had a fight. Doug smashed it on the bathroom floor."

Harper reached for the bottle. Pam's hands were shaking. *Pammy.*

"He cut his foot open," she said, her voice high. "I had to drive him to the ER."

Harper looked up from the bottle to Pam, her face broken into a strange smile.

"What a goddamned fool," Pam said, shuddering with laughter now, "and I mean *me.*"

It was hardly a lynx coat. In fact, Pam could have bought a half-dozen Joys and not matched Jill Fleischer's splurge. It wasn't even as much as some of the handbags the other women were now toting, not to mention Becky Schloss's suspiciously "alert" eyes at the last party, surely the result of some "preventive" procedure performed at the plush, private offices of Doctor Sharrod on the west side.

And it meant so much more.

But Harper wasn't worried about what the other women might think.

"Of course you should have things," Harper said, both of them slinking down the side of the bed to the matted carpet. "But Vivian . . . she's asking a lot of questions."

Pam made a face. "I thought teenagers weren't supposed to care *what* their parents did. We barely knew ours were alive in high school."

"To be fair," Harper said, "they barely were."

Pam laughed. "Pickled and preserved."

"I'm just thinking about you," Harper said. "She talks to her father. She's very protective of him."

Pam smile faded away. "Jesus, Doug gets away with murder," she snarled, poking her fingers into the minivac, tugging loose long, violet strands of Vivian's hair from its teeth. "Why not ask questions about *his* bank account?"

"The point is, you don't want to give him any ammunition," Harper tried again. "You're in this legal thing with him over the trust and you've got this hearing coming up . . ."

All Harper could think about was what Vivian might have said to her father. And what she herself had told him at Rustic Cabins: *I'm part of this women's club now. We help each other with our finances.* What if Doug connected the dots?

"Fuck him," Pam said. "He's still trying to control me. He wants me to suffer in poverty and shame like first wives everywhere. Well, fuck that."

"I agree," Harper said.

"He really broke me, Harper," Pam said quietly. "I was crazy about him and he broke me and I'll never be the same again. I'll never look at a man that way again, like he hung the goddamned moon."

"Well, maybe that's a good—"

"Now *I'm* the one making things happen," she said, with a sudden steeliness that seemed to ring around the small room. "Including get-ting what's owed. Including making my own nut."

Harper started to laugh, wondering where Pam picked up that slang, but something in her sister's expression made her stop.

Pam looked at Harper, and the perfume seemed to hover in the air between them, heavy, formidable.

"It's my turn now."

10

The waiting room was stuffy, but Harper didn't want to take off her coat.

She tried to call Pam a few more times, anxious for her.

She and Doug were scheduled to appear in court that morning in what seemed like the hundredth step in Pam's monthslong effort to force Doug to address the trust fund theft.

But Pam wasn't answering or replying to texts.

"Hey," Perry said, appearing in the doorway, a nurse at his side. "Dead man walking here."

Harper smiled, rising.

"Deb had to drive Stevie to work," she said. "She asked me to get you."

"Lucky you," Perry said, winking.

The nurse helped him with his jacket. His arms, mottled with bruises, were so thin, like tongue depressors. She remembered how, at U-M, he used to row crew.

―――――――

Perry would be fine, probably. That's what the doctors all said.

But he didn't look fine, lately.

He needs a getaway, Debra had told her that morning. She was taking him to Canada next week. She'd rented a cottage on Pelee Island so he could rest, see some nature.

"You never struck me as a nature guy," Harper said on the drive home.

Perry laughed, shivering under blazing heat vents.

"Well," he said, thumping the dashboard, "you never struck me as the minivan type."

"It's Pam's," Harper said, chuckling. "I mean, it was. Just call me Secondhand Susie."

"You'll be upgrading soon enough," Perry said. "Right?"

"I guess."

Perry looked at her and something seemed to pass between them. She wasn't sure what it was.

"It's given Debra something," he said, clearing his throat awkwardly. Perry, like all the men she knew, didn't know how to talk, not about stuff like this.

"I know," Harper said, eyes on the road, giving him his space. "Pam too."

"And you?"

Harper smiled but said nothing. She guessed she didn't know how to talk about stuff like this either. Feelings.

But, for the first time since Leigh swept into her life, she had something, some organizing feeling. Wonder and anticipation, but fear too. A fear that felt so Midwestern, so Detroit, places that had lived through the boom and dwelt so long in the bust:

If it seems too good to be true . . .

———

At work, Harper couldn't concentrate. She was sloppy, forgetting two private lessons, failing to turn in the stable hands' time sheets. Finally, Mr. Bingham told her to go home.

She was worried about Pam, wondering what had happened at the hearing.

She'd tried calling a half-dozen more times, but Pam still hadn't picked up.

It gave her a bad feeling.

Maybe it was the sense that, though she hadn't heard from Doug in months, she surely would soon.

Or maybe it was just the grinding wait for next week, her big night. *The big gold dream,* as Pam called it. And, too, the awareness that the money would be in her hands for such a short time . . . What kind of payoff was that?

But Doug would get his money, a drop in the bucket of all he owed, his debt. And she would be more than halfway out of her debt to him.

She never let herself think about how Pam would feel if she knew about their arrangement. She never let herself do it.

Pam wasn't back at the house either. Harper went from room to room, even though the rental was so small, you could stand on the front porch and everyone inside could hear.

She was standing in Pam's kitchen, waiting for the stained Mr. Coffee to finish its oily dripping, when she saw something.

She was looking out the window at the old elm tree in back, wondering if it would make it through another Michigan winter.

It was so quick she nearly missed it: someone darting through the neighbor's yard. Someone she'd never seen before, a figure in a black parka and gray fleece ski mask.

The sun had just set and it was cold. Fifteen degrees, with that Michigan ferocity. Still, the ski mask felt creepy.

She moved closer to the window.

There was something about the funny way he'd moved, furtive, awkward. A compact man with puffy winter gloves.

She didn't know the neighbors, really. Next door was another rental, the Fisks gone for the winter, their renters always changing. But something about it was strange.

Her hand instinctively reached for the Merry Mushroom cookie jar on the counter.

But then she remembered Pam had moved it. The spot on the counter felt empty, strange.

When Harper looked up again, he'd disappeared behind the garage, a surprising flash of purple against the black, the parka's zipper like a bright snake.

Running down the basement stairs, Harper's eyes went directly to the Tampax box jammed between the washer and dryer. Peeking inside, she saw the mushroom cap handle of the cookie jar. She didn't open it. She had no idea how much cash Pam had there, but it made her sweat.

Jesus, she thought. *Settle down, Harper.*

As if on cue, she heard Fitzie's growl at the top of the stairs, then heard the vroom.

From the living room window, she saw Cassie's yellow Escort whipping around the cul-de-sac and up the narrow drive as if it were the Corkscrew at Cedar Point.

"Auntie H!" Cassie called out from the front seat, her fluffy pink mittens resting like a pair of Sno Balls on the steering wheel.

The passenger door swung open and Vivian bolted out, Fitzie yelping around her, then darted up the lawn, five feet two inches of uncaged fury.

It reminded her of that Easter Sunday long ago when Vivian, age four, threw a temper tantrum over wearing a dress to church. They all watched as she stood on the second-floor landing of Pam and Doug's grand house, screaming with such force and velocity that she tumbled down the stairs, breaking her elbow, knocking out three teeth. It was as if her own rage had propelled her into the air.

"I hate her, that monster bitch," she was shouting, lashing open the kitchen door as Cassie's car peeled away.

"Not Cassie."

"Fuck no," Vivian said. "Mom."

"What's wrong, baby?" Harper asked.

"Did she tell you?" Vivian demanded, stripping off her bright silver puffer, whipping it to the kitchen floor.

"Tell me what?"

"That she's getting Dad thrown in jail?"

As if on cue, Harper turned to see Pam yanking open the kitchen door, purse in hand.

"Vivian, honey, please," Pam was saying, a desperation in her voice, a gust of Jean Patou as she dropped her purse to the floor, rushing to Vivian, "that's not what this is—"

"How could you do this to me?" Vivian cried out.

It was every teenager's lament, and Harper couldn't help but feel its perennial truth.

In her experience, parents were often doing terrible things to their children, their private dramas and personal disappointments wreaking havoc, spilling over helplessly and ruining everything.

It turned out Pam had waited forty minutes in the county courthouse and Doug had failed to appear.

The judge had clacked his gavel and Pam's attorney had snapped his briefcase shut and that was it. After, Pam sat in her car and screamed.

The bench warrant that followed was cold comfort. It was something, but not enough.

For months, Pam had been waiting for this day, waiting for Doug to have to explain what he had done, was doing. Waiting for Doug to look her in the eye and account for stealing from his children, from her.

But he never showed.

Vivian," Harper said, "your mom's not responsible for what the judge decided."

"She's the one who brought Daddy to court!" Vivian said.

"I'm doing this for you," Pam kept saying, planting herself at the foot of her daughter's bed, Vivian's face buried in her pillow. "I'm trying to protect you. Your future, baby."

It went on for hours, at one point Pam even printing off the judge's memorandum of decision on her squeaking, chugging dot-matrix printer to show to Vivian, to try to make her see that she was protecting her and it was the judge who found her father in contempt. And it was her father who had chosen to avoid paying child support and to start draining his children's trust funds.

But Vivian had *zero interest in the judge's fucking memo* and the pain was too deep, in hard grooves on her forehead that made her look ancient, half-ruined at the tender age of sixteen.

By nine o'clock, mother and daughter had beaten each other down. Pam was sobbing in the bathroom with a rawness Harper couldn't remember. It was awful to hear. *She hates me. My baby hates me.*

And Vivian was gone, disappearing into yet another random car, lurking in front of the house like a ghost. Not Cassie but one of Vivian's exes, a girl named Kodi who bussed tables at the Hunt Club and who'd tricked out her Dodge with a sinister neon underglow, like a blue orb hovering.

"Be careful, okay?" Harper said as Vivian charged past her, in sparkly halter top and fluorescent sneakers, a glowing girl vanishing into the glowing orb, Kodi smiling at her with teeth unbearably white.

Four years ago, the judge's memorandum read, *there was $150,000 in the education account of each child. The court has heard evidence that there is now remaining $9,075 in his son's account and $26,000 in his daughter's account. In addition, the defendant is $42,000 in child support arrears.*

Today, the court finds the defendant in willful contempt for failing to produce records regarding the education funds, and for failing to make any payments for current child support and toward the arrearage and orders him incarcerated until he pays $12,000 to purge the contempt.

He's stealing from her," Pam said to Harper that night, recovering with a gin and soda, a cold washcloth over her face. "He's stealing her future and she still defends him."

But no one wants their dad in jail, Harper wanted to say. Even if he deserved it. Which he did.

"I didn't ask the judge to lock him up," Pam said. "But I can't pretend I don't like imagining him in there. Forty minutes without his phone, he'll be crawling the walls."

She looked so vulnerable, pulling the washcloth loose. Her face pink and swollen.

"Walking into the cell with his Italian loafers and his shit-eating grin," Harper said, squeezing her shoulder.

"I hope they steal his loafers," Pam said, a light cackle.

"Remember when Dad had that DUI downtown?" Harper asked.

It was after they repossessed his Lincoln Town Car from the Hunt Club parking lot. Their father, too many martinis at the Rattlesnake Club, weaving all over Jefferson, hitting a traffic pole, running over a newspaper box. He claimed he was unfamiliar with the rental car. He was unused to its steering principle.

"They made him wear those state-issued plastic sandals," Pam said, rolling her eyes.

"Mom wouldn't let him in the car with them," Harper said. "She said they were filthy. She made him stay overnight until she could bring him a pair of his shoes."

They were both laughing now. None of it was funny, but it was always best to make it so.

Besides, they both knew Doug would make bail, somehow.

They both knew you could win every battle with Doug and still lose the war.

11

The early-morning air was thick, sharp, a heavy fog drifting across the riding ring and paddocks.

It was such a relief, the quiet, the cold, the shuffling sounds of the horses in their stalls. The smell of cinders, smoke. It made her remember so much.

Mmm-mmm, I want to linger here. Mmm-mmm, a little longer.

The shhh-shhh of Leigh's breeches as she walked up behind her that first time, slapping her leather gloves against her thigh. The rasp in her own hand, running it along the elegant hooves of Gilda, her Dutch warmblood.

Mmm-mmm, I want to linger here, Leigh's hand on Harper's, Harper's on the glittering rasp, *mmm-mmm, a little longer.*

Those hands, her fingers dancing, the way her breath always caught in her throat.

In the end, it had cost her fifty grand. Leigh had.

Was she worth it?

There was no good answer to that question, so Harper had to stop asking.

Mmm-mmm, a little longer here with you.

When she heard the crack of pine shavings, she thought it might be Charlie, one of the part-time grooms, who sometimes slept one off in the tack room.

"They took my goddamned belt."

Harper whipped around and saw him, Doug, standing in the barn entryway. His hair swept scruffily up his forehead, chinos loose around his waist.

"I guess they thought I might hang myself," he said. "Can you imagine how desperate I'd have to be to hang myself in the same jail I used to get dragged into at sixteen for doing donuts in the St. Joan parking lot?"

"Doug, you can't be here."

She didn't like the look in his eye, the way he was staggering toward her, his face red and strange.

"And then they couldn't find it when I made bail. Can you believe it? One of those lard-assed pricks at county booking swiped my Hermès belt. At least they didn't take my shoelaces," he said. Then, adding, a glitter in his eye. "As you know, I'm a loafer man."

Harper stepped backward.

"Why didn't you show?" she asked tentatively. "For the hearing?"

He laughed, tugging up his chinos and moving closer.

"Your sister threw the father of her children in jail today," he said. "There's only so much a man can take."

"Look, you have an attorney," she said. "That slick one from Lansing. I assume he's the one who got you out of jail. Talk to him."

He pushed the heel of his hand through his hair, brushing it back.

"You think this is *my* problem," he said, that smoker's crack in his voice, "but, honey, this is *our* problem."

"I told you," she said, stumbling over a feed sack, righting herself, "the money's coming. Next week. I told you."

"I've kept your secret and I've waited on your money. Patiently, so patiently. But what are you doing for me, Harper?"

"Next week," she said, backing up further, past the stalls. Something told her to get out of the barn, into the open. "I'll have half the money for you."

"You know how much money I took out of that trust fund?" he said. "My kids' trust fund. What if I told you it was fifty K? Does that number sound familiar to you?"

Harper felt it like a blow to the chest.

She told herself this was typical Doug manipulation. Money wasn't like that. It didn't work like that. The money Doug lent her wasn't the same money taken—stolen, even—from her sister, from her niece and nephew, their trusts. Money was always changing, moving, always just beyond your fingertips. No one knew that better than Doug.

"That's bullshit," she said. "Fifty thousand means nothing to you. You gave it to me because you wanted to and I was grateful. I'm still grateful and it's coming back to you."

He sighed dramatically and leaned back. "The Bishop sisters, preserve and protect at all costs, right?" He looked at her before adding, "But you live under her roof now. You see what's really going on. With Pamela. Her new enterprise, her new passion. The one she's giving her all to, like she did the PTA, the Parents' Club, the goddamned Junior League."

"Stop trying to bring that into it," she demanded. "Pam has a right to make money—"

"Don't we all?" Doug said quietly. "But are you sure you know what Pam roped you into? With your little ladies' group. Your coffee klatch. This club."

"You don't know what you're talking about," she said, then repeated the words she knew so well they fell from her lips: "It's just women helping women."

"Oh, so that's the line, is it?" Doug said grimly. "Do you report that 'help' to the IRS?"

"Doug—"

"I knew the money was coming from somewhere," he said. "The Lexus, the goodies. It sure wasn't showing up in her assets."

"What, *you're* gonna give a lecture on hiding assets?" Harper hissed. As soon as she said it, she wanted to take it back. "Pam's not hiding anything," she said. "She's not doing anything."

"You liked a slush fund when it served you," he said coolly. "When you needed money fast, free."

"Free?" Harper said. "Nothing about this is free."

"It sure ain't."

Harper looked at him, a sinking feeling inside. "Doug—"

She heard a rumble and turned. Mr. Bingham's Silverado in the distance.

"You're not supposed to be here," Harper blurted.

"I can be anywhere I want," Doug said. "I can do anything I want."

But as he said it, a weariness seemed to envelop him.

Adding, under his breath, "I should wring her goddamned neck."

Harper looked at him, suddenly queasy.

"One week," he said, stepping back into the dark of the barn. "I want that money in one week."

"One week," Harper repeated, breathing, barely.

She turned around and waved to Mr. Bingham, getting out of his car. A quizzical look on his face.

"Time's running out," Doug said, a spike of anxiety in his voice. "For all of us, Harper."

That night, she laid in bed a long time, thinking. Wishing she could smoke. Feeling the vibrations of Vivian's music through the wall, that fuzzy, droning music she played all night.

She was remembering something. Pam, a vibrant twenty-six years old, running around her new home, that stately Georgian mansion of theirs just off Windmill Pointe, a few brief miles from the most battered parts of Detroit. One of the great ironies of Grosse Pointe, that the most illustrious homes, the mansions of the auto barons, were the closest to the city those barons had sacked, then abandoned.

But you didn't think of such things back then. Instead, Pam gave Harper and Debra the grand tour of an extravagant renovation in process, tarps everywhere, drop cloths, ladders. Patrick, a toddler then, tumbling over power cords, Pam scooping him up in her arms, stepping over enormous slabs of Carrara marble and the lapping tubs of lime plaster in her sensible Chanel flats.

Fuck me, Debra confided as they stood in the magnificent entryway. *Is it okay to hate my sister?*

The previous owner, a socialite of note, had died in her canopied bed, leaving behind her time-softened carpets, all the tuckered brocade, the WASP tradition of shabbiness-as-style. Pam was stripping it all away, tearing the curtains down like Scarlett O'Hara, ripping down the hand-painted toile wallpaper from the powder room walls, its silk shreds between her fingers.

You should have seen how long it took to pull up all the carpeting, Pam said. *All the chintz! The whole house, trapped forever in 1954.*

Her excitement over all the new: the limestone fireplace, the Viking range, the Sub-Zero refrigerator. All the marble, onyx, quartz, glass, everything a pedestal, a block, a cube, every surface pale, hard, cold, relentless.

Everything made of rock, Harper whispered, *but the beds.*

Give her time, Debra whispered. And Harper couldn't hide her snicker.

Pam heard them and started laughing, too, and their laughter joined, loud and keening, *the weird sisters,* their mother used to call them, watching them through her vanity mirror. And then little Patrick, his fingers stuffed in his mouth, started giggling along with them, giggling until bubbles popped from his mouth, his morning milk spit up all over his Ralph Lauren overalls, the laughter so sweet it made Harper want to cry to think of it now.

But that was so long ago, a blurry dream before everything, and everything else.

Pam was twenty-six and just starting her life, and she thought—was sure—it would last forever. Like everyone did at twenty-six. You think you can only go one way: up. It's the delusion all young people need. The lie we tell all young people until they tell it themselves, until they believe it, cling to it, dream it. We hope they will, against all logic and circumstance, dream it true.

And now, more than fifteen years later, there was Pam in her vinyl-sided rental, the air thick with lake scum, hurtling through the house in a Hunt Club hoodie, a cache of bills in one hand and a highlighter in the other, plunging down the basement stairs to look at the Board. To look at the Board and all its colors and the promise of the next party and the next and see herself stringing pearl after pearl, enough pearls to make a choker, a necklace, a tiara, a crown. To look at it all and instantly feel excited, hopeful, for a glittering future with endless possibility—up, up, up forever.

12

One week later

Tonight, tonight!" Pam sang, hurrying around the kitchen, a dishtowel for an apron, a bottle of wine open despite the early hour, the oven shuddering with heat.

It was Harper's big evening. It had taken more than four months, but it was happening.

She was running the Wheel at last.

And Pam couldn't stop talking about it, preparing for it—*the perfect distraction*, she kept saying, from the fact that she had to face Doug in court the next day, the rescheduled hearing over the trust.

"I'm so happy for you," Pam kept saying, a manic pitch to her voice. "The first time is so special."

"Yeah," Harper said, trying for a smile. Now that the night was here, it felt strangely like a no-turning-back point. She'd woken that morning with a thick dread in her chest.

Just like game days, back in high school lacrosse, she could feel her body rebelling, a sickly feeling rising up in her as she watched Pam's elaborate preparations, which involved puff pastry stuffed with chicken, mushrooms, the fat bacon sizzling on tinfoil. *Everyone loves my vol-au-vents*, she said. *If I don't bring them, they go crazy.*

"Do any women ever stop after the first time?" Harper asked suddenly. "One run of the Wheel and out?"

"What?" Pam said, spoon nearly dropping from her hand. "Why would anyone do that? It's only twenty-five grand—"

"Only?" Harper said, laughing hollowly. Just a few months ago, the five thousand dollar buy-in felt insurmountable.

Pam shook glossy filling off her spoon and looked at Harper. "But why would you stop?"

"I don't know," she said. "It's gotten kind of intense, hasn't it?"

"What, because of Sue's fit over Jill's call-girl lynx?" Pam said briskly, a flicker of annoyance. "She was just being bossy. She was the same way on the PTA. *Everything* had to be laminated."

Harper nodded. There was a long, uncomfortable pause.

"I thought you loved it," Pam said, staring down at the bulging vol-au-vents.

"Yes, but . . ." Harper started, but then she saw a whiff of panic on Pam's face.

"I don't know what I'd do without it," Pam said, nervously tidying the pastries, whisking extra filling off with a wet paper towel. "It's filled up my whole life. It's sisterhood, it's freedom. It's fucking fun. And I'm . . . I'm really good at it, Harper. And I think you are too."

"*You* are good at it, Pam. The best. But maybe—"

"It saved me," Pam said. "Not just the money, but the . . . the power over my own life."

Pam's eyes darkened. It felt like a moment of self-revelation. One so big Harper didn't dare say a word.

In fact, she wished she hadn't brought it up. She knew she couldn't stop now anyway. Her debt was still there. But there was that heavy feeling she'd woken with. It seemed to sit in her like a dark thing.

"Besides," Pam continued, reaching for her wineglass, gulping hungrily, "I brought you in. You can't abandon me now, can you?"

Harper paused, then shook her head.

Pam took Harper's hand in her hot one, squeezing it. "We're closer than ever."

The party was at Becky Schloss's grand house right on Lake Shore Road. No one knew how Becky had managed to hold on to it while her husband served a sixteen-month prison term for witness intimidation. The papers still called him a mob lawyer, which gave him—and therefore Becky—an exotic sheen, though in high school she was known only as the most ferocious striker on the field hockey team, once backswinging her stick in an opposing player's throat with such ferocity, the girl vomited. After that, everyone had to wear neck guards, which they all called Beckys in her honor.

On the back deck, Becky had turned on her hot tub, unused for four seasons due to defaulting on her electric bills. Many women had brought bathing suits despite the forty-degree weather, drinking hot toddies in terry-cloth robes before slipping them off and taking turns inside.

Harper was late, driving around the block three times before she arrived, nearly slinking in through the impossibly tall front doors.

"How are you feeling?" someone cooed, approaching Harper from behind, tugging her arm excitedly.

"Okay," Harper said. "Good."

It was only when she flitted away again that Harper saw it was Pam, free of her Hunt Club hoodie and faded pajama pants and looking impossibly elegant, as if bathed in some special light. Her wine-colored leather dress shone under the pendant lights of Becky's Tuscan kitchen, under the track lights of her grand living room. And her bounty, that fine, golden hair of hers, freshly colored at Jacobson's salon, you couldn't take your eyes off her.

But it was her face, her expression that struck Harper, so forcefully pierced her heart—the joy and confidence as she moved through the space, floating between and among the women, all their eyes on her, the way her new recruits and her past ones reached for her, their hands stretching out for hers, their smiles, toothy and ecstatic.

The belle of the ball, the queen of the prom, she danced among them, giving them all a moment, a squeeze of the shoulder, a whispered confidence, a laugh fluttering up her throat, a promise of something, everything.

This is how she was meant to be, Harper thought. She didn't know what she meant precisely, but suddenly she could picture her sister as the head of a business, a corporation even, mingling with such ease, all attention on her, hoping for a chance to bask in her reflected glory.

Pam, Pammy, you were meant for this, she thought. *And you have it at last!*

Debra was late, too, unusual for her. Harper finally found her coming out of the powder room, her silk blouse wet under the arms, in blotches across her chest.

"I was trying to clean it," Debra said.

On her way out the door, she said, she'd heard a noise from the garage. Perry had fallen, slipping on motor oil. She found him slumped against the fender of the car.

"He gets so dizzy after the chemo," she said. "I had to carry him back inside. I'm so glad we're going up north tomorrow. We've been trying to work out a payment plan for this round and it's just been . . . I just wanted him to take it easy."

Harper remembered how, at one of the parties at Debra's house, she'd snuck in the garage to smoke and found Perry there, drinking from a bottle of Dewar's stashed in his tool bench.

You weren't supposed to drink during the chemo, he explained, offering her a sip. Harper didn't really want any, but he looked so sad and sweet, his strawberry blond hair so thin now, glossy like a little girl's. So she joined him, both of them leaning against the tool rack, sneaking tastes.

Don't tell Deb, he'd said, grinning. Slipping the bottle behind the pegboard.

I promise, she'd replied. *I promise.*

"It'll be okay," Harper said now, but there was a glint of panic in Debra's face that worried her. "You'll rest up there."

"I just need this all to work," Debra said, her eyes scanning the new members, her hand over the water stain on her chest, over her heart.

"It's working," Harper said, but she wasn't really sure what Debra meant, or how to calm her.

B y eight o'clock, the living room swelled with women, far too many to know them all. The five new members seemed to have pushed the Wheel into a whole new category of party, cacophonous and teeming with shiny bobs and velvet headbands, silk scarves and winter white.

And the new members were so conspicuous this time, mostly because Sandy Gutowski's recruit, Lisbeth, a French-braided pixie with gilded angels tattooed on her hands, turned out to be her nineteen-year-old babysitter.

For nearly a half hour, Sue Fox scolded a weepy Sandy in the kitchen, telling her anyone under twenty-one—twenty-five, really—was a liability.

Sandy kept insisting she was as surprised as anyone else that Lisbeth was so young, prompting Beverly Linebaugh to ask, "Didn't the braces tip you off?"

And Becky Schloss was raging because she'd already served *that bucktoothed Lolita* at least two Tom Collinses.

"Sandy," Harper said, pulling her aside, feeling some obligation as the one who first brought her in. "Taking money from a teenager . . ."

"I'm sure she didn't mean it," Debra said, picking at a tray of blinis.

"I'm so embarrassed," Sandy kept saying, her fingers back in her hair, smoothing her curls ceaselessly.

Some day, Harper thought, tired of Sandy already, *all that hair's gonna fall out.*

I t was Pam's new recruit, Dana, however, that caused the greatest hub-bub. A real estate agent from Macomb County, she'd arrived and im-mediately parked herself in the hot tub, smoking filterless Camels and chatting promiscuously.

According to Caroline Collins, Dana was free on bail for crashing her car into her ex-husband's garage door.

"How do you know?" Harper asked.

"She told us!" Caroline said. "She announced it right there on the back deck."

Some story about her husband cheating on her with a waitress at Friendly's.

My ex bought me that car, she'd pronounced, *so it was mine to crash.*

I t was no surprise, then, when Sue called an emergency meeting of se-nior members in Becky's husband's leather-lined den.

"I think you should come too," Debra said, taking Harper's arm.

Becky was standing over a glass coffee table laden with that evening's haul. Thousands of dollars not in the usual fancy envelopes or tufted boxes but a messy twirl of curled and creased bills.

"What's going on?" Harper asked.

"We're short," Debra said, lighting a cigarette with an enormous Lucite table lighter.

"Short?" Harper said. It had never happened before.

"Five grand short. Somebody didn't bring their bite."

Harper looked at Pam, who was unusually quiet as Becky counted the cash again, sticky fivers she had to uncurl with her French manicure.

Debra was looking at Pam too. Like Harper, she knew her sister's tell, those moments she kept her mouth conspicuously shut. Like every childhood Christmas, sneaking into their parents' closet, tallying all the presents. Like high school, siphoning Stoli from their parents' liquor cabinet, sitting silently as their mother refused to let her leave the dinner table until she confessed. She never did, knowing full well their parents would forget in the morning.

"It has to be the juvenile," Sue said. "I mean, how much babysitting money could she get her hands on?"

"No, she had the money," Becky said. "I collected it myself. That's when I saw the braces."

Finally, Pam sighed. "Maybe it's Dana. She swore she had the money."

"I guess she had to use it for bail," Debra said dryly.

Dana was summoned, arriving with a rum and Coke in hand, and there was an embarrassing standoff on the mauve velvet pile carpet.

"I didn't know I needed to bring it the first time," she kept saying, smiling like Sue was being ridiculous, they all were. "I was just window-shopping."

"This isn't Saks," Sue said. "Five K is the price of admission. To see how we work. We need to trust one another, and the money is how we earn trust."

"Skin in the game," Becky said coolly. "It's pretty simple."

Dana said nothing, her smile fading, her rum and Coke tilting precariously in her hand.

Maybe it was because they were standing in the den where—rumor had it—Becky's husband kept a vintage Prohibition-era tommy gun hidden in one of the mahogany cabinets.

Or maybe it was the way the women circled her so tightly, heels deep in the sheepskin rug.

Either way, Dana cracked like fine china.

"But . . ." she stuttered, "I don't have the money on me. I mean, I'm sure I can get it. Tomorrow. I swear."

Harper wanted to feel sorry for Dana. But she didn't. Instead, all she could think was: *It's my night and that's five thousand less for me. Maybe more if they decide the teenager's five grand doesn't count.*

No one spoke, the festive sounds beyond the door, all those laughing, whooping women, the soft plash from the hot tub vibrating through the mahogany.

Suddenly, it felt like that moment in the crime movie when the gun slides into frame.

But, instead, Pam swooped in to save the day.

"I don't see why we have to make such a big deal out of it," she said, reaching into her new LV fanny pack (*Pochette, that's what you call it!*) and pulling out a money clip full of creaseless bills.

They all watched as she counted them out on the table.

No one was taking any chances.

—————

S he can't just keep sponsoring these women," Sue was saying, couldn't stop saying. "It's not how it works."

If a woman cannot fulfill her obligation for whatever reason, Harper remembered from the guidebook, *she must leave the group. If a member wants to sponsor the woman, giving on her behalf, we can make arrangements.*

But Harper felt funny about it too. That five thousand of her twenty-five would come from Pam. It wasn't how it was supposed to work.

"Someone," Sue said, knocking back the last of her vodka, "needs to take her down a notch. Teach her a lesson."

That was the feeling humming in the air as everyone stared at Pam's fanny pack.

Harper looked at Debra. *Should we stick up for her?*

Debra, however, didn't seem to be listening, watching Pam across the room, soothing Dana, stroking her Jacuzzi-pink arm.

B ut, within the hour, all seemed forgiven, all the women's arms linked, encircled.

"This is it," Pam whispered, twining her arm with Harper's. "And it's just the beginning!"

The chant Harper knew by heart now, a soaring intensity to it, the proliferation of women, the alcohol and energy, the faintly illicit aura of Becky's baronial house, with its whispers of fast money, easy money, under-the-table money, endless money.

L ooking at Pam, brimming with pride.

And at Debra, who seemed near tears—so rare for Debra—

embracing Harper with such force. All of that feeling, maybe it was mostly about Perry, her fears about him. Harper hugged her back, assuring her everything was going to be great. Everything.

There it was. All the money, twenty-five thousand dollars, nestled in the lacquered humidor Becky had stuffed it in. The bills limp, curled, stained, fragrant with tobacco.

Around the circle of women—so large now it barely fit in Becky's expansive living room—the humidor went, the laying of hands on it, even the babysitter's tattooed fingers.

Spread the energy!

Feel it, feel it!

She remembered back to her first time, in Beverly Linebaugh's living room.

Did you feel it? they all asked her.

What am I supposed to feel? she'd whispered to her sister.

Power! Pam had replied.

POWER! they had all shouted.

And she had felt it, but now it was hers and it felt different.

It felt less like power than something else.

It felt like something ending and something new beginning.

Something darker, meaner.

Someone needs to take her down a notch.

A rougher beast slumped toward them, conjured by their mighty chants.

13

n Pam's Lexus on the way home, Harper held the cash in her lap, the scent of Cuban cigars filling the front seat.

The streets icy and black and the lights like glowy halos, Pam couldn't stop talking.

She was recounting a conversation she'd had with Sue, Sue going on and on about Pam, accusing her of cheating the Board, poaching, more. "She's the one who said, when she was grooming me to join, *Pammy, we'll all die of global warming or terrorism or a global epidemic before we run out of women who need money.*"

Harper had heard Sue say it before, many times. Only the list of fatal calamities changed. *We'll all die of SARS, from nuclear fallout, from aspartame, from the zombie apocalypse . . .*

"They're such jealous bitches," Pam said in closing. "As if I didn't have enough to deal with."

"What do you mean?" Harper said, not thinking, clenching the armrest as Pam seemed to spin around a sharp corner.

"The hearing," Pam snapped. "The goddamned hearing tomorrow."

"Right," Harper said. She paused, then tentatively asked, "Do you think Doug'll show?"

"If he's not already halfway to Machu Picchu."

The money in her lap, Harper wondered how long she could wait to reach out to him herself. Wondered if he might be tossed in jail again, unable to collect. It almost made her want to laugh.

Neither of them said anything for several blocks. Pam flipped on the radio, the speakers instantly exploding with some dark, doomy song from their own high school days, crooning about *cold leather seats* and *time's tide*. The one that felt like poetry, the kinds of lyrics Harper would copy on the back of her spiral notebooks.

Those songs, that age when it felt like a kiss could change your life, even kill you.

Maybe it could, Harper thought, sounding like Vivian. Feeling like Vivian somehow, that sense of careering into the night, the car rumbling beneath her, a sense of doom, intoxicating.

The singer wondering how a boy like him could come to this.

As if on cue, Harper's phone buzzed in her lap. A text from Vivian.

Cassie broke up with me.

Shit, Harper thought, her stomach turning from the overheated car, the cigar stench, that vodka soda she'd been talked into. And the second after that.

I wanna die. I wanna die.

"What is it?" Pam asked, turning down the radio.

"Vivian," Harper said. "I have to call her."

"We'll be home in two minutes."

"Cassie broke up with her," Harper said, the phone hot against her ear.

"Cassie," Pam said distractedly, turning the wheel. "Is that the one with the funky tooth?"

It never feels good," Pam was saying as they pulled into the driveway. "But she'll be okay. She's always had so many friends."

"Cassie's not her friend," Harper said brusquely. "She's her girlfriend."

Pam looked at her, a streetlight sheeting her face white.

"Shit," she said, shaking her head. "Sorry. I'm an idiot."

"It's okay," Harper said, feeling the nerves rippling off her sister, imagining how much dread she must be feeling about seeing Doug. "It's fine."

Harper huddled with Vivian in her bed, a frothy swirl of dirty laundry and sheets, a tumble of Sour Patch Kids, a spattered nail polish top.

"Everyone saw," Vivian moaned. "She had her head in his lap on the patio at the party."

"That's terrible," Pam said distractedly, walking back and forth in the hallway, peeling down her leather dress, kicking off her heels.

"Some douchebag from Notre Dame," Vivian continued, blinking through her sticky mascara. "Bret, of course his name is Bret. You know what? He used to call her Snaggle Tooth behind her back."

"I'm sorry, honey," Harper said, stroking Vivian's cheek. "It's the worst."

"I hope he gives her chlamydia. All the Notre Dame boys have it. They pass it back and forth between all those Catholic whores."

"Jesus, Vivian," Pam said, stopping in the doorway, her bra straps red against her skin. "You better hope he doesn't."

Vivian's sobs grew harder, so hard they hurt to hear.

Harper looked up at her sister.

"What?" Pam said. Then, her face softening, "I just meant what if you and she . . . Okay, baby, I am sorry. I am."

"You only care about yourself," Vivan was crying out, her voice thundering through the house. "Yourself and your Chanel purses and your new money and your new life. And your club."

"I just don't know how to talk to her," Pam whispered to Harper as they both crowded into bathroom, brushing their teeth.

"She has a broken heart," Harper said softly. "You can't talk about that?"

An hour later, and the shouting had finally stopped.

"I hate her, I hate her," Vivian whispered as Harper calmed her down, letting her sneak a cigarette, turning off her phone. "Dad understands. He loves Cassie. He even let her drive his Mustang. He—"

"Okay, Vivian," Harper said.

It didn't surprise her that Doug "loved" Cassie. He'd "loved" Leigh, too, or so he announced. But, like all his fine gestures, it felt mostly strategic. A way to set himself apart from Pam, her blind spots. A wedge to plant there.

"You of all people should know," Vivian said, her eyes cold, her face slack.

Harper looked at her. "Know what?"

"About Mom," Vivian whispered. "She thinks we're perverts."

Harper didn't know what to say. She knew Pam loved them both. But there was part of them she could never fold into her understanding of life, or of them. It was a limitation. Everyone had them.

J ust after one, Vivian called her brother at school.

Patrick, in his dorm room after his own party, had come to the rescue, his soft, woozy voice so soothing to his sister.

"I'm gonna burn off her tattoo," she was saying. "I'm gonna burn the dove off with acid."

Back in her room, Harper reached for the Benadryl, one, then two.

Her mind still racing from all the drama of the night, the booze and chaos playing with her, making her feel wired, on edge.

Even having twenty-five thousand dollars in cash in the room, in her accordion file under the bed, made her nervous. A stack thick as a brick, a sparkly rubber band plucked, it seemed, from the dainty head of Becky Schloss's ten-year-old daughter.

But slowly, slowly, the slurry of Patrick's lava lamp worked some kind of magic on her, and the dull thump from Vivian's music through the thin wall. That droning, moody bass.

It make a playa like me mean. Make me chunk some green. Make me feel seen. But instead I'm sipping leeann . . .

And soon enough Harper was deep into a dream. She was young again, so young and green. And she was riding Milkshake, a Thoroughbred now twenty years gone. The one she learned to ride on, back when she could do anything, be anything. Everyone said so.

She dreamt of canter pirouettes. Three-loop serpentines.

And suddenly Leigh was beside her, aloft Gilda, her Dutch warm-blood.

Leigh, riding the way she always rode, with such grace, her hands seeming to float in perfect tandem with Gilda, her rhythms.

Something broke in her chest and Harper could breathe, the rush of air into her lungs as if she'd been under water, underground for weeks, months.

She was riding and Leigh was there, and she was perfect and they were and it would never end. How could it?

The sudden clatter woke her, like a junk drawer torn loose.

Harper jumped from her bed, to her feet, thick socks because the house was always so cold.

The kitchen was bright as an operating room, the basement door open, beckoning.

"Pam," Harper whispered, creeping down the stairs, the dense fug of the cellar, laundry hanging, ghostlike, from the clothesline.

In the corner, by the dryer, Pam was bent over, picking up stray bills on the floor, the Merry Mushroom cookie jar under her arm like Winnie the Pooh with his honey pot.

Harper wondered if she was still dreaming.

"Pammy?" she asked. "What's happening?"

Pam turned, her face pale, fist-tight.

"Harper, we have to hide it. All of it."

It wouldn't all fit in the cookie jar, some of the bills wedged deep in the bleach-ridged Tampax Pearl box, and Pam had spent an hour sitting on the cold basement floor, wrapping the bills tighter and tighter and tighter.

Harper had no idea how much money it was, how much Pam had stockpiled, but it was more than Harper had ever seen.

It reminded her, fleetingly, of playing Monopoly as kids, how whoever won—mostly Pam—would wave the money in the air, singing, "I'm in the Money," stomping their feet.

"I saw it on TV," her sister said breathlessly, "how you could fit ninety-eight thousand dollars into a cereal box. You just have to pack it tight enough."

Harper had seen it, too, on the news a few weeks back. The footage of all the cash absconded from a twenty-year-old drug dealer who finally gave up his hiding spot. The federal agents shown shaking Lucky Charms dust off all the bills.

"What's going on?" Harper kept asking, following Pam back up the basement steps. "Why is this happening?"

But Pam would only say she woke with a bad feeling, from a bad dream.

"What kind of dream?"

"I don't know," Pam said, not looking at her, stopping dead in her tracks. "I don't want to talk about it."

"It's okay," Harper said, touching her arm, quilled. "It's over."

But she could tell the dream wasn't over for Pam.

"I ran over something in the Lexus. It was late, and the road curved wrong. I was driving to the old house instead of the new one. It was an animal. Something red, like one of those fox-faced dogs. When I lifted its head, its teeth fell out like little pearls."

Harper could feel it, the fear quaking through her sister.

"Do you want to put your cash in here too?" Pam asked her, thrusting the jar in front of her. "We have to make sure no one can find it."

"No," Harper said. Her money had to go to Doug.

"I should've gotten a safe, like Deb's," Pam said suddenly, breathlessly. It was like a switch went off and she was moving again, swinging open the kitchen door, bursting out into the frozen yard.

"We can get one tomorrow," Harper said, following her into the dark.

"The hearing is tomorrow," Pam whispered, nearly tripping on an old branch, charging toward the back reaches of the shallow yard. "Oh, god. The hearing."

Harper thought suddenly about that stranger she'd seen days before. The one in the ski mask hovering in the neighbor's yard. She'd never told Pam, or anyone, but now it made Harper frightened, the panic catching, snagging her into its whirl.

Should I tell her? she thought. But Pam was already so scared and everything felt so urgent. She'd tell her tomorrow, after everything.

They crouched together, under the brown-streaked elm.

They dug and dug and dug with the shovel furred with rust Harper grabbed from the shed. The metal bucket, the metal spade.

Harper's right knee throbbing, they dug until they couldn't dig anymore, their breath visible, like little puffs of smoke.

Peering down into the shallow grave, Harper watching as Pam emptied the bucket one last time, the cookie jar's mushroom top disappearing, gone.

And the whole time, Pam whispering, the words slithering from her mouth.

"All I want"—her teeth chattering—"is to be innocent again."

14

Harper would remember all of it later, would replay it dozens of times in her head.

It was just after six and Pam was saying something to her through the bathroom door, towel wrapped around her body.

Harper couldn't hear over Pam's blow dryer.

"What?" she asked, looking for her thermos, getting ready to leave.

"Make sure your pearls are large," Pam said, yanking the dryer cord loose from the wall, "and your hips small."

"Mom," Harper said, remembering. "She always said that."

"Her secret to a happy marriage," Pam said.

"What would Mom have known about a happy marriage?" Harper said, pulling on her coat.

And Pam laughed, that big, throaty laugh of hers, covering her mouth so she didn't wake Vivian.

Her face bare, she looked both twelve and a hundred at the same time.

"I'm going to make it up to Vivian later," she confided, shaking her still damp hair. "I'll take her to Sinbad's tonight. She loves the onion rings. I'm gonna make it all up to her."

Harper was glad. Poor Vivian, who would wake to the same heartbreak that had shuddered through her the night before. Poor Vivian, who had to go to school and see Cassie at the attendance office the second she got there, and then everyone else at school, all of whom—according to Vivian—knew about Cassie's low-down hookup with the Notre Dame boy, with Bret, giver of chlamydia.

It was all so different in Harper's day, everything furtive—the romance and heartbreak both. Maybe you couldn't, or didn't, hold hands in the hallway, or kiss under the disco ball at prom, but no one knew either when it ended, when you were dumped, betrayed, forgotten, through.

H er breath catching, Pam ran a pink hand along her Ann Taylor funeral suit, hanging stiffly on the back of the bathroom door.

"The hearing's at ten?" Harper asked, fighting off a bristle of anxiety as they both moved into the kitchen.

She kept thinking of Pam the night before. After they'd buried the money, they'd had one last drink on the icy patio, wind whipping.

I just have this feeling, she told Harper. *I can't explain it. All these bad dreams. Last night I dreamt I was back in the old house, walking through all the rooms. And suddenly I knew that one of the rooms had this . . . this* darkness *in it. And if I opened the wrong door, I would get lost inside.*

"They pushed it—do you think this looks okay?" Pam asked distractedly, her fingers trembling slightly around the suit collar.

"It's gonna go fine, Pammy," Harper said. "You don't even have to talk to him. That's what your lawyer is for."

But her sister wasn't listening, drifting to the kitchen window, ice crystals curling around the pane. A faint smile twitched there suddenly.

Maybe she was looking at the old elm, thinking of her money, hidden deep in the earth.

That was the moment, the one Harper would remember forever. Pam, wrapped like a baby in her towel, looking out into the backyard, the grass iced-white like a fairy tale.

She was smiling like she had a secret, and the secret would keep her safe.

Sisters think they know each other so well, too well, but Pammy had a whole world behind her eyes, in her smile, and you could never come close.

15

Four hours later

Harper's hand was on Jackpot's flank when she heard her name.
It was her favorite thing to do, currycomb in hand, sweeping circles on her caramel coat. Her stiff brush and finishing brush, soft cloths, hoof pick, mane and tail comb, sometimes the grooming mitt, sometimes clippers, a sponge. Careful around her belly, between the back legs. Gentle around the ears.

She could forget about Pam's hearing, Vivian's heart, Doug's threats, the Wheel, Pam's growing empire. She didn't need to think about money.

"Harper!" It was Mr. Bingham, shouting from his office, that crackly emphysemic voice Harper had known since she was fourteen and working as a mucker, cleaning all the stalls. "Go pick your niece up at school."

Harper sighed, setting down her comb. Leaning a moment against Jackpot's burnished coat, feeling the thump-thump of her sturdy heart.

Then, reaching in the pocket of her coat, Harper glanced at her phone bright with texts, voicemail blinks, the hot frenzy of her niece's frantic head, her frantic life.

I need to leave. Mom won't text me back. Can u come get me?

the nurse won't give me any ibu

where is MOM where r u??? PLEASE.

PLEASEEEE can u get me? I feel like I might die.

"Why didn't you call her back?" the police would ask her later.

"I don't keep my phone on in the stables. The horses don't like the sound."

"Was it typical of your niece to call you?"

It was, of course. Vivian pleading migraines, cramps, bad feelings. Cassie would often just sign her out at the attendance office. But when Pam wouldn't get her, or couldn't, Harper was next.

come pick up and let's ride together ok

It usually meant Harper bargaining with Mr. Bingham for an hour to borrow one of the club's horses—usually Jackpot, or Stardew, Vivian's new favorite, *like riding a pillow*, she would say with a wink—before Vivian vanished into somebody's car—lately Cassie's—circling the paddocks with sinister slowness, stereo thumping rhythmically, hungrily. *Vivian, Vivian, c'mon.*

The short drive to school felt strange, the streets gray and empty.

As she approached, Harper saw her, a lone figure, backpack switching up her shoulder, standing forlornly by the school's football field, that defiant jaw of hers turned up, knife-sharp, her lavender wool hat with the puffy white pom and big pink mittens hanging at her side like paws.

"I don't want to talk about it," Vivian said, unusually quiet as she got in the minivan, slamming the door shut.

Harper guessed the morning had been even harder than she expected. Was anyone more cruel than teenage girls?

They drove in silence, Vivian's big fuzzy mittens resting in her lap, the car so cold and the click-click of the turn signal that never seemed to go off in time.

There was something so little girl about the mittens, angora dyed icing-pink, twice the size of her tiny doll hands.

"She could've texted me back," Vivian said finally.

Harper didn't say anything. It really wasn't like her sister not to respond, nor even to scurry off to school still in her pajama pants to rescue Vivian from a stuck tampon, a boy trying to grab her breast in class, an upsetting text from her dad, I'm crying and I can't stop.

But who knew what Doug had sprung on Pam at the hearing, if he'd shown at all? Harper's stomach turned.

Later, she would think she made it up, but it was true. That eerie feeling as they pulled into the driveway on El Dorado Drive. As they exited the car, as Harper followed Vivian, her white pom bobbing, up the driveway.

Maybe it was the way Vivian, in that big silver puffer of hers, its perky hood bouncing, seemed ready for a fight.

"Mother!" she was saying, even before she reached the door. "Jesus, Mom, did you forget to charge your phone again?"

Harper had her key out, but Vivian had already pushed open the door and you felt it instantly: how hot the house was, the furnace chugging and it all happened so fast.

Vivian, her phone curled in her right mitten, stopped short in the doorway.

Vivian, what the—

But then she saw it, too, one of the long cushions from the old sofa in the basement, inexplicably lying on the kitchen floor.

And something beneath it, sticking out.

L *ike the princess and the pea, but backward.*
    Like the princess and the pea, but upside down.

W ait, go back.

L ater, it was hard to remember it all in one sequence. Instead, it was like a stack of Polaroids dropped on the floor, fanned and jagged.

Vivian's low-top sneaker toe pushed against the cushion edge, lifting it.

"What . . ."

There was something beneath it, a red hand curled.

Curled like the Wicked Witch's feet under the house in *The Wizard of Oz.*

A hand like Pam's hand, red and raw from digging in the dirt the night before.

H arper watched as Vivian's toe lifted the cushion, turning it like, *Surprise!*

Because there was Pam, lying on her side, fetus-curled.

Pam in her Hunt Club hoodie and silky pajama bottoms, black

and ivory and made in Paris, the remnants of a long-ago anniversary gift set from Doug.

"Pammy," Harper said, nearly laughing, covering her mouth with her sleeve.

Because it was like, *What are you doing on the floor, Pammy?* Was it a prank or something?

The hood of her hoodie slung across her face, one ankle caught in the basement door, flung open, the boom-boom of the furnace waking up.

"Call nine-one-one!" Vivian was saying, already on her knees, her pom swinging improbably as she wrested her mother onto her back, her head lolling like a doll's before slumping over and landing back on the linoleum with a nasty thunk.

Pammy?

That was when they saw all the blood, a scarlet bib of it starting under her nose, and the thick red on the right side of her face, along her ear and in her hair.

That dirty-blond Bishop hair scattered with Apple Jacks, the cereal box overturned on the counter.

Later, she would marvel at how quickly Vivian moved to action, while she herself could barely stand, her knees swaying beneath her.

Blood everywhere and Pam's eyes open, lashes sticky, as if startled that all this had happened and that her whole rollicking, tumultuous life, with all its love and horrors and beauty, had come to such a surprising, violent halt.

That it was suddenly, instantly over.

We can't let him see!" Vivian kept crying, pointing at Fitzie, scratching at the kitchen door, slammed shut. "We can't let Fitzie see!"

Time had slowed down like taffy and now sped up like a spring.

The kitchen cramped, hot, and Vivian's hands covered with blood.

"You have to come now!" Harper could hear herself saying the words into the kitchen phone, the cord wrapping around her parka. For a few seconds, she couldn't remember the address or anything else.

But it didn't matter, they were on the way, sirens in the distance, a neighbor who heard the screaming and this was Grosse Pointe and no one ever died, not like this.

Vivian panting, crouched over her mother, one pink fuzzy mitten torn off, the other matted red. Both hands on her mother's chest, pressing down again and again.

"Vivian, what you are doing?"

Looking up, a scatter of blood across her face, her niece said, pure and true, "I learned CPR at school."

That's what she said. Then she said:

"I'm saving her. I'm saving Mom."

The paramedics swarmed the kitchen, Apple Jacks crushed under their heavy shoes, all the noise from walkie-talkies and rolling wheels and Vivian screaming as they hovered over Pammy, one of them turning to the other and shaking his head doomily, just like in the movies.

"But she was okay," Vivian kept saying. "I heard her breathing. I felt it. She was breathing on my face." A red spray on her cheek like an atomizer.

"She was already gone, sweetie," one of them said. "You did everything you could."

The screeching ambulance, her arm around her niece, a half-dozen hard turns to St. John's, and none of it was real.

The pink cereal dust on the bottoms of all their shoes.

The terrorizing fluorescents of the hospital corridors, the dark cluster of police in winter parkas at the far end, coffee steaming in their red hands.

How it seemed like they were waiting for her.

The things she would remember: Pam's left hand flung, her tattered fingers brought to blood again after last night's digging.

The basement door swinging against Pam's ankle, every gust from the furnace, from the opening and closing kitchen door.

Vivian screaming, screaming, her mother's blood ringed around her mouth.

At the hospital, two officers had talked to her and to Vivian.

They asked questions, left, and then returned to ask the same questions.

"So what happened when you got home?"

And Harper's lip started quivering, making her feel five again and *where did her sister Pam go,* separated by the crowds in the cavernous mall.

To talk about it would mean feeling all the feelings again, which seemed unbearable.

But she told them what she could remember, and the more she told, the less she could remember.

It hurt to tell it and she knew it was costing her something to tell it, but what choice did she have, really?

When was the last time you spoke to her? Was she expecting anyone? Did she typically leave the door unlocked? Did you see anything like a weapon at the scene?

Then the detective, Conlan—graying blond hair, a fat Masonic tie tack mid-sternum, one of those tall men who were always hunched over—had new questions, returning from *the scene.*

The scene. What an ugly term for her sister's homey yellow kitchen, its shiny, grease-specked 1970s wallpaper, daisies and sunflowers.

And you're sure you saw no weapon of any kind at the scene? Anything on the floor? A flashlight? A wrench?

And then:

Did you notice anything missing?

. . . No.

He showed her pictures. The living room TV, Pam's room, all the tiny rooms.

No, she said, *I don't notice anything missing.*

I t was only when they left her alone a few minutes that she let herself think about the accordion file of cash under her bed.

And far more so: The Merry Mushroom cookie jar buried in the backyard.

The night before Pam . . . the night before *this,* Pam buried all her money under several feet of dirt. What could it mean? Didn't it have to mean something?

But, when the police returned, she said nothing.

She didn't know how to explain about the money, or what would happen if she did.

She needed to think about it.

In the waiting area, Vivian had curled herself up on one of the Formica chairs, knees to her chest, puffer surrounding her like a silver cocoon, crinkling every time she twitched or shifted. The red spray on her cheek now smeared. Harper could see the light of her phone flashing.

One of the officers brought Fitzie from the house. Poor Fitzie, wheezing like a squeak toy, shaken and confused.

"Did you call your brother?" she asked Vivian, but then remembered she herself had, a half hour before.

At first, Patrick didn't seem to believe her until he did, and started crying. A choke in his voice and he couldn't say anything and Harper kept talking, telling him what to do, how to get home.

I don't understand, he kept saying. *I just talked to her this morning. I called to wish her luck with Dad.*

Within the hour, he would be on a Greyhound bus and Harper could picture him sobbing the whole way, his sweet forehead pressed against the sooty window, his oversize headphones on and vibrating softly, promising him that it was all a bad dream.

By two, Debra had appeared at the police station, grappling her handbag across her chest. Perry followed in coffee-stained chinos, collapsing onto one of the folding chairs when Harper confirmed the news.

They'd been driving all day, leaving their house early that morning for the three-hour drive, plus a ferry, to Pelee Island, and then, less than an hour after arriving, getting the call from the police and turning around and coming home again.

"I had to hear it from a stranger!" Debra cried out hoarsely, and Harper wanted to laugh because it was the same old Debra, angry that her sisters had drank the entire pint of peach schnapps they'd found in their grandfather's den before telling her, angry because they'd read their mother's Judith Krantz book (the one about incest) or found their father's secret *Hustler* stash without telling her.

"Deb," Harper had said to her, a spatter of Pam's blood now brown-bright on her coat, "no one's leaving you out of this."

D ad isn't answering his phone," Vivian kept saying. "His voicemail is full."

"Probably from all of us leaving messages," Harper tried. But it hadn't even crossed her mind to call. She wasn't sure why.

"His voicemail is always full," Vivian whispered, shoving her phone back in the inner reaches of her puffer.

Detective Conlan hadn't been able to reach him either.

P am was supposed to see him in court," Harper told them, remembering about the hearing. Had she already told them? She didn't remember. "Maybe he's there right now."

"What time?"

"Ten," Debra said, from two seats down, tissues sticky in her hand. "It's always ten."

"I thought they changed it," Harper said, though everything was a blur.

"What kind of hearing?" Detective Conlan asked. "Custody?"

"A trust dispute," Harper said.

"He was stealing from his kids," Debra said, wadding up the tissue.

Harper looked at her. An old impulse inherited from their mother. *Don't share our dirty laundry.*

"Do you know his attorney's name?" he asked.

"I think so," Harper said, distracted.

She was looking at Vivian, approaching them. How her eyes were glazed, empty. One of her pink mittens, stuffed in her pockets, had fallen loose to the floor, its tip stained red.

16

an't we go?" Vivian asked, back in the waiting area. "Why can't
we go?"

"You can go, but we'll need you at the station tomorrow,"
Detective Conlan finally said. "We'll have an officer go with you."
The officer followed them to Debra's and stayed there.

He stayed all night, sitting in his car across the street from Debra's
house, where everyone was gathering.

Everyone sat in the living room, on their mother's creaking faux-
Regency chairs and on Debra's brand-new, untouched sofa, bone-
white, now with Vivian's flip-flops skittered across it as she tucked her
knees to her chest.

Beside her, fresh off the Greyhound, was a hollow-eyed Patrick, a
two-day beard and an instant alcohol flush from the short one Perry
poured for him.

"What happened to Mom?" he kept asking, a stunned look on his face.

"I talked to her this morning," he kept saying. "I wanted to wish her luck with Dad. She was so happy I called. She sounded good. Really good."

No one knew what to say, so Harper sat down beside him and curled her arms around him and he clambered close like he did when he was eight years old and told her a shambling, funny story about his bus ride home, how the woman sitting next to him nursed her baby for at least two hours *and it was only when we were all getting off the bus that I saw. That was no baby, that was a pot-bellied pig.*

Soon, Stevie appeared, along with a half-dozen second, third cousins— more Bishops but from the west side of Detroit.

Harper knew she shouldn't drink, that it might unleash all the horror of what had happened, but just the sight of Perry rolling out their parents' rickety brass trolley filled her with such relief that she asked for a vodka neat (*only one,* she promised herself).

Perry joined her and discreetly offered the traditional family toast: "Here's how we lost the farm . . ."

There was a clatter of red go-cups, the very ones Debra shamelessly used for the Wheel parties, as everyone began drinking, first shyly and then with fervor.

"Can you have a wake before the funeral?" one cousin asked tentatively, and everyone laughed, the Bishops' gallows laugh that went far back into childhood, their father's first bankruptcy, their mother's first nervous collapse.

How would they speak about it? About what had happened, an event too terrible to utter. They hadn't figured it out yet, not one of them. Besides, this was Michigan, the Midwest. No one ever really *talked* about things, ever.

Instead, Debra fussed over the white sofa. Vivian and Patrick whispered soundlessly to each other through their hoodies.

Perry sat in the corner, dozing off now and then, twitching occasionally to alertness. At his feet, Fitzie sat sentry, even more nervous than usual, his head twitching, his ears raised at every sound.

There was small talk about their various drives, about the weather, about the rancid coffee at the police station, anything to drown out the disbelief and confusion knotted inside and whatever lay beneath that, the grief and rage to come.

But it was only when Patrick pulled one of the old family photos off the built-ins that they tentatively started talking about Pam.

It was an Easter portrait, the family posing at the country club, all three sisters in their pastel dresses and pastel bonnets, pastel eggs nestled in the grass around them.

"She must only be four or five there," Debra said, looking at the picture. "How she hated when Mommy curled her hair like that."

"Because you called her Piglet," Harper said, a laugh and a sob in her throat at once.

"Was this Halloween?" Patrick asked, gesturing to a picture of Pam at seven or eight, posing in a pink Gunne Sax dress, satin and lace.

"No," Harper said, pressing her fingers on the fading photo. "That was the year she was Cinderella."

Debra nodded, wiping her eyes. "We'd go every year," she said. "And then she won."

Their father would take them downtown to Cobo Hall every fall to join thousands of little girls lining up for their moment with the boy who played Prince Charming. One by one, they'd try on the glass slipper.

"Oh, that feeling," Harper recalled, "trying to wedge your foot into that tiny thing!"

"My foot," Debra insisted, "was always too small. I always had such dainty feet."

"Hmmm," Harper said, winking at Patrick.

Harper and Debra, like hundreds of other little girls, received the "consolation prize"—a plastic princess doll, shaped like a bell, with a handle. Harper never forgot Debra dumping hers in the trash on the way out, calling it cheap.

"After, we all watched her ride the float in the Thanksgiving Day Parade," Harper said.

"It was so cold that day," Debra said. "But she was so beautiful."

But the truth was she'd only ridden the last twenty minutes. Their parents had too much to drink the night before, and slept through most of the parade. Debra kept pounding on their bedroom door. *This is Pam's big day! Get up! Get up!*

Sister stuff was so intricate, so full of land mines, booby traps, deep resentments, old jealousies. It was important to remember *this*, Harper thought. How hard they all fought for each other, mama bears all. But Pam the most mama of them all, a pugilist for her siblings, forever telling boys at school, mean teachers, sadistic coaches: *Leave my sister alone!*

Debra pushed the album off her lap, her hand covering her mouth. Breathing, breathing, determined not to cry.

Harper did what she always did when they lost at lacrosse, tilting her head up, widening her eyes, fighting off the tears.

Bishops don't cry, their mother used to say. Before their father's funeral, she gave them each—ages nineteen, twenty, twenty-two—half a Valium. Standing along the pew, their eyelids drooping, their faces soft and strange, they didn't cry at all. Dry eyes and dry handkerchiefs. After, Debra threw up on her Mary Janes, but no one noticed.

L ate afternoon smeared into evening, clumps of extended family, friends of family arriving with their casserole dishes and tinfoil, their Josef's French pastry boxes, Bommarito's cannolis and Polish ham, and there were whispered confidences over the kitchen sink, in the doorway to the powder room, on the back deck slicked with ice.

Vivian and Patrick disappeared with Stevie into the basement, the heady musk of pot slipping up the vents.

It was all so strange, no one knowing what to say or what to think, and as the hours passed, spinning wild speculations, drawing on the latest suburban legends about the imaginary horrors of Detroit to explain the inexplicable.

"Did you see on the news about that new gang? This could be one of those initiations! Did you hear they chopped off the hand of a woman at Eastland Mall to steal her ring?"

"But there's also been a string of burglaries—did you know the Edmundses had their house cleaned out when they were on Sanibel Island?"

"Yes! There's a new burglary ring from Detroit. They come in vans that say Acme Plumbing. They get in through your storm windows. They're escalating to home invasions."

"But nothing was stolen, was it?" Perry asked. "From Pam's."

They all looked at Debra, who looked at Harper.

She thought, again, of the Merry Mushroom cookie jar.

And what led to it. Pam's dream, how it had scared her. Had it been a premonition, or was there more?

Was the cookie jar still back there?

Everyone was looking at her.

"Not that we know of," Harper started. "But the police didn't say—"

"That's not what this was," Debra said. "It wasn't random. There was no burglary."

Harper knew what Debra was thinking. She couldn't say she hadn't thought of it too.

"It was personal," Debra said, adding, quietly, to Harper, "it had to be personal."

Well, I mean, look who's not here," one of the cousins finally said, her go-cup of chardonnay swirling. "Where is he?"

No one had uttered it openly but, as the night wore on, the most furtive, intense conversations inevitably led—again and again—to Doug. Where was he?

"On a plane to Timbuktu," Perry suggested drolly, "with a new name and a new set of fingerprints."

I should wring her goddamned neck. The words suddenly came back to her. Doug's ferocious whisper in the Hunt Club's dark barn just a few days ago.

But that was the way he and Pam spoke to each other, the hyperbole, the high emotions, the threats. In a divorce like that, everyone threatens murder.

They don't know what they're talking about," Vivian was whispering to Patrick. "They didn't see what I saw."

Harper could hear them lurking in the kitchen, eavesdropping. Vivian's arm deep in a jumbo jar of cheese balls, fluorescent, nearly glowing in the dark.

She knew what Vivian meant. The red scrim over her sister's face, smashed, her nose broken from falling to the kitchen floor, or maybe from beating off the blows, fighting off the force charging at her, seeking to annihilate her.

"How dare they? They don't know anything about our life," Vivian said. "They're supposed to be family, but they don't know anything about what's been going on."

Harper could hear Vivian's jaw clicking as she crunched.

D o you think Doug could really . . . ?" Harper asked Debra.
    They were smoking like movie gangsters in the cold garage, the door halfway open, hunched together near the yard rakes and garden spades.

"Well, where the hell is he?" Debra said. "His children's mother is murdered and he can't be bothered to check in with them?"

"Something isn't right," Harper said. For all Doug's flaws, it was unimaginable that he wouldn't even call his kids.

Debra's eyes widened as a pair of headlights flashed across her face, made her white, old.

"Who is it? Who's there?" Harper asked, curling her hand over her eyes and staring down the driveway to see a violet BMW, two faces bright and alarmed through the windshield.

"Sue and Sandy," Harper said. "What the hell . . . they shouldn't be here."

Clack-clack! Stutter-stepping, Debra backed into the hanging tools, rakes, hedge clippers clattering to the floor.

"No," Debra said thickly, reaching for a fallen pitchfork. "They shouldn't."

The four of them huddled together, Sue puffing like a steam train and Sandy, her curls stiff in the cold, her gloves curled around a fogged Pyrex dish.

"It's unthinkable," Sue was saying.

"It is," Harper said.

Sue Fox was the last person she wanted to see, and Sandy was a close second, bouncing on the balls of her feet in the cold garage. The only thing stopping her from drawing her fingers anxiously through her short, springy coils, Harper thought, was the acid-yellow chicken casserole in her arms.

"Why are you here?" Debra hissed.

"It was on the evening news," Sue said. "I can't believe you didn't call."

"Our sister was murdered this morning," Debra said, "so you'll excuse our bad manners."

Sandy gasped faintly.

"Where's Doug?" Sue asked, unfazed as ever, others' emotions rolling off her like a distant breeze. "They said on the news the police can't reach him."

Harper said nothing, throwing her cigarette on the ground, covering her nose from the cloying smell of tuberose.

"This is family time," Debra said. "Thank you for stopping by."

"But, Debra," Sue started, "we *have* to talk—"

"There's a patrol car across the street," Harper said.

"What?" Sandy asked, a shiver in her voice.

Harper had no idea if the officer was still there, but it didn't matter. Sue's back straightened, her eyes darting beyond the garage door.

"He's watching us right now," Debra bluffed. "Writing down your license numbers."

Suddenly, the door to the house shot open, thudding against the wall.

All four women turned, a sliver of light falling across their faces.

"Oh, hey." It was Patrick, standing in the doorway in his gym socks, looking confused.

"Thank you for your condolences," Harper said, swiping the chicken divan from Sandy's hands, "at this difficult time."

It was late, after one A.M., and Harper was alone for the first time since she'd picked up Vivian at school that morning. She thought she would cry, or something.

But she couldn't do anything, sitting on the edge of the futon, picking at its tufts.

Debra had made up Perry's office for her, his aging printer-fax mysteriously buzzing and lurching intermittently all night.

Vivian was next door in Stevie's old bedroom. Earlier, Harper had poked her head in, startled by the dusty Slowdive poster glowing in the dark. She could barely see Vivian, tangled up in yet another crocheted afghan Harper remembered from childhood. *Am I the only sister,* she wondered, *who didn't get one of those florid things?* Brown and orange zigzags recalling dozens of sick days, hangovers, bouts of menstrual cramps, spilling flat ginger ale into its nubs and grooves.

"We can talk about it," Harper had said to her. "If you want."

"About what?" Vivian asked, her eyes big in the dark.

"About what we saw. What happened. Seeing your mom like that . . ."

Vivian didn't say anything for a moment. A husky breathing from under the afghan loops.

"I can't talk about it," she said finally. "I want to sleep."

"Okay," Harper said. "But when you want to—"

"I just keep thinking about those slippers," Vivian said, and Harper could hear the click-click of those teeth of hers, chattering like a Halloween toy.

"Slippers?"

"When I first saw her, I thought she'd slipped on the floor. Because of those goddamned shearling mules she always wears."

"But . . ." Harper rubbed her temples, something twitching between her brows.

"I kept telling her she shouldn't wear those all the time. Inside and outside, with those old pajama pants. It was so embarrassing. Even to take me to school and the heel catching on the brake. I was always saying, *Mom . . .*"

"But, Vivian," Harper said, "she wasn't wearing slippers."

Because her sister's feet were bare, turned opposite ways like a broken doll.

And she could hear her niece swallow hard.

"Oh," she said scratchily and then nothing at all.

Harper wondered how much Vivian and her brother and cousin had smoked today, or what else they might have taken, swallowed, snorted, remembering Patrick and Stevie both climbing up those steps at night's end, their eyes threaded red, the dazed misery on their faces, such handsome boys both so lost, emerging from the dark cave of Debra's rec room.

"Oh, sweetie," Harper said, reaching for her hand, trying to find it under the afghan's sprawl. "Your poor mom."

Vivian wincing as Harper clasped her fingers and Harper throwing the afghan back and seeing Vivian's hands, band-aids like rings over three fingers, including her index fingertip.

Her nails—always manicured and groomed, those weekly appointments at Madame Suzy's, vampish black, so stiletto sharp it made riding hard—now ruined.

"What happened?" Harper asked, remembering Vivian's bloody pink mitten.

"I tore them up," Vivian said, shaking her hand like it was throbbing.

"But how . . ." Harper started, then stopped herself.

"When I was trying to . . . with Mom," Vivian said, flipping her pillow over like she'd flipped the sofa cushion that morning, like she'd rolled her mother onto her back, shouting that she knew her CPR, certain she could save her mother, long past saving.

Harper closed her eyes, thinking of it now. Pam's dirty-blond hair like her own, how Vivian rolled her over onto her back and that swirl across her face, sticky with dark plums of blood. When is a face not a face anymore—

Vivian, how were you able to do that? she wanted to ask her. Act so fast while Harper herself couldn't move at all.

Some people thrived in a crisis, thrived in chaos, and it was reassuring somehow to know that her niece, used to chaos her whole life, must be one of those people.

The digital clock burned red: *2:36 A.M.*

ZZZt. A flutter from Harper's phone.

She fumbled for it, her palms clammy. Squinting at the little screen. *UNKNOWN CALLER.*

"Who is this?"

There were three clicks, a distant voice—female, reedy—said, "Patching you through now."

"What? Who is—"

"Harper, are you there?" His voice sounded gravel-thick, close. Almost like he was in the room with her.

"Doug," she whispered. "Doug, Jesus . . ."

"Is it true? Please, Harper. Tell me."

Harper swallowed hard.

"Where are you?" she demanded. "The police have been trying to reach you. We all have."

"So it's true? It's . . ."

"Where are you?" Harper demanded, more forcefully now, gathering herself. "Where the hell are you?"

"I'm on a business trip, this Volkswagen thing."

"Doug, your kids—"

"She never showed at the courthouse, Harp. I headed straight for the airport after. Connecting flights and a layover, Christ, I saw it on the hotel TV . . . Is she really gone?"

"Yes," Harper said. "Yes, goddammit. You need to get back here. Why aren't you on your way back? Your kids need you. Vivian, she— we found her."

"Shit," Doug said, his voice swallowing itself.

Harper's hand reached for the wall like she might be sick, then thinking of Vivian sleeping on the other side and could she hear?

"And the police," Harper said, her voice gaining urgency. "You see how this looks, right? How bad this looks?"

"Story of my life," Doug said, such a funny thing to say and a strained chuckle before he let out a sob that chilled Harper to the bone.

It was then that she thought—how could she not?—*What if he did. . . .*

"Doug," she said, "you better call the police now."

A staticky sizzle and he was gone. The connection dead.

She knew she should call the detectives, even at this hour, and tell them everything Doug had said and how strange he'd sounded.

But she set the phone down, her mind racing.

She knew she had to call the detectives immediately, but she had been drinking and had taken that Xanax she found in the bottom of her purse and everything felt so real and yet not real at all. The conversation, so brief and confused, seemed to disintegrate in an instant.

She needed to think first. To get it straight in her head. Because Doug, he . . .

She knew she should call the detectives, but somehow she did not.

An hour later, waking up with a jolt, she looked at her phone, its battery dead. She tried to replay the call in her head, but it all blurred together.

Maybe it had been a Xanax mirage. Or a prank. Or a *missed call* from an *unknown number* that had fed its way into her unconsciousness and become a dream. A bleary fantasy.

In the morning, she would think it through.

In the morning, she would know what to do, if anything.

17

---

arper, Harper, your horses await you!

Harper looked up and there was Pam, whisking through the door, popped open in the night by Fitzie.

"Pammy," she whispered, blinking.

She woke with a start.

And in an instant, she remembered everything, swinging her legs over the futon edge.

She remembered everything.

Oh, Pammy . . .

The newspaper article was vague, upsetting.

> Pamela Bishop, 42, was found dead in the kitchen of her residence on El Dorado Drive when police responded to a 10:34 a.m. 911 call reporting an injured person at that address.

Staff at the chief medical examiner's office confirmed her death as a homicide without releasing any further details.

Police Chief Bud Martins said there were no signs of forced entry.

"Why haven't they found Doug yet?" Debra muttered, snapping the paper with her fingers.

"Maybe they have," Perry said, appearing in the doorway, a knot of pill bottles—all his morning meds—clawed in one hand.

They were drinking endless cups of coffee, making a new pot, then one more. Toasting sad English muffins, edges crumbling under the butter knife.

They were waiting to hear from the coroner. *When would the body be released, should we start funeral plans, would the police have some answers?*

"I mean, how far could he get?" Debra said. "In that gatorade-green Mustang of his?"

Harper snuck a look at her phone. The *UNKNOWN CALLER* in the log.

So it had happened, it wasn't just a dream.

Harper opened her mouth, as if to tell them. But nothing came out. She wouldn't know where to begin. Debra's first question would be, *Why is that monster calling* you?

"Do we know if he showed up in court?" Harper asked. It was possible Doug had lied to her on the phone last night.

"He showed," Perry said. "Pam's attorney called. Doug was there. They all waited. No Pam."

"So he showed, so what?" Debra said. "That doesn't mean he didn't kill her before, or after."

Harper felt a chill across her chest. "I don't think he could have done it before," she said. "He'd be . . . he'd be covered in blood."

Debra opened her mouth, then shut it again. No one said anything for a few minutes.

"I know he's been rotten," Harper said, "but do you *really* think Doug would do this? If you had seen what . . . what was done to her . . ."

"It's always the husband," Perry said grimly. Someone finally saying what everyone had been thinking.

I should wring her goddamned neck. That was in fact what Doug had said. She should tell the police. She told herself she would.

"They were fighting over money," Debra said. "Control. Hiding assets. Stealing from his kids. You don't think Doug could lose his mind over that?"

The question made Harper remember something. That time, right before the split, and Pam called her, hysterical. She'd woken up and couldn't find her wedding ring. She tore apart the bedroom looking for it. Harper came over and found her crawling underneath their California king, digging into the carpet, hunting. She made Harper check the sink drain, the shower drain, everything.

It turned out Doug had taken it. Hocked it or pawned it or given it as collateral, something. He was already a million or two in debt by then.

In response, Pam dragged her car keys along both sides of his Mustang. Then she called an attorney and emptied the checking account.

He took my ring while I slept, Pam kept saying. *While I slept.*

need some of my things," Harper said abruptly. "And I should get Vivian's school stuff . . ."

She knew she needed to go to the house. She was thinking of the tree in the backyard. The unsettled dirt. The cookie jar.

213

No one could know about it, right? And what would it mean if the cops found it?

And what would it mean if it was gone?

"No, Harper," Debra said. "You can't go there. I'm sure they've taped it all off. It's still a crime scene."

"I'll call and ask," Harper said, reaching for her purse. "Vivian and I need some of our things."

"Don't call," Debra said. "Do *not*."

"Let them do their work," Perry chimed in.

"Besides," Debra said, "it's not safe."

"Why isn't it safe?" Harper asked.

Debra looked up from her coffee, her blue-gray eyes watery and cool. "What if the murderer comes back?"

Harper didn't say anything. That word, *murderer*. There was a long, awkward moment of silence, the dishwasher churning in the background, the slosh-crunch sound from the living room of Stevie eating cereal on the sofa, watching cartoons with the sound off. Perry crunching his toast.

The kitchen phone drilled. They all jumped.

Perry answered. "Hello. . . . Okay. Sure. Right away."

He hung up and looked at them.

"The detectives have more questions."

The police station was bustling. More crowded than she'd ever seen it, this tiny municipal building, its walls still arrayed with SAY NO TO DRUGS posters from the eighties.

She had vague memories of her mother making her wait in the car while she went inside to pick up their father after his DUI arrest. How ashamed he was, getting in the car, hiding his face, stinking of vodka.

Or the time she went with Pam last year to retrieve Vivian, caught spray-painting a ringlet of pretty penises around the Woods Park cupola.

The detective from yesterday, Conlan, sat across from her, alongside a new one, a young man, freshly smacked with aftershave, coffee on his cuff.

She was afraid they were going to ask about finding Pam again, *finding the body*, and the thought made her stomach turn.

But instead they wanted to talk about Doug.

"Can you tell us a little about your sister's relationship with her husband?"

"Ex-husband," Harper reminded them.

"Was the divorce . . . acrimonious?"

"Aren't they all?" she said, then took another breath. "I mean, yes. It was."

"The family court hearing—she was having trouble getting her child support? And this matter of the trusts?"

"Yes. Doug, he—he was having financial difficulties," Harper said.

The agreed-upon euphemism for the kind of massive debt only rich people like Doug fall into. A complex array of defunct business enterprises unsecured debts, liens, wages garnishment. *Did you know the average millionaire files for bankruptcy three point five times?* he'd asked Pam once when she showed up at his condo after two bounced checks had led to Patrick being thrown off his track team before the regional championships.

"Would you say they had a contentious relationship?" Conlan asked.

This time, Harper did laugh, a bark, embarrassing. "I'm sorry," she said. "Contentious, sure. Divorces are contentious. Acrimonious. Some marriages too."

"Was theirs?"

"Passionate," Harper said, looking down into her coffee, untouched. That's what you call it, she thought, when it's working.

"Was he ever physical with her?"

Harper looked up. "No."

"You're sure? How about threats?"

"They were always saying things," Harper said. "That's how it was."

"Do you think," Conlan continued, "he's capable of harming your sister?"

Harper paused. She was thinking of Pam, the Medusa spread of her pretty hair on the linoleum, the pink cereal like rosebuds, like the rosebuds in her hair at her wedding twenty years ago, the Yacht Club with its fairy-tale tower, white doves, and larkspur spears and her sister in candlelight satin.

"I don't know," Harper said. Despite all Doug's erratic behavior, his vague threats, she still couldn't picture it. But no one ever could, she guessed. "I mean, they fought a lot. He . . . he came to the house just the other day. With all these pennies."

And she told them what had happened. They both looked at her, listening, the younger one with his pen moving, moving, moving.

"Do you know where he might be, Ms. Bishop?"

"No," Harper said. Also true, in a way. "What does his lawyer say? Did he ever show up at the hearing because—"

"But you didn't talk to him when he came to the house, with the pennies?"

"Just to tell him to leave."

"Was that the last time you spoke to him?"

"Yes," Harper lied.

She had to tell them about the call, but she couldn't.

I should wring her goddamned neck. She had to tell them about that too. Why hadn't she? Because she didn't think he was really capable, or because she was afraid of what Doug might say to the police— about her, about Pam, about all the money—the Club, the loan, everything?

If they knew she owed Doug money, everything might look bad. If they knew how she was getting the money, it would bring in everything else. The other women. The Wheel.

She thought about Sue Fox, the night before. *But, Debra, we have to talk—*

If they knew about the money—all the money—everything looked wrong.

Did your sister have any boyfriends? Any former boyfriends?"

"No."

"Did your niece have any boyfriends? Maybe they had a key. Anyone who, if he showed up at the house, your sister might let them in?"

"No," Harper said. "No boyfriends."

"Did your sister have any other interpersonal conflict? With a friend, or family member?"

Harper looked up again. "No. Just the usual, I mean. Family stuff. With Vivian. You know moms and teenage girls."

Conlan looked at Junior, who wrote something down.

"The usual curfew stuff," Harper clarified.

Conlan nodded but said nothing.

A nd that was it.

She waited while Debra and Perry spoke with them.

She waited, wondering about cell phone records, about what Doug might say when he came back, if he ever came back.

Her phone buzzed. *Sue Fox.*

She let it go to voicemail.

Harper, you know how much we loved Pam. These are the times we must be there for one another. We want to help in any way we can. I just think it would be great, wouldn't it, if we could all talk. . . .

It was only when she listened to it that she saw the texts, the messages she'd missed. From Beverly Linebaugh, Caroline Collins, Becky Schloss, all of them . . .

Just let us know what we can do to help. We loved your sister so much.

There was the long voicemail from Sandy too. Listening to it, she could nearly hear Sandy's hand in her hair as she spoke, her voice quivering. It went on and on.

Harper, I want to apologize for intruding yesterday. Sue just insisted. Everyone is heartbroken. Please call me, okay? Maybe I can even help. When my husband died, well, I fell into such a dark place. Did I ever tell you about that? How I found his body. They said he was dead before he hit the floor, but you know, I saw something in his eyes. I really did. So I know what you're going through. Call me, okay?

Harper deleted it. It was too exhausting.

A n hour later, Debra emerged from the interview room.

In the doorway detectives were chatting with Perry in a friendly fashion. It turned out he knew one of them years ago, back when he was still practicing law.

"Look, it's all been downhill since the Tigers left Corktown," Conlan was insisting. "The writing was on the wall."

Debra leaned over, whispering in Harper's ear.

"It was all about Doug in there," she said. "It's only a matter of time."

18

ut I don't understand," Vivian said. "Why didn't they want to
talk to me?"

"They talked to you yesterday," Harper said. "And it's . . .
it's a lot."

Back at Debra's house, she'd found Vivian in the basement with
Patrick, both on the floor, playing a video game she distantly remembered from their childhood. A buxom bounty hunter in neon blue who
could collapse into a ball to move through tight spaces.

"But what did they want to know about?" Vivian asked.

"The same things, really," Harper lied.

"What do they think happened?" Patrick asked. "Do they have a
suspect?"

Harper paused a moment too long, Vivian narrowing her eyes suspiciously.

"Tell us," she said. "Please."

"They didn't say," Harper said, as firmly as she could. It was true, after all. "I think they're still working on the timeline. The physical evidence . . ."

Patrick's face went pale, the game controller slack in his hand.

"I . . . uh, I think I'm gonna get some fresh air," he said, rising, stroking Vivian's hair before he slipped up the carpeted stairs.

Vivian watched him, her thumbnail in her mouth, tugging.

"They're working very hard," Harper said. She didn't know what else to say. She slid off the edge of the sofa and joined Vivian on the shag carpet.

"The last time I saw her, I was such a bitch," Vivian said. "Over all the stuff with Cassie. I didn't want to go to school and she was just, like, suck it."

"Vivian, honey," Harper said, trying for a smile. "That was every morning."

Vivian nodded, a faint grin, then covered her face with her hand. Those shorn nails that hurt to look at. Her face covered and her shoulders trembling.

Harper guiltily remembered that careless comment she made to the detectives. About Pam and Vivian fighting.

"Don't cry, baby," Harper said. "Your mom knew you loved her. She knew it bone-deep."

In the kitchen, she found Debra at the counter, going over cellophane-window bills.

The kitchen, where everything always happened. In their childhood home, the honey-oak kitchen with the hanging wire baskets. At Pam's, she thought with a choke in her throat.

"Is she okay?" Debra asked. "Vivian?"

"I don't know," Harper said.

"I talked to the insurance company today," Debra said. "Everything's tangled up and the funeral home . . . they need a deposit and—"

"Oh, right," Harper said. "I didn't even . . ."

She thought about the twenty-five thousand dollars in cash she'd hidden in her accordion file under the bed. Was it possible it was still there? And that the police hadn't found it? If they had, wouldn't they have asked her about it?

"How much?" Harper said. "I'll pay it. If I can just get my money—back at the house—"

"No," Debra said abruptly. "Perry and I are taking care of it."

"Deb—"

"No," she said. "We can untangle it later, when the life insurance, the estate—all that."

"Are you sure?" Harper asked, gesturing to the bills.

Debra looked down at them, too, then raked her hand across the stack, letting them flutter dramatically to the floor.

"Fuck the healthcare industry," she said.

"Talk about a pyramid scheme," Harper joked. Then, looking at her sister, "But you're sure?"

"Are you kidding?" Debra said, grinning now. "Perry loved an excuse to crack the fancy new safe."

Her phone beeped.

"It's Sue again, Jesus," Debra said.

"Why is she doing this?"

"She says she wants to know about the funeral," Debra said, deleting the text. "Why don't I believe her?"

"Sandy left me a voicemail earlier," Harper said.

Debra didn't say anything, her eyes drifting to the newspaper.

"She wanted to apologize for showing up last night," Harper continued. "She said it was Sue's fault. It was such a nutty message."

"A lapdog forever looking for the best lap," Debra muttered.

"Sue's lap seems pretty bony," Harper said. Then, tentatively, "I guess they're worried about what might come out. With the Club."

She and Debra hadn't talked about it. Neither of them seemed to want to.

Debra was silent, looking at the newspaper, that morning's article about Pam.

"What is it?" Harper asked. "The funeral, we'll . . ."

"Sue saw this," Debra said, her fingers resting over the grainy picture of the house. *Men in white hazmat suits,* the caption read, *could be seen at the victim's house on Tuesday, speaking to neighbors and entering and removing items.* "She wants to know about Pam's corkboard. The Board with the cards, you know."

Harper didn't say anything. She hadn't thought of the corkboard until now.

"The police—if they found any of it . . . Did the Board have our names on it?"

Harper nodded slowly. "First names. Why?"

Debra paused.

"It's just a club," Harper said. "Like a hundred other clubs in town. I mean, it has nothing to do with what . . . what they're there for."

"No," Debra said, letting out a sigh. "You're right."

"You told me not to go over there," Harper reminded her.

"I know," Debra repeated. "I meant it."

All night, Harper held her phone in her hand, wondering if Doug might call, if news might come.

Other than the buzzing fax, the house was silent. Vivian was no longer next door, having decamped to the basement to sleep with Patrick instead, both of them unfurling old sleeping bags. Vivian in Stevie's *Teenage Mutant Ninja Turtles* one, Patrick in Debra's pilled *Xanadu.*

Her brain skipping and thudding, going back again and again to that morning, to the night before. To Doug, to the party, to Pam's frenzied digging, her bad dreams.

That Merry Mushroom cookie jar, its pearly glaze. Its chipped orange mushroom cap top resting on the lid, flat like a thumb. How tightly Pam had packed it, how deeply they buried it.

The Club, it didn't matter, she reminded herself. This was about murder, not about money. But the fact was, if Doug were responsible, wasn't that about money too?

And he knew about the Club, at least some of it. The money.

It was always money. It was always money.

She dreamt of Pam, of course. Pam in her burgundy leather dress, color piping up her cheeks, spinning around on the carpet of someone's dream house somewhere, the ceilings too high to see. Her arms raised high as if she were in church. *Hallelujah! Hallelujah!*

The blessing of the LORD makes rich, and he adds no sorrow with it!

19

It was just past dawn, still ink-black outside, when the newspaper slapped against the door.

Curled tight and shuddering on the futon in Perry's office, Harper heard it and then heard the door squeak open.

And then she heard Debra's thundering voice.

"Goddammit. Goddammit!"

Debra and Perry stood over the paper spread on the kitchen table.

"What is it?" Harper asked, rubbing her eyes, the bright fluorescents raging at her.

Debra smacked the newspaper and let out a cry, high and pained.

Perry curled his arm around her, but Debra could not be comforted.

> Pamela Bishop, a beloved mother and friend, was expected
> in family court for a trust dispute with her ex-husband
> Monday morning.

But she never made it. Bishop, 42, was found dead in her Grosse Pointe Woods home on Monday when police responded to a 911 call reporting an injured person at that address.

Staff at the county medical examiner's office said late Tuesday evening that Bishop died from multiple blunt and sharp force injuries, and confirmed her death as a homicide.

Police have yet to release any information on a person of interest or suspect at this time, but an investigation is underway. An inside source also reported that they have yet to talk to her ex-husband, Douglas Sullivan, with whom she was engaged in a court battle over their children's trust.

Blunt and sharp force injuries.

The words—ones Harper had probably glazed over in hundreds of news articles in her life—made her shudder. And yet they also didn't seem harsh enough, frightening enough. Pam's face—it was so much worse.

Perry kept reading aloud:

Sullivan's office offered a formal statement: "After the hearing, Mr. Sullivan boarded a flight to Germany at twelve hundred hours on a business trip for Volkswagen."

"Twelve hundred hours," Perry said. "What is this, the invasion of Normandy?"

At press time, however, police have been unable to reach him or to confirm the details of his travel with his office or with Volkswagen.

"Volkswagen," Debra said disgustedly. "Give me a fucking break. Show me the pay stubs to prove Doug has been employed by anybody for a decade."

Harper didn't say anything. She didn't know what to say.

"Why am I reading this in the goddamned paper before they tell *us*? The family? We've been waiting for two days and I have to read it here? This pathetic chamber of commerce, town bugle bullshit paper—"

Harper kept staring at the paper, the words blurring together.

"That police department has no clue how to handle a homicide case," Perry said.

Toilet paper vandalism and DUIs, that's ninety percent of the job, someone told her once, an ex-Detroit cop sitting belly to the bar at the Wooden Nickel one night long ago.

Debra was already on the kitchen phone, hand on hip.

"I need to speak to Detective—what's his name again?" she asked Harper.

"Conlan."

"Conlan," Debra repeated into the receiver. "This is the Pam Bishop's sister and we'd all like to know why this glorified pennysaver has the coroner's report before we do!"

Perry kept shaking his head.

"Yes, I'd like a callback," Debra was saying. "And you can tell him we'll be calling the county prosecutor's office about this. The state's attorney, whatever the fuck he—"

But Perry had taken the phone from her.

"Hi, this is Perry Stanton," he said, politely but firmly, into the mouthpiece. "I'm the brother-in-law and an attorney and we would like to speak to Detective Conlan as soon as he returns."

He spoke a few more minutes, then hung up. "They said it was an error. The county jumped the gun."

Debra's face was in her hands. At first Harper thought she might be crying, but then her hands fell again.

"What are they doing, anyway? All those questions about Doug yesterday and he's still nowhere to be found? A man who steals from his children is capable of anything."

"They seem very focused on him," Harper tried.

"They know how guilty all this makes him look," Perry said, pacing the living room.

Harper nodded, distracted. A creaking sound from the basement stairs.

"That bastard is probably lounging on some beach in Bali by now," Debra said. "Meanwhile we need to pick up the paper to find out how he murdered our sister."

"Debra—" Perry said, abruptly clearing his throat.

Harper turned and saw Vivian in the basement doorway, hoodie and boxer shorts, her eyes red. Patrick stood beside her, his face heavy with sleep.

"You all think he did it," Vivian said, her voice husky. "You all think our dad's a . . . murderer."

"Vivian, we didn't mean . . . We're upset," Debra said.

But Vivian was looking at Harper. "I never expected it from you."

"I was only talking about the police . . ." Harper started, rising.

But Vivian's face made her sit down again. There was something in it, her eyes slitted.

"You do," she said. "You all think he's the one with all the secrets to hide."

"No, honey—" Debra said, softening.

"Well, he's not the only one," Vivian said, "with secrets."

Harper and Debra exchanged looks.

"I don't want to stay here anymore," Vivian said, grabbing her backpack from the coatrack, her sneakers from the floor. "I'm going to Cassie's."

"Vivian, you're not going anywhere," Debra said, pushing the newspaper out of sight. "It's not safe."

But Vivian was gone, shooting past them, the kitchen door rattling shut.

They all watched her pace in the driveway a few moments, talking into her phone. Her bare legs bright in the dark.

Debra looked at Harper. "Who's Cassie?"

Harper sighed. That question. Like sister, like sister.

"She's her girlfriend," Patrick said, standing in the doorway.

"I'll get her," Harper said, but again she didn't move.

"Let her be," Perry said. "Let her be."

Patrick reached for the newspaper. No one stopped him.

Instead, they watched Cassie pull up the driveway in her yellow Escort and Vivian disappear inside.

I guess they made up, Harper thought. *In grief, forgiveness.*

"Maybe," Patrick said, looking at the article, "it was a robbery gone wrong."

Everyone was quiet again.

"Maybe," Perry offered doubtfully. "Some druggie, looking for cash. Thought no one was at home."

"Maybe," Harper said, thinking. "Sure."

Debra's eyes flickered over to Harper.

Patrick leaned against the doorjamb defeatedly.

"Except, was anything taken?" he asked, his voice breaking a little.

He was asking the same question she had been asking herself. The one she needed an answer to. She couldn't wait any longer.

"I mean," he said, looking—it seemed—straight at Harper, "was there anything in there to take?"

Harper made an excuse—*I need to talk to Mr. Bingham, pick up my check, tell him I need time*—and drove around for a half hour, to Windmill Pointe and back. Along the bottomless lake, steel-gray today, furred with mist.

Her eyes on the rearview mirror the whole time.

But no one was following her. Yesterday's patrol car was nowhere to be seen. She felt silly. There was nothing suspicious about going to the house. There were plenty of reasons she might go to the house.

Still, as soon as she turned the corner onto El Dorado Drive, she started to lose her nerve.

She pulled over a half-block away, several yards before any safety cones or yellow tape.

The house looked lonely, forlorn, as it always did, the last on the block and pitched up a small icy slope of grass. No trees around it, so bare, so unlike the leafy crowned manor she and Doug had lived in, the one the bank now owned.

She sat in her minivan a long ten minutes. She saw no police cars, but there was a Crown Vic parked in front of the neighbor's house.

The quiet was worse than anything.

There was something she needed to check, to see. It would help her figure out what to think about everything. What to believe.

230

She parked down the block and cut through one of the neighbors' yards. The Fisks were in Sarasota for the winter. They'd never know.

Yesterday's roadblocks were gone, a forgotten safety cone lay crunched on its side.

Yellow tape was everywhere, but no officers in sight.

Maybe it was a bad idea, but it was, after all, where Harper lived. She had a right, or at least a reason, to be here. And no one had told her she couldn't come back. To get some things.

It definitely *was* a bad idea, but it was far from her first. *Without bad ideas, nothing would ever happen, you'd never have an adventure, get into trouble, fall in love.* That's what one of her first girlfriends had told her, furtive midnight swims at summer camp, tugging down Harper's halter, slipping her hand into the spandex crotch.

The locker room, horse camp, slumber parties, sleepovers. They were full of mysteries and exploration. That was what they were for.

It was all so much easier back then. No one would ever believe you if you told them that, but it was.

Harper pushed into the side door, ducking under the yellow tape.

At first, other than the shoe treads on the carpet, the coffee table tilted on its side, everything looked normal.

But you could feel the strangeness everywhere, like an invisible presence, heat.

She passed by the kitchen without looking inside.

The bright hank of her sister's hair on the floor, the scatter of Apple Jacks, Fitzie's wheezing breaths and pained squeaks, the way he kept turning in circles like a cartoon.

No. She would not go into the kitchen. Not yet.

In the bathroom, the smell of Pam's shampoo, sweet and flinty, rosemary and mint. Harper covered her face, pushed the tears back in.

Vivian's room, chaotic and perfumed, terrified her with its teen mayhem, a water bong, a half-stashed bottle of Stoli, a ringlet of thongs hanging over the vanity mirror.

Her legs shaking, she sat down on the bed for a moment, a sequin-laced blanket, a bohemian rhapsody of purple-dyed fleece and faux satin sheets and tufted pillows smelling like sex, toothpaste, saliva.

Her heart was doing funny things. She could hear the wind whipping outside, something knocking against the house, a tree branch, something.

She was remembering everything.

Rising quickly, she turned to her niece's closet, mindlessly grabbing a duffel bag, a few pairs of jeans, and, ducking down, Vivian's favorite sweatshirt, tufted haphazardly on the floor.

In Patrick's room, she reached into the filing cabinet where she kept her clothes, snatching jeans, a sweater.

The wind kicked up again, the knocking louder, more insistent. Harper looked out the window, but the only tree she could see was the towering elm, its bare branches still. The one they'd dug under. That Merry Mushroom jar, a living thing now, rattling in her head like the telltale heart.

She waited last to look under the bed. For the creased brown accordion file into which she'd shoved her twenty-five thousand dollars, gathered tight by a sparkly rubber band.

Part of her dreaded seeing it. Everything had curdled. That money she'd done so much for, how much of her life and her sisters' lives it had dominated—and now it was a dark thing, a hole you fell in, one you'd spent the rest of your days trying to dig yourself out. Maybe it always was.

But she needed it.

Her arm reaching, gathering dust tendrils, knuckles scraping the carpet, feeling the scrape of an old binder clip, a scatter of Patrick's rolling papers, curled and crisp. Nothing.

The accordion file was gone. Her twenty-five grand gone.

Maybe the police didn't know anything about homicides, but they knew how to look.

"Easy come, easy go," she whispered, a shiver scissoring up her spine.

She stood in the kitchen door a long time, its heavy wood cabinets glossy with decades of cooking grease too thick to penetrate.

The tape was still up there, across the doorframe, and she ran one calloused finger along the edge.

Stray latex gloves like violet petals, black powder scattered, reminding her of the roach powder along the floorboards at the Parkcrest Inn after Leigh left and she'd spun out.

The floor, like mud tracks. The blood like mud now.

They'd taken pictures of her shoe treads at the police station, and Vivian's. She only remembered it now, pulling off her boots, one sock going with it, embarrassed at her red, rough feet.

It was then she noticed a long strip of the yellow linoleum gone, pulled back like a shorn nail, like Vivian's shorn nails, bleeding through her mitten in the ambulance.

Vivian's shorn nails—

Bzzzt! Her phone in her pocket and she jumped, grabbing for it, dropping it on the linoleum.

Kneeling down for it, a smell overtook her and she keeled back on the heels of her hands.

A missed call from Debra. Another from Perry.

Suddenly, dizzily, she was on her feet again, her arms reaching out for the walls, stumbling through the house, forgetting the duffel bag of clothes, whirling around to grab it again, abandoned on the matted carpet.

In the basement, everything looked the same.

Except the sofa, its center cushion missing. The one that Vivian had hurled off her mother's body.

The police must have taken it, she thought. Of course they did. It was a clue, something.

Without its center cushion, the sofa looked naked somehow. A mouth missing its front teeth.

She thought of something Debra had said. *The police—if they found any of it . . . Did the Board have our names on it?*

But the Board was still there, behind the dented furnace.

Harper pulled it out and stared at it.

One by one, she plucked all the index cards off the cork, tacks scattering, first shoving them in her coat pocket. But they kept falling out, so she dropped them down her shirt front.

Better safe than sorry.

On her way out, she glanced between the washer and dryer, looking for the blue sheen of the Tampax Pearl box, the jaunty string of pearls graphic on the side. It wasn't there.

She couldn't remember what Pam had done with it once she'd emptied it of bills three nights ago. *Did she take it upstairs?* she wondered, her foot landing in spilled detergent, her phone buzzing again.

Her eyes flashed over the window screen: *Debra, missed call.*

She had to go.

But she hadn't even done what she was here for. She should have done it first.

If it was still there, it meant one thing, or maybe nothing. But if it were gone, well . . .

She pushed through the screen door to the backyard, gazing out to the elm tree, deep in the long, frost-blistered back lawn.

The sky above, that dirty white of Michigan winter, and a hard, cold wind coming off the lake a few blocks away.

He'll find it, Pam had said, her hands covered in dirt.

Or was it: *She'll find it.*

Or was it: *They'll find it.*

The pronoun lost in the wind, in Harper's own panting as she had swung her shovel.

There was no way anyone could know about it, she told herself. The police didn't excavate the backyard, after all. They had no reason to even look.

The only way anyone could know was if they'd seen Pam and Harper out there that night, digging.

The Merry Mushroom cookie jar, buried deep in the cold earth, but maybe not deep enough.

She was so exposed out there.

She should have come at night, she realized now, peering deep into the yard.

It had snowed, a dusting, the ground newly frozen over and she would have to hunt for the loose dirt, the exact spot under the elm tree.

She didn't move, couldn't.

She wished she'd taken Fitzie, who was back at Debra's, curled up in the dog bed of Perry's late, beloved terrier. If she'd taken Fitzie, she could—

She was crying now, wiping her face with the back of her sleeve. Her phone falling to the ground, its plastic cracking.

"Ma'am . . ."

Harper whipped around.

"Ma'am, turn around slowly and drop the bag."

20

They were talking down the hall.

The detectives, stoop-backed Conlan and the young one, whatever his name was, very young and bouncing nervously on the balls of his feet.

She guessed they didn't think she could hear, that she was invisible somehow, seated on the plastic molded chair, waiting for them. Middle-aged woman in a parka, who would ever notice.

"Multiple scalp lacerations," Conlan was saying, looking at a file in his hand. "Rounded contusions. Then chop wounds to the face."

"Still no weapon," the junior detective said. "But the coroner thinks—"

"Miss Bishop," Conlan said abruptly, noticing Harper at last, flashing a look at his partner.

"They picked her up at the house," the junior detective told Conlan.

"Call me Harper," she said.

Conlan opened the door for her, waving her into a conference room.

Her duffel bag, the one the officer had taken from her, sat on the table.

"Didn't anyone tell you, Harper?" Conlan said, a polite smile. "You can't go home again."

Then, as if remembering why she was there, the smile disappeared.

F irst, we want to apologize for not contacting you before the county chose to speak to the press," Conlan was saying. "Reading it in the paper must have been—"

"The paper said blunt force," Harper said, the words fumbling in her throat. "What does that mean exactly?"

"It can be a fall," the junior detective said, taking her too literally. "And she did fall."

"But not sixteen times," Conlan said. "These were blows with a blunt instrument."

"But you haven't found the weapon?"

"Not yet," Conlan said. "We were hoping you could help. Given there are no signs of forced entry, the assailant may have picked up something on the scene."

"Brick, bat, pipe . . ." Junior said, looking at the report in his hand.

Harper winced with each word, each time a flash of those red smears, gapes, puckering strawberries on her sister's face, temple, her bright hair glossy with blood. The mottled pink starburst on her sister's right cheek that reminded her of looking through the big telescope once in elementary school.

". . . or a hammer," Conlan said.

"Coroner's hot on the hammer," Junior noted. Harper squinted at him, the pale young man with a square jaw that made him look like a cartoon hero, the barrel-chested blond boy from *Scooby-Doo*.

"Maybe claw or framing," Conlan said, looking at the report now too.

"Explains the sharp force injuries," Junior said.

"Something about the shape of the wounds."

"Excuse me," Harper said, "but are you going to share that report with me—"

"But no hammer found," Conlan said, ignoring her.

"No brick, no bat either," Junior added.

Harper studied them. The way they were talking to her—what had changed in a day, she wondered. Or maybe she hadn't noticed, still so caught up in the horror of the blood, the chaos, the sticky linoleum under the heel of her hand. *She isn't breathing!* The bloody bubble frothing in her sister's mouth.

"This is my sister you're talking about," she said.

Conlan looked up at Harper. "Did she have a hammer?"

"Doesn't everyone have a hammer?"

She thought of Pam, trying to defrost the freezer with their father's hammer and her hair dryer, risking ice in the eye and electrocution at once.

"We didn't find any hammer," Junior said, looking in the folder. "Where'd she keep it?"

"It was always around," Harper said.

"Could you describe it?"

"It had a pointy end," Harper said. "And my dad's monogram. WBE."

The two men looked at each other.

Junior cleared his throat.

Conlan set down the folder and looked at her.

"Would you like to tell us what you were doing at your sister's house this morning?"

She followed his eyes to her parka, the bright skein of yellow tape on one sleeve. She hadn't even noticed it.

Because suddenly all she could think about was the index cards she'd shoved down her shirt. *Sue, Sandy, Beverly, Caroline, Jill, Becky, Debra, Harper.* Every time she moved, she could feel their sharp corners.

"It's still an active crime scene," Junior said, slapping on a pair of gloves, reaching for Harper's duffel bag. "Didn't you see the . . . barriers?"

"I needed a few things," she said, "Vivian and me."

"If you need anything," Conlan said, watching Junior unzip Harper's duffel bag, "we can send a deputy."

"Otherwise," Junior said, "it's criminal trespass."

"I'm sorry," Harper said, wondering if they could search her.

"Why were you in the backyard?"

"I don't know," she said. "I needed some air. It was a lot."

She watched the young detective dig through the duffel with a small flashlight—the tangle of turtlenecks, stiff jeans, Vivian's favorite fuzzy low-tops, neon thongs—poking and prodding with care.

"Better not shake it," Harper said, "or the hammer might fall out."

Conlan snorted.

Junior set the bag back on the table. The two men looked at each other.

In some ways, she couldn't believe they didn't ask her to take off her coat, didn't try to pat her down. But they didn't.

That police department has no clue how to handle a homicide case, Perry had said.

"Did you find Doug yet?" Harper said, changing the subject. "How hard can he be to find? I'd like to know what happened to my sister. I have a right to know—"

"Not yet," Conlan said, closing the folder. "But we will."

———

*B*lunt and sharp force injuries.

That was what the coroner had said. The detectives.

They didn't say anything about what her sister's sweet face had looked like. What it was like to look at her sister, her sister with the same bracing blue eyes as her own, *like Wedgwood china, their mother used to say*, the same straw-colored hair and snub nose. And her sister's dimple, which you couldn't see anymore, a slick of red where her face had been and even that snub nose turned to its side.

When they were little, she and Pam coveted Debra's Madame Alexander doll, the Spanish dancer with the black lace mantilla, with the perfect curl in the middle of her forehead. *Debra knows how to take care of her dolls,* their mother told them. *So she gets the nice ones.* Debra sticking out her tongue at them. It felt like a taunt and dare to Pam and Harper. That very night, they'd set upon the doll, pulling out all her hair, smushing in her pretty vinyl face with the rubber reflex hammer from their toy doctor kit, flattening it with such force that one of her blinking lashed eyes popped loose.

Just like Pammy, Harper thought now, the red socket where her sister's eye had been.

Oh, you little monsters, their mother had said, trying to be stern as Debra sobbed beside her, as Debra sobbed and sobbed until their father bought her a Snow White and the best of all: the one he called a Carmen Miranda with rickrack trim and a fruit bowl piled on her head.

Money hadn't mattered then, long ago. They never thought about what it meant to destroy an expensive doll. It never even crossed their minds until they were in college and their father was laid off and there were no executive jobs to be had anywhere, no auto industry at all anymore.

They never thought about money until it was gone and then it was all any of them thought about. And it had stayed that way.

They'd given her a ten-minute break. They had some more questions. First, Harper ducked in the restroom and, struggling in a stall, gathered the index cards.

She thought about flushing them down the toilet, but what if they clogged? Instead, she wedged them tightly in her waistband. If they were going to pat her down, they would have done it already.

Five minutes left, she stood outside, trying for a smoke, some time to clear her head.

She tried Debra's house, but the answering machine picked up.

She tried Debra, who was at the doctor's office with Perry, getting his chemo, that awful drip, the wheezy pump.

"You were right," she said. "I shouldn't have gone to the house."

"Imagine that," Debra said.

"Did Vivian ever come back? I got some of her things."

"I thought she was with you," Debra said, her voice tight and tired.

"What?"

"Aren't you at the police station?" Debra said.

"Yes," Harper said. "Wait, is Vivian *here*?"

The detectives had called Debra. Apparently, Vivian had showed up at the station, demanding to know the status of the investigation.

"She talked to them for a while, I think," Debra said. "I drove over there, but I couldn't find her."

"Really," Harper said, thinking.

"They had more questions for me, too," Debra said. "They wanted to know how Pam seemed the night before, stuff like that." She paused, then lowered her voice. "And then, well, you should know this."

"Know what?"

"Well, they had all these questions about where everyone was that morning."

"But we already told them all that."

"Yeah, but they wanted to, um, confirm it. They said it was just a formality."

"Okay."

"So, well, I gave them my toll receipt. From the tunnel to Canada. I had to dig it out from the bottom of my purse. And they were satisfied."

"What?" Harper asked. "I don't . . ."

"They said it was a formality," she repeated. "You know, collecting everyone's . . ."

"Alibis," Harper finished. What was her own? The six horses she'd tended to that morning? "I thought it was all about Doug for them."

"I'm sure it is," Debra said. "It's just—"

"A formality."

They were both quiet for a second.

"Harper," Debra said after a pause, "be careful."

s my niece here?"

The desk officer looked up, phone tucked under her chin.

"The detectives are waiting for you," he said.

Harper turned and saw them, Conlan and Junior, a fresh coffee cup extended to her, beckoning her back inside.

"Where is my niece?" Harper asked, tugging the police tape off her parka, charging toward them. "Why didn't you tell me she was here?"

"She just left. Her friend picked her up."

"What were you talking to her about?" Harper asked. "I'm her guardian and I don't like you talking to her alone—she's only sixteen."

"Your sister gave us permission," Conlan said, handing her the new cup of coffee. "So did you."

"That was two days ago."

"We wanted to go through the timeline again. On Monday she was, understandably, quite upset."

"She was able to provide a very lucid account," Junior said, looking at his notebook. "Much more detail."

"She was very helpful," Conlan added. Junior nodded in agreement.

Harper wondered what that meant. She couldn't remember the last civil conversation Vivian had had with an authority figure, daily tangles with the attendance office until Cassie started working there, her world civ teacher, the school parking lot monitor . . .

"Look, why am I here anyway?" Harper asked, following them inside the room. "I've told you everything I know. Shouldn't you be out investigating?"

"Who do you think we should be investigating?"

"Aren't *you* supposed to know?" Harper felt a sheen of sweat developing. She didn't like all this attention, wasn't used to it. "I mean, isn't it always the husband?"

It just slipped out.

Conlan looked at her. Junior looked at Conlan.

"Do you think he's responsible?"

Harper didn't say anything. She didn't know why she was so mad, but it was the feeling the detectives were furtively circling something, the wrong thing.

"Why did you go back to the house?" Conlan asked again.

"Like I said," Harper repeated. "I needed a few things."

"Like money?" Junior asked.

"No," Harper said, waiting. She could nearly feel her hand on the cool ceramic of the cookie jar. There was no way they could know.

"Because we found some money," Conlan said finally. "In the room I believe you were staying in."

The accordion file, of course.

"Yeah," Harper said. "I noticed that was gone."

Conlan smiled a little, despite himself.

"Twenty-five thousand dollars," Junior said. "A lot of money to stuff under your bed."

"That's my nest egg," she said.

"Quite a nest egg to have in cash," Junior said.

"I worked hard for that money," Harper said, folding her hands in her lap. "Extra lessons. Private clients. Parents prefer cash and so do I."

"IRS, not so much," Conlan pointed out. "Did anyone know you had that kind of money under your bed?"

Harper paused. Every woman in the Club knew she had the money, but none of them knew where.

"No," she said, on the technicality. "Look, I'm trying to save. Put a little money from each paycheck—"

"Most people just go to a bank," Conlan said.

"Do they?" Harper said. "How many banks have failed in the past year?"

They both looked at her.

"A pretty big nest egg for someone with money issues," Conlan said, his pen flipping the accordion pleats, making an annoying little *tuh-tuh-tuh* sound.

"Who says I have money issues?" Harper asked.

"Staying in your nephew's bedroom," Junior said. "In your sister's house. Don't you drive your sister's old minivan?"

"I didn't realize my financial well-being was at the center of this investigation."

"It's not," Conlan said, "but maybe it's part of the picture."

"I didn't go back for the money," Harper said. "I knew if you did your job half-right, you'd find it. Does it become part of your department slush fund now?"

Junior smirked this time.

"Right now it's evidence," Conlan said.

"How about that?" Harper said, gesturing to the duffel bag. "Are my niece's freshly laundered thongs evidence too?"

"No," Conlan said.

"So I can have the bag back?"

"Sure," Conlan said, sliding the duffel halfway between them. "Just one more thing first."

"What?" Harper said, grabbing the bag.

Junior clicked his pen, flipped the page in his notebook as Conlan leaned back, swirling his coffee mug like it was a glass of cabernet.

Harper took a long breath, the hidden index cards pricking her chest.

"What can you tell us about this club?"

"Club?" Harper asked, her voice creaking now.

Conlan looked at her, said nothing.

"Yeah," Junior said, leaning back now too. Tell us about the club.

21

arper wondered the last time she'd eaten anything, the caffeine whirring, blurring her brain. The fluorescents above spotting her eyes.

She cleared her throat and shrugged, shifting in her seat.

"It's just a social club. For women. There must be a hundred in the Woods alone. Gardening, weight loss, bridge."

"And you and Pam were both in the club?"

"Yes. We meet every few weeks. Like a book club without the book."

"Sounds like my wife's book club," Conlan said, writing something down.

"So you, what, gossip, get loaded?" Junior asked, a grin dancing there.

"Sure. Gab about boys," Harper said. "Braid each other's hair."

"How many women are in the club?"

"I don't know," Harper said. "It changes based on people's schedule. It's very casual."

She was surprised how easily she lied.

"Okay," Conlan said, clicking his pen. "Thanks."

Inside, Harper could feel her heart ricocheting in her chest.

She rose unsteadily, the coffee cup they'd given her tilting in her shaking hand.

"Are you okay, Miss Bishop?"

"Yeah," Harper managed, her legs like overstretched springs. "I'm just . . ."

"Are you okay?"

"Yeah," Harper said, letting Junior take the coffee from her clawed grip. "I haven't . . . eaten."

"Let's get you something from the vending machine."

Ten minutes later, Harper was sitting in her car, a bright orange packet of peanut-butter crackers crushed in her hand. Her right leg shook like a wishbone, twanged.

It's okay, it's okay, it's okay.

There was no need to tell them the truth. If they disapproved of cash for lessons, they certainly wouldn't like the Club.

One thing has nothing to do with the other, she thought.

This needs to be about what happened to Pam.

What happened to Pam has nothing to do with—

But only one person might have told them about the Club. Or at least one person she knew they had just talked to. One person who had volunteered some information.

---

have some of your things, she texted Vivian. Do you want them?

She waited a long five minutes before Vivian texted back.

Ok, I'm at Cassie's

Cassie's house was modest, a duplex with a metal awning near Schum-mer's Ski Shop. A *divorce house,* Vivian once said. It was something they had in common.

Harper honked the horn once and Vivian came charging out.

"Where's my stuff?" she said, a snarl over her brow like she was talking to her mother.

"Don't be mad at me," Harper said, handing over the duffel bag, stripped of her own things. "Everyone's just . . . none of us are ourselves right now."

"I am," Vivian said. "I'm myself. I don't go around accusing people of horrible . . ."

She stopped, her voice shaking.

"No?" Harper said. "Then why did you take it upon yourself to go talk to the detectives today?"

Vivian looked at her, pale and eyes clouded.

"I just wanted to know what was going on," she said, stroking her hair with one hand, the duffel bag strap knotted around the other. "He's my dad. My dad."

Harper paused, her throat tight.

"I know. I do," she said, finally. "But we all want the same thing. To find out what happened."

Vivian nodded, rubbing her face exhaustedly.

"What did you talk about?"

"Just how we found . . ." she started, her throat caught. "About Monday. They made me go through it again. All of it."

Harper felt something twist inside. She reached across the open window for her niece's arm.

"They're assholes, those cops," Harper said, still trying. "I'm sorry you—"

Vivian's arm jerked back, her legs sliding under her, her whole body, her whole everything pulling away.

"They're just doing their job," Vivian said. "And if you don't tell them important information, that fucks it up for them."

Harper didn't know what to say. There was a bristle of mistrust between them. She wasn't sure where it came from, but it was there.

"Your dad will call you, honey," Harper said. "I know it."

Vivian's eye twitched. She pressed her finger against it.

"Why are you telling me that?" she asked. "Did you hear some-thing?"

"No," Harper said. "But I know you're worried about him."

But Vivian wasn't even looking at her, untangling the duffel strap from between her pink fingers, three Powerpuff Girls band-aids tied tight. You might think, like her teachers did, that she wasn't even lis-tening. That she was just some sullen teen, hearing you only as that *mwah-mwah* warble of adults in *Peanuts* cartoons.

But Harper knew better.

"Did you," she asked finally, "tell them about your mom's club?"

"My mom's club," Vivian said, raising an eyebrow. "Isn't it all of yours?"

Harper shook her head. "You shouldn't have done that, honey. It has nothing to do with anything."

"Then it doesn't matter, does it?" Vivian said, looking back up at the house. Cassie at the window now, that blur of her pretty hair. "I just think they should have all the information before they go around thinking—"

"But the club, it's just going to confuse everything," Harper continued. "We want to let them do their job. Focus on the evidence . . ."

"Why are you yelling at me?" Vivian asked, her voice cracking.

Harper didn't think she'd been yelling. Had she?

"I'm not mad at you, Viv," Harper said. "But what did you tell them? About the club?"

"There's nothing to tell," Vivian said, stepping backward, a funny look on her face now, "is there?"

Driving back to Debra's, Harper wished she'd handled it all differently. She didn't like hearing herself. She didn't like talking to Vivian like that, a mix of evasion and worse.

She could feel a distance growing between them, a heavy expanse.

She couldn't guess what was going on behind her niece's sparking eyes.

She thought of Vivian and Cassie inside the house, curled up under a comforter, curled around each other for comfort, warmth, whispers, and confidences, a romance threatened and now restored.

Everything was different these days, she thought, a flicker of envy, or something.

I told you not to go to Pam's," Debra reminded her. "Half the police force is patrolling El Dorado Drive. It's the only game in town."

She was standing at the sink, staring out the window, the same cherry-sprig curtains their mother had. Maybe the same exact ones, remembering how, more than twenty years ago, the three sisters had only a day after the estate sale to clean out the house before the bank took it. Oh, how they'd fought like packs of hyenas, Pam and Debra both tugging opposite ends of their mother's fingertip mink coat until they tore an arm off and somehow Harper ended up with it, the least suited to it, but she'd used it as a blanket for years until she finally pawned it in rougher days.

"Never miss a chance for a second I-told-you-so, do you?" Harper said, poking her lightly. "Maybe I needed to see it again. To see if it was real."

But it still hadn't seemed real, a technicolor nightmare, Pammy's bright hair, the fluorescent cereal, the forest-green Hunt Club hoodie, the gasping blood beneath.

"Now the cops are wondering about you," Debra said, a cigarette burning in her right hand, resting on the sink edge. Perry's chemo had her smoking again. "Is that what you want?"

Harper paused, working up her nerve.

"They found my money," she said, finally. "My twenty-five K."

"Okay," Debra said, stabbing the cigarette butt on the sink edge. "Well."

"I think it's okay," Harper said. "I told them it was from private lessons."

"Sure, that makes sense."

"But," she said, bracing herself, "they also asked me about the Club."

Debra twitched backward ever so slightly.

"What about it?" she whispered.

"They just asked what it was. I told them it was just like any other women's group. You know how they think."

Debra nodded, turning to the coffee maker. Busying herself with making a new pot. She made four or five a day, black as pitch, like tar in your mouth.

"Wait," Debra said, "who told them about it?"

"Vivian, I think," Harper said. "But she doesn't know anything."

"Why would she tell them about that?" Debra said, a fierce whisper. "It has nothing to do with Pam's—what happened to Pam."

"I don't know," Harper said. "She's worried about her dad."

Debra didn't say anything for a second, staring at the coffee maker.

"I keep thinking about Sue and Sandy coming here," Debra said, shaking a filter loose. "They shouldn't have done that."

Harper took one of Debra's cigarettes. Debra lit another one.

"Did Sandy call you again?" she asked. "She's such a weirdo."

Harper shook her head.

"She talks too much. We should keep an eye on her."

"If she ever stops moving," Harper said.

"Jesus, do you think they found Pam's stash?" Debra asked. "I kept telling her to take care of that. Were they in the basement?"

"I don't think so," Harper said. She didn't want to get into it with Debra about the cookie jar, the late-night burial.

"You went down there? To the basement?"

Harper nodded slowly, then reached up inside her sweater.

Debra watched as Harper shook loose the stack of index cards, letting them tumble to the counter like the blades of a fan. *Sue, Sandy, Beverly, Caroline, Jill, Becky, Debra, Harper . . . Pam.*

Debra turned to the sink in silence, pushing the garbage disposal button.

Harper watched as her sister raked the cards into the sink, down the meaty hole.

"I doubt it'll come up again," Harper said, over the grinding. "Maybe it won't."

"We're going to need to do something," Debra said, turning off the disposal. "Give everyone some guidance. This needs to be about Pam."

Harper nodded again, so close to her sister, the smell of the doctor's office, a rippling anxiety. The coffee maker beeped and flashed.

"We didn't do anything wrong," Debra said. "That's what we need to remember."

Harper reached for a coffee cup, holding it out to her sister.

"Right," she said. "Nothing at all."

Perry was in the den, stuffed in his recliner, his face gray, the remote control poking through the afghan as he watched his programs, Golf Classics, the History Channel, just the WWII documentaries, or anything about Ulysses S. Grant.

"How'd it go?" Harper asked.

"The chemo? It was a gas," he said. "But not as exciting as getting arrested."

"I wasn't arrested," Harper said, smiling, "yet."

He laughed, their long history unfurling before them for a moment.

Time was, back when he and Debra were newlyweds, they would always be fighting, over money, over baby plans, and Perry would show up at Harper's old apartment with a bottle of rum and they'd play war or gin rummy until Debra finally called, crying. *Put my husband on the phone! You always take his side!*

Harper always gets along with the husbands, she once heard Debra say to Pam.

And that knowing look Pam had given Debra in return. Like this was an area where Harper couldn't be trusted. Her sympathies suspect.

She supposed it was true, but sisters were so much harder.

She smoked outside at dusk. She was thinking about Doug. She was thinking of the things she could, and probably should, tell the detectives about him. How he'd threatened to wring Pam's neck. Most of all, how he'd called her the night of Pam's death. Time was running out. Standing on the frozen earth of Debra's backyard, she thought again of that Merry Mushroom cookie jar. She could almost feel it beneath her feet. It was as if, three miles away in Pam's yard on El Dorado Drive, the jar were shaking, its top rattling, demanding to be heard.

22

No one knew how they'd pay for any of it. The burial fees, the hearse transport, the hand-carved rose mahogany casket with piano gloss finish that Vivian and Patrick had picked out. The champagne velvet lining that Vivian stroked over and over with her index finger in the big book of samples the funeral director had shown her. It was a gesture Harper remembered from Vivian as a child, the pink center of her stuffed rabbit's ears, how she'd caress it until she fell asleep.

Mommy should have everything, she kept saying the day before, the sample book spread in her lap. *Everything she deserved.* Her voice the softest Harper had heard from her niece in years, so soft it almost didn't seem real or true.

Patrick, beside her, couldn't stop crying, smelling heavily of vodka, sweat.

There was still great confusion about life insurance, the estate, everything. And Doug's absence only confused things further. So much had been litigated and re-litigated, a puzzle too great for anyone to ponder quickly.

So, as promised, Debra and Perry paid all the deposits without saying a word, opening their Sentinel Plus TL-15 floor safe and emptying it wordlessly the day of the funeral.

"It'll sort itself out," Perry said, watching Debra count bills.

"I wish I could help," Harper said softly.

It felt so strange, returning to the Verheyden Funeral Home, with its white columns and white shutters, the very one in which their father and then their mother had lain in state all those years ago.

The lobby was crowded, thick with the cloying scent of lilies, wool, sweat. Moving through the throng, Harper kept feeling the tickle of petals and stiff ribbons on her hands, neck, two dozen or more garish floral displays, furry white wreaths and brash easel sprays, an elaborate three-foot-high white mum cross from Doug's Catholic mother.

In the reception room, everything felt the same: the gold wall-to-wall and long curtains, pocket doors and hushed voices, women clasping their husbands' arms and men coughing politely into handkerchiefs, everything so polite as to seem not really real. Like if they opened one of those maple caskets, they might find wax dolls instead of their parents.

But everything was different now, with Pam. Her parents, even though they had both been only in their fifties, had seemed impossibly old when they died, and so battered by life, by fortune's fall.

Not Pam. Despite everything she'd been through, she still felt so alive, a moving thing, perpetual forward motion, crackling and buzzing with energy. Vibrant and bruised, buoyant and relentless.

"It just can't be," Harper found herself whispering, tugging at the black stockings she'd bought an hour before at Bob's Drugs. Tacky to the touch, they reminded her of the ones that used to come in those plastic eggs when she was little.

What the fuck is that?" Debra said. "What kind of monster sends that?"

They were in the parking lot, ready to leave for the church when the assistant funeral director, a slight man with a narrow moustache, appeared, chasing after them with a late arrival, a six-foot-high arrangement that he unveiled with great ceremony.

"I thought you might want to take it to the service," he said.

It was a standing spray of deep red roses curled into a bulbous misshapen heart from which hung long, veinous crimson ribbons pooling on the ground.

Harper looked at it, stunned.

"He sent it, didn't he?" Debra said loudly. "Doug sent it. Only a fucking psychopath would send that."

The assistant director looked up from the easel, his eyes wide with surprise.

"It's a Bleeding Heart," he protested. "One of our most expensive arrangements."

Debra reached toward the bulging heart, plucking loose a white card knifed into its center.

"I fucking knew it," she said, waving the card at Harper.

All my love, it read, *Dad.*

"Deb," Perry whispered, hands on her shoulders. Discreetly gesturing toward Vivian and Patrick, draped around each other near the car.

But it was too late.

"What *is* that?" Vivian asked, stutter-stepping toward them, staring at the display.

"It's from your father," Harper said to Vivian, extending the card.

"Dad?" she whispered, reaching for Patrick's arm. He seemed nearly to hold her up, her voice suddenly small. "But where is he? Where's Dad?"

"The Cayman Islands?" Debra snorted. "Playing sixteen holes with OJ?"

"Deb," Perry said again, more firmly this time.

"He asked," the assistant director offered, clipboard shaking in his hands, "for the most sumptuous arrangement."

Bleeding Heart. Leave it to Doug. A heart long stopped but still bleeding all over the floor.

He can't show for his kids, but he can send an arrangement?" Perry said once Vivian and Patrick were out of earshot.

"The cops can't find him, but he can fucking throw it in our faces?" Debra said.

But Harper had a feeling.

"I think he's coming back," Harper said. "I think something's happening."

23

Harper was supposed to speak at the service but, a half hour before, she knew she wouldn't be able to, her legs shaking like jackhammers in Debra's stiff black dress.

It had been five years or more since she'd set foot in Christ Church, stone Gothic and severe. The last time was that Christmas concert when Patrick played guitar and Vivian sang a solo from Bach's *Christmas Oratorio* that made everyone cry, those last moments before puberty and maybe the divorce, too, stripped the sweetness from her voice forever.

All the Bishops were there, and their significant others, exes, prodigal children. All sixteen cousins, Stevie in his father's repp stripe tie, his face shaved and pink and his hair slicked back like a little boy's. And there was Pam's divorce attorney, Marty—that tall, pink-faced man with thinning colorless hair—along with several of Pam's old neighbors and a half-dozen sorority sisters and fellow PTA members. A sea of black wool and pearls.

Harper scanned the crowd obsessively, on alert for Sue Fox or any of the women from the Club. She guessed they were all in constant communication with one another and she wanted no part of it.

But, of course, it was Doug whom she dreaded the most. It would be so like him, she thought, to make a grand entrance, like a character on a soap opera back from the dead. First the flowers, then Demon Doug himself.

When the organist finally took her seat, the pews nearly full, Harper let out a gasp of relief, trying to catch Debra's eye. *We're safe.*

But then, just as the organ started, the double doors creaked open.
"Shit," Debra whispered, putting her glove to her face, shaking her head.

Harper turned and saw them:

The entire inner circle of the Club marched in formation, their heels clicking on the flagstone, a skulk of well-appointed, middle-aged ladies, handkerchiefs in hands, their mascara dappling, exuding a kind of glamour like a chorus of Italian widows in a Puccini opera.

First, Caroline, Jill, and Becky, all three salon blondes, their arms locked, in black crepe Talbots fit-and-flares.

Next, long, tall Beverly in a black-brimmed hat and the same Swiss-dot hose she wore on New Year's Eve when she'd stood on a case of Veuve and toasted, her voice husky with pleasure, the Power of the Wheel.

Bringing up the rear was skittish Sandy in cap sleeves and an astonishing amount of décolletage.

Then Sue herself, striding to the front, reaching across a full row to try to clamp her hand, knotted with heavy rings, onto Debra's shoulder.

As the organ boomed, they finally assembled themselves across two rows near the back as Harper tried not to look, tried not to scream.

"What are they doing here?" whispered Debra, leaning across Perry's lap, smacking her hand over Harper's. "I made it very clear."

"Just ignore them," Harper said.

"I'll talk to them after," she said, through gritted teeth.

"Debra, *don't*," Harper said.

Perry nodded, too, vigorously. "It'll only draw attention."

"Attention from who?" Debra asked.

But, as soon as she said it, she knew the answer, spotting Detective Conlan and Junior making their way down the aisle before taking seats in the rear pew like a couple of ghouls.

Of course, Harper thought. *Of course.*

It was just like in the movies, the detectives hovering in the back of the funeral, looking for suspicious behavior, clues, a sign.

The reverend spoke with a soaring, shaking voice, his tremor giving everything extra meaning and weight, and Harper reached for Vivian's hand, cold and dry, the Powerpuff Girls band-aids gone, making her fingers look pink and withered, nails jagged. One of them seemed to be missing its nail entirely, which made Harper wince.

Before the service, Patrick had given his sister his last Xanax, and now she had dead eyes as Patrick wept beside her.

But she looked so lovely in the lace cardigan Debra had forced on her to cover the black scoop-necked club dress she'd chosen. Her hair pulled back, her ears—usually studded extravagantly or covered in headphones—were bare and babylike and Harper remembered all those times when she held her as an infant, how hot and feverish her body always felt in her arms, how delicate and forlorn.

But she had Cassie, at least. It seemed they really had reconciled and when she arrived, she'd embraced Harper, smiling through tears, showing that sweet crooked front tooth of hers. But Cassie seemed overwhelmed by it all, too, swathed in a hand-me-down black blazer that ran to her knees. The two of them like a pair of hungover club kids stumbling into the Vatican.

"I don't think I can go up there alone," Debra murmured, staring at the pulpit.

So Perry, stuffed into one of his old court suits, went with her and—when she couldn't speak—stood beside her at the lectern and spoke about his charming and beloved sister-in-law until Debra finally managed a whispered story of when Pam first joined her at U of M, a blooming freshman to Debra's steely senior and how, within two weeks, Pam seemed to have made a hundred friends, snared bids from all the most prestigious sororities, and snagged herself a football player boyfriend.

"Everyone wanted to be around her," Debra said softly. "I was the big sister, but she . . . she didn't need me. Instead, I needed her. In fact, I still do."

Her face hot with tears, Harper reached into her pocket for another wet packet of tissues. But as she did she saw Vivian staring at her. Staring at her with such iciness, she would later think she'd imagined it.

"Viv . . ." she started.

But Vivian turned away, burying her face against her brother's chest. Patrick looking at Harper with an expression she couldn't place.

Something had happened, had come between them. She'd suspected it the day before, but now it seemed confirmed.

She supposed she was part of the enemy camp now, one of the ones pointing the finger at Vivian's father. It seemed unfair, but how could you argue fair when it came to her beloved dad? You couldn't.

We were always allies, Harper thought. But Vivian seemed so far away from her now. She felt the loss keenly.

———

After the service, Harper hovered in the mahogany stairwell, sneaking a smoke, one of its heavy casement windows hand-cranked open a few inches.

She watched the mourners, nervous little black tufts, all the heads slumped low, men with graying hair combed smooth, fidgety children in snug suits and dresses, shoes polished and gleaming, shuffling across the marble floor, dark wool overcoats and white pocket squares and even a few hats, the older women who still wore hats to church, to weddings, to funerals.

It might, she thought, have been fifty years ago, or a hundred, because of the occasion, because their hometown never changed anyway, and in some ways Eisenhower was still president here, the kind of place people still casually drove after four cocktails and everyone hid their problems and murder investigations were shocking, *shocking*, like one of their private brick homes riven open, revealing all the secrets you never dared share.

A sound rippled through the crowd below and echoed up, up, up. A loud sob, so loud in such an echoey space, bouncing off every eave.

It was Sandy Gutowski, crossing the lobby below, her face red, one hand raking through her curls.

Instantly, Debra appeared, hooking her arm around Sandy's narrow shoulders with the force of a nightclub bouncer, both of them disappearing through the heavy wooden doors of the ladies' room. The other women swiftly followed.

Harper thought again of those voicemails Sandy had left on her phone.

Hey, Harper, wanted to check in on you. I've had so much loss, you know. My mother, my brother, my husband. It changes you. I'd love to talk to you about it.

She wondered what Sandy really wanted, because they had never been close, and if it was Sandy, it was probably money.

No parties, no money. The Club was on ice.

She could almost hear Pam giggling in her ear. Because Sandy cried at everything—cried at commercials, the news (especially fires), and cried extravagantly each time any Club member received her gift, her *hot box of cash,* as Pam liked to call it.

She wants you to think she's crying because she's so happy, Pam used to say at every Club party, *but she just wishes that twenty-five grand were hers!*

D ebra's voice, stern and impatient, radiated through the ladies' room door.

"We can't have you here, do you understand?" she was saying. "Not at the burial, not at the house after. Nowhere. Save your casseroles, your condolences. For everyone's sake: Stay the fuck home. Am I clear?"

Pushing the door open, Harper saw Debra standing in the very spot their mother used to slouch, glamorously, dragging on one of her Parliaments as slowly as possible, in slow motion nearly, until the minister stopped speaking and the bells came.

Sue, Caroline, Beverly, Jill, and Becky, a clutch of black crepe, all turned to look at Harper.

"Is it true?" Sue asked her. "Did the detectives ask you about . . . our thing?"

Harper looked at Debra, surprised.

"I told them," Debra admitted to Harper. "They need to know that we're on their radar. They're watching us. All of us."

"What exactly did they ask you?" Sue said, hand on her hip.

"What we do," Harper said. "Our activities. I told them it was social."

Debra gave the women her signature *I-told-you-so* look, one Harper had known since childhood.

"Deb, we all get it," Beverly said. "The need for discretion. But what about the newer members? I mean, how about that looney one, Dana, the one Pam brought in?"

"The one who crashed her husband's car into the garage door?"

"She never even paid her five," Beverly said. "What if she talks?"

"The point is, we don't know what the police know," Debra said. "They're all over my sister's stuff right now. The stuff with Doug—that makes them look at money."

Jill gasped softly. "I put the lynx in cold storage. I . . ."

"They could be watching us," Debra continued. "Monitoring our phones."

"Oh, come on," Caroline said, lighting a Merit in the corner. "Our phones? They really want to bother with my beauty salon reminders and my mother's weekly lectures on varicose vein prevention?"

"You think they're *not* interested in what you might have on that phone?" Debra said. "Or what Pam might have on hers? On her computer?"

Pam didn't have a computer, but Harper didn't say anything.

"Deb's right," Becky said suddenly. "We don't want them looking into our shit."

Harper hid a smile. Of course Becky didn't, given her husband's business activities, the IRS audit they suffered through after his clients were indicted on wire fraud.

"We're just trying to show our friendship by being here," Sue said coolly. "Pammy was our friend."

There was something in the way Sue said it, Harper wanted to smack her.

"If she was your friend," Harper said, "then you'll shut the fuck up."

Sue raised her eyebrows. Sandy let out a little yelp.

"Or what?" Sue said, folding her arms. "A horse's head in my bed?"

"Or," Debra said, "the detectives might get the idea to look into bank records. Tax returns."

"Or," Harper added, "they might just find that corkboard in Pam's basement, the one with all your names on it. And they might wonder what it means and where the money went."

A bluff, sort of.

"Did they find it?" Sue said, more softly now. "Did they . . . find Pam's stash?"

Harper looked at all of them, their faces tight and jaws clenched, their makeup thick under the lights, these masks they wore.

"Maybe," Harper said. "You want to take that chance?"

The church was nearly empty as they hurried toward the exit. Debra held her arm tightly, like she used to after Harper dominated at a lacrosse game.

"I don't think they'll come to the house," Harper whispered.

"No," Debra said, hiding a grin, proud of her sister. "I shouldn't think so."

In the parking lot, she saw them.

Detective Conlan and his partner. They were talking to her boss, Mr. Bingham, and writing things down fervently.

My alibi, she thought. *Good.* She had nothing to hide on that front, after all. Not on that front.

But Mr. Bingham, with his veinous, rosy nose, a cigarette hanging from his hand, kept nodding and talking. Talking and nodding.

She didn't think she'd ever seen Mr. Bingham without his Triple Crown Feed cap and barn jacket. She didn't think she'd ever seen Mr. Bingham talk so much.

And there was something about their intensity, the detectives, a tension in them that worried her.

"Um, Aunt Harper?" A voice behind her, too small and sweet to be Vivian's.

Harper turned and saw Cassie, trembling in her thrifted peacoat, her hands purpling in the cold.

"What is it, honey?"

"I just . . ." she stuttered, looking around the lot, then back at Harper. "Vivian and me—we're back together."

"I'm glad," Harper said, reaching for Cassie's arm. "She needs you now."

"I know," she said, the wind pushing against them, Cassie holding her coat collar up around her bare throat. "That's what I wanted to tell you. I work at the attendance office, you know. It's my work-study. In the mornings."

"Okay," Harper said, distracted again by an approaching police car, weaving fast around exiting mourners. Heading straight for the detectives.

She watched it pull up beside Conlan and Junior, window down. The officer at the wheel saying something, his face red.

"I was there that morning," Cassie was saying. "So everything's okay."

"Wait, what?" Harper said, turning around to face Cassie again.

"Everything's okay," she repeated, backing away from Harper, her eyes on Vivian, in the distance. She stood near Cassie's weather-beaten Escort, her arms wrapped around her tiny frame. Staring out at Cassie and Harper, her face too far away to read.

"Cassie . . ." Harper started, but the girl was already running toward Vivian, her shiny Doc Martens slapping on the brittle concrete, skidding over the ridges of ice.

By the time Harper whirled around again, Mr. Bingham was alone, cigarette back in his mouth, staring off into the jumble of cars, their exhaust pipes pluming.

The detectives and the police car were gone. Running to the far end of the lot, Harper could hear a squeak of wheels on the icy concrete in the distance.

The siren came next, the wail of it, and a second police car arriving, turning around with a screech and disappearing too.

Something was happening.

Everything was happening. She just didn't know what yet.

24

Debra's stubby brick bungalow heaved with mourners, the furnace rumbling, hot dishes steaming from every surface, the tiny oven swollen with a tray of stuffed mushrooms and a glistening, fulgent ham, and everyone clustered in groups, sweating, tugging their black crepe or striped ties from their throats.

Harper kept moving, from room to room, unable to sit still, her mind racing.

Passing the den, she saw Perry drinking with all the older men, uncles and husbands, suit and sports jackets stripped off, bloodshot eyes. Gossiping, speculating like a clutter of fishwives.

"Did you see those goddamned flowers?" Perry was saying. "Who does he think he is, Don Corleone?"

"Money can't buy class, and he hasn't even got the money anymore."

"But do you really think he could do *that*?"

A brief pause, a stifled cough.

Then: "C'mon," someone said, "only an ex-wife could piss you off that much."

A snort of laughter, muffled. A faint cackle.

Desperate, Harper swung the door open for a breath of icy air.

Stepping outside, she saw someone cutting across the lawn. It reminded her, eerily, of the man she'd seen in the neighbor's yard at Pam's house.

But it was only Stevie, emerging from the garage with a case of beer.

"Hey, Auntie," he said softly. "Join us?"

Harper nodded, following him to the cramped porch, filled with cousins, teenagers curled around Patrick, exotic now that he was in college, his eyes red and face drawn.

"Hey, Aunt H," he said, extending his arm, offering her a joint tucked behind his jacket.

All the girlish and boyish faces upturned from their makeshift seats on old planters, their phones glowing in the dusk.

"No, thanks," Harper said, smiling. Eyes darting from the joint to the lostness in Stevie's face. The forgotten child, so easy he was forgotten.

Then, looking at the joint again, she added, "Well, maybe a little."

An hour passed, the teenagers laughing in that way you do at formal, serious events when you're self-conscious, bewildered what to do, how to make small talk, or say the right thing. She only took a few hits, but it was what she needed, that tingling feeling that seemed to surround you, keep you a foot or two apart from what was happening, from your own bad thoughts.

"Is that Vivian?" she said, spotting her niece, her phone to her face, sitting on the cold ground near the garage.

"Yeah," Patrick said hesitantly. "Talking to Cassie, I guess."

Harper looked out at her, hunched over her phone, half in shadow, half in brilliant light from the security lamp.

Maybe it was the joint—shot through with her own grief and confusion—but there was something in Vivian's eyes, glossy black. A numbness she'd never seen before. An eerie blankness.

And the way her niece's body was keeling, like a ship that couldn't right herself. Her knees tucked to her chest now, rocking slightly, a kind of seething rhythm to her, like someone infinitely capable of rage and abandon—how could you know what they could do, even if they might regret it the instant after?

Through the haze of the joint, she remembered something. That thing Pam had said the night of Patrick's graduation, all those months ago.

Now it's just me and Vivian. One of us is coming out in a body bag.

She didn't know why the memory came to her now, but it did.

I'm worried about her," she said to Patrick, pulling him aside.

"The thing about V," Patrick said, "she comes at everything with anger. She thinks it protects her, or something."

Harper nodded. It seemed true. But that anger had never been directed at her and it felt different, painful, strange.

"And how about you?" Harper asked. "How are you?" With everything in the world folded into that question.

"I'm not the same person I was a week ago," he said, looking away. "I guess . . . I guess that person's gone forever."

"Oh, Patrick," Harper said, curling his face in her hand. Then lying, "You'll feel like yourself again, I promise."

"Sure," he said, his eyes filling, "I'm so stoned anyway."

Upstairs, she found Debra in her bedroom, ashing her cigarette in the palm of her hand, one of their mother's old tricks, a matriarchy of stealth smokers.

"They're not down there, are they?" Debra said. "The detectives."

Harper shook her head, handing Debra a lukewarm cup of white wine.

"I half expected they'd show up here, for the buffet. Can't you picture the hunchbacked one jamming pigs in a blanket in his mouth?"

"They left right after the service," Harper said. "Peeled out of the parking lot like a bat out of hell."

"And it looks like we kept the wailing widows away," Debra said, peeking through the window blinds, likely checking for Sue's violet Beamer.

"Showdown in the powder room," Harper smirked.

"Turned out all I needed to do was let you loose on them," Debra said, grinning.

"For now," Harper said.

She was thinking of Sue, hard charging on the lacrosse field. The look on her face, like a warrior unleashed. The same look on her face whenever she unsnapped money bands, when she counted the pot . . .

"I wanted you first," Debra said abruptly. "I wanted to invite you. Pam said it wasn't a good idea."

Harper looked up, surprised. "To the Club?"

Debra nodded. "Pam said it might not be a good idea."

"Okay," Harper said, wondering where this was going.

"She said you were too . . . emotional. Maybe indiscreet."

Harper nodded, her head instantly throbbing.

"She thought you couldn't keep a secret," Debra said, "or a promise."

Harper winced. "I get it, Jesus, Deb—"

Debra put her hand on Harper's, a fleeting gesture, her hand cool. "She was wrong."

Harper didn't want to think about it, or why Debra had told her. Like in high school, Debra telling her Pam wished Harper would grow out her hair, *or at least comb it, Christ.* Pam denied it. *Deb's the one who said that, Harper. Don't you get it? That's what she does.*

Right now, she didn't want to think about anything.

Downstairs, everything got loud all of a sudden. A rumble of voices, feet. Almost like a real party, when there's an exciting late arrival, or your cousin returns with more beer and it's a big *whoop!*

Except it wasn't like that at all, Perry and Stevie standing in the center of the living room, various stray mourners cluttering the corners. On the sofa, Patrick was hunched over, his head in his hands.

The TV was on, Debra's new flat-screen monstrosity, plastic film still on the corners.

Husband turns himself in, the news crawl read, *for questioning in the bludgeoning death of his ex-wife in her home on Monday. . . .*

"That must've been it," Debra said, looking at Harper. "Why the detectives took off so fast."

"Thank Jesus," Perry murmured.

There he was, on all three local news broadcasts, making his grand entrance: Doug striding into the police station, batting off the cameras like Princess Diana.

"*Turns himself in,*" Debra said, rolling her eyes. "That's rich. Like a rat as the trap snaps shut."

On the screen, Doug looked sunbaked, serene in his sports jacket, chinos, dark sunglasses. His lawyer, in a searing coral golf shirt, followed, head lowered.

They couldn't stop watching, all of them.

Doug, Harper thought, shaking her head, *did you have to dress for the perp walk?*

He looked so guilty.

It made her think of something Pam said, years ago. After everything with Leigh, the breakup. When everything was going wrong and Harper was drinking too much and Pam kept interfering, wanting Harper to *get over it and just move on.*

I just want to help you, she said. *You don't have a husband to protect you.*

And Harper replied, *Like yours protects you?*

Which one of you did it?"

Everyone turned in unison to see Vivian in the doorway, her black minidress riding up her thighs, her phone hanging from one hand.

Her eyes on the TV screen, the pixelating image of her father, sunglasses flashing, teeth so white they were nearly blue.

"What, honey?" Harper asked, moving toward her.

"Which one of you ratted out my dad?" she said, voice husky with smoke and cold air.

The room fell silent, Vivian picking at the scabs on her hand and forearm. Those glancing cuts now caked over. They looked infected.

"Oh, Vivian," Harper said. "No one did anything. He turned himself in. He's doing the right thing, your dad."

"First time for everything," Debra said, dropping a cigarette butt into a random go-cup. "The chickens are finally coming home to roost."

Harper looked down at Vivian, her face hidden behind all her hair, and she couldn't tell if her niece was crying or raging. With Vivian, the difference was pin-thin.

Harper couldn't sleep. Stuffed in the office, cords tangling at her feet, she couldn't keep any of it straight. Taking one Benadryl, two, four, brain furred.

Vivian left again, her puffer coat a streak of silver down the driveway.

For hours, Debra and Perry had sat at the kitchen table, nursing a misty bottle of Cutty salvaged from the basement, waiting for news updates, speculating about Doug.

Patrick, stoned and dreamy, kept trying to call his father, even though everyone told him it was no use.

"He came back for us," Patrick said. "That's what I think, anyway."

"See how hard it is," Debra said, after he disappeared into the basement, "to turn your back on your father? See what he can do and they still forgive." She looked at Harper, eyes glossy. "It's something to see."

It wasn't like Debra to be sentimental, Harper thought. It must've been the Cutty.

All night, she kept waking up, thinking of things. What Doug might be telling the police. She could only guess how desperate he was. What he might say to save his own skin.

At some point, she dreamt. She was back in Christ Church, the organ booming, pews creaking. But she was up in the pulpit this time, everyone waiting for her to speak about Pam, to extol Pam, to remind everybody why we all loved Pam so much.

They were all there, Debra and Perry weeping in the front row, Patrick, eyes red and glassy, his arms wrapped around Vivian, covering her face with those big pink mittens she'd been wearing when they found Pam, their tips heavy with Pam's blood.

And Doug coming up the aisle late, his wrists cuffed in front of him, arms wrapped around his heaving bank sack of coins—pennies scattering across the aisle like confetti at a wedding.

Everyone was waiting and Harper kept closing her eyes, trying to think about Pam. Beautiful Pam, beloved Pam. Her Pam.

But when she opened her mouth, no words came out, her throat dry, gasping, and everywhere she looked she saw them.

The Club members, that tight knot of them, black hose and crumpled tissues, sharp elbows bent at the pew. The cool blondes, tight-faced, bright-teethed, and deep-tanned, their funeral crepe crinkling as they shifted and turned. Sandy sobbing operatically, a wet stringing sob that rose up the belfry, a widow's wail.

Sue Fox, her black bob shining, bracelets clinking as she wrapped an impossibly long arm around the other women, an arm so long it gathered all of them into its embrace.

25

The dawn light purpled the window blinds.

Harper hadn't slept more than an hour or two.

Aren't your hands cold? she heard herself saying. *Where are your mittens?*

Then she remembered: Cassie in her peacoat in the parking lot, her hands mottled red.

How she'd approached Harper after the service, bouncing on the balls of her feet in the cold.

I wanted to tell you, she'd said in her cracked little voice, tongue thrusting against her crooked teeth, *I work at the attendance office. I was there that morning.*

Then, seeing Vivian waiting for her, how she quickly backed away.

So everything's okay.

Everything's okay.

The kitchen was already bright, Debra and Perry at the tiny table, as if they'd never gone to bed at all, as if they'd stayed there all night, rooted in place.

Through the doorway, Harper could see Patrick dozing on the living room sofa, cartoons playing with the sound off, a bowl of half-eaten Lucky Charms tipping onto the carpet.

"That's tight," Perry was saying to Debra.

"Tight, but doable."

Perry had pulled out a water-soft road almanac, trying to figure out if Doug would have had time to kill Pam after she'd returned from dropping Vivian off at school and still get back to court in time.

Yesterday, they'd wept over her sister's body—the supreme awfulness of which Harper had tried to push away with static, wine, tobacco, the thrum of voices, the gallows humor, her own powerful ability (gifted from her childhood) to scrub pain from her brain—and now they were drawing a little map on the back of the memorial program with Perry's stubby golf pencils: HOME TO SCHOOL and COURTHOUSE TO AIRPORT?

"At eight-fifteen," Debra said, "Pam drops Vivian off at school."

"We know that for sure?"

"That's what Vivian said."

Harper looked up.

It was only then she let herself think what Cassie's cryptic assurance might have meant. *Was Cassie saying she'd confirmed Vivian's alibi?*

Or that she'd given her one?

Debra was writing something on the map. Writing so hard she broke the pencil tip.

"Then Pam drives the ten minutes home," Perry said, "where she is confronted by the killer."

279

"By ten, Doug is in court, a thirty- to forty-minute drive away."

"Just before eleven, Harper picks Vivian up from school and they discover the body."

"He could have done it at eight-thirty. He could have been waiting for her and done it and still been in court in time."

"Killed her and, what, showered and changed?" Perry said. "Like Harper said, he'd have had blood all over himself. He'd be covered in it."

Harper shut her eyes.

Debra paused, the golf pencil tight in her hand.

"I'm sorry," Perry said. "I just . . ."

Debra shook her head and he stopped.

Harper looked down at Perry's map, the stick figures he'd drawn. The one of Pam sprawled in the center of the square of her house.

Something slapped against the back door. They all jumped.

"Paperboy," Perry announced, rising. Then adding, *Boy*—he's my age. The delivery guy. Probably used to run General Motors."

Patrick appeared in the doorway, staring at his phone. "Vivian talked to him," he said. "She just talked to Dad."

They heard Perry fumble at the back door, then say, "Son of a bitch."

Debra looked at Harper. "They released him."

"Sure did," Perry said, returning to the kitchen. "I guess they didn't have enough to hold him. But he remains a person of interest."

"A person of interest," Debra said, slinking back into her chair. "Fuck me."

The court clerk confirmed that Mr. Sullivan was on the premises from nine-thirty A.M. until approximately ten-ten, at which point the judge granted a delay due to the victim's failure to appear," read Perry from the newspaper, wet from the front porch.

"Shit," he said, leaning back. "That's pretty definitive."

Harper felt a hand on her shoulder. It was Patrick, rubbing his eyes, studying the stark timetable Debra had made.

"He's a compulsive liar," Debra said, taking the paper from Perry. "I still don't believe any of it. And I still think he had the time. Maybe after. She doesn't show, so he goes to the house, kills her—"

"And then gets on a plane within the hour?" Perry said. "Like OJ?"

Harper nudged Perry, pointing to Patrick. *Enough with the OJ.*

But Patrick still had his head bent over the timetable. "Why does everyone keep saying ten?"

They all looked at him.

"The hearing was at ten," Debra said. "So she would have left the house at nine-fifteen at the latest—"

"But they moved it later," Patrick said. "Didn't they?"

Debra set her coffee down. "What do you mean?"

"When I talked to her that morning," Patrick said. "Mom. She said they changed the time to two."

Harper looked at him, a ghostly flicker of something rising inside her.

"She mentioned it to me too," she said, then looked at Debra. "I told you I thought they changed it."

They pushed it, Pam had said that morning, her hand trembling on her Ann Taylor suit.

"She said she was glad it got moved," Patrick continued. "It gave her more time to polish her pistols."

Harper started to laugh, then stopped herself. *Polish her pistols.* It was so Pam.

"Wait, who changed it?" Debra said, pushing her chair back from the table.

Patrick shrugged. "She said someone called. Some lady."

"A lady?" Debra asked. She looked at Harper.

"Was it the clerk?" Perry asked. "The police can check on that. The phone records. Hopefully they already have."

"Don't count on it," Debra said. "It's probably a mistake—"

"Did she say anything else?" Harper asked, turning to Patrick. She was thinking of something. A vague notion blinking faintly in the corner of her brain.

Patrick paused a moment. "It was a message. She told me they left a message."

Harper and Debra exchanged looks.

Perry rapped the pencil on the pad. "Maybe it's still on the machine."

"Maybe," Harper said, thinking.

Twenty minutes later, they were driving to the police station.
She had an idea. She was guessing, of course. There was only one person who benefited from Pam not showing up in court. Even as she still, despite everything, struggled to imagine Doug as a murderer, better him than—

"Should we call Vivian?" Patrick asked as they pulled into the lot. "Should she come too?"

"No," Harper said. "Not yet."

26

The detectives looked tired today.

"Homicide is murder on our budget," she'd overheard the desk sergeant say, laughing at his own joke. "The overtime alone."

They were back in the same small room, the punishing fluorescents, the laminate table.

Patrick, nervous and twitchy, kept trying to explain.

"She said someone called. The hearing time got changed."

"And you just remembered this?" Junior asked Patrick.

"I didn't put it together," Patrick started, his face red. "I didn't know it had anything to do with— I'm sorry."

"She mentioned it to me too," Harper said. "She said it got pushed."

Conlan looked at her, then Patrick.

"The point is," Harper said, "Pam told him someone left a message. On the machine. And maybe Pam didn't erase it."

"And you think that means what?"

"I don't know," Harper said. "A mistake, maybe. Or maybe someone wanted to make sure Pam was home."

Conlan looked at her, his eyes dancing a little. She had his attention now.

"Someone," he said. "Like . . . ?"

"Maybe," Harper said carefully, "Patrick can take a break."

Conlan nodded, rising.

"Patrick," he said, "how about you get a pop or something and we'll call you back in a little bit?"

Patrick nodded, relieved.

Don't you get it?" Harper said. "Someone tricked her. Someone who wanted Pam to be home at a particular time. A time when he had an airtight alibi."

"And by *someone*," Conlan said, "you mean your former brother-in-law?"

"You tell me," Harper said. "You had him in here last night."

Conlan and Junior looked at each other. Whether it was their third coffee or the information, she had their full attention now.

"Your nephew said it was a woman who called," Junior pointed out.

"So he had someone call for him!" Harper said, exhausting herself. "His secretary, his girlfriend of the week. What does it matter? Do you have her answering machine here? I mean, there's no way you missed that, right?"

They both looked at her.

"We have it," Conlan said. "But we're still waiting on the phone records. Time stamps. To match."

"Whoever left the message," Harper said, "might be the key."

Conlan leaned back, his fingers gently squeezing his Styrofoam cup.

"Coincidence," Junior said. "Amateur sleuths never met a coincidence that they couldn't spin into a conspiracy."

"Probably a coincidence," Conlan said, "but let's get that answering machine."

Moments later, an officer brought Pam's dusty, cord-tangled answering machine into the room. They all watched as he plugged it in.

Harper noticed the familiar fluorescent orange Detroit Tigers decal on the side, slapped on there by Patrick a decade ago. She wanted to reach out and touch it.

After the officer left, Junior pressed *play.*

A woman's voice, clipped and brisk, said, *Mrs. Sullivan, I'm calling from the clerk's office. Due to scheduling issues, the hearing is now at fourteen hundred hours. Courtroom C. Good day.*

"Fourteen hundred hours," Conlan said. "They got former drill captains working at the courthouse now?"

Harper pushed her fingers to her temples, thinking.

It was so familiar, not the voice itself but—

"His assistant," Harper blurted. "That's his assistant. Doug's."

Conlan looking at her. "You recognize the voice?"

Harper shook her head. "He told me she was in the reserves."

She could still picture Doug, so charming and menacing under the Christmas lights at Rustic Cabins. *Army reserves, no shit. She keeps me on schedule with military precision.*

Junior sighed, unimpressed.

"What about that statement his office issued?" Harper said, putting all the pieces together. "It said his flight was at eleven hundred hours."

"We should get the phone records today," Conlan said, tapping his pen energetically. She could tell he believed her, or wanted to.

"Can't you bring her in?" Harper asked. "Right now."

"You let us deal with that," Conlan said. But she could tell he was thinking.

"It doesn't change much," Junior said. "Let's say this *is* his assistant. *He* still has the same alibi."

"You don't think it's suspicious?" Harper said.

"That he wants to stall the hearing so he doesn't have to pay up?" Conlan said. "Look, if he's behind this, it's a kind of fraud. We can take it to the prosecutor. But what does it prove?"

"It proves he's a liar," Harper said, her voice shaking. She didn't even know what she herself thought anymore. "He had a motive. He fled. Who knows what evidence he destroyed, gone all that time? Blood on his clothes—"

"He still has the alibi," Junior repeated.

"Maybe he hired someone," Harper tried.

"That's Hollywood bullshit," Junior said.

"Why did you let him go?" Harper asked. "He'll run again. I—"

"He's not gonna run," Conlan said. "We got a tail on him."

Harper tried not to roll her eyes.

"Have you talked to your niece about this?" Conlan said. "She has very strong feelings about all your very strong feelings. She thinks you're all trying to railroad her dad."

Harper wanted to pound the table.

"Of course she does!" she said. "He's her dad."

There was a knock on the door and an officer brought in more coffee, three Styrofoam cups nestled between his big man hands.

"Did Pam hide money in the house?" Conlan said, shaking a stirrer loose from a plastic sleeve.

Harper felt her shoulders sink. It was the risk she'd taken. That it would come back to this.

"Money?" Harper said, buying time. "What do you mean?"

"We mean money."

"Not that I know of."

"The money we found under your bed," Conlan said. "Are you sure it's not your sister's?"

"Why would my sister's money be under *my* bed?"

Conlan played with his coffee stirrer, red as a maraschino stem.

"Maybe you took it," Junior said with a shrug. "Before you killed her."

Harper felt it like a punch in the throat.

The room was close, oppressive, an ancient space heater humming hotly in the corner.

A moment ticked by, then two. They were looking at her, blank-faced.

"Were you involved in some kind of profit-making scheme with your sister?" Junior asked.

"I can hardly balance my checkbook," she said. Maybe she even smirked.

Inside, she was frantic. Had Doug told them about the money she owed? She knew he would do anything to protect himself. *He's the one you don't want in the Donner party*, Pam used to say.

"I don't know what you've heard," she said, making her voice even, firm, "but the money under my bed was mine. If I took it from her, would I just shove it under my bed like my nephew with his *Playboy*s?"

They both watched her for a long moment.

"I would *never* hurt my sister," she said, her voice breaking. "Never. Ever."

Junior twirled his pen.

"Maybe the scheme went south," he said, staring at her. "She made more bank. You didn't like it. You took her stash and bopped her."

Harper nearly laughed, but instead she thought she might be sick. What had Doug told them? Everything and more.

Conlan raised his eyebrow at Junior. She could read it: *Easy, boy.*

"Why would I ever do that?" Harper said, trying not to lose her mind. That's what it felt like. Like she might explode into a thousand pieces. "Why would I ever hurt my sister? Take a goddamned hammer to my sister's face? Why would I ever do that?"

"Maybe it wasn't money," Junior said, twirling the coffee stirrer between his pink knuckles. "Maybe you had beef."

"Sisters have beef," Conlan said, nodding.

Harper shook her head. Shook her head over and over until she felt it might fall off.

"Maybe she didn't approve of your lifestyle," Junior said, another shrug.

"My lifestyle? Bridling and saddling rich people's horses—Buttercup and Cinnamon and the Gipper—picking gravel from their hooves, sweeping manure from their grooming bays?"

"Your personal life," Conlan said, clearing his throat. "Perhaps it was a source of tension."

She knew what they meant, of course. But they couldn't say it, so why should she?

"My sister loved me," Harper said, a tremble in her voice. "You can't talk about my sister that way. She loved me."

You'll never understand, she wanted to tell them. *It was complicated like every family is. Like sisters are. Your sisters will always break your heart, pierce straight to the center of it and split it in two. And your sisters will always make it whole again. It's what we do. What sisters do.*

The detectives looked at each other.

Conlan pushed a Kleenex box toward her.

"We talked to your boss," Conlan said, finally. "Les Bingham."

"And?" Harper said, bracing herself. "Because I was in the stables most of the time, but—"

"He confirmed your alibi."

Harper leaned back, breathing. *Thank you, Mr. Bingham....*

Both men continued to look at her. As if still deciding something. Or deciding they weren't sure.

H ow was it?" Patrick asked, sliding on his coat. "Do they need me again?"

"Not right now," Harper said, breathing deliberately, trying to slow her breath. Then to Debra, newly arrived after dropping Perry off at the doctor: "Can you take him home?"

Debra looked at her, trying to read her face. To figure out what was happening.

"I feel like I did something wrong," Patrick said, eyes darting between them.

"You didn't," Harper assured him. "You're helping. We'll know more soon."

Patrick nodded, looking at his phone. "Dad's been calling."

There was a long moment, Patrick's eyes so sorrowful.

"It doesn't mean he did anything," Patrick said. "Dad. Even if he was behind that call."

"That's right," Debra said, her voice clipped. "It just means he wanted your mom to miss the hearing. Over your trust."

Harper threw a look at Debra. *Don't.*

"It just means," Patrick admitted, defeated, "he really, really didn't want to give us our money back."

Sitting in the minivan in the parking lot, she knew what she had to do, but she was screwing up her nerve.

She'd come to them with proof—or proof enough—and they were treating her like the number one suspect. Whatever Doug had been pouring in their ears had had its effect.

You lit the fuse, Doug, she thought, *now watch out.* There was so much she knew, countless Demon Doug deeds. The slush fund he'd hid from Pam. But to tell them about that would be to tell on herself, the money she'd taken from him. She would have to be careful, so careful.

A flicker in the rearview and a car pulled up behind her.

That familiar powder-blue Ford Escort, its muffler hanging low. The shiny MGM Grand parking tag hanging from the rearview.

Not now, she thought with a groan.

Instantly, Sandy, stuffed in a black parka, darted from her car, running to Harper's window.

"Sandy," Harper said. "I don't have time to—"

"It's important," she said, moving quickly around the minivan to the passenger side.

Reluctantly, Harper unlocked the door and Sandy jumped in.

"I need to talk to you," she said, tearing off her puffy gloves. "It's absolutely critical."

"I don't have any money, Sandy," Harper started. "The police seized it—"

"I think you and Deb should know," Sandy said, her red hand on Harper's arm. "The other women—they're really worried. I'm worried. It's getting scary."

"You haven't talked to the police, have you?" Harper asked, gently pulling her arm away. She couldn't imagine anyone worse to talk to the police. Under questioning, Sandy might very well confess to the Kennedy assassination.

"I'm no rat," Sandy said, and Harper wanted to laugh. "I would never do that. I took the oath."

"Okay," Harper said. "Then there's nothing to worry about. If everyone keeps quiet, everything's going to be okay."

"But you don't know what's happening!" Sandy insisted, grabbing her phone from her parka pocket. "There's all these texts and, Harper, I swear, I keep seeing people in my yard."

Harper turned off the ignition and looked at her.

"Who?" Harper asked.

"I don't know," Sandy said, shaking her head. "I see their feet in the morning frost."

"Really?" Harper said. She thought again of the man she'd seen in the neighbor's yard at Pam's. The one in the ski mask. Each time she remembered it, it felt stranger.

"And I found something," Sandy said, her voice dropping to a whisper, "on my porch this morning."

"What?"

"A rabbit," Sandy said, blinking twice. "Dead."

Harper looked at her, confused.

"There was no blood on it, just frost all over like lace," she continued, "I knew it was meant for my eyes only."

Harper felt instantly exhausted. Sandy, always weird, was getting weirder. She guessed they all were.

"Wild cottontails are everywhere, Sandy. It drives the Hunt Club gardener crazy—"

"It's a warning. A threat. From someone in the Club."

"Who? What kind of warning?" Harper said. It reminded her, vaguely, of high school hockey games. *Who threw the octopus on the ice?* An obscure Detroit Red Wings tradition.

"A warning not to talk," Sandy said, tugging at her neon zipper. "To the police."

"Ten to one, it was your cat. They sometimes leave animals—"

"Pepper would *never* do that."

"Sandy, are you suggesting one of us killed an animal and placed it on your porch? Rather than just say, *Keep your goddamned mouth shut?*"

Sandy said nothing for a few seconds, her whole body seeming to vibrate. Then, unable to help herself, blurted:

"Sue—she keeps sending us these texts."

"What kind of texts?"

Sandy pulled out her phone again and showed Harper her tiny flip screen.

REMEMBER WHAT WE PROMISED.

Harper sighed. Sue loved all caps.

"Well," she said, "she's just reminding everyone we pledged to keep the Wheel to ourselves."

Sandy flicked the screen to another text:

ONE OF US TALKS, WE ALL GO DOWN.
I WON'T LET THAT HAPPEN.

Sandy was silent. Harper could hear her breathing.

She told Sandy not to worry. That she'd take care of it, and she was sure it was nothing.

It took several minutes, Sandy's eyes darting around like she hadn't slept. A coffee ring around her mouth. Poor Sandy.

"I just knew I should tell you," she said. "The women aren't telling you things anymore. Because of . . . what happened. And—"

"I have to go," Harper said, more forcefully this time. "There's someone I need to see."

"Okay," Sandy said, finally, opening the door and exiting, but not before once turning around, her puffy glove tapping on the window. "You're sure you can't spot me fifty? Until we can start the parties again?"

27

The drive downtown along Jefferson was one Harper had known her whole life. But it was always a fresh surprise when the leafy lulls and lifeless brick colonials and chilly stone manors disappeared precisely as one crossed Alter Road, the infamous dividing line between the city and the suburbs, and instantly one landed in one of the hardest-hit corners of Detroit, now half-scraped clean by the city's economic woes.

Careening past the crumbling pilasters and sooted gargoyles always made Harper sad, stunned. *The city will rise again*, her father used to proclaim over G&Ts at the club, as if he and all his peers had played no role in its struggles. They were not a family that talked politics, certainly not race, but you couldn't grow up where you did without an awareness of the history of plunder and abandonment, exploitation and desertion.

The city will rise again, and maybe it would, but would it ever be so majestic again, would anything in America, as the boom-time ballyhoo of the first half of the century, the days when American cars ruled the land, and Detroit was its mighty center?

Those days were going or long gone before she and her sisters were born, but the notion of a fallen empire of steel had hummed in the air their whole lives, a mournful feeling. Remember when . . . remember when . . .

Nostalgia is always a trap, she thought now. It made you forget the things you didn't want to remember, the ugly things that keep you honest, true.

But then she saw it, a spectacle born in her lifetime: the Renaissance Center, as optimistically named as El Dorado Drive. A once-glittering, futuristic marvel of cylindrical steel and glass built in the seventies, it promised to be *the city within the city!* Shopping mall, movie theaters, offices, a luxury hotel, the optimistic assertion of Detroit's longed-for return to glory after "everything"—a word that held all the intricacies of the city's complicated history, but just barely.

As little girls, she and her sisters used to love to take one of its famous glass elevators all the way to the top (*Twelve minutes! And your ears would pop!*) and dine in the rotating restaurant.

Now it was the now shaggy, louche place made for now shaggy, louche Doug.

Harper hadn't stepped inside the Renaissance Center in years, and had certainly never seen Doug's apartment, only heard reports from a stunned Patrick and Vivian, who couldn't believe that their father lived downtown, and in the RenCen, of all places. It might as well have been a Roman ruin as far as they were concerned.

When their father first moved out three years ago, Vivian and Patrick felt sorry for him, blaming their mother for his exile into what they decided was a fallen place. And they loved to tell heavily embroidered stories of finding a hank of hair trapped under the new paint in his apartment and the time Patrick got stuck in a stalled elevator with a friendly sex worker who saved the day with a screwdriver in her handbag.

That, of course, was all Harper could think of as she rode up the sluggish elevator this time. It was easier than thinking about anything else.

She had no idea what to expect when she buzzed Doug's twitchy buzzer.

But she didn't anticipate such a buoyant greeting when Doug opened the door.

"There she is. There's my girl," he said, eyes glinting, as if he'd been waiting for her.

Or maybe he'd just been drinking. In fact, she was sure he had, his shirt untucked, and his hair uncombed and something pink and unwashed about him, like a businessman on a bender.

Harper stepped inside, a whiff of old deodorant on him, crushed cigarettes.

"They probably saw you, you know," he said, peering through the bent blinds on the floor-to-ceiling windows. "The dicks. The badge men. The po-po. Hope you don't get any blowback."

"I think you're confusing yourself with a KGB spy," Harper said.

"There's at least one cop downstairs," he continued. "Could be one next door right now. There's a lot of vacancies in here. Fifty percent. I thought I heard a whirring sound through the walls, like someone might be recording—"

"We need to talk," Harper said, ignoring him, stepping farther into the sunken gray living room, gloomy and dark. The windows, floor to ceiling, left unwashed.

"How does it feel," he said, clearing newspapers off the sofa for her to sit, "being a hammer's breadth away from the man who murdered your sister?"

Harper looked at him.

"You think if you say that, you sound innocent," she said. "But, Doug, you have never sounded innocent."

He laughed grimly and took a seat across from her, smoothing his hair, straightening an invisible tie.

"I know what you did," she said. "Giving Pam the wrong time. The court hearing."

He leaned back, raising an eyebrow.

"I listened to the message. With the police. We listened to it together. You had your assistant give Pam the wrong time."

"Why would I do that?" he said, blinking twice, three times.

"To give yourself an alibi."

"An alibi for what?" Doug said, smiling greasily. "So I'm *not* a KGB spy but I *am* the kind of guy who, what, contracts out my wife's murder? Is that what you're suggesting? You give me too much credit. I don't have *those* kinds of connections."

Harper didn't say anything.

"And to what end?" Doug said. "What does that get me?"

"Money," Harper said. "Why do you do anything?"

"What money?" He laughed, leaning back now, enjoying himself.

He was baiting her, she thought. He must know, she thought. He must know Pam had money in the house and he wanted her to confirm it. She said nothing.

"Did I have Monique call?" he said, reaching behind his chair and emerging with a bottle of Jim Beam. Doug, always the magician. "Sure I did. Was it stupid? Supremely. I was just buying time."

"You might have gotten her killed," Harper said, wanting to make it hurt. "If Pam had been at the hearing, it never would have happened."

"I'm not proud of it," he said, pouring the bourbon into a sticky glass on the sticky glass coffee table. "I'm not proud of anything."

"What have you been telling the police?" Harper asked, her voice straining. "About me? They were asking me terrible things. Like I stole from her and . . . hurt her."

Doug stared at her, his face half-hidden in shadow.

"I think," he said, "you've half convinced yourself you have nothing to hide."

"I borrowed money from you. What does that have to do with Pam?"

"You knew things, Harper," he said. "I had the money to give you *because* I hid money from her. Of course I did. We were splitting up, she was a vengeful bitch—"

"Don't you dare—"

"But you took it. That dirty money. And then when Pam accused me of stealing from her, you played the innocent. You—"

"Stop it," Harper cried out. "Please."

He took a long sip. "Did you forget?" he said, eyes glossy now.

"Forget what?"

"I know she's sainted now. Our Pammy. She's gone and we all miss her. Even me. But did you really forget how she could be? Her judgment. Her high and mighty judgment. About the way you live. You know what I mean."

Harper didn't say anything.

She thought again of what Vivian had said: *You know how Mom is.* About girls loving girls. It was *fine, whatever works for you,* but it wasn't—could never be—serious.

Doug looked at her, fingers delicate around the glass rim. "There's a reason you came to me for that money. And I gave it to you. Not her. Me."

"I'm out," Harper said, rising, moving away from him.

"Wait, wait," Doug said. "I'm just saying—look, money mattered to her."

"It matters to all of us."

"Not you," he said.

"Are you kidding me? That's how I got stuck in this . . . this thing with you," she said. "It's like an affair I'd never have and now can't escape."

"All three of you, the beautiful Bishop sisters, to the manner born. With your cashmere sweaters and your Tiffany bracelets. And Daddy went broke and it all went away," he said. "But Pam cared most. And Pam married me—"

"She loved you."

"She loved the man she thought could bring it all back," he said. "She loved the big house on Windmill Pointe with the Juliet balconies and the reflecting pool. She loved her flamenco-red BMW and our boat slip at the Little Club and those long summer Sundays at the Hunt Club—"

"Stop it," Harper said, her voice unaccountably high, pained.

The memory came back to her, of Pam at twenty-six, sweet toddler Patrick in her arms, showing off her Georgian mansion to her sisters. The limestone fireplace, the Viking range, the Sub-Zero. The elation on her face. *Look! Look!*

But Doug had it all wrong. He didn't get it. When you grow up in comfort and it all falls away—and your parents with it—money isn't about money. It's about security, freedom, independence, a promise of wholeness. All those fantasies, illusions. Money was rarely about money.

That was what the Club was about, too, that yearning, that longing, that desire for a return to an imagined place of safety—like childhood. A place that probably wasn't so wonderful to begin with, but it was yours.

You're wrong," Harper said, gathering herself again. "You never understood my sister at all. You tried to poison her kids against her and you've always been shit and you still are. Slithering out of your obligations. Abandoning your kids when they needed you most. You left them here to deal with all of it. You should see Vivian, defending you to everybody—"

"I never asked her to—"

"The daughter you couldn't bother to call after her mother was murdered. And she's the one out here banging the drum for your innocence. Protecting you."

Doug leaned back, his eyes glinting strangely.

It was a long moment, charged with a meaning Harper couldn't quite grasp.

"Have you considered," he said slowly, "that I might be the one protecting her?"

Harper looked at him, a sharp pain in her chest. "Bullshit."

Doug sat for a minute, his hands on his flannel pants. "I came back for Vivian. Because of Vivian. Do you honestly think we haven't talked since this happened? We've talked."

Harper sat down again, her knees buckling. She was afraid of what Doug was about to say.

A feeling slowly sinking in her, one she'd felt for days with Vivian's coolness toward her, her sudden secrecy. But it couldn't be—

"She called me that morning," he whispered gravely. "The morning Pam—the morning it happened. She called me right before the hearing."

"Why?" Harper covered her face.

"She was upset. About her girlfriend."

At last, Harper thought. At last one adult in this family referred to Cassie as Vivian's girlfriend. Too bad it was Doug.

"She didn't want to go to school," Doug continued. "She was crying. Something about a fight. Pam was insisting she go. Jesus, she was hysterical. She kept saying she hated her. *I hate that bitch.*"

Harper took a breath, trying. "Teenage girls and their mothers—"

"It was different," he interrupted. "Vivian was heartbroken. Your first heartbreak. You never forget it."

Harper nodded. *Dad understands,* Vivian had told her. *He loves Cassie. He even let her drive his Mustang.* Doug gave her something her mother kept failing to. And it meant the world.

Doug looked at Harper. "You know how Pam could be. You, of all people, know."

Harper guessed she did.

"But Vivian, she—it was bad," he said. "The way she sounded. She sounded broken. Wild. She sounded out of control."

And Harper could see it, hear it. She had. The way Vivian felt things so deeply, to the bone. The things she'd said the night before Pam had died: *You only care about yourself. Yourself and your Chanel purses and your new money and your new life. And your club.*

Pam saying, *One of us is coming out in a body bag.*

What are you trying to say?" Harper asked finally, afraid of the answer.

Doug set the glass down, a haunted look in his eyes. "I don't know."

"You didn't tell the police," Harper said.

"Of course not," he said. "Look, I know she'd never . . ."

Doug trailed off, resting his face in his hands.

Harper didn't say anything. She was remembering something. That time Pam had caught Vivian *with her hand literally in the cookie jar* before relocating it from the kitchen counter to the Tampax Pearl box, between the washer and the dryer.

She thought it was pizza money, Pam had said, laughing dryly.

She was thinking, too, of all Vivian's questions about the Club. *But, I mean, where's the money coming from?*

"You couldn't possibly think Vivian could . . ."

Neither of them wanted to finish the sentence.

"You didn't see Pam," Harper said. "Her face, how it looked. Her ruined, ruined face."

She felt her voice catch, stutter nearly into a sob.

"If you saw it," she finished, "you would know your daughter never could have done that."

"And *I* could?" Doug asked, eyes wide. "Harp, do you really think I could do that?"

Harper paused a moment, looking out the streaked window, the gray river beyond.

She was thinking about Vivian. How she always told Harper about even her minor skirmishes with her mother, but that morning, when she'd picked up that nervous, sparking wire of a girl in the school parking lot, Vivian had never said a word.

In fact, on the ride home, she'd been unusually quiet, remote, those big fuzzy mittens resting in her lap. Those mittens, so unlike Vivian, so girlish, cotton-candy pink.

And how quickly Vivian moved to action when they found Pam's body. How Harper couldn't even understand what she was seeing when Vivian was already on her knees, trying to make her mother breathe again.

"People," Harper said, echoing his favorite phrase, "are fucking inexplicable."

"Until they're utterly predictable," he finished. "They showed me the photos, Harper."

He couldn't speak for a second, his face in his hands.

"And, yes, I'm a scoundrel," he muttered, before letting his hands fall again. "A cheat. A coward. But I'm not . . . I'm not *that*."

"No," Harper said, shaking her head. "No. I don't believe any of this."

"I hope you're right," Doug said. "Vivian said they checked her alibi. Someone at the attendance office."

Harper felt her chest grow cold. Cassie. *I was there that morning,* she'd told Harper. *So everything's okay.*

A re you alright?" Doug said, looking at her.

Harper was standing now, her legs soft and strange. She had to leave, to get out of there.

"We don't know anything," she said, her voice stilted, not her own. "The police—we'll see what they've found. What they still could find. Prints, blood, hair. Neighbors. We have no idea what—"

"You have a lot of confidence in our little Mayberry R.F.D."

The apartment was so hot. The blinds ticking against the windows, the rising whirr of ancient ventilation. Crumpled newspaper sections shuddering to life. Nothing felt right.

"I have to go," Harper said, stepping backward, nearly stumbling on the sofa edge.

"Harper," Doug said, "listen to me. I didn't do this. I—"

"I have to go," Harper repeated, trying to catch her breath. When did the apartment get so dark? Michigan winters, four P.M. and everything starts to go dark.

"Harper, one last thing—"

"Good luck, Doug," she said, not wanting him to touch her, moving swiftly to the door.

"Maybe," Doug said, more gravely now, "you should be more worried about yourself."

"I'm not," Harper said. "I have an alibi. I have nothing to hide."

"Nothing to hide," Doug said, rising too now, "except that club of yours. You can't honestly think that thing is legal, can you?"

"You don't know what you're talking about."

"Did you ever think maybe everyone's looking in the wrong place?" he said. "That it's not about trust funds and this goddamned endless divorce, but about that pyramid scheme your sister's running?"

Harper looked at him. Demon Doug was back. "That's not what it is."

But Doug just shook his head. "We'll see how the police define it."

"Is that a threat?" Harper asked.

"No," Doug said "I'm just saying—we all have secrets, Harper. All of us."

But did you really forget how she could be? Doug had asked her. *Her judgment. Her high and mighty judgment. . . . You know what I mean.*

Of course she knew.

Harper, Pam had said when everything was falling apart with Leigh, *do you really want to break up a family? Is that what you want?*

It was near the end of Pam and Doug's marriage and maybe that explained it, the shrillness in Pam's tone, the horror on her face.

Harper came to her—desperate, frantic—asking for the money for Leigh.

Pam, she needs it or her husband will take her kid away.

But Pam kept shaking her head as Doug watched from the sofa.

It's not that I don't want to help you, Harper. I do. But Leigh has a family. She— I can't be a part of that.

Instantly, Harper had regretted ever sharing anything with Pam about Leigh, all the drinking and deceit, the hours Harper was left waiting for her in parking lots, diners, and dive bars deep in Macomb County, that motel near the airport. *She's a wife and a mother,* Pam had insisted, clucking her tongue. *Let her find her own way out of what she's done.*

It was the only time Harper had ever cried in front of her sister and she could tell it made her uncomfortable, confused.

You're so self-righteous, Harper had said. *You think your life is so perfect, that nothing could ever happen. I can't wait until it does.*

But Pam was unmoved. Hurt and unmoved, disappearing into her bedroom.

I can't wait until it does.

It was only when Harper had left, already in her minivan, catching her breath, pulling herself together, that the knock came on the window and it was Doug, telling her to meet him that night, at Dawn Donuts. He'd have the money, cash if she wanted. *My life hasn't been perfect,* he said. *And I may be an SOB, but I'm still a romantic.*

He'd given her the fifty thousand that Pam wouldn't. He'd understood what Pam couldn't, or refused to try. That was something. It wasn't nothing.

Pam hadn't given her the money and Doug had. Was it that simple? You couldn't decide about a person, a loved one, based on the time they'd failed you, or the one weakness or limit they'd revealed.

Pam loved her, loved everybody. No person was ever just one thing.

28

Why didn't you tell me about the fight with your mom?

Harper sent the text, then waited, sitting in her minivan inside the massive RenCen parking structure.

It was a risk, but she took it. She felt like she was running out of time.

Her phone hummed. *Vivian.*

You told me when you love someone you should do anything for them, Vivian's text read. Or it means nothing.

Harper stared at it, not sure what Vivian meant, or didn't mean.

Yes, Harper texted back. I guess I did.

A beat, then Vivian again:

Meet me at Cassie's. Wait out front. Don't honk.

Harper pulled up in front of Cassie's duplex, the curtains shuddering in the front window.

Moments later, the front door opened and Harper saw a flare of pastel hair as, puffer open, Vivian charged across the lawn into the minivan.

Except it wasn't Vivian. It was Cassie, hoisting herself inside the minivan, a flutter of nerve and spirit. The giddy sugared Bath & Body Works smell.

"She won't come out," Cassie said, rubbing her hands together, pressing them against the vents. "Her dad called and she's upset."

"I'm just trying to find out what happened," Harper said.

"I know," Cassie said, not quite looking at Harper. "But she doesn't want to talk to you."

Something in Cassie's tone seemed off, different. All her liveliness muted.

"Her dad," Cassie said. "You all keep coming for him."

Harper looked at her. Sweet Cassie suddenly didn't seem so sweet.

"I'm not coming for anyone, Cassie."

"I thought you were helping her," she said, looking at Harper at last. "I thought you were on our side."

"Of course I'm on—"

"Her dad, he sees her. He really *sees* her. That counts for a lot."

"I know it does," Harper said, her voice cracking. "Believe me, I do."

Cassie blew on her hands. Harper looked at them, red and trembling.

"Where are your mittens?" Harper blurted.

Cassie let her hands fall to her lap. "Inside."

Harper nodded, thinking. Staring at Cassie's cold, cold hands.

"Can I ask you a question?"

Cassie looked back at the house, the front window, the curtain twitching. "Okay," she said, hesitantly.

"Those mittens Vivian was wearing," she said. "The morning her mom . . . Were they yours?"

She could nearly picture it, Cassie tugging them off her hands to cover Vivian's battered ones. Mittens to hide torn-up nails because

Vivian had already done something unfathomable by the time Harper picked her up at school.

Harper thought she might be sick.

Cassie didn't say anything, one hand covering the other.

"Because I've seen you wear those pink mittens many times," Harper said. "In fact, just a few weeks ago."

She could see it, so vividly it was like a piercing pain. Cassie waiting in her car, her hands on her steering wheel, like two Sno Balls nestled close.

"Everyone has those mittens," Cassie said, eyes darting at the house, its front window.

"Cassie, it's important," Harper started. "Did you give her those mittens that morning?" Then, remembering the rest: "Did you lie to the police about her being at school?"

There was a brief silence.

"Whatever you think," Cassie said finally, her eyes wide and desperate, "you're wrong. You know a few things and you think that means the big thing. But you're wrong."

Harper opened her mouth but said nothing. She was thinking, in some subterranean way, how lucky Vivian was. And Cassie. To have each other, and believe in each other so deeply, to believe in the "us" of them so deeply. It made her want to cry.

Cassie's arm jerked, her hand reaching for the door handle.

"I have to go now," she said. "She needs me."

"No," Harper said. "I need to talk to her. To both of you."

But Cassie was already sliding the door open, one sneaker landing on the footrest, then both slapping on the asphalt.

"Wait—"

"Don't worry," Cassie said, turning around. "I won't ever tell her."

"Tell her what?"

"What you thought," Cassie said, looking at her, the wind whipping her cottony hair. "That she could do that. I won't tell her."

"Cassie—" Harper said, her voice cracking.

"You're her favorite person, you know," Cassie said, backing away, up onto the lawn. "You're like her hero."

Harper nodded, her throat tightening.

As if on cue, the curtains jerked again and Vivian appeared in the window, her face pale and drawn.

Cassie stopped midway up the lawn.

"Can I ask you something?" she said, whirling around, shouting over the wind. "Vivian can't talk about any of it, but I've been wanting to ask, did they talk to that neighbor? The cops, I mean."

"Which neighbor?"

"I don't know. I saw her back there last week. Maybe she saw something that morning."

Harper felt something unlatch inside of her. "She? Are you sure?"

"I think so."

"Was she wearing a black parka and a . . ."

"Ski mask. Yeah. I figured she went outside to smoke, but it'd be pretty hard to smoke in a ski mask," Cassie said, laughing a little. A nervous laugh as she looked at Harper.

"I don't think that's a neighbor," Harper said, her hand reaching for the gear shift.

She was thinking back to something Sandy had said: *I keep seeing people in my yard. I see their feet in the morning frost.*

Could it have been the same person Harper had seen the week before? That Cassie had seen?

The streetlights flashed and Harper heard herself talking out loud, her brain hot, thoughts racing. She was thinking of those all-caps texts from Sue, the ones Sandy had shown her, phone curled in her sweaty little hand: ONE OF US TALKS, WE ALL GO DOWN. I WON'T LET THAT HAPPEN.

It was how Sue talked, the big drama of it. But the texts felt like screams now.

Maybe it was the way Sandy's hand trembled at the thought of what the other women—or Sue, at least—were capable of. And that knot of fear at the center of her face. Sandy seemed to live constantly in a crackle of tension you could almost feel like a physical thing, but was it ever like this? So scared she thought one of the women might have actually killed an animal and dropped it on her front porch as a warning? Remember, Sue's text demanded, what we promised.

It reminded her faintly of that final night, Pam waking her from her sleep, all that wild energy, as if springing from a cage. What had made Pam so agitated?

Was it anticipatory nerves about the court hearing, or something else?

She thought about all the ire at the party, Sue raging over Pam. *Someone,* she'd said, downing the last of her drink, *needs to teach her a lesson.*

That was when she remembered the dream that had woken Pam.

I ran over something. It was an animal. Something red, like one of those fox-faced dogs. Its teeth fell out like little pearls.

Something red, like a fox. Sue Fox.

29

here was no time, or it didn't feel like there was.

She tried to catch up Debra on everything, but it was hard to walk her through it and make her see what Harper now saw. That it didn't seem to be about Doug anymore, or Vivian either. (*Vivian?* Debra said, alarmed.) It was about the money. It was about the Club.

"So you're saying Doug made sure Pam missed the hearing, but that he had nothing to do with what came next? That she just happened to be murdered?"

"I am," Harper said. "Because there's something else."

"What?"

"I saw someone. At Pam's."

"What do you mean?"

"A few days before it happened. Someone was hurrying across the next yard. A person in a, well, a ski mask."

"What?" Debra said, a hot whisper. "Why didn't you tell—"

"It didn't mean anything at the time. Or even after, really. But Cassie saw him too. Except she thought it was a woman."

"Okay," Debra said, turning from her, reaching for her coffee. "But what does that mean, really? A random neighbor—"

"Who knew Pam had money in the house?" Harper said. "The Club. The women in the Club."

"Sue," Debra blurted.

"Including Sue," Harper said carefully.

"Why didn't I think of it?" Debra said, hand tight on her mug. "She was the one that was so angry at Pam that night. About her sponsoring that woman. And bringing in women who couldn't be trusted."

Someone, she'd said about Pam, *needs to take her down a notch. Someone needs to teach her a lesson.*

"Maybe Sue," Harper said cautiously. "Or one of the others. Maybe one of the new women."

"Like that Dana chick, the new one who came empty-handed. What do we really know about her?"

"Nothing other than I wouldn't want to be her ex."

"But you think whoever did it came for Pam's stash," Debra said. "That's what you're saying, right?"

"And Pam surprises them. She's not supposed to be home. She's supposed to be at court. So it's someone who knows about the hearing—"

"*Everyone* knew about the hearing," Debra said. "She was always talking about it. She mentioned it at the party."

"She did?" Harper said, though she wasn't surprised. "But Pam *is* home. And it all goes . . . wrong."

She thought suddenly of the sofa cushion.

The cushion had been in the basement, on the frenetic pink-and-lilac sofa from their childhood. How did it get in the kitchen?

Had the killer—*the murderer*—been in the basement first?

Because the killer—*the murderer*—had gone looking for the money they thought was there?

It was possible Vivian knew about the money hidden down there, in that Tampax Pearl box. And if Vivian knew, then Doug might too.

But it was also possible, maybe more possible, that it was someone in the Club.

They'd all talked about where they hid their money.

It's still in the cookie jar, Pam had confided to them at that party just a few weeks ago, *but the jar's now in the basement.*

It was a clue. It was, maybe, *the* clue.

But Pam's money—whoever did this, they took it?" Debra said. "The cookie jar?"

"No," Harper said. "I don't think so. It wasn't in the house."

It was time to tell her, she knew. So she explained about that night, after the party, Pam's hands covered with dirt, the way they dug so far into the cold earth.

She told her and, in telling her, it felt so vivid and real again. And now so much darker, Pam's cresting terror. *Is it gone, is it really gone?*

"It was as if Pam knew," Harper said. "Knew someone might come for her winnings."

Debra didn't say anything for a moment, looking down at her hands.

"Are you okay?" Harper asked, even as she felt it too. How frantic Pam had been that last night, but how undeniable too. That feeling radiating off her that she'd made it, her life was beginning, beginning at forty-two, and no one was going to take it from her.

"I just hate to think of it," Debra said softly. "It's so much worse somehow. Worse than Doug."

Harper nodded.

"I wish you'd told me," Debra said, eyes narrowing. "So many se-crets."

Harper sighed. It was just like Debra to say it. Always accusing Harper and Pam of confidences, of excluding her—even now. But somehow, this time, it didn't seem like an accusation. It seemed like something else. Like she wished she'd been a part of it, those last vital moments with her sister the night before she died.

"I'm sorry," Harper said. "I should've told you."

"I still think it's Doug," Debra said, wiping her face on her sleeve like a little girl.

Harper held her hand and knew something she should have known before. She knew that Debra needed to believe it was Doug. She had to, or even that it was Vivian or an intruder or anyone else at all. Because, as painful as that was, the alternative was even more so.

The alternative, the only one that made sense now, was that it was one of them. Someone in the Club. That they had made this thing, birthed this monster, and now their sister was gone, lost inside it. Lost to them forever. All that hunger, you had to pay the price.

Harper's phone was ringing. It was Mr. Bingham at the Hunt Club. "Sorry to intrude," he said, "but I wanted to make sure this was all okay with you."

"What was?"

"The meeting. In the clubhouse."

"What meeting?" Harper asked.

"Your friends. That little brunette lady kept insisting she has per-mission since she's a member. When I told her that we don't open the clubhouse after hours, she used a few choice words, then dropped your name."

"Sue Fox," Harper said. "When was this?"

"Just now," Mr. Bingham said. "The brunette and a herd of blond ladies filed into the clubhouse like it was Saks Fifth Avenue."

"I'm on my way," Harper said, gesturing to Debra to get her purse, her keys.

Harper supposed Sue thought it was the most discreet location. Not at anyone's home, not in a public place. After hours.

"Discreet," Debra muttered as they turned down Cook Road. "Like no one will notice the lights blazing from the clubhouse at eleven P.M. on a Sunday."

"What do you think she has in mind?" Harper asked, pulling into the side entrance.

"Judas," Debra hissed. "She's trying to cover her ass."

Harper seldom went into the clubhouse, not after Mrs. Calhoun reported her for dragging dirt into the dining room a decade ago. Mrs. Calhoun, who had been a friend of her parents', so close her mother even stayed with her for a few days after Mr. Calhoun dislocated his wife's shoulder, shoving her down the stairs. *She needs someone to hold her in the shower, to help her dress.* That was the first time Harper realized she was no longer a Bishop here. She was a service employee. The help.

But, as they entered the vestibule, all that went away and her childhood came flooding back. The Easter brunches, baskets heavy with pastel eggs from the hunt on the lawn ringed around their wrists. Countless summer Sunday dinners, hair stiff with chlorine, chasing her sisters in the coat room, sneaking old-fashioneds off the busboys' tray stands.

———————

N ot yet," Debra said, her hand on Harper's arm.

They hovered in the vestibule shadows, watching.

The women were arrayed around the stone fireplace in the Great Room. The very one they sang Christmas carols around when they were little girls, a garland of little girls, gingerbread crumbs crusted on their joined hands.

Arrayed like sorority sisters, they had the hectic, nervous energy of Rush Week, except now, instead of piling hoodies and puffers on the chintz sofa, it was camel and cashmere, Becky Schloss's mink, Jill Fleischer's new white lynx, which, apparently, had not been placed into cold storage after all.

The exception was Sandy, slumped in a wing chair, parka still on, her curls slack and dirty.

Poor Sandy, Harper thought. She was never cut out for the Club and she certainly wasn't cut out for this.

"We must remember what we pledged," Sue was saying, slipping off her lambskin gloves. "We all became a part of this for different reasons and those reasons are private, personal."

The women nodded in unison.

"And what we do together, in support of one another, is private too," Sue said. "We must never share with anyone outside this room, our circle. Remember our promise."

"Women trust," the women recited, "women give, women protect."

"But should we even be talking about this?" Sandy asked, squirming in her seat.

"This is a safe space," Sue said. "These clubhouse walls are seventeen inches thick."

"We need a plan," Beverly Linebaugh said. "We're all hearing rumors. I heard they seized Pam's address book, her day planner—"

Sue raised her hand to silence Beverly.

"Unfortunately," Sue said, "the tragic death of one of our members has made us vulnerable to prying eyes. I invited only the core members here tonight so we could prepare what to say in case investigators contact one or all of us."

A quiver of panic ran through the room.

"Sue, you told us your husband reviewed all our guidelines," Jill Fleischer said. "He's a CPA. That's what you said."

"And that Caroline's husband reviewed it," Beverly said. "And he said there was nothing to worry about."

"Ex-husband," Caroline said, fiddling nervously with her bracelets. "His specialty is copyright infringement, but he did review it."

"Do you think they've gone through Pam's phone records?" Beverly asked. "I bet they have. Texts. Emails."

"What matters here is that we're on the same page," Sue said. "You all have your talking points about the Club, its purpose. Female empowerment. Stick to them. And remember their priorities are not necessarily our priorities. Debra and Harper—it's best we distance ourselves from them. Because they may say things that put us at risk."

Hiding in the vestibule, Debra looked at Harper, eyes black.

"Jesus," Caroline said, shaking her head. "This is what happens when we invite women who are so . . . indiscreet. Pam's disgraceful ex-husband, that wild daughter of hers. Now we have to count on them to make sure we don't get arrested? Pam's mistakes become ours."

Before Harper could stop her, Debra charged forward into the room, making a beeline for Caroline.

"Shut your goddamned mouth about my sister," Debra said, Harper lunging for her arms, trying to hold her back.

All the women turned to face them. "I see what you're doing,"

Debra said to Sue. "Stoking division. Using what happened to my sister to take over everything. Why weren't we invited to this meeting?"

"You wanted us out," Sue insisted, hands on her hips. "You kicked us out of your house, you kicked us out of the funeral reception."

"I was protecting all of us," Debra said. "Do you really want the cops digging into our finances?"

Jill Fleischer shivered by the fireplace. "I had a friend in Oakland County," she said softly. "The IRS audited every member of their club. One of them was just charged with filing a false tax return."

"Did you read about those women in Grand Rapids?" Caroline asked, her voice so low Harper could hardly hear. "They went to prison. Conspiracy to commit to defraud the IRS, conspiracy to commit wire fraud—"

"Wire fraud?" Becky said, suddenly more attentive. It was her husband, of course, whose clients were convicted of wire fraud two years ago, leading to their own audit, leading to bankruptcy and to, well, here. The Club.

"Should we call our attorneys?" Beverly asked, one hand curled around her wrist.

Everyone looked at one another.

"Should we have drinks first?" Caroline piped in, and everyone laughed nervously.

"I have Valium," Jill said, opening her purse so swiftly it emptied on the floor, a tumble of prescription bottles, lipstick, crushed cigarettes.

A loud clang echoed through the room.

Sue, her hand curled around the blow poke by the fireplace, was rattling it against the grate—so loud Sandy covered her ears.

"We need to focus, ladies," Sue said, swinging the blow poke at her side. "The bottom line: There's nothing for them to find. But what matters most is that we keep our mouths shut. So I'm asking you to reach out to those you recruited and remind them in strong terms to be discreet, to remember what we all promised."

"Snitches get stitches," Becky Schloss said dryly.

"But these new recruits—they haven't run the Wheel yet," Beverly said. "They put in their five and got nothing in return. How loyal will they be?"

"That's why we need to tread carefully with the virgins," Sue said. "Which brings me to Dana. The new one Pam brought in."

"You mean the one out on bail?" Caroline said wryly. "Why wouldn't she be trustworthy?"

"You said you talked to her," Debra said to Sue. "You said you had her locked down."

Harper looked at Debra, surprised. Maybe she hadn't told her sister everything, but Debra definitely hadn't told her she was still talking, strategizing with Sue.

"I did talk to her. It seems Pam didn't bother to do her research on Dana," Sue said, her jaw tightening. "Or she might have learned Dana's brother works for the DOJ."

"*What?*" Harper said. The women exchanged glances.

"Who told you that?" Debra asked.

"Dana," Sue said. "Yesterday. She showed up at my house. I'm guessing she wants money. To keep her mouth shut."

The room fell silent for a minute.

"What does the Justice Department have to do with us?" Jill asked, nervously stroking her lynx.

"Nothing," Sue insisted. "It's just some bullshit white-collar-crime unit. They like to poke their noses into places they don't belong."

Harper looked at Sue, thinking. Sue was always calculating. She was calculating now. It wouldn't surprise her if it turned out Sue had talked to the DOJ herself, the county prosecutor herself, the detectives herself.

"Well, we have to give it to her, don't we?" Beverly said softly. "Money. To this Dana woman. If we all pitch in—"

"This is bullshit. Fuck the DOJ. We're not criminals," Becky insisted, a hard edge to her voice. "This is our money to do with as we please."

Harper couldn't listen to it anymore. None of it mattered to her anymore.

The anxious whirl of voices.

"I don't like what you're suggesting," Harper said to Sue. "About Pam. That she brought in someone who—some kind of rat."

"I'm saying no such thing," Sue said. "But we all know Pam was playing fast and loose with the rules. Letting anyone into the group. Poaching recruits."

"We all know *that*? Who knows that?" Harper demanded. "You? Maybe you're just jealous because she was better at it than you. Than all of you."

Debra's eyes lit up as if she suddenly remembered why they were here to begin with. She turned to Sue.

"Where were you Monday morning, Sue?" Debra asked, marching toward her. Getting in her face.

"Deb," Harper cautioned. Something told her this was the wrong time. The wrong play.

"What does that mean?" Sue said, forcing a laugh. "What are *you* implying? That I'm some kind of killer?"

All the women averted their eyes, the moment so heavy and confusing. Debra had gone too far too fast.

"Debra's just saying everyone better have their alibis ready," Harper said. "I was in the stalls. Debra was halfway to Canada. Where were all of you?"

———————

Suddenly, there was a low moaning sound.

For a second, Harper thought it was one of the barn cats mewling outside.

But it was Sandy, sliding off the wing chair and moving toward them, slinging her beat-up Dooney & Bourke bucket bag behind her.

"I want . . ." she said, "to talk about the rabbit."

Harper wanted to roll her eyes and throttle Sandy. *Not the rabbit thing, Sandy.*

"What?" Sue said impatiently. "What rabbit?"

"The rabbit one of you bitches left on my porch."

As they all watched, Sandy turned her bucket bag upside down and shook it onto one of the mahogany side tables.

Out tumbled a pristine rabbit head, its ears soft and pearly lilac, its eyes red as cherry sours.

There were gasps, a strangled yelp from Beverly Linebaugh.

"God," Beverly said. "What happened?"

"I bet it was an owl," Becky said. "One of them got my neighbor's kitten . . ."

"Sometimes a snowplow will . . ." Jill Fleischer started, her hand over her mouth.

"There was no blood at all," Sandy said, eyes wide, "just frost everywhere, like a wedding veil. I took a picture. I have proof."

"You don't really need a picture," Caroline said, looking down at the rabbit head, its red-jellied eyes, "when you have the head right there."

"You think one of us did *that*?" Sue said, her lips pursed in disgust. "Why?"

"Sandy," Harper said wearily, "I think you—"

"It's bullying," Sandy whispered, sinking back down into the wing chair. "Whoever did it. It's terrorism."

The fireplace whooshed and the rabbit head skittered off the table's edge, landing in Sandy's lap.

"Jesus Christ," Sue said. Then, turning to the women, "We can't let her near those cops."

The women kept exchanging looks. Debra caught Harper's eye. *This is bad.*

A faint odor wafted from the rabbit's head.

Sue looked at Harper. "She's yours. Your recruit."

Harper turned to Sandy, the rabbit's head balanced between her knees. "Let's go, okay?"

"I'm sorry," Sandy said, looking up at her. "I'm sorry. Nothing makes sense anymore."

Harper had dealt with many unstable souls in her time. You don't spend late nights at Club 500 or the Wooden Nickel or Rustic Cabins—or Chi O for that matter—without seeing sad women unspooling themselves, unfurling their sorrows and confusion. Crying in bathroom stalls. Smashing bottles, glasses, jukebox plexiglass, windshields.

But Sandy seemed a different kind of fragile, her hand shaking on her car keys, dropping them once, twice, three times.

They stood in the dark parking lot a long time.

Harper tried to tell her it was going to be okay. IRS agents weren't going to show up at her house. The DOJ wasn't going to knock down her door. She wasn't going to land in prison for wire fraud. Things Harper didn't know were true, but she knew to say them.

At first, Debra stood with her, arms wrapped around herself, the wind—so cold it felt like glass, like tiny chips of glass against your skin.

"Sandy, you're acting like a lunatic," Debra was saying. "Get your head right."

A sternness in Debra's voice that reminded Harper of early child-hood, bossy Debra, forever shushing her little sisters, who only laughed, giggling under the covers at Dumb Deb, poking their Barbie dolls against each other, refusing to play nice.

D eb," Harper said, handing her the keys to the minivan, "how about you head home? I'll have Patrick pick me up or something."

"I don't think that's a good idea," Debra said.

But Harper could see Debra was making it worse, Sandy shrinking under Debra's big voice, her irritation.

"Sandy, how about I drive you home?" Harper asked, her arm around Sandy, walking her away from Debra. "Get you settled. Your kids—"

"My kids," Sandy whispered, slumped against her car door. "My kids. My kids sure miss their dad."

"I know," Harper said, even if she didn't. She wasn't even sure how many kids Sandy had—was it two? "How about you give me your keys?"

Sandy nodded but didn't move, her bucket purse hanging open, empty now of the rabbit head (Sue promised to take care of it, which surely meant she'd leave it to a member of the janitorial staff to handle). There was still that smell, meaty and sulfurous.

Harper waited a long moment. She noticed Debra hadn't left yet, lingering in Harper's minivan, a worried look on her face.

"Harper," Sandy said at last, staring at Harper. "We can go now."

H arper drove slowly, the car unfamiliar to her, its steering loose and unpredictable.

At first, Sandy didn't say anything, gazing out at the lonesome stretch along Kerby Field, the ghostly baseball diamond, its silver spoked batting cage like a giant spider.

"I guess I was just having a bad spell," Sandy said, a vague smile on her face. "I've been on some medication. My doctor, he says I'm too high-strung. He— Anyway, I feel better now."

Bad spell, like their mother used to call it. A phrase that carried within it everything from too many of those diet pills that made her heart feel funny, to a four-martini dinner party, perhaps to some private horror she never ever would share.

"I'm glad," Harper said. "This is a hard time."

"This reminds me of driving home from the lacrosse tournaments together," she said. "Remember? The bus rides from Shaker Heights, Columbus. Those were my favorite times. I never wanted to go home. Nothing good ever happened at home."

Harper didn't know, or remember, what home was like for teenage Sandy. There was something in the back of her head, something about a brother and how they had to take him out of school. He'd disrupted some school assembly, insisting that the voices from the PA speakers were telling him things, whispering secrets to him.

"And that bus ride back from Stoney Creek," Sandy said. "We listened to your Walkman, one headphone for each ear. Remember? We held hands inside my letter jacket."

Sandy was looking at her, flushed, a little shy. Harper wondered: *Did she have a crush on me?* The kind of question you asked yourself a hundred times a day, back then.

"Sure I remember," Harper lied.

She didn't recall Sandy specifically, that time so full of feeling, all the girls so close after the heady experience of the game, the faraway town, the sneaky sips of Jack Daniel's from someone's pilfered pint. She was still figuring things out back then, even as, deep down, she knew. But it was really all about Stephanie Modelli and her French braids and the three beauty marks below her collarbone that Harper liked to rest her fingertips on. Stephanie wore thin gold rings on her fingers and one with a fat pearl that rolled. She'd roll it between Harper's thighs, rolling it to just the spot, beneath her underpants, that made her see a scatter of lights, feel a tight throb she never wanted to end.

"I felt so safe," Sandy said, looking at the road again. "It was the safest I ever felt."

Harper understood then that for Sandy the memory was romantic, but in a way beyond sex or desire. Maybe Harper taking her hand on that bus stood in for something else in Sandy's jumbled, frightened mind. The promise of belonging, of security, of connection.

"So when you came to the library all those months ago," Sandy said, "it was like you took my hand again. And saved me."

Harper looked at her but didn't say anything.

She thought of Sandy that day at the circulation desk, her desperation. And at the casino downtown. Her face lit by the slot machine, her body tense, excited.

We always want other people's desires to be simple and defined—sex, love, money—but in Harper's experience, it never worked out that way. There were all kinds of wanting. And the seduction of the Club was that it promised so much. Whatever you wanted and couldn't have—the Club could give it to you.

The road was darker after they crossed Mack Avenue, the cracked roads near the freeway. The wheel jerked in Harper's hands, the tires pulling right.

"What's that sound?" Harper asked, a funny rattle shuddering through the car.

"I wonder," Sandy whispered as Harper pulled over under a streetlamp, turning the ignition off.

"Maybe that pothole," Harper said, opening the door, the wind pressing against her, so cold it seemed to cut her face.

She moved quickly around the car to look at the rear tires.

The lights bright and the road empty.

Something was wrong right away, so wrong she couldn't believe she hadn't noticed it when they got in the car.

The smell so strong now, she covered her nose and mouth with her arm.

Bending down, she saw something immediately, a strip of fur on the rear tire and a flash of something—a carcass caught in the undercarriage and wheel wells. Its head gone.

Once, a few years ago, she'd found a cottontail, its throat torn, at the Hunt Club. Its limpness, its struck beauty, it made her want to cry. This was so much worse.

"Sandy," Harper said, slowly realizing, "about that rabbit . . ."

"Oh," Sandy said, opening her door slowly, walking toward Harper, her eyes wide and glazed. "Oh, no. Oh, no."

"It's okay," Harper said. "I'm sure it was an accident. They dart out so fast. I'm sure you didn't realize you'd done it. . . ."

Sandy nodded loosely, like her neck couldn't quite hold her head.

"I wasn't sure it happened," she said. "That it was real."

Harper looked at her, a sickly feeling. Everything was starting to make some kind of sense even if she couldn't quite grasp it yet.

"Do you have something to clean some of this off?" Harper said.

Sandy nodded again. "Some old towels. In the trunk."

Harper walked back to the front seat and leaned inside to pop the trunk.

She could hear Sandy mumbling, her voice so strangely childlike.

"It wasn't supposed to go that way," Sandy was saying. "You need to understand that. But it was dark and she didn't see me."

"It's okay," Harper said, lifting the trunk all the way up. In the back, she spotted an old beach towel with a faded Tweety Bird. "It happens. We should probably call—"

"She wasn't supposed to be there," Sandy continued. "She came out of nowhere at the top of the stairs and she scared me so bad. And then she hit me with it."

Harper turned and looked at her. "Sandy, what are you talking about . . ."

Sandy tilted her head toward her, and under the streetlamp, Harper could see it. A scabbing hole between her springy curls right on the crown of Sandy's head.

"Maybe she thought I was a burglar," Sandy added. "Because she hit me. The hammer came down right on my head."

Harper was listening but not listening. She was looking at something resting under the Tweety Bird towel. Something glinting under the streetlamp.

At first, she thought it was the tire iron. But it wasn't.

It was the mason's hammer. With her father's initials. *wBE*.

"It all happened so fast. I grabbed it from her just like this," Sandy said, her arm darting past Harper, grasping the hammer handle in her hands. "I hit her and down she went. And then I had to keep on hitting her."

"No, no, no," Harper said, trying to keep her voice steady even as her heart ricocheted in her chest. "Sandy, what are you telling me?"

"I'm telling you about Pam," Sandy said, staggering back with the hammer in both hands. "It was dark and I was only defending myself. She hit me first, remember. So I hit her. And then she popped up again, so I had to keep hitting her, over and over, to keep her down."

"Sandy, why would you ever . . ." Harper started. But she couldn't even say it. She could only think of Pam's face after. Loose and ruined. Thick with blood.

"I needed money," Sandy said flatly. "And we all knew about that cookie jar. She wasn't supposed to be home. All I had to do was go down there and get it. But then she hit me in the dark. I have to defend myself."

The wind gusted up, elm trees shuddering, the distant whine of a car somewhere, and Sandy looked suddenly exhausted, her arm dropping, the hammer hanging from her hand.

"Sandy, just give me the hammer and we'll talk," Harper was saying, even as she was discreetly scanning the dark trunk for a flashlight, a tire iron, something, anything.

"Don't move," Sandy said dully, her eyes unfocused, her hand tightening around the hammer again. "I have to defend myself."

Then, once more, "Don't move."

Harper staggered back as Sandy raised her arms above her head, the hammer glinting under the streetlamp.

That's when Harper saw the flash of Sandy's parka zipper—a sizzle of purple. A roar of recognition. She didn't need to see the ski mask to know.

The hammer came down once, slicing through the air, the sharp end landing hard in Harper's arm as she reeled back, her foot catching on the front of the tire.

The hammer came up again just as a pair of searing headlights illuminated everything, Sandy's face made white, featureless, her eyes burning as a vehicle seemed to leap up from the dip in the road.

"Stop!"

Harper heard her sister's voice, the lights blinding her as Debra leapt out of Harper's minivan and crashed against Sandy, knocking her down, the two of them rolling, grappling for the hammer.

Harper frantically turned to the trunk, now illuminated, a tire iron wedged in one corner.

Grabbing it, she swiveled around just in time to see Sandy swing the hammer against Debra's face, her cheek instantly heaving blood.

The sight seemed to stun them both and Sandy fell back on the ground, Debra jumping on top of her, plunging her thumb into Sandy's eye, a squealing sound Harper knew she'd never forget.

Leaping forward, Harper swung the tire iron against Sandy's back, the hammer skittering on the ground, straight into Debra's outstretched hands.

The crack was loud, thundering as Debra swung the hammer, missing Sandy and landing straight on the asphalt, sparking.

Like a jack-in the-box, Sandy sprang to her knees again, lunging for Harper, knocking her flat on her back, the tire iron leaping from Harper's hand.

"Harper!" Debra called out.

But Sandy was already on top of Harper, pinning her down with both knees, her red hands gripped around her throat, fingers punched against her windpipe until Harper saw darkness, then stars.

But then she heard the sound, a whir like the spinning slot machine, as Debra rose behind Sandy, swinging the hammer sidewise, whizzing through the air, its steel head landing with a whistling pop smack in the side of Sandy's curly head.

Sandy's body slumped on top of Harper, then rolled, her eyes meeting Harper's one last time before her skull hit the pavement with a muted crack.

Those eyes, Sandy's eyes, for the first time in maybe ever, were neither frightened nor desperate. Those eyes, nearly serene. It was over now, it was done.

———

For several seconds, Harper and Debra stood, breathless and ragged, looking down at Sandy, flat on her back, lashes blinking, blood pooling beneath her. Her mouth opening and closing, like a little girl blowing bubbles.

Finally, Harper, hands shaking, reached for her phone.

"Yes," she said to the operator, "this is an emergency."

Debra sank slowly to her knees, holding the side of her face, dizzy from all the blood.

"It was dark," Sandy whispered. "Debra, it was so dark."

30

The black, ice-ridged street swarmed with life.

The flaring reds and blues of the ambulance, two police cars, a dozen or more neighbors shivering in flannel robes, puffers thrown over plaid pajamas, ankles red with cold stuffed in slippers. The skitter and static of the police radio. *Dispatch, looking like a 1302, ambulance on site. . . . Next car in, if they could block eastbound traffic Mack and Brys. . . .*

Later, Harper would only remember it in flashes. The police officers covering their noses and mouths as they peered under the car. Detective Conlan, face drawn, asking her question after question as she leaned against his car, one hand on her bandaged arm. Junior swinging the plastic evidence bag heavy with the hammer. The soft gauze wound around Debra's cheek, how it kept unfurling, like a ribbon wheel spinning loose, curling at her feet.

Perry, stepping out of his car, his face bristled with fatigue, the terror in his eyes as he moved toward them, his hands shaking at his sides. The way he hurtled toward Debra, crying out, and the way she watched him, something lost in her eyes. Everything they'd been through in the last few hours. Harper didn't know if her heart would ever slow down.

She's in critical condition," Detective Conlan told them. "We should know more soon."

It seemed impossible that Sandy was still alive, or even more that she could ever be dead, so vital, terrifyingly so, springing at them again and again like a windup toy.

At the police station, Harper and Debra sat with the detectives in separate rooms, telling the story again and again. Each time she told it, Harper felt it slipping away from her. It became the story of what happened, solidified, even the words and phrases feeling comfortable on her tongue: *She swung the hammer down on Deb's face and . . .*

She wouldn't stop, there was no stopping her.

I think she would have killed us both.

It had felt that way and somehow still felt possible, her chest pounding so hard she ached inside.

"It's just too much," Perry was saying to the police chief as Harper came out, her mouth burnt from all the coffee, her legs weak. "They should have an attorney with them anyway."

"If you want," the police chief was saying, "but I don't think that's necessary."

No one seemed to doubt their story and even when Detective Conlan said he wanted them back in the morning, there was a gentleness in his voice. Or maybe it was just exhaustion.

But something was hanging heavily in the back of Harper's head. A feeling that it wasn't over and they weren't through it yet.

Maybe it was because, as she stepped outside with Debra and Perry, she found herself stumbling backward, sure that Sandy would appear from around the corner, from the dark stretches of the parking lot, moving straight toward them with that same adrenalized relentlessness, her head dented and heavy with black blood, their father's hammer swinging clumsily at her side.

I t was just before three A.M. when they returned to the house. Patrick was still asleep, blissfully unaware. No one had called Vivian, still at Cassie's.

"Let's just wait until the morning," they all kept saying. No one knew what to say yet. It was too baroque, too extreme to feel true, even though it was true, it did happen.

The kitchen lights were on, the refrigerator door left open, leaking on the floor.

"I left in a hurry," Perry said. "I was so damned scared."

Reaching to close the door, he slipped, nearly falling.

Debra, her face hollowed out, helped him gain his footing, both of them trembling, and it became a funny kind of dance as their sneakers skidded on the linoleum.

Harper started to laugh as Perry, ever the ham, swept Debra fully into his arms as if to twirl her.

Cheek to bandaged cheek, they danced for Harper, Debra laughing, too, a kind of antic squeak, her throat strained from all the talking, all the screaming. Calling out, fighting for their lives.

N o one knew what to do next, how they would ever sleep.
It was Perry who suggested a drink. It felt forbidden somehow, like they were teenagers again, sneaking tilted pours from their parents' bottles of V.O. and Glenfiddich.

The cabinet was nearly bare, only a few inches of bottom-shelf vodka left, but Debra found a nearly rancid can of orange concentrate in the freezer and they made screwdrivers, which felt nearly right, the acid tang, their hands sticky, a mere hour or two before rosy-thumbed dawn.

"Your wife saved me," Harper found herself saying as Perry filled her glass. "She saved my goddamned life."

"That makes two of us," Perry said, smiling through his four o'clock shadow.

"I just had a bad feeling," Debra said. "I couldn't just let you go off with her. Not after how she was acting."

"You saved me," Harper repeated, her heart going again at the memory.

Debra reached for Harper's hand, their fingers locking momentarily, then she pulled away, drinking long and deep from her tall glass.

Soon enough, Perry fell asleep on his leather recliner, snuggled under the prickly tartan blanket their parents used to take to U of M games.

Harper and Debra returned to the kitchen to try for one more round, the last stinging drops of the Smirnoff.

Debra decided the screwdrivers would taste better frozen, yanking an ancient, avocado-colored blender off the top of the refrigerator.

"Won't that be too loud?" Harper asked, recognizing the blender as their mother's, its buttons forever stained from long-ago grasshoppers.

She wondered if she was the only sister who hadn't pillaged their mother's house after she died.

"You're probably right," Debra said, sighing, sitting down again.

They were quiet for a moment.

"I just hate to think of Pam so scared," Harper whispered.

"I know," Debra said. "Finding crazy Sandy in her basement. Can you imagine?"

"No," Harper said. Something was hovering over her ear, a thought she couldn't quite hold on to.

"There might be one more bottle in the garage," Debra said, shaking the jug over Harper's glass. Adding, with a wink, "Perry always stashes something under his tool bench."

"I'll get it," Harper said, rising.

She wanted the squeak of fresh air, the house so hot, overstuffed.

The garage door was open a foot or two so Fitzie could slink in or out. And there he was, curled in the corner on a pile of clothes ready for Goodwill.

His soft wheezing so soothing, Harper made her way through the rakes and snow shovels, paint cans and half-frozen sacks of potting soil to Perry's tool bench, its plywood top piled high with recycling, stacks of grease-stained cardboard bound with fraying twine.

Behind the pegboard she found Perry's Dewar's and, amusingly, a tower of Dixie cups like you might see at the dentist, but as she tried to retrieve the bottle, the pile of flattened boxes scattered to the floor like giant playing cards. Stroh's, Vernor's, Kirkland—

It was only when she bent down, bottle under her arm, that she saw the Tampax Pearl box, pancake-flat.

A coincidence, she thought at first, her palm resting on the sapphire cardboard, the familiar illustration: a string of fat pearls.

Maybe an old box, maybe a used box like you pick up at the warehouse store.

Except for the telltale bleach stain from when it sat in Pam's basement, between the washer and the dryer.

It was dark, Sandy had whispered, lying on the cold asphalt a few hours ago, her skull sunken, blood spreading beneath her. *Debra, it was so dark.*

Debra, she'd said, *it was so dark.*

Without stopping to think, Harper carried it back into the kitchen, Debra looking up, her eyes on the Dewar's.

"Thank god," she said, extending her hand. "Is Scotch and orange juice a thing? I don't think I can drink that straight. It reminds me too much of senior prom."

She laughed, was still laughing even as Harper slapped the cardboard box on the kitchen table.

"Is this your way of telling me you need a tampon?" Debra said. But her fingers were trembling as they curled around the Dewar's neck.

"*She came out of nowhere at the top of the stairs,*" Harper said, reciting Sandy's words. "That's what Sandy said. How did she know to look in the basement?"

Debra looked at her, her jaw tightening.

"She guessed," Debra said with a shrug. "Or Pam told her. Pam was always telling people things she shouldn't—"

"Someone told her," Harper said. "Someone told Sandy that all she had to do was go down there and get it. If only that someone hadn't told her the wrong time."

"Sue," Debra said, the Dewar's tipping in her hand. "Sue Fox, then."

"I don't think so," Harper said.

They both watched the bottle fall, roll across the tabletop before Harper caught it with her hand. Harper was thinking of so many things.

"She was just supposed to get the money," Debra said finally, her eyes dark. "Only the twenty-five from Pam's last win. We were going to split it. Pam wasn't supposed to be home. She was just supposed to get the money."

Harper sank down into her chair.

It couldn't be true. It couldn't.

"Harper, you need to understand. Pam poached Maggie Mueller. I'd been working Maggie for months, every Sunday at church. All through the blood drive we ran. And Pam swept in one Sunday—the first time she'd set foot in Christ Church in years—and poached her. She poached two of my book club members—"

"*So what?*" Harper said. "Who fucking cares, Deb? Jesus—"

"And you," Debra said, her voice shaking. "She poached you."

Harper looked at her.

"It was my idea and she just took it," Debra said, that familiar aggrieved look on her face. "I knew you had debts. They were holding you back. We talked about it and then . . ."

Harper didn't say anything. She remembered what Debra had confided the day before: *I should tell you: I wanted to invite you first. Pam said it wasn't a good idea.*

I wanted to invite you first.

"That was my money," Debra whispered. "Mine."

Harper looked at her coolly. "Okay, Deb," she said. "Then why the hell didn't you just ask her for it?"

Debra looked at her, her eyes dark and lost. "It was all so easy for her. Everything was always so easy for her."

Harper said nothing. She'd heard it before. Or felt it. How Debra looked at Pam. The rising-star husband, the luxurious house, the galas, the picture-perfect family. *Fuck me,* Debra had said, touring Pam and Doug's luxurious home. *Is it okay to hate my sister?*

But that was all years ago. And nothing since had been easy for anyone.

"So you had Sandy do it," Harper said, finally. "And cut her in."

"She was in trouble," Debra pleaded. "You know she couldn't help herself. The slots, she couldn't kick them."

Harper remembered begging Debra to pick Sandy up at the casino that time. She was at work, she couldn't do it, and Deb saved the day.

"So you told Sandy where the money was," Harper said. "It was just a matter of when. And she'd been casing the house. I saw her. Cassie saw her. Hiding in the backyard."

Debra looked at her. "I didn't know that. I didn't know she was so . . . unstable."

"But *you* had an alibi for Monday," Harper said. "And Pam was supposed to be in court. So you told Sandy that Monday was the day."

Debra nodded. "But it wasn't there, and Pam was. Because of Doug. Demon Doug."

Harper shook her head. It was true, but what did it matter?

"She called me right after," Debra continued. "I was in the car with Perry, already across the border. I couldn't say anything. I couldn't . . ."

She explained how Sandy was waiting for her back at the house. How she made her wait in the garage until Perry was changing to go to the police station.

How Sandy was fresh out of the shower when she arrived, her hair soaking wet, but brown blood still under her fingernails. Debra saw it and was sick.

How Sandy had the Tampax box in her arms like it still might yield something, like if Debra dug deep enough inside, the slick-wrapped tampons tumbling to the floor, the cookie jar or the money might still be at the bottom.

Sandy told her how she was coming up the basement stairs when she heard a gasp and then a blow, like something had fallen on her head.

She could feel her legs crumple beneath her, one hand gripping the stairwell. It was only then that she saw her, Pam's blond hair glowing at the top of the stairs, the hammer in her hands like a baseball bat. How frightened Pam was, then how surprised Pam was to see her—*Is that Sandy?*—peering down the steps.

Oh, no, Sandy, she'd said, her arm dropping to her side. *I'm so sor—*

It was only then that Sandy felt the warm wetness coming down her forehead. And the blood scared her and when Pam extended her hand to help her up the steps, she charged at her, knocking the hammer free, knocking Pam down. The hammer now in her own hand and swinging it, swinging it. The more Pam squirmed, the harder and faster the hammer fell, like it was its own thing, not in her hand but its own thing.

"She couldn't explain it," Debra said. "The shock of Pam hitting her. The fear, the adrenaline shooting through her. It was almost like she couldn't believe she'd done it."

Not until she saw Pam on the kitchen floor. She ran downstairs and grabbed the sofa cushion, something, anything to cover her. She couldn't look at her. All the blood, in hot gashes. Pam's eyes open like a doll.

Then Debra started crying, her hands covering her face. The sound was a sound Harper had never heard from her sister, an animal sound, full of sharp pain.

"I told her to get rid of it," Debra whispered. "The hammer. Drop it in the lake, the sewer. Sandy could never do anything right."

Harper didn't know what to say. It was too big to say anything.

"Maybe," she said finally, her fingers running along the cardboard ridge of the Tampax box, "you didn't need to recycle this."

Debra almost smiled and then they both fell silent.

———

The phone started ringing on the wall behind Debra but neither of them moved.

"Harper, I need you to understand," Debra said. "I didn't need a Lexus. A fur coat. I had real reasons."

"Okay," Harper said.

"These medical bills—you never get out from under them," Debra said. "What do you do? Say, *Don't try that treatment*? *We can't afford those drugs?*"

Harper looked at her. She wanted to take her sister's hand but couldn't.

I just need this all to work, Debra had said at that last party, a dozen hours before Pam died. How she didn't know how they were going to pay for the latest chemo round. Harper had listened, sympathized, but she guessed she'd never understood how desperate Debra had been.

It's our secret now, Harper," Debra whispered, almost like a prayer. "Like all the secrets you and Pam always had. This is ours now."

They could hear Perry stirring in the other room. Harper pictured him untangling himself from the blanket, tripping off the recliner, stumbling toward the cordless in the living room.

"Hello?" Perry said. "Yes. . . . No, they just said she was in, uh, critical condition. . . . Oh, she did? Is she fully conscious? . . . Well, okay. . . . Yes, we will. Thanks, Detective."

Harper and Debra looked at each other, their hands on the table between them, the wood sticky with Scotch.

"Deb?" Perry called out.

They could hear the floor squeaking, Perry walking to the kitchen, his socks shushing on the carpet.

Harper could hear her heart beating, and Debra's.

"Deb?" Perry called out again. "Sandy woke up. She's alive. She's alive and, uh, talking, I guess."

When his face peeked around the corner, Debra wouldn't turn to look at him.

Neither sister could look at him, move, or say anything.

31

Six weeks later

It looks different," Vivian said as they stood on El Dorado Drive, peering up the short slope of lawn to the house.

"Bigger or smaller?" Harper asked, Fitzie leaning against her legs, letting out skittering barks.

"Both," Vivian said.

Harper knew what she meant. It did look different, but she couldn't say why or how. Maybe it was the overgrown lawn, a half-dozen blue plastic newspaper sleeves strewn along the front path. Or maybe it was the new, swollen buds ringleting the sweeping elm tree behind the house, some scattering across the roof itself.

Or maybe it was the absence of things: the screen door constantly screeching on its rusty hinges, the low, heavy-lidded thump of Vivian's music, the forever fogged windows from all the energy—Pam's energy—churning inside.

"Do we have to go through everything?" Vivian asked, moving to bite a nail, then letting her arm fall again.

"No," Harper said, reaching out to stroke Vivian's hair, temporarily back to her natural dirty blond, its texture just like her mother's. *Magic hair,* she used to call it, how it always tumbled right back into place. "We don't have to do anything."

So much had happened and now everything had changed.

Patrick was reluctantly back at school, Doug improbably offering to drive his son to Chicago himself, even staying an extra four days to help him get settled. Still, it was no surprise when, two days later, Patrick called to say the bursar's office wanted to know when his father planned to post his overdue tuition payment and to warn him he couldn't enroll in next semester's classes until an arrangement had been made. *Dad dadding,* Patrick said over the phone with the bemused sigh of someone twice his age.

Perry finished chemo, Harper taking him to his last three sessions, sitting beside him in the infusion room, playing gin rummy with him, making sure he had warm socks.

We're gonna beat this case, he kept telling Harper. *Deb, she just got overwhelmed. She was so damn worried about me. She wasn't thinking straight. They're gonna see it.*

In the meantime, however, Debra silently endured the humiliations of house arrest, an ankle monitor strapped tight. At night, Harper would hear it thud against the walls as her sister moved through the house, unable to sleep. She said she could always hear it buzzing, feel it vibrating on her anklebone, a phantom pulse, a beating heart.

The dreams, Harper, Debra confided. *The dreams are worse than anything.*

The plea negotiations seemed promising, but everything was moving in slow motion. Sandy was still in the hospital, her long-term head trauma issues unclear. *She's got bigger problems than a hammer to the head.* That's what Debra's lawyer said.

And the U.S. Attorney's Office had begun making queries, approaching the women in the Club, one by one. Harper knew it would be her turn soon enough. She could only dodge the calls from the IRS Criminal Investigation unit for so long.

Speculation abounded—felony conspiracy, tax and wire fraud charges, violations of securities laws—but no one knew if they had the goods, if anyone had flipped, if Sue Fox's defiant stance would hold or if she'd make a deal.

You are going to hear of investigations, Sue kept telling the other members, *and rumors of investigations. But we must remain steadfast.*

They're trying to scare us, to intimidate us. Another way they try to stop women from making money, controlling their own assets, gaining power.

She was surprisingly persuasive, energizing to the other women. *Sue gets it,* they told Harper. *She's not gonna give it up to the Man.*

Harper sometimes wondered if Sue, with her monogrammed sweaters and grosgrain headbands and circle pins, was on her way to becoming radicalized. She half hoped so.

Inside the house, the air was fizzy with bleach. They'd paid a service to come in and clean up the kitchen. Harper didn't want Vivian to ever have to see it as it was. They'd torn out the floor, save a few scraps of peeling linoleum. Fitzie moaned when he saw it, a mournful sound that echoed in the small space.

But many of their belongings were still exactly where they'd left them that awful morning. Vivian nearly tripped over Pam's hair dryer cord, still plugged in. Her court dress still hung on the back of the door.

"I just wish," Vivian said, her hand pressing against the silk, "the last time had been different. I hate that it'll always be *that* last time."

They had yet to talk about it. The fight between Vivian and her mother that morning. The one Doug told her about.

"I . . . I can't," Vivian said.

"Sure you can," Harper said, taking her hand.

At last, Vivian took a breath and told Harper. How she woke up that morning, her face stinging with salt, still crying from the night before, from the breakup with Cassie.

Please, Mom, don't make me go to school, she kept begging.

But her mother was distracted, anxious, brusque. They fought in the kitchen, Vivian knocking the cereal box off the counter, showering the floor with Apple Jacks.

They were late. Her mother told her to get in the car now, goddammit, she couldn't deal with this, she had enough on her hands with her father. Grabbing Vivian's wrist to get her moving, leaving scratches on her hand.

They'd fought even in the car, in Pam's grandma-gold Lexus, nearly swerving into traffic, the wheels screaming as they pulled into the school lot. Bolting from her seat, Vivian stumbled, her hand catching on the car door, her nail tearing on the handle.

Running up to the school, her bleeding finger throbbing in her mouth, Vivian turned around once to look back at the car and the pained expression on her mother's face, so full of regret. Her lips mouthing, *I'm sorry, sweetie. I'm sorry.*

When she got to homeroom, Cassie saw her and took pity on her. In an instant, everything—the boy, the breakup—fell away and Cassie stripped off her own mittens and gave them to Vivian to protect her bleeding hand.

"I just couldn't make Mom see about Cassie, about the breakup,"

Vivian said, sinking to the floor, the crusty rug. "I just couldn't make her see . . ."

"—you," Harper finished. "You couldn't make her see you."

Vivian nodded, her jaw tight, trying not to cry.

"She knew you loved her," Harper said, sliding down to the carpet with her niece, putting her arm around narrow shoulders. "She just had trouble sometimes. Understanding things."

"Like us," Vivian said, nodding at Harper.

"Like us," Harper said, squeezing her shoulder. "But she was trying. She really was. She was getting there."

Vivian wiped her face with the back of her hoodie sleeve and nodded.

"She wasn't perfect," Vivian whispered, "but she was Mom."

"She wasn't perfect," Harper said, "and we loved her anyway."

"You never . . . you never really thought I could hurt her, did you?" Vivian asked.

"No," Harper said, even if she wasn't quite sure. At one point, she would have believed anything rather than the truth. That the truth would be even closer than that.

Did you ever think maybe everyone's looking in the wrong place? Doug had said. That it might not be about the family but about the Club. It turned out it was both.

"I just don't get it," Vivian said. "Aunt Debra."

"Vivian—"

"I never cared about money," she said. "Not like you guys."

"It wasn't the money. It was about getting something back."

"The Big Before," Vivian said. "You all talk about it so much. How amazing things used to be. The old days, with all the money, like it could never end. And nothing could ever go wrong."

It was so hard to explain. How much of their adulthood was about mourning the life they'd lost, secure, comfortable, serene. A life they were born into by chance, luck. But had it ever really felt secure or comfortable or serene? Their parents, with their gin and tonics and private miseries, mostly offered dry kisses, closed bedroom doors. It was really in one another that the sisters found their anchor, their buoy.

"We thought it would fix things," Harper tried to explain. "The Club. Solve everything. Heal everything."

It was even harder to explain how the energy of the Club took over anything, how everything else just fell away. And once you'd committed—hustled for your buy-in and then for your new recruits—it seemed impossible to stop or even hesitate and think about what you were doing, what it meant to bring other women in, especially the easiest marks, the desperate ones, the vulnerable, the easily led. Soon enough, you would do anything to keep it growing, moving, expanding. You wouldn't even think about it anymore. The fog of war.

The truth was, at some point—at different points for all of them—they had all decided *not to know what they knew*. That was the only way to keep going. And you had to keep going.

What would happen if you paused and thought about it? Would the weight be unbearable, like it was now?

All I want, Pam had said, that night before she died, *is to be innocent again.*

For the first time, she knew what her sister had meant. But innocence, like our childhoods, our first loves, our broken families—you don't get it back, and if you thought about it, you wouldn't want to. It made you who you were, who you are.

"All I want," Vivian started, even sounding like her mother, "is to stop feeling everything."

"You think you want that," Harper said. "But you don't."

———

They were packing boxes, mounds of clothes, knickknacks, sticky old photo albums.

It all felt random and perplexing. What would they do with any of it?

No one had even figured out where Vivian would go. She was still staying at Cassie's and Harper was trying to find a two-bedroom rental near the school. No one really rents in Grosse Pointe, or so the real estate agent with the Burberry scarf warned her. *It isn't really a place for transients,* she added briskly, scanning Harper's application.

Soon enough, they were sweeping things into garbage bags: Vivian's and Patrick's mildewed stuffed animals, action figures, old Game Boys, hockey sticks, the wispy-haired troll dolls Vivian used to collect, the detritus of childhood.

"Mom told me something," Vivian said, moving toward the window. "When she wanted you to move back in. She said it was important to her. That she owed it to you."

"To me?"

"She said you asked her for something once. Something you really needed."

Harper felt a warmth under her eyes, pressing her hand there. *It's not that I don't want to help you, Harper,* Pam had said. *But Leigh has a family. . . . I can't be a part of that.*

"And she didn't give it to you," Vivian continued. "And she always regretted it . . . because you'd given her so much."

Harper didn't say anything. She couldn't speak at all, her throat thick.

They both looked into the backyard, still ravaged by the Michigan winter, the grass frost-scorched, the patio tiles sunken, everything silver and lovely and dead.

Even the soaring elm looked different, its bottom branches eerily black and bent like a finger hooked.

"That tree's probably a hundred years old," Harper said, "and we killed it in less than a year."

"No, that branch is just singed," Vivian said, a smile creeping up her face. "From the party. Patrick's graduation."

Harper smiled. "Those string lights. Your mom screamed like a banshee."

Vivian giggled. "I heard this big whoop and Patrick flew past me with this giant cooler of beer."

"The bucket brigade," Harper laughed, remembering how it was just like *Little House on the Prairie,* a line of townspeople passing pails of water from hand to hand.

And how, the rest of the night, guests kept slipping on ice shards, slick grass, dented cans spinning under their feet. *Oh, no, darling!* Pam would say each time, running around the yard with a broom even after she cut her own foot, even after she'd been dancing for hours on the grass, her feet battered and green.

It's my fault, all those lights, she confided to Harper later, *everything beautiful is dangerous, isn't it?*

Not everything, Harper thought, looking out onto the frozen lawn.

Come outside," Harper said suddenly, grabbing Vivian's hand, a sureness inside her she hadn't felt in so long, maybe years. "Come with me."

This time, she needn't worry about the police watching, about anyone. It was time.

Vivian sprinted ahead of her through the storm door, and the cold felt bracing, delicious, and Harper ran ahead of her to the tiny toolshed, her sneakers crunching on the stiff grass.

She could hear it beating, under the soil, earth. It had been beating all this time.

Hoisting opened its squeaky door, she grabbed the same rusty shovel, the same metal spade, dirt still on its tip from that night with Pam.

I'*ve never done anything,* Pam had said the morning of Patrick's graduation, stuffing an envelope with cash for her baby boy, *but I can say I did this.*

It wasn't true, of course. Pam had done many things, countless gestures of love and a few fumbled moments of failure, but Harper knew what she meant, knew the purity of the feeling behind it, knew the desperation to fix things, to give more than you got, to make meaning of all the meaninglessness they'd given themselves over to. They had gotten lost, all of them, but there were ways to light the flare on the dark road.

I've never done anything, Harper said to herself. *I never even got started.*

But I can say I did this.

Under the tree," Harper said, looking around into the darkening yards beyond. Seeing no one, hoping no one saw.

"What is it?" Vivian asked as Harper shoved the spade in her hands, as she plunged the shovel into the hard earth.

In seconds, they were both digging, their breaths frenzied, Fitzie catching up with them, swirling around them.

Vivian, now on her knees, was nearly laughing it all felt so deranged.

Harper looked down at her, Vivian's golden head so like her mother's, and it was like time had shuttled back to that ancient night less than eight weeks ago.

"Vivian," Harper whispered, the lustrous top of the cookie jar beginning to appear. "Vivian, your mom wanted this for you."

Vivian's hands dove into the cold earth, that relic of her childhood, Harper's childhood slowly appearing, the dirt scattering away to reveal its ceramic top.

Vivian was crying now, leaning back on her knees, trying to catch her breath.

"Keep going," Harper said, her hands aching.

Tear up the planks! she wanted to cry out. *Here, here! It is the beating of all our hearts!*

And Harper could feel Pam watching over them as Vivian yanked the Merry Mushroom cookie jar free from the earth, its top jostling loose, a curl of bills tumbling out.

Just like that night at the graduation party when everything felt so precarious and no one had yet done anything wrong.

That night Pam made everything work and hum and sing, Pam the center of the party, the life of the party, the party herself.

Harper could see her there, in the dying sun, spinning into an exultant little dance on the brown grass, her smile veiled and mysterious.

Twirling away from her, then twirling back, her apron falling to the ground, her head tilting back in laughter, Pam smiling at both of them and blowing them a kiss.

ACKNOWLEDGMENTS

Gratitude feels too small a word to cover the massive efforts and peerless instincts of Sally Kim and Daphne Durham, each of whom brought their incredibly intelligent, incisive, and transformative instincts in shaping this book. Two of the greatest editors in the business and I feel wildly lucky. Also big thanks to Katie Grinch, Alexis Welby, Ashley McClay, Shina Patel, Tarini Sipahimalani, Aranya Jain, Brianna Fairman, and the whole outstanding team at Putnam.

And I'm forever in debt to both Stephanie Rostan at Levine, Greenberg, Rostan Literary Agency and Dan Conaway, as well as Maja Nikolic and Chaim Lipskar, at Writers House. To the invaluable Sylvie Rabineau at WME as well as the dynamic duo of Bard Dorros and Robyn Meisinger at Anonymous Content.

Perhaps none of my books owes a greater debt to my family, with whom I spent the first eighteen years of my life in Grosse Pointe, the setting of this book. Foremost: Patricia Abbott, Josh Abbott, Julie Nichols, Kevin Abbott, and Karen Nichols. And with gratitude to the endlessly supportive Nases: Jeff, Ruth, Steve, Michelle, Marley, and Austin.

And to my muse, stalwart, and queen Alison Quinn; my dear friend (and de facto psych consultant) Darcy Lockman; and my saviors: Jack, Ace, Bill, Jimmy, Theresa, Angela, Katie, and the whole extended Oxford family.

Big thanks, too, to my partners in petty crime. You know who you are.

Photo Credit © Nina Subin

Megan Abbott is the Edgar Award–winning author of eleven crime novels, including *You Will Know Me, Give Me Your Hand,* and the *New York Times* bestseller *The Turnout,* winner of the *Los Angeles Times* Book Prize. She received her Ph.D. in English and American literature from New York University, and her writing has appeared in *The New York Times, The Guardian, The Paris Review,* and *The Wall Street Journal. Dare Me,* the series she adapted from her own novel, is now streaming on Netflix. Her latest novel, *Beware the Woman,* is now in paperback.

VISIT MEGAN ABBOTT ONLINE

meganabbott.com
𝕏 MeganEAbbott
🖸 MElizaAbbott
🅕 MeganAbbottBooks